"With her usual gift for creating imaginative plots fueled by scorchingly sensual chemistry, RITA Award–winning Ashley begins a new sexy paranormal series that neatly combines high-adrenaline suspense with humor."
—*Booklist*

"Delve into a gritty world where inequality and prejudice are the realities of shifter life. Award-winning Ashley develops a new series, Shifters Unbound, that is sexy but with a hard edge." —*Romantic Times*

"A whole new way to look at shape-shifters . . . Rousing action and sensually charged, Mapquest me the directions for Shiftertown." —*Publishers Weekly*'s Beyond Her Book

"Absolutely fabulous! . . . I was blown away by this latest release. The action and romance were evenly matched and the flow of the book kept me glued until the last page . . . Paranormal fans will be raving over this one!"
—*The Romance Readers Connection*

"Ashley has created a riveting tale that . . . explores different interpretations of human and nonhuman interaction."
—*Fresh Fiction*

"A very promising start to what should be a fresh take on a well-worn idea . . . A clever, quick book with some interesting twists that has whetted my appetite for more."
—*The Good, The Bad and The Unread*

continued . . .

LADY ISABELLA'S SCANDALOUS MARRIAGE

"I adore this novel: It's heartrending, funny, honest, and true. I want to know the hero—no, I want to *marry* the hero!"
—Eloisa James, *New York Times* bestselling author

"Readers rejoice! The Mackenzie brothers return as Ashley works her magic to create a unique love story brimming over with depth of emotion, unforgettable characters, sizzling passion, mystery, and a story that reaches out and grabs your heart. Brava!" —*Romantic Times* (Top Pick)

"A heartfelt, emotional historical romance with danger and intrigue around every corner . . . A great read!"
—*Fresh Fiction*

"Skillfully nuanced characterization and an abundance of steamy sensuality give Ashley's latest impeccably crafted historical its irresistible literary flavor." —*Chicago Tribune*

"A wonderful novel, filled with sweet, tender love that has long been denied, fiery passion, and a good dash of witty humor . . . For a rollicking good time, sexy Highland heroes, and touching romances, you just can't beat Jennifer Ashley's novels!" —*Night Owl Reviews*

THE MADNESS OF LORD IAN MACKENZIE

"Ever-versatile Ashley begins her new Victorian Highland Pleasures series with a deliciously dark and delectably sexy story of love and romantic redemption that will captivate readers with its complex characters and suspenseful plot."
—*Booklist*

"Ashley's enthralling and poignant romance . . . touches readers on many levels. Brava!" —*Romantic Times* (Top Pick)

PRIMAL BONDS

JENNIFER ASHLEY

BERKLEY SENSATION, NEW YORK

THE BERKLEY PUBLISHING GROUP
Published by the Penguin Group
Penguin Group (USA) Inc.
375 Hudson Street, New York, New York 10014, USA
Penguin Group (Canada), 90 Eglinton Avenue East, Suite 700, Toronto, Ontario M4P 2Y3, Canada
(a division of Pearson Penguin Canada Inc.)
Penguin Books Ltd., 80 Strand, London WC2R 0RL, England
Penguin Group Ireland, 25 St. Stephen's Green, Dublin 2, Ireland (a division of Penguin Books Ltd.)
Penguin Group (Australia), 250 Camberwell Road, Camberwell, Victoria 3124, Australia
(a division of Pearson Australia Group Pty. Ltd.)
Penguin Books India Pvt. Ltd., 11 Community Centre, Panchsheel Park, New Delhi—110 017, India
Penguin Group (NZ), 67 Apollo Drive, Rosedale, North Shore 0632, New Zealand
(a division of Pearson New Zealand Ltd.)
Penguin Books (South Africa) (Pty.) Ltd., 24 Sturdee Avenue, Rosebank, Johannesburg 2196,
South Africa

Penguin Books Ltd., Registered Offices: 80 Strand, London WC2R 0RL, England

This is a work of fiction. Names, characters, places, and incidents either are the product of the author's imagination or are used fictitiously, and any resemblance to actual persons, living or dead, business establishments, events, or locales is entirely coincidental. The publisher does not have any control over and does not assume any responsibility for author or third-party websites or their content.

PRIMAL BONDS

A Berkley Sensation Book / published by arrangement with the author

PRINTING HISTORY
Berkley Sensation mass-market edition / March 2011

Copyright © 2011 by Jennifer Ashley.
Excerpt from *Wild Cat* by Jennifer Ashley copyright © by Jennifer Ashley.
Cover art by Tony Mauro.
Cover design by George Long.
Cover hand lettering by Ron Zinn.
Interior text design by Laura K. Corless.

ISBN: 978-0-425-24078-6

BERKLEY® SENSATION
Berkley Sensation Books are published by The Berkley Publishing Group,
a division of Penguin Group (USA) Inc.,
375 Hudson Street, New York, New York 10014.
BERKLEY® SENSATION and the "B" design are trademarks of Penguin Group (USA) Inc.

PRINTED IN THE UNITED STATES OF AMERICA

10 9 8 7 6 5 4 3 2 1

ACKNOWLEDGMENTS

Heartfelt thanks go to my editor, Kate Seaver; her assistant, Katherine Pelz; publicist Erin Galloway; and everyone at Berkley Publishing who makes a book happen.

I also want to shout out a big thank-you to my readers who loved *Pride Mates* and asked for more Shifters! This book would not have happened without you. For more details on the series, please visit the Shifters Unbound page at www.jennifersromances.com.

CHAPTER ONE

Andrea Gray had just set the beer bottle in front of her customer when the first of the shots rocketed through the open front door. The bar just outside of the Austin Shiftertown had no windows, but the front door always stood wide open, and now a cascade of gunfire poured through the welcoming entrance.

The next thing Andrea knew, she was on the floor with two hundred and fifty pounds of solid Shifter muscle on top of her. She knew exactly who pinned her, knew the shape and feel of the long body pressing her back and thighs, trapping her with male strength. She struggled but couldn't budge him. Damned Feline.

"Get *off* me, Sean Morrissey."

His voice with its Irish lilt trickled into her ear, swirling heat into her belly. "You stay down when the bullets fly, love."

A ferocious roar sounded as Ronan, the bouncer, ran past, heading outside in his Kodiak bear form. Andrea heard more shots and then the bear's bellow of pain. Bullets splintered the bottles above the bar with a musical sound, and colorful glass and fragrant alcohol rained to the floor. Another roar, this one from a lion, vibrated in the air, and the hail of bullets suddenly ceased. Tires squealed as an engine revved before the sound died off into the distance.

Stunned silence followed, then whimpers, moans, and the angry voice of Andrea's aunt Glory. "Bastards. Human lickbrain assholes."

Shifters started rising, talking, cursing.

"You can get off me now, Sean," Andrea said.

Sean lingered, his warm weight pouring sensations into Andrea's brain—strength, virility, protectiveness—*You're safe with me, love, and you always will be.* Finally he rose to his feet and pulled her up with him; six-feet-five of enigmatic Shifter male, the black-haired, blue-eyed, Collared Feline to whom Andrea owed her freedom.

Sean didn't step away from her, staying right inside her personal space so that the heat of his body surrounded her. "Anyone hurt?" he called. "Everyone all right?"

His voice was strong, but Andrea sensed his worry that he'd have to act as Guardian tonight, which meant driving his sword through the heart of his dying friends to send their bodies to dust and their souls to the afterlife. The Sword of the Guardian leaned against the wall in the back office, where Sean stashed it any night he spent in the bar. Since Andrea had come to work there, he'd spent most nights in the bar, watching her.

She'd also seen in the two weeks she'd lived next door to Sean Morrissey that he hated the thought of using the sword. His primary job was to be called in when there was no longer any hope, and that fact put a dark edge to his entire life. Not many people saw this, but Andrea had noticed.

Andrea was close enough now to Sean to sense his muscles relax as people assured him they were all right. Shifters climbed slowly to their feet, shaken, but there was no one dead or wounded. They'd been lucky.

The floor was littered with glass and splintered wood, the smell of spilled alcohol was sharp, and bullet holes riddled the dark walls. Half the bottles and glasses behind the bar had been destroyed, and the human bartender crawled shakily out from under a table.

A wildcat zoomed in through the front door and stopped by a clump of humans not yet brave enough to get up. Feline Shifters were a cross between breeds: lion, leopard, tiger, jaguar, cheetah—bred centuries ago from the best of each. The Morrissey family had a lot of lion in it, and this wildcat had heavily muscled shoulders, a tawny body, and a black mane. It rose on its hind legs, its head nearly touching the ceiling, before it shifted into the tall form of Liam Morrissey, Sean's older brother.

The human males at his feet looked up in terror. But what did the idiots expect if they hung out in a Shifter bar? Shifter groupies baffled Andrea. They wore imitation Collars and pretended to adore all things Shifter, but whenever Shifters behaved like Shifters, they cringed in fear. *Go home, children.*

"Sean," Liam said over the crowd, eyes holding questions. "No one in here got hit. How's Ronan?"

"He'll live." The anger on Liam's face mirrored Sean's own. "Humans, a carload of them." *Again,* he didn't say.

"Cowards," Glory spat. Eyes white with rage, the platinum blonde helped another Shifter woman to her feet. The Collar around Glory's neck, which she wore like a fashion accessory to her body-hugging gold lamé, emitted half a dozen sparks. "Let me go after them."

"Easy." Liam's voice held such calm authority that Glory backed off in spite of herself, and her Collar went silent. Liam's Collar didn't spark at all, although Andrea felt the waves of anger from him.

One of the Shifter groupies raised his hands. "Hey, man, it had nothing to do with us."

Liam forced a smile, stuffing himself back into his ostensible role as bar manager. "I know that, lad," he said. "I'm sorry for your trouble. You come back in tomorrow, why don't you? The first round's on me."

His Irish lilt was pronounced, Liam the Shiftertown leader at his most charming, but the humans didn't look comforted. Liam was stark naked, except for his Collar—a large, muscular male, gleaming with sweat, who could kill the men at his feet in one blow if he wanted to. As much as they pretended to want the thrill of that danger, Shifter groupies didn't like it when the danger was real.

Ronan staggered back in, no longer in his bear form. Ronan was even bigger than Liam and Sean, nearly seven feet tall, broad of shoulder and chest, and tight with muscle. His face was sheet white, his shoulder torn and covered with blood.

Andrea shook off Sean's protective hold and went to him. "Damn it, Ronan, what were you doing?"

"My job." The amount of blood flowing down his torso would have had a human on the floor in shock. Ronan merely looked embarrassed.

Sean got to the man's other side. "In the back, lad. Now."

"I'm fine. It's just a bullet. My own fault."

"Shut it." Sean and Andrea towed the bigger man to a door marked "Private," and Sean more or less shoved him into the office beyond.

The office was ordinary—cluttered desk, a couple of chairs, a storage cabinet, shabby sofa, and a small safe in the wall that only the bar's human owner was supposed to know the combination to. Andrea knew good and well that Liam and Sean knew it too.

The Sword of the Guardian leaned against the wall like an upright cross, and threads of its Fae magic floated to Andrea from across the room. Andrea had no idea whether pure Shifters could sense the sword's magic as she, a half-Fae, half-Lupine Shifter could, but she did know that the Shifters in this Shiftertown regarded the sword, and Sean, with uncomfortable awe.

Sean pushed Ronan at a chair. "Sit."

Ronan dropped obediently, and the flimsy chair creaked under his weight. Ronan was an Ursine—a bear Shifter—large and hard-muscled, his short but shaggy black hair always looking uncombed. He didn't have an ounce of fat on him. Andrea wasn't used to Ursines, having never met one before moving to Austin. Only Lupines had lived in her Shiftertown near Colorado Springs. But Ronan had proved to be such a sweetheart he'd quickly overcome her uneasiness.

"I can't stay in here," Ronan protested. "What if they come back?"

"You're not going anywhere, my friend, until we get that bullet out of you." Sean snatched a blanket from the sagging sofa and dropped it over Ronan's lap. Shifters weren't modest as a rule, but maybe Sean thought he needed to protect Andrea from a bear in his naked glory. Ronan, admittedly, was . . . supersized.

"I thought I'd be away from the door maybe a minute." Ronan's deep black eyes filled. "What if someone had gotten hurt? Or killed? It would have been because of me."

"No one got hurt but you, you big softie." Sean's voice took on that gentle note that made Andrea shiver deep inside herself. "You frightened away the bad guys before anything worse could happen."

"If I'd been at my post, I would have blocked the door, and none of the bullets would have gotten inside."

"And then you'd look like a cheese grater," Sean said. "And be dust at the end of my sword. I like you, Ronan. I don't want that."

"Yeah?"

Andrea set down the first-aid kit she'd fetched from the cabinet and perched on the edge of the desk, her hand on Ronan's unhurt shoulder. "I don't want that either."

Ronan relaxed a little under her touch—he needed touch, reassurance, all Shifters did, especially when injured or frightened. Andrea wanted to give Ronan a full hug, but she feared hurting him. She kneaded his back instead, trying to put as much comfort as she could into the caress.

Ronan grinned weakly at her. "Hey, you're not so bad yourself, for a Fae."

"Half Fae."

Anyone else mentioning her Fae blood made Andrea's anger rise, but with Ronan it had turned into friendly teasing. Ronan squeezed her fingers in his pawlike hand.

"This is going to hurt like hell, big guy," Sean said. "So just remind yourself who you'll have to answer to if you turn bear on me and take my head off."

"Aw, I'd never hurt you, Sean. Even if I didn't know Liam would rip my guts out if I did."

"Good lad. Remember now. Andrea, hold the gauze just like that."

Andrea positioned the wad of sterile gauze under the ragged hole in Ronan's shoulder as Sean directed. Sean sprayed some antibacterial around the wound, reached in with the big tweezers he'd dipped in alcohol, and yanked the bullet from Ronan's flesh.

Ronan threw his head back and roared. His face distorted, his mouth and nose lengthening to a muzzle filled with sharp teeth. Blood burst from the wound and coated first the gauze, then the clean towel Sean jammed over it. Ronan's hands extended to razorlike claws, which closed on Sean's wrist.

Sean pressed the towel in place, unworried. "Easy now."

Ronan withdrew his hand, but not before a blue snake of electricity arced around his Collar, biting into his neck. He howled in pain.

Damn it. Andrea leapt to her feet, unable to stand it any longer. She batted the surprised Sean's hands aside and pressed her palm directly to the wound. Folding herself against Ronan, she held her hand flat to his chest.

The threads of healing spiraled in her mind, diving through her fingers into Ronan's skin, swirling until she closed her eyes to fight dizziness. She sensed the threads of Fae magic from the sword across the room drifting toward her, as though drawn by her healing touch.

Ronan's skin knit beneath her fingers, tightening and drying, slowly becoming whole again. After a few minutes, Andrea opened her eyes. Ronan's breath came fast, but it was healthy breathing, and the blood around the wound had dried.

Andrea drew her hand away. Ronan probed his injury,

staring at it in amazement. "What the hell did you do to me, Andy-girl?"

"Nothing," Andrea said in a light voice as she stood up. "We stopped the blood, and you heal fast, you big strong Ursine, you."

Ronan looked from Sean to Andrea. Sean shrugged and gave him a small smile, as though he knew what was going on, but Andrea saw the hard flicker in Sean's eyes. Oh, goody, she'd pissed him off.

Ronan gave up. He stretched and worked his shoulder. "Slap a bandage on me, Sean," he said in his usual strong voice. "I need to find my clothes."

Sean silently pressed a fresh wad of gauze to the wound, secured it with sterile tape, and let him go. Ronan kissed the top of Andrea's head, clapped Sean on the shoulders, and banged out of the office, his energy restored.

Andrea busied herself putting things back into the first-aid kit. Sean said absolutely nothing, but when she turned from tucking the kit back into the cabinet, she found him right behind her, again invading her personal space.

It was difficult to breathe while he stood over her, smelling of the night and Guinness and male musk. She had no idea what to make of Sean Morrissey, the Shifter who had mate-claimed her, sight unseen, when she'd needed to relocate to this Shiftertown.

A mate-claim simply meant that a male had marked a female as a potential mate—the couple wouldn't be officially mated until they were blessed under sun and moon by the male's clan leader. All other males had to back off unless the female chose to reject the male's mate-claim.

When Andrea had wanted to move to Austin to live with Glory, her mother's sister, Glory's pack leader had refused to let Andrea in unless she was mate-claimed. The pack leader had the right to disallow any unmated female to enter his pack if he thought that the female would cause dissention or other trouble.

Andrea, a half-Fae illegitimate Lupine, was considered

trouble. When Andrea's mother, Dina, had become pregnant by her Fae lover, Dina had been forced from the pack. That same pack now didn't want her half-Fae daughter back. But Andrea had needed to flee the Shiftertown in which she'd been living in Colorado, because a harassing asshole, the Shiftertown leader's son, had tried to mate-claim Andrea for his own. He hadn't taken her answer—*no way in hell*—very well.

Glory had turned to Liam, the Austin Shiftertown leader, as was her right, to appeal her pack leader's decision to keep Andrea out. Apparently the arguments between Glory's pack leader and Liam had been loud and heated. And then Sean had cut the arguments short by claiming Andrea for himself.

Why he'd done it, Andrea couldn't figure out, even though Sean had explained that it had been to keep the peace between species in this Shiftertown. But if that was all it was—a formality to satisfy a stubborn pack leader— why did Sean watch Andrea like he did? He'd not been happy with Liam for hiring her as a waitress, and Sean made sure he was at the bar from open to close every night Andrea worked. Didn't the big Feline have better things to do?

Sean was tall and blue-eyed, and he radiated warmth like a furnace. Andrea loved standing close to him—*How crazy is that? I'm hot for an effing Feline.* She'd thought that after what Jared, the harassing asshole, had done to her, she'd never have interest in males again, but Sean Morrissey made her breath catch. To her surprise, Sean's mate-claim had awakened her instincts and made her come alive. She'd never thought she'd feel alive again.

"What?" she asked, when Sean made no sign of moving.

"Don't play innocent with me, love. What did you just do to Ronan? I watched with my own eyes while that wound closed."

Andrea had learned to be evasive about her gift for her own safety, but she somehow knew Sean wouldn't let her. If she didn't answer, he might try to pry it out of her, maybe by seizing her wrists and backing her against a wall, looking down at her with those blue, blue eyes. Well, a girl could hope.

She made herself turn her back on his intense gaze—not easy—and start straightening the shelves in the cabinet. "It's something I inherited through my Fae side. Of course it's through my Fae side. Where else would I have gotten it?"

"I didn't notice you mentioning that you had healing magic when you arrived. I didn't notice Glory mentioning it either."

"Glory doesn't know," Andrea said without turning around. "I had a hard enough time convincing Glory's pack to let me move in with her, not to mention the pair of Felines who run this Shiftertown. I figured, the less of my Fae part I revealed, the better."

Sean turned her to face him. His eyes had gone white blue, an alpha not happy that a lesser Shifter hadn't bared every inch of her soul to him. As much as Andrea's gaze wanted to slide off to the left, she refused to look away. Sean might be an alpha, but she'd not be a pathetic submissive to his big, bad Feline dominance.

"Why keep such a thing to yourself?" Sean asked. "You could do a hell of a lot of good with a gift like that."

Andrea slid out of Sean's grip and walked away. First, because it proved she could; second, it got her away from his white-hot gaze.

"The gift isn't that strong. It's not like I can cure terminal diseases or anything. I can boost the immune system, heal wounds and abrasions, speed up the healing of broken bones. I couldn't have magicked the bullet out of Ronan, for instance, but I could relieve his pain and jump-start his recovery."

"And you don't think this is something we should know about?"

When she looked at Sean again, his eyes had returned to that sinful, summer-lake blue, but his stance still said he could turn on her anytime he wanted. If Andrea hadn't been

intrigued by Sean the moment she'd laid eyes on him in the
Austin bus station, the man would terrify her. Sean Morrissey was different from Liam, who was a charmer, in your
face, laughing at the same time he made damn sure you did
whatever it was he wanted. Sean was quieter, watching the
world, waiting for something, she wasn't certain what.

It had been one hell of a long ride from Colorado to
central Texas, but Andrea had had to take the bus, because
Shifters weren't allowed on airplanes, nor were they allowed
to drive cross-country. Glory had brought Sean with her
when she'd picked up Andrea from the station. Tall, hard-
bodied, and black-haired, Sean had been dressed in jeans
and a button-down shirt, motorcycle boots, and a leather
jacket against the February cold. Andrea had assumed him
to be Glory's latest conquest until Glory introduced him.
Sean had looked down at Andrea, his hard-ass, blue-eyed
stare peeling away the layers she'd built between herself
and the world.

She remembered thinking, *I wonder if he's black-haired
all the way down?*

Sean, being the alpha he was, had sensed her distress
and exhaustion and pulled her into his arms, knowing she
needed his touch. He'd smelled of leather, maleness, sweat,
and cold February air, and Andrea had wanted to curl up
in a little ball against him like a wounded cub. "You're all
right now," Sean had murmured against her hair. "I'm here
to look after you."

Now Sean stood patiently, waiting for her explanation.
The damn stubborn Feline would stand there all night until
she gave him one.

"I wasn't allowed to talk about it in Colorado," Andrea
said. "The Shiftertown leader gave my stepfather permission to let me use it, but they didn't want me telling people
how I healed them. I understand why. Everyone would have
freaked if they thought I was using Fae magic on them."

"That's a point," Sean conceded. "But we're not as easily, as you say, *freaked*, around here. You should have told
me, or Glory at least."

Andrea put one hand on her hip. "My life as a half-breed illegitimate orphan hasn't exactly been pleasant, you know. I've learned to keep things to myself."

"And you thought we'd treat you the same, did you, love?"

Damn it, why did he insist on calling her *love*? And why did it sizzle fire all the way through her? This was crazy. He was a *Feline*. If Sean Morrissey knew little about her, Andrea knew still less about him.

"Well, you're part of us now." Sean came to her, again stepping into her space, a dominant male wanting to make her aware just what her place was. "You're right that not all Shifters are comfortable with Fae magic, but my brother has to know about your healing gift, and my father. And Glory has a right too."

"Fine," Andrea said, as though it made no difference. "Tell them." She moved to the door, again deliberately turning her back on him. Alphas didn't like that. "We should go help clean up out there. Does the bar get shot up often? I should get hazardous duty pay."

"Andrea."

He was right behind her, his warmth like sunshine on her back. Andrea stopped with her hand on the doorknob. Sean rested his palm on the doorframe above her, his tall body hemming her in. She remembered the feel of him on top of her on the floor, the tactile memory strong.

"Glory says something's been troubling you," Sean said. "Troubling you bad. I want you to tell me about it."

Andrea shivered. Damn Glory, damn Sean, and no, she didn't want to talk about it.

"Not now. Can we go?"

"It's my job to listen to troubles," he said, breath hot in her ear. "Whether I'm your mate yet or not. And you will tell me yours."

Andrea's tongue felt loose, her pent-up emotions suddenly wanting to spill out to this man and his warm voice. She clamped her mouth shut, but Sean stunned her by saying, "Is it about the nightmares?"

She hadn't told anyone about the nightmares, not Glory, not Sean, not anyone, though Glory might have heard her crying out in her sleep. The nightmares had started a week after she'd moved in with Glory, when they'd risen in her head like a many-tentacled monster. She didn't know what they meant or why she was having them; she only knew they scared the hell out of her. "How do you know about my nightmares?"

"Because my bedroom window faces yours, love, and I have good hearing."

The thought of Sean sitting in his bedroom, watching over her while she slept, made her shiver with warmth. "There's nothing to tell. When I wake up, I can't remember anything." Except fear. She had no idea what the images that flashed through her head meant, but they terrified her. "I really don't want to talk about it right now," she said. "All right?"

Sean ran a soothing hand down her arm, stirring more fires. "That's all right, love. You let me know when you're good and ready."

From the feel of the very firm thing lodged against her backside, Sean was good and ready now. One part of him had definitely shifted.

Andrea deliberately leaned on the door and pressed back into him. A jolt of heat shot through her, the fear of the nightmares dissolving. After Jared, Andrea thought she'd be afraid of Sean, turned off, ready to run. Instead, Sean made her feel, for the first time in years . . . playful.

"So, tell me, Guardian," she said, lowering her voice to a purr. "Is that where you carry your sword, or are you just happy to see me?"

CHAPTER TWO

Damn but the woman could ignite the mating frenzy without even trying.

Andrea's backside fit right into Sean's groin, her wriggle of hips teasing his hard-on for all she was worth. She smelled good, better than good. Even her overlying Fae scent couldn't change the sensory goodness that was Andrea.

The frenzy wasn't supposed to start until they were officially mated in ceremony, blessed by the clan leader under sun and under moon. Then they would be a recognized mate-pair, similar to a human marriage, together until death. The mate-claim alone shouldn't be enough to start the frenzy. But Sean's libido and instincts were busily overriding the stringent Shifter rules drilled into his head since before he could talk.

Andrea had pulled her ringlets of dark hair into a ponytail tonight, baring her slim neck to his delectation. Sean leaned down and bit her skin, right above her Collar.

"Not now," he growled.

"Are you implying that there will be a later, Feline?" she asked in that throaty, sexy voice.

"If you want one." His own voice sounded thick, his tongue wanting only to taste her.

She had no right to smell this good. She was a bloody Lupine, like Glory. Sean had never understood his father's fixation with Glory, but damn it, Andrea was getting under his skin. He couldn't make himself stay away from the bloody woman. And then she did things like *this*.

Sean wanted to jerk Andrea back into him, peel off her clothes, make love to her on the sagging sofa or maybe the desk. He wanted to lift her in his arms, rush her home, and tell Liam he was ready for the mate blessing. *Under sun and under moon; get on with it, man.*

"Not now," he said again, directing the words to himself.

Andrea straightened and turned, putting her back against the door, her stormy eyes making him wild with wanting. "You know I'm grateful for what you've done for me, Sean."

"Aye, and your undying gratitude is what I live for."

"Really?" She looked him up and down with a hint of a smile.

"Sure it is." He heard the bitterness in his tone, but he couldn't keep it out.

Her brows moved upward, her smoke-colored eyes looking straight into his heart. He had to wonder what she saw there.

Sean had pictured her, before he'd met her, as a submissive little she-wolf—shy and scared, grateful to him for making it possible for her to relocate to Austin. But what he saw in front of him now was a sensual, curvaceous female with eyes the color of smoke, who lifted her head and met his gaze without flinching. She didn't glance to the side or bow her head, as someone low in a pack should. It was as though Andrea couldn't be bothered to remember she was supposed to be a submissive little she-wolf.

"We should go," Sean heard himself saying. "They'll be wondering what we're doing back here. You know how Shifter gossip is."

"Rampant," Andrea said.

So was Sean, at the moment. He leaned down and nipped her cheek. "I'll walk you home."

"That's sweet, but Glory's walking me home. She's plenty scary. I'll be fine."

"And tonight, with humans running about shooting up places, I go with you."

Andrea squarely met his gaze. She always did that, making it clear that she knew that Sean was dominant to her but she didn't give a damn. Her mouth softened into a smile. "What an offer. A walk with something that worships a scratching post."

Her teasing made him want to pin her against the door and nip her until she couldn't speak for laughing. "Lupine humor, as inventive as ever," he said, exaggerating his Irish lilt. "I'd offer you a doggie biscuit, but I don't want to soil me dignity."

"Not a rawhide bone? Stingy."

He leaned toward her again, heart pounding. "If I were to offer you a bone, that's not the type I'd be thinking of."

Her answering smile fanned the fires all through Sean's body. "Good answer, Guardian. There's hope for you yet." She turned the knob behind her, and Sean forced himself to let her go.

S ean did walk home with Andrea and Glory, letting the two females stride ahead, the pair of them talking like they hadn't seen each other in days. The bloody women lived together; you'd think they'd have had enough time to talk about shoes and things without having to go on and on about them now.

Mostly Sean walked behind them so he could watch Andrea's sexy rear end sway beneath her jacket. The feeling of it rubbing against him in Liam's office still tingled across his crotch, guaranteeing 'twould be another sleepless night.

He was trying to go slowly with Andrea, knowing that she was worried and uncertain after what that bastard in her old Shiftertown, Jared Barnett, had done to her. When Andrea had rejected his mate-claim, as was a female's right, Jared, amazed and affronted, had terrorized the hell out of her. He'd followed her around, threatened her and her stepfather, had his friends leave roadkill or lighted rags on her doorstep, and even had them beat up her stepfather. It got to be so bad that Andrea hadn't been able to leave the house. Her stepfather's pack refused to extend her protection: first, because she was not related to them by blood, and second, because they thought she should take Jared's offer. Jared was giving Andrea, a nobody Lupine half Fae, a chance to be safely mated, and she'd had the gall to refuse.

Andrea had finally managed, with her stepfather's help, to sneak away to Colorado Springs to the human government's Shifter oversight office and request a transfer to the Austin Shiftertown. A lot of paperwork and calls to Texas later, and Andrea had their approval. Which had led to the problem of Glory's pack accepting her, and then Sean's mate-claim.

And now his wanting for the woman was driving him insane.

Andrea and Glory said good-bye to Sean in front of Glory's house. Sean pulled Andrea into a full embrace, inhaling her scent. He liked that Andrea hugged him back, not fighting the Shifter way of saying good night. Her body felt good and warm, the strength and softness of her making him want to hold her for hours. Glory's hug wasn't nearly as intoxicating, and her embraces were always accompanied by a flood of perfume.

Sean waited until Andrea had safely shut the front door behind herself and Glory before he jogged next door and up the steps to the Morrissey house. Sean went straight to his room to put away the sword and from there heard Liam come in and up the stairs. In the hall, Sean found his sister-in-law, Kim, Liam's human mate, in the doorway to the master bedroom, arms folded over her pregnant abdomen.

Kim was petite by Shifter terms, though humans might consider her about average, maybe a little smaller. She always insisted that she was fat, which baffled Liam and equally baffled Sean. Women *should* have generous breasts and nice bums. If Kim was a little plumper now, it was because she was carrying Liam's cub. That made her beautiful. Sean suddenly imagined what Andrea would look like, thickening with Sean's child.

Kim caught sight of Sean and transferred her glare to him. "Sean," she said in a voice that brooked no argument. "Tell Liam that he is *not* to don a bullet-proof vest and go off chasing the bad guys."

Liam looked aggrieved, but Sean agreed with Kim. Liam was hotheaded enough to do something daft like hunt down a carload of trigger-happy humans by himself.

"Liam," Sean said. "You are not to don a bullet-proof vest and go off chasing the bad guys."

"Don't start, little brother," Liam growled.

"She has a point. Your cub in there will need his dad."

Liam slid his large hand lovingly over Kim's protruding abdomen. Ever since Kim's announcement that she was pregnant, Liam had been perpetually worried. He ought to be. Though Kim was robust and though Shifter-human pairings were not unknown, having the child would be tough on her.

"We have good people," Sean went on. "Including me. Use them."

This shooting hadn't been the first one. A similar incident had occurred just prior to Andrea's arrival in Austin, humans driving up to a Shifter bar, unloading bullets, and screaming off again. No one had been hurt, thank the Goddess. Sean had talked to the police, but they'd put it down to gang violence and didn't seem very interested, not when the potential victims were only Shifters.

"Fine." Liam frowned, and Sean knew that the preliminary

round of this argument had been won. By Kim. Again. "Kim, go back to bed," Liam said.

Kim's blue eyes sparkled. "*You* come to bed."

"I will. I need to chat with Sean a bit, then I'll be up."

Kim slid his hand from her belly but gave him a smoldering smile. "I'll still be awake."

"I'm counting on that, love."

Sean rolled his eyes in mock irritation. "Don't tell me the two of you will be keeping the rest of us awake again."

Kim blushed, but Liam only grinned, his good humor restored. The two brothers went downstairs as Kim retreated into the bedroom.

"Andrea all right?" Liam asked Sean when they reached the kitchen. Liam opened the pantry, extracted two bottles of Guinness, and handed one to Sean. Though they'd learned to drink lager cold after twenty years of living among Americans, they still agreed that stout was best at room temperature. "She wasn't hurt?"

"No, she's fine," Sean said absently. He knew he needed to tell Liam about Andrea's healing gift, but he didn't want to yet. Sean's newfound protectiveness of Andrea exerted itself even against his own brother. Besides, at the moment, he was remembering Andrea doing a little booty dance for fun behind the bar earlier that evening. Andrea's body had moved in a sinuous rhythm, and every unmated male in the place, including Sean, had gone alert and hard.

"Sean." Liam snapped his fingers in front of Sean's face. "Dreaming are you? Anyone would think you were smitten."

He was laughing, and Sean started to answer, but they were interrupted by Connor banging in the back door.

Connor, their late brother's son, had recently turned twenty-one. While that made him an adult by human standards, by Shifter standards he was still a cub, still waiting to find his place in the clan. In a few more years, though, Connor would be a formidable contender for dominance and ready to find a mate. Connor had enough of his father,

Kenny, in him to make him tough, strong, and a force to be reckoned with.

"Hey, Liam. Sean," Connor said. "Ellison wants to know when we can go hunt down the humans and kick some gobshite ass."

CHAPTER THREE

Sean started to grin, doubting that Ellison, a steadfast Texan who lived across the street, had used the term *gobshite*, but Liam growled. "Ellison can keep his Stetson on and his mouth shut."

Connor went to the refrigerator and helped himself to a chilled beer. His movements were restless, angry, a young Shifter impatient to make his place in the world. "They invaded our territory, or as good as. They put our females in danger. I say Ellison's right. We fight."

"Since when do you listen to Lupine assholes like Ellison?" Liam's voice had an edge to it. "We'll get them, lad."

"By sitting around drinking Guinness?" Connor took a swig of his beer, swallowed, and wiped his mouth. "Fine leaders you are."

"I talked to the human cops before I closed up," Liam said. "Sean's going back downtown tomorrow morning to speak to the detective he talked to last time. Ronan at least remembered the license plate of the car. Not that it will help much—the last car turned out to be stolen."

Connor swung a punch at air. "The police should let *us* track them. And then take them down."

"Sure, lad," Liam said. "We'll find the humans and jump on them, and then our Collars will go off, and won't we look like fools rolling around, screaming in pain? We'll get them, Con, but another way."

Connor thumped down on a chair. "Why can't we just get these damned Collars off of us?"

Liam and Sean exchanged a glance. Last summer, secret experiments by Shifters on removing the Collars had produced some horrifying results, and Liam had declared that the experiments were to be terminated. But Sean knew full well that Liam and their father, Dylan, were still working on it, looking for a safer way for removal. They hadn't told Connor about it, or Andrea, though Glory and Kim knew, because they'd been involved. But it was strictly a need-to-know basis.

Connor shrugged, a picture of youth frustrated. "Sometimes it looks to me like you're not doing anything."

"That's when I'm most dangerous, lad," Liam said. "Anyway, what were you doing rushing off with Ellison? You were supposed to stay here and guard Kim."

"I was only across the street. I could see the house the whole time." Connor wriggled on his chair, too energetic to keep still. "It's not fair, is it? The humans snap Collars on us and make us work shit jobs—they make it so we can't fight back, and then they try to shoot us. We were just lucky no one got killed."

Liam only nodded, but Sean was pulled to Connor's distress. Sometimes Liam's stoic "don't worry, I have it" attitude wasn't exactly reassuring. Sean moved behind Connor and wrapped his arms around his nephew.

"We have the luck of the Goddess on our side," he told him. "And the Irish."

"Yeah, that potato-famine thing was sure lucky," Connor growled, but Sean felt the lad's body relax under his touch. Sean rubbed Connor's arms, kissed his hair.

Take care of Con for me, Kenny had whispered the

night he'd been killed, his broken body in Sean's arms. *Promise me, Sean.*

Sean had promised to protect Connor with his life as he'd held his brother close and come apart with grief. Kenny had died before Liam and Dylan could arrive, and Sean had rocked Kenny's body and wept.

Then Sean had gently laid his brother on the ground, taken up the silver Sword of the Guardian, and sent Kenny to dust. That had been the hardest night of Sean's life.

Under Sean's light massage, Connor calmed. He reached up and rubbed Sean's hair, indicating he felt better. Sean released him, and Connor went back to drinking his beer. Connor had insisted on buying his own beer and going to the bar now that he'd reached the lofty human age of twenty-one.

Sean kissed the top of Connor's head, touched Liam's shoulder as he went past, and told them both good night. He went up to his room, the smallest in the house, but Sean didn't need much. A bed, a desk for his computer, a place to stash his clothes, and life was good.

The wooden case that held the sword—polished, inlaid, velvet-lined—rested on his dresser, the elegance of the case incongruous with the functional sword inside it. The Sword of the Guardian itself, made more than seven hundred years ago, was fairly plain, with runes covering the magically hardened silver-alloy blade.

The hilt was unadorned and easy to grip, though runes had been etched on it as well. It was an ancient thing, made by the best swordsmith in the old kingdom of Kerry, a Shifter called Niall O'Connell, and passed down through the generations. The Morrisseys were descended from the smith, through his offspring from his first mate, a Feline Shifter who'd died, leaving him two sons. Naill had taken as his second mate the Fae woman who'd woven her spells through this sword, the legends said.

Sean turned off his light and sat on the end of the bed. From this position he could look across the yard that separated the two houses to Andrea's bedroom window. She'd pulled the curtains closed, but light glowed against them, and he could see Andrea's silhouette moving about the room.

He watched Andrea's shadow pull off her top and slide down her jeans, and Sean's mind filled in what he couldn't see. The curve of her waist, the slashes of lace that would be her bra and panties, the soft round of breasts that had teased him from behind her tight shirt all night.

He adjusted himself on the bed, his skin hot, his arousal hard and painful. She was a delectable woman, and this edge of mating frenzy was driving him crazy. He'd told Andrea that she could leave his mate-claim unanswered for as long as she wanted, to give Wade's pack time to get used to her. Sean wouldn't force the issue, but he might burn up and die before she made her decision.

The light went out in Andrea's bedroom, and the night flowed into silence. Andrea had closed her window against the cold, but Sean knew when her nightmares began. Andrea cried out in her sleep, tossing and turning, the frightened noises she made heartbreaking.

"Hush now," Sean whispered. "Hush, love."

As though she heard him, Andrea quieted and settled into even breathing. Sean made himself lie down and pull the covers over himself, but sleep eluded him for most of the night.

The next day, Andrea had time off from the bar, but Glory had business to take care of—she wouldn't say what. Whatever it was, it made her spend forty-five minutes in the bathroom before she waltzed out again bathed in perfume and every hair in place. *Meeting Dylan?* Andrea wondered.

Dylan, Sean's father, had been living here with Glory but had left for who knew where the night Andrea had moved in. That had been two weeks ago, and Glory had been in a foul mood ever since.

Andrea had long ago given up trying to figure out her

aunt Glory. Glory was nothing like what Andrea remembered of her mother, Dina. As far as Andrea knew, Dina hadn't worn outlandish outfits, mile-high shoes, and rivers of Oscar de La Renta. Andrea's mother's scent had been like warm baked bread overlaid with the freshness of the outdoors. Andrea remembered her mother's touch, the hand on her back when she went to sleep at night, reassuring Andrea that whatever happened, her mother would be there to protect her. Until one day, she wasn't.

After Glory left, Andrea ate a little breakfast, then returned to her room and took out a file folder she'd stuck under her mattress. She sat on the bed and opened it, flipping through her notes and maps, the sparse information she'd gathered about where exactly her mother had met her father.

Forty years ago, the Lupine pack that had contained Andrea's mother and Glory had been living in Colorado, isolated in the mountains. The pack hadn't been very big then. By now it contained fifty or sixty Lupines, but back when Shifters had been wild, low fertility rates had been good at keeping their numbers down.

Andrea's current map of Colorado contained colorful lines that marked roads and highways, noting scenic views and tourist attractions. She overlaid it with a map she'd made herself, a transparent sheet covered with crisscrossing lines of a different kind.

These were ley lines, magic currents that ran under the earth. Much the same way fault lines formed where geologic plates met, ley lines marked where magic rammed together and flowed along the path of least resistance. Northern Europe contained a huge number of lines, which stretched from there to all corners of the planet. Interestingly, on Andrea's map of Texas, a line snaked along the Colorado River that ran through Austin on its way to the Gulf Coast. There was a concentration of magic right under the Congress Street bridge—Andrea wondered whether that was why the bats liked it there so much.

The maps didn't tell Andrea any more today than they

had yesterday. She hadn't learned anything new about her real father, or how he'd crossed from Faerie to this world and where, or how he met her mother, or why he'd left again. Glory's only explanation for him was a long, foul-worded diatribe against the Fae, nothing very helpful. When Dina's pregnancy was discovered, she, a mateless female now smelling strongly of Fae, had been cast out of the pack. Glory hadn't been able to stop it.

Dina had survived only because a Lupine of another pack, Terry Gray, who was now Andrea's stepfather, had found Dina, fallen in love with her, and mate-claimed her. The mate blessing had been allowed, because females were scarce and Terry could have more Lupines with Dina once her Fae-get was born. Andrea's stepfather had been commanded to kill Andrea at birth, and Terry, for the first time in his life, had disobeyed his pack leader.

He and Dina had protected Andrea with everything they had, and once Andrea had learned to shift, she'd been grudgingly accepted if not trusted. Accepted because Andrea had been damn careful to hide any part of herself that was too Fae, like her small healing ability. But Glory hadn't been allowed to see Andrea at all, and once Glory's pack had been relocated to Texas after taking the Collar, all chance of them meeting had gone.

Andrea sighed, put everything back into the folder, slid the folder under the mattress, and went downstairs. She planned to continue tracking the ley lines, mapping them through Austin, but she'd need to get a car. She was saving every penny she made at the job Liam had given her toward one, but vehicles were expensive, even ones Shifters were allowed to buy.

Outside it was freakishly warm for midwinter, but the weather here could swing like that, Glory had told her. Colorado Springs would still be buried in snow, but temperatures today in Austin were pushing eighty. Andrea hopped up on the wide balustrade at the end of the porch to enjoy a patch of warm sunshine.

The Morrisseys' house next door was a mirror image of Glory's, a two-story bungalow with a deep porch and Craftsman-style windows. It was a homey place, kept freshly painted, the yard trimmed. The curtains on the downstairs windows were wide open, letting Andrea glimpse the cluttered living room beyond, a contrast to the neat yard outside.

Three men lived in that house—Liam, Sean, and Connor—with Kim the only female. Andrea imagined that Kim had her hands full keeping the place straight, and she smiled in sympathy. Andrea had lived with her stepfather in a tiny house and knew firsthand how messy males could be. And how they blinked in surprise whenever a female commented on it.

Glory's house, on the other hand, was pristine. Maybe another reason Dylan had fled?

Andrea hadn't sat there long before Sean rode up on a black motorcycle, already out and about for the day. Andrea wondered what he'd been doing, where he'd gone. She had no idea what the man did all day, only that he was around to watch her all night. What did Guardians do in their spare time?

Sean pulled onto one of the two strips of concrete that made the driveway, turned off the motorcycle, and dismounted.

Andrea swung her leg, foot bare in a sandal, and gave him a smile. "Morning, Sean."

Sean nodded. "And a good morning to you."

He fetched a toolbox from the porch, slid off his leather jacket, and squatted down to examine something on his motorcycle's engine. Andrea wasn't familiar enough with motorcycles to know what he was doing, but she enjoyed watching his biceps play and his thighs move under his jeans as he worked.

A Shifter woman emerged onto the porch of the house beyond the Morrisseys', another Feline, dressed for the warm weather in a low-cut sleeveless top and shorts. She hopped up on her porch railing and dangled her legs as Andrea did. "Hey, Seanie."

Sean gave her a brief glance. "Caitlin."

"I've come home from San Antonio."

"I can see that."

Andrea watched Caitlin grumpily. If the woman leaned any farther forward, she'd fall off the porch, not to mention right out of her blouse.

"You should come over and say hi, Seanie," Caitlin said. "A girl might think you'd forgotten her."

Sean grinned but kept his gaze on his motorcycle. "Oh, I haven't forgotten you, Caitlin."

Andrea's chest burned. Goddess, she wasn't jealous of that overly obvious Feline girl, was she? Andrea had always thought her Fae blood suppressed her mate-possessive instincts—she'd never had them for any other male she'd ever met. But the minute this woman with her breasts spilling from her top cast a glance at Sean, Andrea's fighting instincts stirred to life. She growled low in her throat.

Oh, gods, she *was* jealous. Proprietary and jealous, like a she-wolf in heat.

"Hey, Sean," Andrea couldn't stop herself from saying. "Thanks for walking me home last night."

Sean glanced up at her expressionlessly. "Just doing my job."

"Seanie likes his job," Caitlin sang. "He's a sweetheart. So *protective*."

Sean returned his attention to his motorcycle, not bothering to answer.

"Well, well," another female voice drawled. "If it isn't Sean Morrissey."

A woman stopped on the sidewalk in front of Sean's house and folded her arms. She was a bear, tall like Glory but more muscular, though her muscles didn't detract from her beauty. She was strong but thoroughly feminine.

"Rebecca," Sean greeted her, voice neutral. "How are you this fine morning?"

"Better now that I've taken in the sights."

Andrea stifled another growl. These females were perfectly in their rights to flirt with Sean, because according to Shifter rules, Sean would not be off-limits until he and Andrea had the official mate blessings. Until then, Sean was fair game.

In the unfair world of Shifters, however, the mate-claim put Andrea *off* the market, females being scarce and jealously guarded. No other male would dare try to move on Andrea until she rejected Sean's claim, unless that male wanted to challenge Sean for her. And Andrea had the feeling that no sane male would challenge Sean. The aura of raw power he walked in would make them run away in terror before they even got close.

"Go on with you now," Sean was saying to Rebecca. "You must have better things to do than watch a man fix a bloody stubborn bike."

Rebecca shook her head, still smiling. "Not really."

"Me either," Caitlin called from the other porch. "I could watch you all day, Seanie. In fact, why don't you bring that bike over here, and I'll make us some lemonade?"

"Or you could come to my house," Rebecca said. "I'd give you Guinness."

Rebecca was a little older, probably more experienced than Caitlin, who wasn't much beyond cub years. Neither of them were looking for mates, Andrea could tell. Just mat*ing*.

"What we really want is to see all you've got, Sean," Andrea called. She barely stopped herself from snarling, her fingers wanting to turn to claws. "We *say* we'll give you lemonade or Guinness, but it's only to get you out of those sweet jeans."

Sean glanced up, the skin around his eyes tightening. "Is that so?"

"That is so. Right, ladies?"

Rebecca laughed. "You are so right. Is it boxers under there? Or a thong?"

Sean's brows rose. "So, you're taking bets on my underwear now?"

"Come on, show us what you've got, Seanie," Caitlin said.

"Yes, come on, Sean," Andrea said, forcing herself to remain relaxed. "Settle the bet. *I* say briefs."

"You don't know Seanie then," Caitlin almost crowed. "It's boxers. Black satin."

Rebecca touched her lower lip. "I'm holding out for a thong."

Sean stood up, socket wrench in hand, his gaze locked on Andrea's. "You're serious."

Andrea gave him a slow smile. "You betcha. Who's right, *Seanie*?"

Sean fixed his unreadable blue gaze on her for a long moment. His eyes sucked her in, made her want to leap off the porch and fall at his feet, begging him to be gentle— but not too gentle. She'd be down there kissing his boots in a second. Pathetic.

Andrea met his gaze with a steady one of her own, challenging, daring.

A smile of pure sin spread across Sean's face. "If I settle the bet, will you ladies let me get on with some work?"

"Depends on the answer," Andrea said. "Go on, Sean. Make our day."

Sean kept up the wicked smile a few seconds longer. Then he shrugged, dropped his wrench, unbuckled his belt, and slid his jeans down his backside.

He wore no underwear at all.

Caitlin and Rebecca screamed in delight. Andrea remained silent, but her heart pounded so hard she heard a rushing sound in her ears.

Sunshine touched a backside that was slightly paler than the rest of Sean but still tanned. He must expose his entire body from time to time, probably right after he shifted. Sweet thought. Andrea wanted to leap down and bite that firm, bare ass, nip it, taste it.

The show lasted only a few seconds before Sean pulled up his jeans again. "You all lose," he said as he buckled his belt. "Satisfied?"

Rebecca ran her tongue over her lips. "Oh, I might be

satisfied for the rest of the week." She turned away and walked on, her low laughter drifting behind her.

Caitlin lingered awhile, all but rubbing herself on the porch railings as she cooed at him, but Sean switched his entire focus to the bike and paid no attention. Playtime over. Caitlin evidently didn't like being ignored, so she said a sugary good-bye and waltzed back into her house.

Andrea lifted herself from the porch and made her way down to Sean's driveway. Her body was shaking and hot, but she pretended coolness as she stuck her hands into her back pockets and watched him work.

"Is it a Feline thing?" she asked. "Going commando?"

Sean kept tinkering. "No, it's a 'no clean laundry' thing."

Andrea tried a grin, but her heart was still pounding. "What, won't Kim wash the big, bad alpha's underwear?"

"She's a modern woman, Kim is. Which means she'll look after her mate but not his good-for-nothing brother. She makes Connor do his own laundry too. Says it builds character."

"She makes you males work the washing machine? That must be something to see."

"Oh, I know how to," Sean said, still not looking away from his task. "I just forgot to."

Andrea leaned down, hands on her knees, and got lost in watching the muscles in his arms work as he tried to wrest a stubborn bolt loose. He smelled like sunshine and dust, and she didn't blame Caitlin and Rebecca for wanting to grab him and haul him off.

"While you're standing there all pretty," Sean said, grunting with effort, "will you come down here and grab on to this stiff thing for me?"

Rowr. Hot words to make her hot. *I'll hold anything you want me to, Sean Morrissey.*

She crouched down. "To what?"

The glint in his eyes told her he'd phrased the question that way on purpose. "Right here." He steered her hand to the handle of a wrench that was closed around the bolt. "Just keep a grip on it, and don't let go."

Andrea touched her tongue to her lip. "You'd be amazed at what a tight grip I have."

Sean growled low in his throat. "You walk the edge, Andy-girl."

She did, and Sean always made her want to leap right over it—to land right on top of him. He steadied her hand again with his strong one, and she held the wrench as he loosened a piece beneath it. The whole assembly came out, Sean and Andrea lifting it away together.

Nice. Sean's face hung near to hers, a smudge of grease on his cheek. He smelled of sweat and bike grease, the outdoors, and all she could think of was the sunshine kissing his sweet backside.

Sean set the piece aside. He started to reach for the next thing he wanted to yank off, but Andrea touched his shoulder. Sean turned back to her, his breath on her face, eyes darkening.

Andrea was never sure who leaned forward first, but she was melting toward him and, next thing she knew, felt the scalding pressure of Sean's mouth on hers. He kissed with strength, barely masking his power, and Andrea closed her eyes and drank it in. His hand stole to the back of her neck, arching her up to savor more of her.

"Come inside with me," he whispered against her mouth, and she tasted his breath. "You can make sure I wash my underwear. How's that?"

She wanted to; oh, she wanted to. No one was home, and they could explore what they'd started. More kissing, more touching, and Andrea could slide her hands into his jeans and cup his firm, sun-touched backside.

She pulled away slightly. He watched her, wanting and yet cautious, trying not to scare her. That worry for her twisted her heart around, and at the same time, she wanted to lick the moisture from between his lips.

"Your pants are vibrating," she whispered.

"What?" Sean jerked. "Aw, damn it." Andrea watched with amusement as Sean unfolded to his feet and yanked his cell phone from its holder.

As she rose with him, she heard the grating tones of Sean's father, Dylan, come clearly over the line.

"Son," he rumbled. "Fetch the sword. You're needed."

CHAPTER FOUR

The warmth and vibrancy drained from Sean's eyes. "I'll be right there." He clicked off the phone, looking grim.

"What is it?" Andrea asked. "What's happened?"

Sean shoved the phone back into its holder. "My cousin Ely in San Antonio. Another drive-by shooting. Dad says he's still alive, but . . ." The way Sean trailed off said it all. "He's asking for the Guardian."

The darkness Andrea sensed in Sean came forward with a vengeance. His smiles were gone, as was the charming lilt with which he'd asked her to go inside with him. Then he'd sounded like a warm man seeking pleasure on a sunny morning; now he was the cold man who'd looked upon so much death.

"Sean, I'm sorry." Andrea rubbed his tight forearm. "I don't understand, though. The San Antonio Shiftertown has a Guardian, doesn't it? I thought the humans made each Shiftertown use its own."

"That Guardian is Lupine, and Ely's my kin. Dad says Ely wants me, and I don't care about the human rules right now. They think what we do is only ceremonial anyway."

Sean looked down at her, his eyes tight with pain. "Come with me?"

Andrea started shaking her head before he finished the sentence. "I can't. I shouldn't. I'm a half-Fae Lupine. His family won't want me there."

"Doesn't matter. You might be able to help."

"If you're thinking of my healing gift, I told you; it's not very strong. It might make no difference at all."

"Damn it, Andrea, we have to try."

The desperation in Sean's eyes caught at Andrea's heart. She hadn't recovered from his smiling suggestion that they go into the house—no one was home; she knew that. She'd wanted what he offered so much it worried her.

But their personal lives had just dwindled to background noise. Once again, Sean was being asked to go and watch someone die.

Andrea drew a breath. "All right." She might be able to ease Ely's pain a little, at the very least.

Sean looked at his bike in pieces, then turned away, sunshine dancing in his dark hair. "Dad left his truck in the back. The keys are in it. Fetch it and meet me round front."

Andrea nodded. Sean wiped off his hands, picked up his tools, and disappeared into the house without a word.

He'd gone to get the sword. Andrea's heart beat faster. Sean's expression, before he'd turned away, had been so empty that she'd wanted to put her arms around him. She hadn't had the heart to refuse his request to accompany him, though she still wasn't sure how much good she could do. Her healing talent had fixed up Ronan, but that had been the equivalent of bandaging a skinned knee. Kodiak bear Ronan was tough and strong, and he had an amazing metabolism. A few bullets in the shoulder were to him what bee stings were to everyone else. If Sean's father had told Sean to bring the sword, it meant that Dylan thought Sean's cousin beyond saving.

Andrea found the white pickup parked behind the house, keys hanging from the ignition. No Shifter would take another Shifter's vehicle, and few humans ever ventured into Shiftertown without invitation, so the chances of someone stealing it were slim to none. Despite the fact that the truck was ten or more years old, Andrea knew, as she started it up, that it would be in perfect condition. Shifters learned to keep vehicles running in top shape, being forbidden to buy brand new ones.

She pulled the pickup through the alley and around to the front of the house. Ellison Rowe, another Lupine and a friend to the Morrisseys, came out of his house across the street and jogged over.

Ellison's pack had been relocated here when Shifters took the Collar twenty years ago, but by all evidence he loved being a Texan, even by adoption. He never left home without his big belt buckle, cowboy boots, hat, and Texas drawl.

"What's up?" he asked, leaning on the open window.

"There's been another shooting. Down in San Antonio. Sean's cousin."

Ellison's face changed. "Aw, shit, not again. What the hell is going on?"

"Must be a new hobby for humans."

"Damn," Ellison growled. "Come and play Shoot the Shifter. Step right up, have a good time. Assholes."

Sean emerged from the house in a button-down shirt in place of his T-shirt, the sword strapped to his back. Ellison straightened up. "I'm sorry, man," he said.

Sean nodded his thanks. He approached the driver's side, and Andrea slid over to let him get in. Sean carefully laid the sword across the seat, but the pickup was narrow, and the hilt had to rest on Andrea's lap.

"Goddess go with you," Ellison said as Sean buckled his seat belt. "Andrea, don't let this Feline get you into any trouble, now, hear?"

"No worries there," Andrea said, giving him a little smile. "Will you tell Glory where I am if she comes back?"

"You bet." Ellison patted the top of the truck and stepped away as Sean pulled the truck away from the curb. Ellison watched them go, his stance somber.

Sean was silent as they rolled through the streets outside Shiftertown. As though a switch had flipped in him,
Sean had gone from a Shifter male flirting with a female
to a man with the weight of the world on his shoulders. His
blue eyes flickered as he gave the traffic on Ben White a
steely gaze, his hands tight on the steering wheel.

"Sean," she said softly. "Please don't count on me to
save your cousin. Ronan's was a flesh wound. If vital
organs have been hit, that's different."

Sean acknowledged this with a tight nod. "I know that,
love. But I can't not try."

"Oh, I'm willing to try. I just don't want you to get your
hopes up."

"I like hope," he said, his mouth softening. "Hope—it's
a fine thing."

The sheathed sword's hilt was hard on Andrea's lap. She
brushed it with her fingertips and felt the Fae magic in it, a
tingle that worked its way through her body. Andrea could
see it in her mind, golden threads of Fae spells wafting
from the metal.

She saw those same kinds of threads in her nightmares
too, shimmering wires that sought to bind her, to trap her.
Last night, she'd fought them again, flailing and thrashing
to get away, and they'd drawn tighter, tighter.

She drew a sharp breath.

Sean glanced at her, his face too tight. He was nearly
vibrating with tension, his grief and anger held too closely
inside him. Shifters shouldn't do that; it ate them up.

Whenever Shifters became overwhelmed with an emotion, especially one like grief, they withdrew from the
world, taking time alone to work through it. This instinct
had kept the pack from weakening in the wild, because
the pack leader wouldn't have to worry about protecting a
Shifter too grief-stricken to fight. But Sean could never disappear for weeks while he licked his wounds, because the
clan always needed its Guardian. The Guardian freed souls
with one thrust of the sword but was never free himself.

Andrea lifted the sword and slid over in the seat until her

thigh touched his. Sean's need for touch screamed itself at her, and she couldn't justify denying him comfort because she wasn't certain how she felt about his mate-claim.

The Shifter in her recognized that Sean had ten times the strength of Jared, physically and emotionally, not to mention in the dominance department. If Sean ever decided to force the mate-claim, Andrea might not be able to withstand him. Sean could have forced it today—hell, any time since she'd arrived. But he hadn't. He'd soothed her fear with his Shifter touch and told her he'd wait for her. That put Sean a hundred times higher in her estimation than spoiled-brat Jared.

Andrea slid her hand around Sean's arm, shivering a little at the hardness of the bicep under her palm. Sean looked down at her, eyes deep blue.

"Thank you, Andy-love."

"Keep your eyes on the road, hot ass. Austin traffic is insane."

A tiny smile brushed his mouth. "Isn't it, though?"

"It is. I'm used to wide open roads and mountain vistas."

"You'll not be getting that here, love. But I can show you some beautiful places. It's not so bad."

"Says the man from Ireland, where mountains don't exist."

Sean took his hand from the wheel to rest it over hers, rough fingers tightening. "We had some grand hills there." His voice matched hers, two people trying to say light-hearted things to keep from thinking about terrible ones. "You should see the black cliffs tumbling into the sea in County Kerry. 'Tis a beautiful sight."

"But it's not the Rockies." While she spoke, Sean squeezed her hand ever-more tightly. "You look at those mountains, and you know no one rules them. Not humans, not Shifters. They've stood there for eons, dominating the edge of the plains, fearing nothing."

"Same thing in Kerry. 'Tis an old place, ancient. You can feel it in your bones. All this—Shifters, humans, Fae—doesn't matter."

"You miss Ireland."

"Aye. But it's grand here too. No more hunger, no more struggle. Just time to watch Connor grow up, see Liam mated and about to become a father. We're stronger now, more likely to survive." His jaw hardened. "Except for humans and their stupid weapons."

"They won't win," Andrea squeezed his hand in return, noting that Sean's body smelled damn good.

"No, lass, they won't."

He fell silent, concentrating on the traffic bottled up on the interstate. In impatience, Sean shot off the freeway to take a back highway that headed straight south.

The clinic lay just inside the city limits of San Antonio on the southeast side. Not many places treated Shifters, and ones that did were quickly deserted by their human clientele.

Sean parked in the clinic's small lot and came around to open Andrea's door for her. She handed him the sword, which he strapped to his back, and they went inside to the clinical smell of disinfectant.

Shifters were clumped inside the waiting room—they'd be friends and members of the clan. When they saw Sean walk in, his big sword on his back, some turned away and murmured prayers; others simply looked at him. They all knew what his presence here meant.

Andrea walked beside Sean without meeting any gazes. She saw nostrils widen, eyes snap to her as they smelled Fae, but no one moved to stop her. They wouldn't while she was with the Guardian.

Dylan waited for them near a nurses' station in the hall beyond. The nurse there, human, came out from behind the desk when Sean and Andrea entered, her already fierce expression turning to one of outrage.

"You can't go in there," she snapped at Sean. "Not with *that*."

She held out her hand as though Sean would meekly unstrap the Sword of the Guardian and give it to her, like an unruly pupil handing over a toy to his angry teacher.

Sean walked by her without a word, and Dylan fell into step with him.

"You can't go back there! I'm calling security."

Andrea turned back and stepped squarely in front of the woman, putting just enough growl into her voice. "Leave it."

The nurse stared, stunned. Andrea smelled her fear but also her cunning. She'd be on the phone as soon as Andrea moved to follow Sean.

Swallowing a sigh, Andrea gripped the nurse's wrist and yanked her along with them. The nurse's protests died when they walked into the room at the end of the hall, which was full of Shifters and the smell of impending death.

CHAPTER FIVE

The grief in the room was palpable. It was difficult not to feel anything but compassion when Andrea beheld Sean's cousin Ely lying in the hospital bed, his face sunken, his Collar a dark streak on his pasty throat. Tubes snaked into his arms, human machines gently beeping around him.

Ely wasn't much older than Sean, maybe at his century mark. His mate curled on the bed next to him, a ball of misery. Four younger men and a young woman—Ely's cubs, she guessed by their similar scent—stood in positions of resigned grief. An older man waited on the opposite side of the room, just as grief-stricken. Ely's father.

Andrea tasted rage against the humans who had done this. No Shifter of venerable years should have to watch his son die; no cubs should have to watch their father cut down before them. And no mate should have the love of her life yanked away from her. The woman's grief would bury her for years. It had already started.

Sean moved to the side of the bed and touched Ely's shoulder, his voice softening to gentleness itself. "Now,

Ely, lad, what did you do to attract all those bullets to you? Magnetized yourself, did you?"

Ely smiled, his face drawn in pain in spite of the liquids that dripped into his arm. "That's me, Sean. Too damned attractive." His whisper rasped. "Thank you for coming."

Andrea watched Sean suppress all his own rage and grief to caress Ely with a reassuring hand. "Look who I brought with me," he said. "The pretty she-wolf that lives next door to me. Glory's niece, the one I mate-claimed. Isn't she a fine one?"

Sean stretched out his arm, indicating that Andrea should come to him. Andrea had to let go of the nurse, but Dylan moved to block the nurse's retreat. She'd never get past Dylan.

Sean drew Andrea to him, arm around her waist. Ely's mate lifted her head in anger.

"The half Fae," she spat. "Get her out of here."

Sean ignored her. "Let Andrea touch you, Ely. She can ease the pain."

Ely dragged in a shallow breath. "Hell, I'm all for that."

Andrea felt the waves of outrage from Ely's children, from Ely's father, even from the nurse. Collars or no, these Shifters were on the verge of violence. If Andrea made one wrong move, they'd take her down. They might do it anyway, angry at her for being here at this private time. If Andrea had any sense, she'd shake off Sean, rush back out to the truck, and take off. She'd heard the River Walk was nice this time of year . . .

But Andrea couldn't walk away. That was the problem with the healing gift—she couldn't look upon Ely's suffering and turn her back on it. She'd never deny a man relief from pain just because his family's anger made her uncomfortable.

Sean eased the blanket from Ely's torso and parted the hospital gown, and Andrea stifled a gasp. Ely's pale abdomen was crisscrossed with pink puckered wounds held together with steri-tape where surgeons had tried to sew his shredded insides back together. Half his stomach had been gouged out by the look of things, and unhealthy red streaks striped his stomach. This man was chopped up, infected, dying.

His hurts were well beyond Andrea's gift. The most she could do was ease Ely's pain, perhaps make his death easier. She glanced at Sean, and he gave her the faintest of nods, telling her he understood.

Andrea let out her breath, ducked out from under Sean's arm, and laid her hands very carefully on Ely's abdomen.

Ely grunted, and the machines beeped faster. The sons and daughter started forward, only to be curtailed by Dylan.

"Let her do what she can," Dylan ordered. He outranked them, and the others fell silent.

"Go on, love," Sean said softly.

Andrea closed her eyes. Whenever she used her healing gift, she visualized a snarl of threads that she had to untangle and lay straight. Sometimes it was easy to unravel the hurt, as it had been with Ronan last night, sometimes impossible.

Ely was pretty tangled up. From the shredded mess inside him, Andrea could tell he hadn't been shot with a simple pistol. An automatic weapon had done this, probably with bullets that expanded on the inside and did bad things. To think, humans put the Collars on the Shifters.

Andrea pictured herself working out the threads, one by one, as though she pulled apart a mangled attempt at a complicating knitting pattern. This would take time, and she wasn't certain Ely had time. The man bravely sucked in breath after breath, but despite whatever painkiller he'd been given, Andrea knew that it wasn't adequate for the high metabolism of a Shifter. His pain had to be intense.

With her eyes closed and the healing flowing, Andrea could see the faint aura of each person around her. Ely's fire was at the lowest ebb, warmed somewhat by his mate's next to him. The sons, daughter, and father had formed a circle around the bed, ready to begin the ritual of grieving.

Dylan, a hotter fire, still holding the quivering human nurse, stood behind them.

And Sean? He was like a living flame. There could be no doubt to anyone with the slightest hint of magic that Sean Morrissey was Goddess blessed. Andrea had a vague idea of how Guardians became Guardians—the sword passed in a ritual to an of-age member of the clan who was closely related to the old Guardian—a son or nephew or grandson—but there must be more to it than that.

Sean was an upright fire, the sword a gleam of brightness on his back. He had no Fae blood in him, but even so, the glitter of magic wound tightly through him, independent of the sword.

Andrea's sudden insight told her it wasn't just the Sword of the Guardian that sent the Shifter into the afterlife. It was the combination of the sword and what was in the man, the Guardian himself. Did Sean know that?

Ely's wound was impossible. Andrea knew she'd never be able to help him, not in time, and the thought filled her with despair. She'd have to open her eyes, raise her head, tell the family he was about to die. Ely's glow dimmed even as she thought it, his tiny flame almost burned out.

The sword glistened on Sean's back, its magic like hers, singing to her.

Andrea snapped open her eyes. "Sean," she said in a quiet voice. "Draw the sword."

Ely's mate moaned; his daughter clung to one of her brothers. Sean's lips tightened.

"No," Andrea said quickly. "Not for that. Not yet. Just draw the sword."

Sean frowned at her, but he whispered a prayer and drew the blade. The metal rang in the stillness, and Ely opened his eyes.

"Sean." Ely smiled. "Thank you."

Andrea lifted her right hand and wrapped it around the blade. Sean blinked, checking his start so he wouldn't cut her.

The edge nicked Andrea's palm anyway, and the trickle of blood that followed warmed her skin. She closed her eyes, pulled on the Fae magic of the sword, and twined the threads of it with her own.

It hurt. Andrea swallowed pain as her magic wove with that of the sword's. The sparkling threads dove into her, gleefully wrapping her in a gleaming wiry mesh.

Andrea's blood turned glacial. Her nightmares were like this, a cocoon of burning threads that tried to bind her, to suffocate her. Whatever was in her nightmare wanted her death.

She realized after a few seconds of blinding panic that what happened to her now was different. She'd never had the feeling in her dreams that it was her own healing magic, similar to the magic of the sword, that was trying to kill her. The mesh that attacked her in the nightmares came from something else, something horrific.

Drawing a steadying breath, Andrea directed the bright threads from herself and the sword straight into Ely's abdomen.

And the wounds began to heal. Strand by strand, the bright magic of the sword and her gift untangled the snarl of Ely's hurts and rewove them into smooth, healthy tissue. Muscle and bone, blood and organs, all moved and changed under her touch.

She'd never heal him completely; Andrea knew that. Ely would not leap from the bed, yank the tubes out of his body, and dance out the door in his hospital gown. But the healing had started, the magic giving the natural process a huge boost. With Shifter metabolism as strong as it was, Ely would continue healing on his own and live. His mate, children, and father would not have to perform a grieving ceremony today.

The machines started beeping a different tune, and the nurse exclaimed. Dylan let her go as Andrea opened her eyes.

Ely was regarding Andrea over his half-healed stomach, his eyes wide. His face was flushed, lips healthy red, gaze Shifter strong.

Andrea let go of Sean's sword and sat back, blowing out her breath. The nurse fiddled with the machines in amazement, not bothering to explain to the rest of them what the change in numbers and sounds meant. Andrea's hand stung where the sword had cut it, but the threads of magic had flowed away and dispersed.

Ely's mate was crying, clinging to Ely in joy. Ely stroked her hair but was staring over the foot of the bed at Andrea in amazement.

"What did you do to me, Fae-girl?" he asked, voice ringing. "That fucking *hurt*!"

S ean walked Andrea out of the clinic with his hand firmly on her shoulder. Andrea's eyes were dark with shock in her white face, her gait unsteady. But his girl held it together while they passed all those Shifters in the waiting room, who rose to watch them go by.

They'd all heard what had happened, and the weird thing was, they supposed Sean had worked some kind of miracle. But Sean knew it had been all Andrea. He'd felt the magic of the sword change when she touched it, felt the magic remake itself. The sword had helped drive life back into Ely, to seal his soul to his body.

Sean had no idea how that had happened, and by the look on Andrea's face, she didn't understand either.

The Shifters reached out to Sean. "Guardian," some murmured. They touched him as he passed, but Sean kept walking, acknowledging them but not stopping.

"Goddess bless you, Sean Morrissey," one man said. His mate, in the circle of his arm, brushed a hurried finger over Sean's sleeve.

Sean and Andrea made it out of the clinic into the crisp air of a day turning cold. Texas winters were like that—a morning could begin warm and fine and end up bloody freezing by nightfall.

Dylan's white pickup waited incongruously in the lot. When they reached it, Andrea collapsed against it, breathing hard in relief. Sean stashed the sword in the cab and went to her, rubbing her chilled arms. "You all right?"

"I don't know. What the hell happened in there?"

"They think I worked a bloody miracle. You and me together."

"Didn't we?"

Her body was tight, her eyes flicking from feral wolf to human and back again. Sean had felt the sword's magic go into her, had felt the tug of it through the hilt, pulling on his own flesh. It had been strange, frightening, and heady at the same time.

"You worked the miracle, Andrea."

She shook her head, her warm ringlets brushing his hands. "I just used the sword to enhance my magic. The sword's a Fae artifact; its magic is the same as mine. Maybe that's what happened." She shivered. "Stop looking at me like that, Sean. You want me to have answers, and I don't."

"There's more to you than meets the eye, Andy-love, that's for damned sure."

Andrea gave him a shaky smile. "And you still want to claim me as mate?"

Fire streaked through his body. Andrea had saved Ely's life, had given Sean's cousin the chance to see his children mated and his grandchildren grow up. She'd made certain Sean hadn't had to lift the sword and drive it into Ely's heart. Sean could now ride home with his arm around his girl, happy and warm, not scoured empty inside, drained by grief. She had given him that gift.

"Hell, yes." Sean slid his arms around her until her soft breasts pressed his chest. "You're a beautiful woman, Andrea Gray, even if you are a damned Lupine."

"Go on and flatter me, now."

Sean laughed. It felt so good to laugh. He scooped her to him and pressed a hard kiss to her lips.

She tasted like orange juice, sensuality, and sex, plus the sparkling of magic still flowing between them. Sean caressed her mouth open, tongue sliding inside to be met with the hot strength of hers.

Unlike their leisurely kiss in his driveway, Sean sought her with a kind of desperation that was echoed in her. He felt her Faeness in the fine bones under his fingertips, the satin of her skin. So delicate, and yet at the same time, so damn strong. The little noises she was making in her throat drove him wild.

She hooked her fingers around his waistband, hips moving as she kissed him. She might not realize she was rubbing against him, but his hard-on responded.

"I'll flatter you more than that when you're in my bed," he said. "With me seeing if I can feel that magic deep inside you."

"Hormones," she murmured.

"What, love?"

"Shifter males are a walking mass of hormones."

Sean stroked his fingers over her throat. "Is that why your own pulse is beating so fast? Don't pretend you're above a little mate frenzy yourself."

"I'd never be in a mate frenzy." She licked across his mouth. "I'm much too sensible."

"Oh, yes?" He felt the grin spread across his face. "Andy-love, one day soon, we'll have a chat about female and male lust." His gaze swept to her bosom bared by the V neckline of her shirt. Her skin had broken out in goose bumps in the cold—she had dressed for the warmer weather of this morning. "It'll be a fine talk."

"Keep dreaming, cat-boy."

Sean laughed again. She loved to tease him, and he loved being teased by her. It felt good to laugh now that the pall of death had lifted from his heart.

He shrugged off his leather jacket and wrapped it around her shoulders. The coat was covered with his scent, and now she would be too. *You can deny it all you want to, lass, but your frenzy's as hot as mine.*

Sean held the jacked by the lapels and bent to kiss her again, just as Dylan came out of the clinic and made for the truck.

The tightness in Dylan's jaw told Sean that he'd seen the kisses. Sean had made the mate-claim without asking

Dylan's opinion, which Sean knew had to sting. Dylan had slipped in the hierarchy recently, and Sean's claim without consulting his father had driven that fact home.

Without saying a word to either of them, Dylan climbed into the passenger seat of the pickup, moved the sword, and waited.

Sean pressed one more kiss to Andrea's mouth and released her. She stepped away and shot him a challenging smile, though she didn't shrug off the coat.

A tingle of anticipation heated Sean's blood as he stepped back to let her scramble into the pickup. He still hadn't recovered from the body blow he'd received when she'd walked toward him across the bus station, beautiful and elegant and unafraid. He wanted to hold her hard, stroke fiercely into her mouth, learn every corner of her. At the same time he determined to reward her well for the beautiful gift she'd given him today. For the first time in all the years that he'd been Guardian, he'd been able to watch certain death back away and life blossom in its place.

S ean examined the sword later that night in the living room while Connor lounged on the floor, pretending to watch television. Liam was working at the bar, and Kim had gone there with him after winning a heated argument. Liam had wanted Kim to stay safely home; Kim had insisted on going to the bar to make sure he didn't do anything stupidly dangerous, like dive in front of bullets.

Liam had finally conceded. He'd asked Sean to stay home and look after Connor, who was furious at being forced to remain behind. Though he seethed, Connor wouldn't disobey Liam's direct order. Andrea had the night off, so Sean had no problem staying here where he could also keep an eye on the house next door.

The sword looked no different than it had before. Long ago, the Shifter Niall O'Connell and his Fae mate had forged the sword, he working the metal with his amazing artistry, she weaving Fae spells into it.

Today, a half-Fae Shifter had taken the magic from the sword and bent it to her will. Sean recalled the amazed look on Ely's face when he'd realized he wouldn't die, at least not today.

What had Andrea done? She hadn't said one word about the healing on the drive back to Austin, and Dylan hadn't brought up the topic either. Though Dylan was of course relieved that Ely had lived, he hadn't hidden his deep disturbance about the event. Sean knew that Dylan made Andrea plenty nervous, so the ride home wasn't as joyous as it could have been.

Sean had dropped Dylan off at the bar on their way into Shiftertown, and he and Andrea had ridden the rest of the way in silence. In equal silence, Andrea had handed Sean his jacket before hurrying alone into Glory's house.

The coat still smelled of her. Sean would carry it upstairs and lay it on his bed, hoping the scent would seep into his sheets. Then he could dream of her, maybe of her wearing nothing *but* the jacket. And a pair of spike-heeled shoes. Now there was a picture.

Someone came in the back door. Both Sean and Connor jumped to alertness, but they recognized the scent and relaxed. Sean propped his sword against the wall and went into the kitchen.

"Dad."

Dylan pulled Sean into a brief, tight hug before helping himself to a Guinness.

"Are you full up here?" Dylan asked. "Or do you have a corner left where your old dad can sleep?"

Sean leaned against the breakfast bar to watch his father take a drink. "Sure we do. But I thought your move in with Glory was permanent."

Dylan hard face cracked a smile. "Is anything with Glory permanent?"

"You tell me."

Pain laced Dylan's eyes, and he covered it by taking another sip of beer. "I loved your mother, Sean."

Sean shrugged, as though they hadn't had this discussion

many times. Sean and Dylan, Dylan and Liam. "I know you did. But she of all people wouldn't want to see you buried in grief after fifty years. She'd say, 'What is wrong with you, man? You'd best be getting on with life.'"

The smile flitted across Dylan's mouth again. "I can hear her saying that. Funny thing, I can hear Glory saying it too."

"Well, then."

Dylan retuned his attention to his beer. "It's not an easy thing. It never will be." He clicked the bottle to the counter. "I didn't come to talk about my troubles, Sean; I came to talk about yours."

"About Andrea, you mean."

"About Andrea and you." Dylan's dark blue eyes were serious. "It was a good thing you did for her, claiming her so she could relocate. But she'd not an ordinary Shifter, son, and I'm not just talking about what she did for Ely today."

"I take it you're meaning more than her being half Fae?"

Dylan nodded. "I've met half Fae before, even half-Fae Shifters. Andrea is different from any Shifter, half Fae or otherwise I've ever known. She's not dominant. Glory isn't top of her pack, and Andrea is well beneath her in the hierarchy. But Andrea acts more like an alpha."

"No, she doesn't." Alpha females were rare and had to fight hard for pack or pride dominance, with the males below her always ready to take her down. The few alpha females Sean had met were more ruthless than any alpha male and would rip the heart out of said male the instant he couldn't make eye contact with her. With alpha females, a male had to be constantly on guard, or preferably, in another state.

"Not quite what I mean, no," Dylan said. "Andrea isn't an alpha. But at the same time, she doesn't give a damn how alpha anyone else is. When Glory brought her home, Andrea walked right up to me and looked me in the eyes. No avoidance, no submissiveness. Her stare wasn't bravado or defiance; she just didn't care. Glory still has a hard time meeting my eyes, even after all these years, but not Andrea. I see Andrea do the same to you. It's as though she has no interest in the hierarchy, like she's somehow outside it."

Sean had noticed that, and her lack of fear somehow spiked his libido. "Maybe she learned the trick because she grew up more or less at the mercy of her own pack. The Colorado Shiftertown is pretty insular, and they always treated her like an outsider. It couldn't have been easy on her, poor lass."

"Granted. But it's something to watch." Dylan came to Sean, put his strong hand on his son's shoulder. "Be careful of her."

"Don't worry. I plan to watch Andrea very closely." From an inch away, if Sean had his way. Better still, from even closer. "Are you staying here tonight then?"

Dylan let his gaze drift to the eastern window, through which they could see the line of Glory's house. "No," he said quietly. "No. I'll be next door if you need me."

Sean nodded, and then father and son stepped together and shared a long embrace. Sean and Dylan were the same height, Dylan's hair as dark as Sean's except for a bit of gray at the temples.

"You need her, Dad," Sean said. "Shifters, we're not meant to be alone."

They released each other, and Dylan stepped back. He broke eye contact first, and that fact pulled at Sean's heart.

"Good night, son."

"'Night, Dad."

Dylan left. Sean watched with mixed emotions as Dylan crossed the yards between the houses and lightly ran up onto Glory's back porch, entering the house without knocking.

Sean's father *did* need Glory, as interesting as that lady was. Dylan was slowly conceding his place in the pride to Sean and Liam, and he needed someone to both soothe him and distract him from the pain of that.

Andrea had the nightmare again. This time the threads that bound her were white, so bright they blinded her. She fought, screamed, kicked as they wound tighter and tighter, ivylike fingers slicing into her wrists and ankles.

Andrea. It was a whisper, the silver threads of it tangling around the wires that already held her. *Andrea. Beautiful one.*

Andrea screamed loud and long.

"Andrea!"

Andrea jumped awake and sat up straight. Sean Morrissey stood inside her open window, in his underwear, the glare from the harsh streetlight streaming in behind him.

CHAPTER SIX

Andrea yelped and yanked the covers up to her shoulders. "Sean, what the hell are you doing in here?"

"I heard you yelling," Sean said, as calmly as though they stood in the middle of a park. "My window, it faces yours. And you left yours unlocked." He turned and pulled down the sash, closing off the frigid air.

"I'm on the second floor. In the middle of a well-patrolled Shiftertown."

"A second floor easy to reach by climbing onto the porch roof. Piece of cake to a cat."

As he came closer to the bed, Andrea saw fully what he was wearing. Or not wearing. A T-shirt and underwear, easy to peel off for the shift, to slide back on once he made it to the roof.

"Briefs," Andrea said. "I knew it."

"Have you got a blanket I can wrap myself in, love? It's bloody cold in here."

"You're the one who decided to turn into a cat and climb in through my window."

"I did. Had to leave most of my clothes behind to do it too."

He sounded so nonchalant, as though this were nothing unusual. And maybe it wasn't to Sean. Not that Andrea could imagine any ladies locking the window to keep him out. He stood tall and tight, his hands on his hips, silhouetted against the light outside. His body made the wolf in her want to howl.

Hurried footsteps sounded in the hall, and the door of her bedroom swung open to reveal Glory, resplendent in silver pants, camisole, and gauzy robe. She was tense, poised to shift, but she relaxed when she saw Sean.

"Ah." She gave a throaty laugh. "I guess it's Felines for both of us tonight."

"Sean and I are just chatting," Andrea said before he could speak. "Everything's under control."

Glory's smile spoke volumes. "Of course it is. Good night." She turned, robe floating, and closed the door behind her.

"About the blanket," Sean said. "It's still bloody cold."

"I thought you were a big, bad Feline Shifter."

"I am. Now I'm a cold one."

"I also thought you were leaving."

"I never said that." Sean sat on the edge of her bed. "You're shaking like a leaf and you smell of fear. Tell me about these nightmares, love. After you lend me a blanket."

He was right about the fear. Sean waking her abruptly had sent the nightmare fleeing, but Andrea couldn't stop shivering, even though her skin was clammy with sweat. The dreams were incoherent but at the same time terrifying as hell.

Sean might say he was cold, but his body radiated warmth. So much warmth. She wanted it. Her libido noted every line of his strong, hard body; the curl of his hair at the base of his neck; the sensual mouth that had kissed her so masterfully today. Twice. But right now, she longed even more for his Shifter touch, his comfort.

She eased down a corner of the covers and moved over, inviting him in.

Sean's eyes glittered as they flicked to her, his chest

rising with a quick intake of breath. Just when Andrea thought he'd refuse, Sean took hold of the covers, lifted them, and slid into the bed with her.

Sean laid himself down next to Andrea, wondering if this weren't the biggest mistake of his life. She had a double bed, so there was room for him, but the damn bed wasn't *that* big. Not big enough that his legs didn't touch hers, that when he put his head on the pillow, her face wasn't inches away from his.

Her breath was warm on his cheek, her hair mussed and spilling over her pillow. She smelled of sleep, damp and sultry, and the bed was a fine place of heat, where a Shifter male could curl up and be touched by his sweetheart of a mate.

"You're a dangerous one," Sean said. He thought about what Dylan had said about Andrea not respecting the hierarchy, and sure enough, Andrea was gazing straight into his eyes. No evasion of the submissive, no awkwardness, no hesitancy.

"Me? Dangerous?" Andrea shrugged. "It's cold, and if you want to talk, this is the warmest place. Anyway, there's nothing dangerous about me."

"You're dangerous, because you can make the Shifter-town leader's baby brother dance to your bidding."

A smile touched her mouth. "Do you? Dance to my bidding?"

"I'm dancing a jig right now, love."

Her red lips curved. "You're the dangerous one, Sean Morrissey. Here you are climbing through my bedroom window."

"Because I was worried about you."

"That's what makes *you* dangerous."

Her eyes were silver in the moonlight, her face a curve of marble. Her beauty did something to Sean's soul, and her eyes looked deep into his heart. He was never going to survive her.

Sean smoothed a lock of hair from her cheek. "Tell me about the nightmares. Do you dream about Jared? The things he did? He can't touch you by law, Andrea, you know that, now that you've been mate-claimed by me. Besides, I'll kill him if he comes near you."

"No." Andrea's mouth went tight, the pucker of the word remaining as she frowned. "The nightmares aren't about Jared. They're about—I think about what happened today."

That surprised him. "What, you mean with Ely? The healing?"

"I think so. But . . . I don't know."

"Why don't you tell me, and I'll be the judge."

Andrea wet her lips, the moisture gleaming in the dim light. Sean remembered kissing those lips and the warmth and pressure of her mouth in return. Her breasts pushed at the neckline of her pajama top, and his legs told him she wore no pajama bottoms.

"I see threads," she said. "No, that's not right. They're more like wires, tangling me up, trying to smother me. I can't get away. But whenever I heal someone, I also see threads. I'm not sure if I really see them or I just picture them to help me focus. Today I saw them coming from your sword, and I used them to help heal your cousin."

Interesting. "But the dreams, they're nothing about healing?"

"No. I don't know what they are."

From the worry in her eyes, he feared she did know, and that it wasn't good.

"Something to do with the Fae?" Sean asked.

"I don't know," she repeated, voice sharp. She smelled of fear, anger, distrust.

Sean stroked her hair, calming her with his touch. He didn't mind doing that for her, running his fingers through her silky hair, finishing the stroke on her cheekbone.

"You can trust me, sweetheart," he said.

"Can I really?"

"Yes. My dad is shagging your aunt, probably right now. That makes us almost family."

A slight smile rewarded him. "If we're related, you can't claim me as mate."

"I didn't say blood relation. I said *family*. Mate is the best kind of family."

A sigh. "I wouldn't know. My stepfather loved my mother, but his people never took to her. They were relieved when she died."

"All deaths are grief," Sean said, running his fingertips across her lashes. "For all Shifters. We all grieve."

"You do, maybe."

Goddess, she was so brittle. That was Andrea, brittle and fragile at the same time. She'd been hurt, and Sean wanted to erase that hurt. He wanted to wipe out her nightmares and destroy everyone who had ever caused her pain.

"You can trust us, Andrea," Sean said. "You can trust me. Whenever you think you're alone, you won't be."

Her expression softened, and she grinned. "Fine words from a man who climbed in through my window and got into my bed."

Sean propped himself on his elbow. "You invited me to do the last bit, love."

He let his fingers trail down her cheek to her neck, around the neckline of her pajama top, which came to a V below her Collar. He touched the Collar's Celtic knot that rested against the hollow of her throat. He wished he could have seen her before the Collar had been fused to her skin to keep her tamed for humans. He could have pressed kisses down her neck to her shoulders, nuzzling in under her hair. He still could, but he longed to taste her, not the metal bite of the Collar.

She watched him while he touched her, gray eyes big. Many Lupines had gray eyes, but they were light gray, like Glory's. Andrea's were the color of deep smoke, of leaden skies over an Irish sea. Her lashes were dark, thick, and full, which went with her lush black hair. *Black Irish,* she'd be called where he came from. Dark hair and creamy skin, gray eyes that recalled the Sidhe, the Fae, the Fair Folk.

Fair bloody bastards. They'd created Shifters for their own pleasure, so Shifters could hunt for the Fae and entertain them. Animals that could turn human and back again, *Oh what fun we can have with them!* But they made Shifters too strong. Shifter had allied with Shifter, and they'd turned on their Fae masters and driven them back to Faerie. Good riddance.

Once in a while, a Fae emerged and coupled with a Shifter or a human to produce a half-Fae offspring. Those were the dangerous kind. The half Fae could live among humans—they weren't as fragile as the full-blooded Fae who weren't easy with all the iron now in use in the human world. Half Fae weren't affected by iron, and they had that Fae charm. It had been a half-Fae human and his son who'd helped convince the human government that Shifters were dangerous and needed to be kept on a leash—the Collars had been the half-Fae human's idea.

And now there was this half Fae, half Shifter. Andrea Gray, scared and angry, the Shifter-Fae war being fought inside her own body.

You can trust us, Sean had said. He'd really meant, *You can trust* me.

Andrea touched his throat, tracing Sean's own Collar. Sean closed his eyes to enjoy. The feel of her light fingers around the edges of the Collar was erotic and enticing, and yet, he also loved simply bathing in her warmth and the scent of her.

Sean jumped when her lips brushed his chin. He opened his eyes to find her face an inch from his, and then she closed the space between them and kissed him.

A slow, leisurely kiss. A slide of lips, moist with heat. She smelled good, like honey and that bite of mint that was the Fae in her.

Her mouth moved on his, and Sean answered, licking, stroking. He caught her tongue and gently suckled it, and she made a sound in her throat that made his already hard cock lift.

But this wasn't a night for mating frenzy. It was cool in the room, they were warm snuggled under the blankets. This was a time to kiss, touch, nip, getting to know each other. Shifters mated for life. If Andrea accepted his claim, there would be time. So much time.

Andrea nipped and tasted Sean back, her touch light on his shoulders. She was fragile and strong at the same time, her body honed but fine boned, her curves round and delicious. Shifter but different.

Sean nuzzled Andrea's cheek, and he feathered kisses along her jaw. Her hair smelled good, a fine place to bury his nose and inhale.

"Dylan will know you're here," she whispered.

He bit her earlobe. "Of course he knows I'm here. Even if Glory didn't tell him, he can scent his own son."

"He doesn't like me."

Another bite. "He likes you fine, love. He's uncertain, but he was clan leader for all his life. It's his job to be suspicious of anything different."

"Different like me."

"Give him a chance. He's giving you one."

"Is he?"

Sean left off the enticing fun of licking the shell of her ear. "Love, if Dad didn't want you here, you wouldn't be here. Never mind that Liam's now Shiftertown leader. If Dad thought you a true threat, your request would never have been approved, no matter what your pack leader wanted, no matter how many times I insisted on making the mate-claim."

Andrea looked puzzled. "Dylan doesn't have say over Glory's pack leader. He's Feline and not the leader of Shiftertown."

"Doesn't matter." Sean wanted to laugh. "You think power only flows within a pack or a clan? That nothing outside can influence it? Living in a Shiftertown has taught me a lot about dominance and power, leadership and control. It's not who wins in the pecking order, it's who has true dominance. And my father has it. Liam's leader now, but he still listens to Dad."

"What about you?" Andrea's mouth softened into a smile. "Do you listen to your father?"

"Mostly." Sean traced her lips. "But he also listens to me. If I say you're the one for me, he'll concede. Eventually."

"I never know what to make of you, Sean Morrissey."

"Not many do. Come here." Sean kissed her again, soft touches, his hand stealing around her back. She responded by nibbling his lip, running fingers through his hair.

Sean kissed her lips and face and throat, then he gently rolled her so that she faced away from him. He spooned up against her back, arm around her waist. "You sleep now. No more nightmares. I'm here to drive them off."

"With your big stick?"

Sean chuckled and moved his hips, his hardness through his briefs finding the cleave in her panties. "Bikinis," he said. "I knew it."

"We're strangely fond of each other's underwear."

"I promise not to wear yours if you don't wear mine."

Andrea started to laugh, her body shaking in a wonderful way. Sean hid a groan. He had to be crazy, lying here with her, promising himself he'd leave her alone.

"The big, bad Guardian in women's underwear," she said.

"You hush now." Sean kissed the soft skin behind her ear. "Sleep."

She giggled some more, a sound that drove heat into his bones. "I'll dream about that. You big, strong Shifter, you."

Sean turned the kiss to a nip. "Hush."

"No doubt about who's the dominant in *this* room."

Andrea laughed again, the sound softer as she relaxed back into him. Sean held her in a safe embrace, cradling her like a cub until she fell into limp, dreamless slumber.

When Andrea awoke in the morning, Sean was gone. She didn't like the bite of disappointment that gave her.

Last night, Sean had held her like a mate would, kissing and cuddling, touching, nuzzling. Shifters did that in their animal forms, curving around each other and basking in the safe joy of being together. Her stepfather had done so when she was little, holding her after her mother died, the two of them united in grief.

She'd not had the comfort of such a thing in a long time. Sean was tearing down the walls Andrea had built against the world, and she wasn't certain whether to embrace that or cower in terror.

Andrea showered, dressed, and went downstairs to find Dylan in the kitchen drinking coffee, alone. Cowering in terror started to sound good. Glory's scent was all over Dylan, and from the way his eyes flicked to Shifter white and back to blue, Andrea knew that he could smell Sean's scent all over *her*.

"Nothing happened," she said as she moved to the coffeepot.

"Sean is almost at his century mark," Dylan said in a dry voice. "He can sleep with whatever female he likes."

Andrea poured herself coffee from an old-fashioned percolator pot, carried the cup to the table, and sat down across from Dylan, making herself face him. Andrea remembered how he'd looked at her the night Glory had brought her home, with a white-hot stare that Sean must have learned from him. Dylan had blue eyes, like his sons', and a touch of gray in otherwise black hair, but he possessed a grim darkness that Liam and Sean both lacked. Dylan was a few centuries old, born long before the Shifters ever considered making themselves tame for humans. His eyes carried the weight of his years, and he hadn't hidden the fact that a half-Fae Lupine was not someone he wanted living in the same house with him.

"You know, I didn't come here to make trouble," Andrea said. "Not between you and Sean, or you and Glory. Honestly. I just wanted somewhere to lick my wounds, somewhere to find my equilibrium."

Dylan nodded, eyes settling again to human blue. "And this is a fine place to do it. You're safe here, Andrea. I promise you."

Andrea turned her coffee cup on the placemat, breathing

the coffee smell to keep up her courage. Dylan might not be Shiftertown leader anymore, but that didn't mean he'd run off with his tail between his legs. Slipping in the hierarchy meant that he was only a *little* less powerful than Liam.

She drew a breath. "Sean told me that if you hadn't wanted me to come here, I wouldn't have been allowed."

"True."

"Then what made you let me?" Andrea sipped the coffee, cool enough to drink now. It was rich and good; Glory's coffee always was.

"Glory. She's fond of you and thought it would be best if you came here. I trust her judgment."

Oh really? "Then why did you take off the minute I walked into the house?" That still bothered her. "I didn't even know you lived here. Glory sprang that on me when I was walking up the porch steps. 'Oh, by the way, I've shacked up with the most powerful Feline in South Texas.'"

Dylan didn't smile. "Liam is the most powerful Feline in South Texas. Sean and I are neck and neck for second, though Sean will pull ahead soon. He's younger, and I'm tired of the game."

Andrea traced the rim of her coffee cup and made herself look into his intense blue eyes. "You didn't answer the question. Why did you leave the moment I arrived?"

"Clan business." Dylan raised his cup, took a sip. "Nothing to do with you."

"And it's coincidence that this business happened the same night I got here?"

His smile was so quick she would have missed it if she hadn't been looking hard at him. "Yes."

"I'll have to take your word for it."

"You will, yes."

Glory clicked down the stairs and into the kitchen at that moment, tall and slim and dressed from head to toe in hot pink. "Oh, good, you're chatting. Sean went home?"

"Apparently," Andrea said.

Glory smiled. "But you didn't have any more nightmares, did you?"

"No." Something tight loosened inside Andrea. "No, I didn't."

"Good. Dylan's going to make breakfast, then we're having a pride meeting at Liam's bar. About the shootings."

Andrea looked at her in surprise. "Do you want me there? I'm not part of the pride." Neither was Glory.

Dylan rose and headed for the stove. "You're a witness. You and Glory and Ronan. So, yes, Liam and I want you there."

He proceeded to clatter frying pans and cook up an amazing concoction of sausage, eggs, and potatoes. Discussion over.

An hour or so later, Andrea found herself seated next to Kim Morrissey in the closed bar. Liam lounged on a chair next to Kim, his long legs up, feet propped on the table. Like Sean, Liam wore motorcycle boots, although Sean's were hooked around the legs of his chair as he sat backward, arms on the slats.

Remembering how good Sean had felt curled up behind her made Andrea flush. She didn't know why—they hadn't done anything sexual. Kim caught sight of her flush and smiled knowingly, which made Andrea blush even harder.

Ronan was there too, the big Ursine giving Andrea a wave. Ellison came in behind him. Ellison, as usual, had dressed in cowboy boots, a black shirt, a big silver belt buckle, and a black hat, which he hung up near the bar, smoothing out his honey-colored hair.

Annie, the other waitress, was there, with a tall human man that Annie had her arm around. Annie had mentioned her human boyfriend in passing, a friend of Kim's, she'd said, but Andrea hadn't met him yet. The thin man didn't look frightened to be in a roomful of Shifters, but Annie's stance was protective. *Hurt him and you're toast,* her body language said.

"The owner of the bar wanted to close it because of the shooting," Liam began without preliminary. "I convinced him to keep it open and not give in to terror tactics. Besides, how would poor Shifter bar managers and the waitresses make any money?"

Liam flashed his charming Irish smile, and the Shifters smiled with him. Silas, Annie's human, looked a little confused, but Andrea understood Liam's joke. If humans were too short-sighted to catch on to how Shifters could survive on part-time pittance, then they deserved to be duped.

"But this is a serious situation," Liam went on. "Sean's been talking to the police. Sean?"

"I had another chat with the detective yesterday morning," Sean said. "She didn't have much more to tell me."

"She?" Andrea asked.

Sean didn't seem to notice Andrea's sudden possessive growl. "The woman didn't look happy to have our problem dumped on her, but I managed to talk her around."

I'll bet. Andrea imagined him smiling his quiet smile, and the female detective being unable to resist his charming blue eyes. She wondered if the detective had realized that Sean had gone commando that morning, and she wanted to growl again.

"She said she'd continue to look into it," Sean said. "But she suspects it's gang kids who have decided to make Shifters their target. Sort of counting coup, she said. She looked up the license number of the car, and as you suspected, Liam, it was stolen. In her opinion, it's kids up to no good. The shooting in San Antonio yesterday didn't change her mind, at least it hadn't when I spoke to her again this morning. Random, she said. No one seems very interested in our little problem."

Sean delivered the story in a calm voice, but Andrea sensed his simmering anger.

Liam listened without changing his expression. "Ronan, what's your assessment?"

Ronan shrugged his big shoulders. "At first glance, a lowrider full of gang kids, like the cop said."

"And at second glance?"

"It was too organized, and they weren't kids. In human terms, adults. The attack was exactly timed when there weren't a lot of people outside the bar and when I went off to use the gents'. I kinda do that every night at about the same time. Usually there isn't anyone but Shifters in here then, although we got some humans out barhopping that night."

Liam took this in. "So a planned hit at a time there would be only Shifters inside—they thought—when they know the guard steps away from the door."

"Sorry, Liam," Ronan said. He no longer looked mournful, but his eyes held shame.

Dylan, standing behind him, put a hand on Ronan's shoulder. "Not to worry, my friend. No one blames you."

"Dad's right," Liam said. "You chased them off, Ronan, before they could do more damage. Well done." He flicked his gaze to Dylan. "Now, we move on to the shooting in San Antonio. Dad?"

"I've been down in San Antonio for a while, cleaning up clan business," Dylan said. There were knowing nods around the table, indicating that everyone but Andrea and Annie's friend knew what he was talking about. "Ely Barry, one of our clan, and his family were at a café in Alamo Heights. He was having lunch—a double cheeseburger, he made sure to mention. A car drives up, two young men get out, unload their weapons, jump back in, and roar away. Most of the Shifters hit the deck, but Ely had to be a hero and pull a cub out of the way. Cub was fine; Ely took four shots to the stomach."

Andrea was aware of the glances in her direction. Ely had been dying, and Andrea and her Fae magic had ensured that he'd live to eat another double cheeseburger.

"Good for Ely," Ronan said.

"Don't worry, he's milking it for all it's worth."

The Shifters laughed, happy that tragedy had been dodged.

"The point, my friends," Liam said when the laughter trailed off, "is that we have someone targeting Shifter establishments—that is to say, human establishments that have a large Shifter clientele. Is their goal to punish the human owners or to frighten Shifters away from said establishments?"

"Does it matter?" Kim asked. She moved her hand to her abdomen. "They're shooting and maiming people. Killing them but for luck and Andrea."

Sean rested his arm across the back of Andrea's chair. "And Andrea can't be everywhere."

"The question is what are we going to do about it?" Kim continued. She had been a courtroom lawyer, and though she was seated, in a loose dress with her Shifter mate at her side, her voice was still crisp and lawyerlike. "Stay home and lock the doors? Or figure out who is doing this and put a stop to it?"

"That's my girl." Liam grinned at the others. "Didn't I pick out a fighter?"

"We'll just have to convince the police this is serious," Kim went on.

"Good luck with that," Ronan muttered.

"I know people," Kim said.

Annie's human boyfriend, Silas, spoke up for the first time. "So do I. I can put a word in with my police contacts if you want."

Andrea leaned in to Sean. "Who is he?"

"Friend of mine," Kim answered for him. "He's a journalist."

"A reporter?" Andrea stared in disbelief. "You let a reporter in here?"

"Silas likes Shifters."

Andrea met Silas's gaze—briefly; he had to look away.

Andrea's experience with reporters had been all bad. One had once come out to the Colorado Shiftertown to nose around, and the next thing they knew, the reporter had hinted that the Shifter males, because of a lack of females, kidnapped human women and made slaves of them. This told to the reporters by a human Shifter groupie who'd been dumped by her Shifter boyfriend. Humans had been so outraged, they'd wanted Shifters rounded up and shot, and Shifters had to scramble around to prove that wasn't true. That had been ten years ago, but the worry of it still hung like a pall.

"Silas is fine," Sean said, with a glance at Silas that told the tall man he'd better be fine.

"I don't mind you trying," Liam said. "Not that I have much hope for your chances, but it can't hurt. In the meantime, the bar is open for business. I've convinced the owner to hire a second bouncer to help out Ronan."

"The café in San Antonio is now barred to Shifters," Dylan said. "I couldn't convince them not to do that. But I can't really blame them. They're scared."

"I'll keep the bar owner as calm as I can," Liam said. "If we can find the perpetrators, so much the better."

"I disagree."

Sean's voice was so quiet that Andrea almost missed it. But at his words, the bar went silent.

"Sean?" Liam looked over at him, eyes still. "What do you want to say?"

All gazes turned to Sean, sitting strong and quiet beside Andrea with an air of power that matched Liam's.

"It's fine for us to find these gobshites and stop them," Sean said. "And by all means, we will. But you're saying you'd risk lives—the lives of Andrea, Kim, the life of your unborn cub—to prove that you're not afraid of humans? I'm thinking that's not wise, Liam. We shut the bar and find the bastards, while we keep our families safe."

CHAPTER SEVEN

The room got very quiet. Andrea saw Kim start to speak but one look at Liam made her close her mouth again. Dylan's hands tightened on the chair he leaned on, but even he kept his lips firmly together.

Liam's tone was light when he answered. "So, should we show the humans that we scramble into our holes the minute they make a threat?"

"No." Sean said it emphatically. "We find them and make the bastards pay. But we also shouldn't encourage Shifters, especially the cubs and the mates, to be in a position to take more bullets."

Liam and Sean studied each other across the table, neither giving way to the other. Liam's eyes flicked to Shifter white, cat pupils slitted, before they snapped back to human. "I never meant that we should dance in front of human guns in our altogether, Sean."

"I know." Sean's words were flat. Simple.

Liam couldn't be seen looking away first. He was leader, the alpha of this entire community. Sean had to drop his gaze before Liam did or risk his gesture being taken by the others as a challenge. If Sean challenged, especially in public, he and Liam would have to fight. And watching them now, Andrea understood that the fight would be close. Too close to call.

Sean knew this too. He held Liam's gaze a little while longer before he gave his brother a faint nod and looked away. Liam blew out a breath.

"I think we're done here," Liam said. "Business as usual, but extra security, extra caution."

It was a dismissal. The Shifters drifted away from the pulled-together tables; Silas went with Annie. The others were talking together, Ellison laughing about something with Glory.

Sean rose and silently left the bar. Andrea followed him out.

She easily caught up to him at the field that was the shortcut to Shiftertown. Sean wasn't walking fast but contemplating the world with a slow stride. Andrea knew he heard her, even though he didn't look at her. He'd scent her, feel her warmth at his side.

"Liam is different from any pack leader I've ever known," Andrea said, sticking her hands into her pockets.

Sean still didn't look at her. "Is he?"

"Of course he is. He let you have an opinion. Not only that, he let you voice it in front of everyone. My pack leader in Colorado would have been across the table clawing out your throat for challenging his decision."

"Good thing Liam isn't a bloody self-centered Lupine then."

"He didn't like what you said, but I think he agrees with you."

Sunlight glistened on Sean's silver sword. "Maybe."

Andrea walked a few more paces in silence, hands digging farther into her pockets. Shifter males *never* challenged their dominant in front of others, unless they wanted to be used to wipe the floor, but Sean had fearlessly said what he thought, disagreeing outright. Once again, Sean was proving himself different from any other Shifter Andrea had met.

"You're not a coward, Sean."

"I'm not? Whew, good to hear that."

"But I think Liam's right. If we give in to the shooters and hide, they'll just keep coming. They'll know they can win."

"I never said anything about letting them win." Sean finally looked at her, and she suddenly understood why Liam had backed down from him in there. Yes, *Liam* had done the backing down, she knew, and probably Dylan had understood that too. Sean had shielded his eyes first, sure, but he'd let Liam know he was breaking eye contact on purpose, so that Liam wouldn't lose face.

"Do you think I want to see my nephew bloodied up like Ely?" Sean asked. "Or my father? Or you? Especially not you." He stopped and faced her, his breath streaming like fog. "It's a damn scary thing claiming a mate. I want to protect you all the time, and never stop."

Andrea tried to smile. "Maybe you should have considered that before you claimed me."

"I did. I've thought about it a lot. For ten years I've pondered it."

His gaze was intense, but Andrea looked back at him in surprise. "Ten years? You only met me a few weeks ago."

"Ten years ago, my brother Kenny died. Ten years before that, Kenny lost his mate, Sinead. Both of those nights were the worst of my life, together with the day we lost our mum. All three of those times, I thought I'd die from the grief."

Andrea knew what he meant. She's been tiny when her mother had died, but the loss still pulled at her heart. "I'm sorry."

"When Dad arrived the night Kenny died, when he and Liam saw that Kenny was already dead, Dad just folded up on himself. Right there on the ground, curled into a ball. I'd lost my brother, but he'd lost a cub, a child he'd made with my mother. The mate bond between Dad and my mum was strong. And now Dad had lost another link to her." Sean cupped Andrea's shoulders, his fingers points of strength. "Is that what taking a mate is, ultimately, Andy-love? Nothing but loss?"

A lump formed in Andrea's throat. "I don't know." The mate bond, that almost magical quality, had nothing to do with the mating ceremony itself, but made mates live and die for each other. "My mother and stepfather were mate blessed but never formed the bond," she said softly.

Sean raised his brows in surprise. "I'm sorry, lass. If they didn't, that's a tragedy."

"I was little, but I could tell. My stepfather adored my mother, but she didn't love him the same way. She was grateful to him, fond of him, but there was no bond. She'd never got over my real father, you see. The Fae."

Sean's eyes flickered. "That so, love? I thought . . ."

"That he raped her?" Andrea's smile was wry as she shook her head. "That was the official story. Less humiliating for the Lupines if she didn't go willingly to a Fae, isn't it? But she loved my real father. She never stopped loving him."

"Damn. That must have been hard on you."

"My stepfather is a kind man, and I love him. My mother knew he'd not harm me when I was born, even knowing I'd been sired by a Fae, and he didn't. He loved me for her sake. But she accepted his mate-claim out of expediency, not love."

Sean touched the curls at the base of her neck. "That doesn't mean *you* need to accept out of expediency, lass."

"I know. But it made me not want a mate pairing without the mate bond, which was why I said no to Jared." Andrea grimaced. "Well, that, and he's an asshole."

"Even though the mate bond can tear us up in the end?" Sean slid his hands around her waist, under her coat. "In there, thinking of you being shot, falling at my feet, me having to stick my sword through you, like I had to with Kenny." He swallowed. "I don't ever want to have to do that, love. Never, ever."

So that was the difference between Sean and Liam.

What Liam saw as giving ground and retreating, Sean saw as keeping loved ones safe. Because Sean was the one who'd have to look at those loved ones last.

The thought made Andrea want to hold him. She slid her hands up his arms, loving the feel of the firm biceps beneath his coat, and locked her fingers behind his neck. Such strength and such compassion rolled into one male.

"Then you've changed your mind about wanting me as your mate?" Andrea had the right to walk out of the mate claim, but then, so did Sean. But the thought of him turning away from her made her heart suddenly ache.

"I should. To save myself from the hurting."

"Can we ever? Hurting is part of life, isn't it? So is happiness."

Sean caressed the small of her back. "When did you become the wise one?"

"The day I told my whole Shiftertown I wouldn't mate with that sorry excuse for a Lupine, no matter how much he and his friends terrorized me."

Sean's touch became stronger, his mouth relaxing. "I'd have given a lot to see that. I bet some wolf jaws dropped."

"They didn't exactly applaud me."

"And you knew they wouldn't. But you did it anyway. That's my girl." He sounded proud, which warmed her.

"Scariest thing I've ever done." Well, that and meeting Sean for the first time, but the fear had been markedly different.

Sean's mouth softened even more. "But you being brave doesn't mean you're strong enough to take a bullet through your body. Liam's determined to keep the bar open, but I don't want you working there for a while. Not until we get this thing solved."

Andrea stepped back. "Wait a minute. Not go to work? Screw that."

Sean looked at her in surprise. What, he was expecting her to meekly say, "Yes, Sean," and obey? Looking into his eyes, she saw that he did. Oh, he did, did he?

"Andy-love, if I hadn't thrown you to the floor that night, you'd have been hit. You were right in the line of fire."

Andrea planted her hands on her hips. "If Liam can hire more guards and keeps the damn door closed, we'll be fine."

"Right. You'll be fine walking home alone at night from the place. Fine stepping out in the dark to empty the trash. You don't need to work; you're provided for. Dad made sure this Shiftertown was filthy rich. The jobs are to give the human social workers something to put in their reports."

"I know that. It's not the point."

"Waiting tables at a bar isn't freedom, love. It's showing humans what they want to see."

Just because Sean was sexy, and she hoped they could form the mate bond, didn't mean he couldn't drive her crazy. "No, it's helping out Liam. It's the side bet I have with Annie on who can get the best tips out of the humans. It's me with a bit of money of my own so I can buy myself a car and not have to depend on Morrissey handouts. It *is* freedom. To me."

"But it isn't safe." The growl came into Sean's voice. "Let Liam and me find these bastards and stop them first."

"You and Liam don't know who these people are or what they want or what they'll do to get it. You'll run off after them and get yourselves shot. Me, I'm just waiting tables in a bar protected by some very tough Shifters."

Sean's growl grew more pronounced. "So, what, you got yourself away from a crazed gobshite just to let yourself get offed in a drive-by?"

"What do you expect me to do?" Andrea didn't bother to keep her voice down. "Lock myself in the house and never leave it? Or maybe in *your* house?"

"At least there I could keep an eye on you."

"No." She poked Sean's chest. "I just got away from a creep who wanted to lock me up until I gave in to his mate-claim, every wolf in my pack happy to let him. Do you think I came here to hide myself away, cringing from every sound? Well, forget it. I'll take my chances with the trigger-happy humans."

She wrenched her boot heel from the muddy soil and marched away, but Sean was beside her in an instant. "You're brave, lass, but stupid."

"Oh, thank you very much. I understand, all right? You don't want me to die, and I appreciate that. I don't want to either. But I need to live my life, make my own decisions, take my own risks."

"Be a lone wolf?" Sean laughed, but the laugh held no warmth. "We couldn't afford that in the wild, and we can't now."

"This isn't the wild. This is Shiftertown, in the twenty-first century. And I'm tired of Shifter males trying to bully me."

Andrea started stalking away again, and in her heels, she could work up a really good stalk. Sean, though, could stride along there with her.

"Not bully, love. Protect. Jared deserves to die for trying to keep you submissive, trapped, and vulnerable. That's not how we cherish a mate."

"You are the most idealistic male I've ever met."

Sean slid his warm, strong hand into hers. "Someone has to be."

"I'm not giving up my job, Sean."

"Mmm."

He stopped arguing but didn't agree either. Andrea clenched her jaw even as she twined her fingers through his strong ones. They'd argue some more later, she knew that, but as long as they were fighting it out, that meant Sean hadn't won yet.

That night Andrea had the dream again. The threads that sought to bind her glittered evilly, the metallic cords tightening to crush her.

Andrea.

It wasn't Sean's voice this time. She had no idea who it was, and terror kept her from placing it, kept her from thinking.

Fight it, Andrea. Get free.

"I'm trying!" she shouted.

The threads choked her, suffocated her. Incoherent screams left her throat, and then something else bound her, iron bands, bigger, stronger, thicker than the threads. She clawed at them, dove upward from a well of sleep to find Sean in bed with her, his strong arms hard around her.

"Hush now," he murmured. "You're all right. I've got you."

Part of her wanted to struggle away, to yell at him. But terror drowned her, and she welcomed the warm, safe haven Sean offered.

Her body relaxed as he kissed her hair and drew her back against him. Andrea's eyes closed as he continued to cradle her, and she drifted into exhausted slumber.

When morning light touched Andrea's face, she sat up to find Sean out of bed and moving to the window, though the mattress still held his warmth. He wore only black briefs and a white T-shirt, the clothing molding to his body. A beautiful sight to wake up to.

"Sean."

Sean turned. "I didn't mean to wake you, love."

Andrea hugged the pillow he'd slept on to her chest. "You know, I've never yet seen your wildcat."

Sean studied her a moment, hands on hips, then he grinned. The smile warmed every part of her, and so did him tugging the T-shirt off over his head. His wide chest was dusted with dark hair, tight muscles moving under liquid dark skin. Sean obviously spent his summers shirtless in the sun.

Looking away was out of the question. Especially not when his hand went to his waistband, and the briefs slid down.

Strong, tanned legs. Narrow hips. A phallus thick with desire, rising from a dark thatch.

Yep, I was right. Black-haired all the way down.

Andrea saw this only briefly before Sean's limbs distorted with his shift. Claws sprouted on his hands and feet, which almost instantly turned into paws. His face elongated into a feline's, eyes becoming white blue, lips lifting from a row of pointed teeth. He dropped to all fours and shook out a lion's mane that grew down past his huge shoulders. It too was black.

Growling, Sean started for her. His paws were gigantic, his tail long, his eyes in his broad face light blue. Sean came for the bed, his intent clear.

Andrea held up her hands. "Don't you dare jump up here. Glory will never let me hear the end of it if you break the bed."

Sean put his forepaws on the mattress. Andrea found herself on her back, covered in warm fur and hot wildcat breath. His mane ticked.

Sean gave her face one long lick.

"Cat spit. Yuck."

Sean licked her again, thoroughly wetting every inch of her face. He moved to her neck, then her chest, burrowing into the top of her pajamas.

"Sean Morrissey, you stop that." Laughing, she shoved at him, but she couldn't budge him an inch.

His growls sounded smug, the look in his eyes satisfied. He nuzzled her with his huge velvet nose, which was like being nudged by a thousand-pound kitten.

"Damned Feline." Andrea stroked his face, reveling in the warmth of Sean's fur, the wiry heat of his mane. She'd never touched a Feline Shifter before, and their fur was different from wolves'. Softer, less shaggy, more like hot silk. She pressed a kiss between Sean's eyes, and he closed them, rumbling in his belly. Purring.

"Are you staying for breakfast?" Andrea asked him. "Should I tell your dad to make enough coffee for you? Or maybe pour out a bowl of milk?"

The purr turned to another growl. Sean backed off the bed, shook himself like the cat he was, and strolled to the window.

He was a beautiful beast. Each Feline's coat was different, and Sean's was lionlike, tawny with a hint of the broken spots of the jaguar. He gave her a look over his shoulder, one that said he knew that she liked what she saw. Conceited shit. Sean climbed over the windowsill and out onto the porch roof.

Andrea slid out of bed and went to the window in time to see him crouch on the edge of Glory's porch roof. She bit her lip, then let out her breath as he leapt gracefully across the space of the yard between the houses and landed on the Morrissey porch roof.

On his feet, of course. Sean sent her another look over his shoulder before he climbed into the open window to his own bedroom.

Andrea closed the window on the cold air. She'd been a little worried that she'd find Sean repugnant in his Feline form, but no. He didn't repel her at all. He was gorgeous in any form he wore.

Sean had left his T-shirt and underwear on the floor. Andrea picked up the briefs, looked at the waistband, and grinned. At least now she knew what size he wore.

Andrea had never been to a human clothing store before. The Colorado Springs Shiftertown had been isolated, it had been difficult to get into town to do any shopping, and Andrea's stepfather had never had a car. Andrea's usual practice was to order her clothes from a catalog, and they'd been delivered to a post office that served all of Shiftertown.

Glory swept up Andrea and took her to a street she said was called South Congress, or SoCo, with funky shops and flea markets, one of the few shopping areas that allowed Shifters. Andrea approached the shopping trip with excitement and guilty pleasure. She knew Sean would have a conniption if he knew she and Glory had left Shiftertown on their own, but Sean had driven off on his motorcycle earlier that morning, probably to talk to the police again about the shootings or maybe on some other errand for Liam.

Andrea had the feeling Sean was going to be very nice to Liam for a while after nearly making a leadership challenge the day before. Knowing Sean, he'd do that to keep the peace, not because he thought he'd been wrong.

Glory parked her small car in a tight space right on the street the instant another car deserted it. While humans got busy gawking at Glory's six-foot, svelte body in skin-tight black leather, Andrea was able to browse the flea markets without attracting much attention.

On this cold Saturday, Andrea's sweater and leather coat hid her Collar. Her Fae blood made her a little shorter and slimmer than Glory, and she could walk right past most humans without them realizing what she was.

Of course, she thought wryly, whenever Glory was nearby, Andrea could stride around naked with a big arrow pointing to her Collar, and no one would notice.

Glory walked into a store that carried men's and women's clothing similar to what Glory liked to wear. The girl behind the counter, who made bright red and yellow vinyl look cute, snapped her gum and said, "Hey, Glory. How are y'all?"

"Not too bad, Mabel. Need to pick up some things for my honey."

"Y'all know where to find them. You need any help, you just let me know."

Glory nodded in a friendly way and led Andrea to an aisle filled with men's T-shirts and boxer shorts in all colors and designs. Shelves and racks also held gadgets, the function of which Andrea had no idea and wasn't sure she wanted to.

Glory snatched up some black satin boxers covered with big red hearts. "How about these for Dylan?"

Andrea burst out laughing. "For Dylan?"

"You're right. He's not so flamboyant. I'll go with sub-dued." She picked up some bright blue ones, with two golf balls surrounding a disproportionately large golf tee printed on it. "Dylan's mentioned golf."

"He has?" Andrea moved to the stand that displayed briefs.

"In passing. Mostly to say that only humans would invent a game where they hit a ball and then chase after it themselves."

"Not an aficionado then."

"No." Glory put back the boxers and moved to browse the gadgets.

Andrea picked out three pairs of briefs, the designs of which made her laugh. She pictured Sean's face when he opened the package and laughed harder.

A waste of money, really, Andrea thought as she took the briefs to the counter. Sean would either get the joke or look disgusted, but either way he'd throw them away.

But what the hell? It was Andrea's tip money, and who said she couldn't have fun with the mating dance? If Sean insisted on holding her when she had bad dreams and wor-rying about her getting hurt, she got to tease the hell out of him.

"Oh, those are cute," Mabel at the counter crooned. "Are you a Shifter?" she asked as she put the purchases in a bright red shopping bag. "You don't look like one."

Andrea pulled down the edge of her sweater to reveal her Collar. "'Fraid so."

"No offense. All right?" She had a musical Texas accent and winning smile.

"No offense."

"How's that Connor doing? Tell him to come in more often. I'm starting to think he's forgotten about me."

Mabel looked too sane to be a Shifter groupie. She didn't wear Collar-like jewelry or have the frenzied look many groupies had. She had dark, friendly eyes, and maybe she just liked Connor.

Andrea smiled at her. "I'll tell him."

Glory bought a couple of the plain black satin boxers, a bottle of flavored lube, and a few toys Andrea pretended not to notice. Mabel laughed and cracked her gum, telling Glory her boyfriend was so lucky.

"Y'all come back now," she said as Andrea and Glory left the shop.

"Wish all humans were that friendly," Andrea said.

"She will be until Connor breaks her heart."

Andrea glanced back at the brightly painted shop. "You think he will?"

Glory shrugged. "It's inevitable, isn't it?"

She had a point, unfortunately. The store clerk was about the same human age as Connor, but Connor wouldn't take his place in the pride for a few more years and probably wouldn't be looking for permanent connections for another ten years after that. Humans aged quickly, so the girl might be middle-aged before Connor got around to taking a mate.

Kim and Liam had gotten around the age problem because of Fae magic, which would lengthen Kim's lifespan to match Liam's. This was a secret bargain made between the Fae and Shifters long ago, that if a Shifter had to take a human mate, a Fae had to agree to lengthen the human's lifespan. Andrea wasn't sure why or how this had come about, but the bargain was still honored.

Glory led Andrea across the street to a little bakery that served luscious-looking ice cream. Glory ordered two heaping cones of three different flavors, handed one to Andrea, and shoved the cash across the counter to the server. Andrea licked her cone as she followed Glory to a tiny table. The ice cream was delicate and good, and happily, Shifters could devour large quantities and burn it off later with a good run. There were advantages to being Shifter.

A serious-looking man in a suit stopped in front of their table. "Excuse me, but you can't be in here."

Glory looked up in surprise. "I come in here all the time. Ask them." She waved her ice-cream cone at the humans behind the counter.

"New policy. You can buy the ice cream, but then you have to go. No Shifters lingering in the store."

Glory gave her ice cream a long, almost sensuous lick. She looked up at the man over it, and he started to sweat.

"Why not?" Andrea asked him.

He wiped his forehead. "Not when establishments that allow Shifters are getting shot up. The management decided. I'm sorry, ladies. I have to ask you to leave."

CHAPTER EIGHT

The man's stern stance faltered as Glory rose, her six-foot height made higher by four-inch heels. She pinned him with her Shifter stare, and he swallowed hard, trying to stand his ground.

Glory ran her tongue around the ice cream. "Are you telling me you're kicking us out?"

"Leave him alone," Andrea said quickly. "It's not his fault."

"But he looks like he'd taste good," Glory purred.

Andrea got up. She was about the same height as the man, and she knew she looked positively harmless next to Glory. Good Shifter, bad Shifter. Andrea gave him a sweet smile. "You'll be fine if you back away slowly. Give her a little more ice cream, and she'll leave."

Glory continued to lick her cone and give the man her hungry stare. The manager swung around and signaled to the servers behind the counter, who were watching with wide eyes. "Give them whatever they want. No charge." He gave Andrea a pleading look. "And then you really have to go. I'm sorry. It's not my decision."

"We understand." Andrea asked for a couple of pints each of dark chocolate and vanilla-cinnamon, and the servers scrambled to pack the tubs.

Glory continued to lick her ice-cream cone, watching the man with a cold stare. Andrea took the bag with the pints of ice cream and urged Glory to come with her.

Glory gave her melting ice cream one last lick, dabbed a bit onto the man's nose, and handed him the half-empty cone. She sauntered out as only Glory could saunter, aware that all eyes were on her.

Andrea and Glory held it together until they reached the little car down the street, then they dropped inside it and collapsed into laughter. Glory high-fived Andrea, started the car, and ruthlessly backed out into traffic.

"This is bad, though," Andrea said as they drove north across the Congress Street bridge. Rain was just starting to patter down, the scent of the bat colony that lived beneath the bridge filling the humid air.

"I know." Glory swung around a slowing car. "Fucking humans. The Collars aren't enough?"

"Maybe this is what the shooters want—terrifying humans into keep us penned in the Shiftertowns. Why, I wonder?"

"Does there have to be a reason? Humans are afraid of us, and people act like assholes when they're afraid."

"I know that, but I mean, why now? It's been twenty years since humans have known about us. They know what we can and can't do by now—or what we will and won't do. It seems like there's something more behind this."

"Whatever." Glory was furious, which added to her already maniacal driving. Andrea sank back in her seat, holding on and speculating the rest of the way home.

"Hey, Glory left her bag here," Connor said from where he sat with Kim on the other side of the kitchen.

Sean flipped burgers on the griddle, cooking inside because it was too rainy to do it outside. Glory had stormed in, vented her spleen about being kicked out of her favorite bakery, and stormed out again. Andrea hadn't said much to Sean, just looked concerned and presented Connor with a pint of dark-chocolate ice cream, his favorite.

"These aren't Glory's," Kim said, rustling the tissue paper in the red bag. "Andrea told me what Glory bought."

Connor helped Kim pull out the tissue paper and then the rest of the bag's contents. Connor held up a pair of black briefs that had the word "Fine" printed on the back. "Did you buy these for Liam, Kim? I dare him to wear them."

Sean froze, spatula in midair, grease dripping to the floor.

Kim's blue eyes went bright with amusement. "Not me. I haven't been shopping in a while. I think Andrea left these."

"What for?" Connor stared at the briefs before his puzzled look gave way to a smile. "Oh, these are for, *Sean*." He cackled with laughter as he shook out another pair that had a cupid's bow and arrow on the crotch. "Hey, what do you think *this* means?"

Sean jerked back to the stove and slid his spatula under a burger before it burned to a crisp. "Bloody hell."

Damn Andrea, she was as changeable as the sea. Staring him down, telling him she wanted her freedom one moment, buying him sexy underwear the next. Not giving it to him, but slyly leaving it where the rest of his family could find it. Either she was signaling her intentions or making him a laughingstock. Or both.

So she wanted to play, did she? Lupines were like that, playful about the most serious things. Look at Ellison, dressing up in his Stetson as the overboard Texan, or Glory in her spike heels and black leather. Cats had much more dignity.

But if Andrea wanted to challenge him, Sean was up for it.

Connor pulled out the last pair of briefs, blue and covered with smiley faces. "Try these on Sean. I have to see this."

"Shut it, Connor. I—"

The scent came to him like a stinging slap. Sean dropped the spatula, and grease flew.

"Sean?" Kim's concern cut into his alertness, but not far. He smelled woods, mint, and the acrid tinge of the otherworld.

"Son of a bitch." He ran for the living room, grabbed his sword, and bolted out the back door.

Connor shouted after him. "Sean, what is it? What's wrong?"

"Stay inside," Sean shouted back. "Guard Kim."

Rain poured down as Sean ran, the cold casting fog in the green yards behind houses. Nothing was fenced in the back—the yards ran together under stands of towering trees, providing space for kids to run and play, although not today. The sun was setting, the fog darkening.

Sean found him in the middle of a circle of trees not ten yards from Glory's house. The man was tall and unnaturally slim, his hair hanging down his back in a braid like twisted white silk. His face was clean shaven, unlined, perpetually young, and bore a cruel sharpness. He wore, not robes, but a mail shirt that looked to be made of beaten silver, leather leggings, boots, and a longbow across his back. Dressed for battle in a *Lord of the Rings* sort of way.

Sean unsheathed the sword and pointed it at the man's chest, feeling a hell of a tingle as the sword touched the gate between the worlds. "What the fuck do you want?"

The man looked down at the blade in some disdain. "Feline. *She* summons me. Don't interfere."

"Who? No one here would be daft enough to summon a Fae . . ."

He trailed off as the man's cold black gaze moved to Glory's house. Andrea was in there, alone, because Glory had gone off to find Dylan.

"Shit," Sean whispered.

He ran for Glory's house, finding the back door unlocked. He pounded through the unlighted kitchen and up the dark staircase to Andrea's bedroom, bursting in to find Andrea on her bed in a fetal position, her eyes closed, her breathing rapid.

"Andrea, wake up. Wake up, love."

She wouldn't come out of it. Sean dropped the sword and got up on the bed with her, shaking her. "Wake up, now."

Andrea's eyelids fluttered. She looked at Sean in half-focused confusion, then awareness hit her, and she gasped. "Sean."

Sean gathered her into his arms, kissing her damp forehead. "It's all right, love. What were you dreaming?"

She shuddered. "The same. The same nightmare, except . . ."

"There was someone there."

Andrea nodded, her eyes full of fear. "I hear his voice sometimes. This time I could see him."

"White-haired Fae bastard with ice-cold eyes?"

"Yes," she said, then she jerked in his arms. "How the hell do you know?"

"I just saw him. He says you summoned him."

"Saw him? What you mean, *saw* him?"

"He's standing out in that circle of trees behind this house, large as life."

Andrea gaped. "But I didn't summon anyone. I never would."

"Not on purpose. You did it through the dream."

Her eyes darkened with fear. "Oh, Sean. Oh, crap."

"Not your fault." Sean rubbed his hand down her back. "Not your fault."

She raised her head. "I need to see this Fae."

"Not a good idea."

Andrea wrenched herself from his grasp. "I don't care. Stop protecting me. Show me where you saw him."

"Andrea."

She was strong and fast as she twisted away and to her feet. She was halfway to the dark window before Sean got off the bed, but instead of climbing out and running off, she stopped and pulled off her shirt.

Sean couldn't move. He saw black lace cupping the generous curve of her breasts before Andrea unhooked her bra with one hand and started peeling off her jeans with the other.

Her naked breasts were firm and high, round peaches tipped with dusky red. Another slash of black lace enclosed her hips, and Sean lay transfixed as she stripped off the panties. Her slim waist flared to lush hips, with a wisp of black between her thighs. For one instant, Andrea and Sean looked at each other, she a woman bare for the man who wanted her. Then she shifted.

Shifter wolves were larger than natural, wild wolves, the females almost as large as the males. Andrea wasn't as big as Sean's wildcat but looked every bit as strong. Her fur was black, like her hair, her gray eyes the same shade as her human eyes, which was unusual. Most Shifters' eyes changed with the shift—Sean's became very light blue as did Liam's; Glory's turned to silver. Not Andrea's. Hers stayed the same, smoky gray and beautiful.

These thoughts shot through his head seconds before Andrea turned and gracefully leapt out onto the porch roof. Sean sprang from the bed, tore off his clothes, shifted, and followed her.

Andrea, as a wolf, nosed around the clearing behind the house. The rain had stopped, the wind tearing gashes in the clouds, revealing the waxing moon. Sean sniffed the wind, but the air was clean. All scent of Fae had gone.

Sean shouldered past Andrea to the spot where he'd seen the Fae. He watched as Andrea, doglike, sniffed the dead leaves, pawing at them with one large foot. She looked up at Sean with her smoke gray eyes, again meeting his gaze without fear.

The dominance roles of Shifters were more obvious when they were animals, when verbal communication didn't interfere. A thorough discussion of the Heisenberg uncertainty principle was out of the question, but Shifters could communicate basic emotions, the most simple signals being dominance and submission.

A submissive Feline or Lupine would keep his head lower than the dominant's, or run a few paces behind them, or move aside for those more dominant in the pride. That was survival—the leader kept an eye out for enemies, and one growl sent the pride or pack either into hiding or into defensive positions. Stragglers or wanderers couldn't be guarded. The leader protected, and the rest stayed out of his way or obeyed his commands without question, for their own safety.

What they didn't do was stand in front of the dominant and look him straight in the eye. They didn't deliberately turn away and start investigating the area of danger, not letting him take the lead. They didn't twitched their tails derisively when the dominant growled at them to stay back.

Sean didn't want Andrea walking across the place that the Fae had occupied. The line between the real world and Faerie blurred in places, and who knew whether that doorway would open suddenly, the warrior Fae ready to drag her in. He shouldered Andrea away from the spot, rumbling a long lion growl.

Andrea gave him a glare and curled her lip. The words *bite me* might as well have been stamped on her forehead.

So, Sean bit her.

Andrea whipped out from under him, whirled, and clamped her jaw around his throat. Sean snarled and shook her off. He shoved her to the ground with one big paw, the temper of his beast aroused.

Sean had wrestled with his brothers growing up, but he'd never fought with Lupines. The interspecies truce that kept them from tearing each other apart cautioned against even playful wrestling matches. Sean guessed Andrea had never read the pact or wouldn't care if she had.

Andrea squirmed out from under him, rolled to her feet, and sprinted away. Sean sprinted right after her. Andrea stopped, then spun and faced him, down on her forepaws, rear in the air.

Oh, she wanted to play, did she? Sean let out a roar as he leapt at her. At the last moment, Andrea sidestepped, and Sean tumbled through air where she'd been. He scrambled to regain his feet only to find her behind him, her teeth in his tail. He yelped, whipped around, and this time sent her to the ground with him on top of her.

Under him, Andrea shifted back to human. "Get off me, you great big hairball."

Sean held her down, her scent in his nostrils, her warm body writhing beneath his. *You shouldn't do that to a horny Shifter.*

Andrea wound her bare arms around him, hands in his mane, with a smile that would melt stone. "You're so warm. Like a fur coat."

Sean's growl softened. He nuzzled her cheek, liking the feel of her human body against his furry one. He licked her gently between the breasts, her salt taste heady.

He couldn't take this. He had to have her. He licked her again as he let his body shift back to its human form.

Andrea found herself holding a very naked, very aroused human male. Sean's eyes changed from pale, slitted cat's to dark blue, but the look in them was still untamed. He brushed his mouth over hers, then again and again. Her own longing coiled through her body, and she kissed him back with matching hunger.

Sean's skin was slick with sweat under her hands, his mouth hot, body heavy. Excitement gripped her as Sean's kisses opened her mouth, tongue sliding in, tasting, seeking.

Andrea's blood pounded, her body singing as his hands heated her skin. His knee parted hers, his penis touching the opening that was wet and ready for him. She'd be lying her ass off if she said she didn't want him.

His body enclosed hers as he kissed her, a Shifter protecting his mate even as he devoured her. Clouds shrouded the moon again, and it was dark under the trees, hiding them from watchers.

Sean bit her neck. He was silently urging her to raise

her hips so he could slide inside, but at the same time he was holding himself back, every muscle shaking with the strain of it.

"Sean," Andrea murmured, and it wasn't a murmur of protest.

"I need to stop." Sean's voice was tense, his eyes flicking again to white blue. "But I can't when you say my name in that fucking sexy voice."

"I could always hit you with a stray branch."

He growled deep in his throat. "Don't. Let me fight this, or I'll take you. I don't want to hurt you."

"I'm not screaming and trying to get away," she said softly. "You might have noticed."

"I want this mating. I want it fierce. I want to be inside you and not come out for days."

That could happen. If the mating frenzy was hard enough between Shifters, they could hole up and screw until exhaustion sent them into a weeklong slumber. Right now, that didn't sound like such a bad thing.

Sean was damn big. Big body, big cock. Nice. Andrea was smaller than most Shifter women—she wondered with a touch of both fear and excitement what would happen when they joined.

She touched his lips. "Sean, I've never . . ."

Sean's eyes snapped back to blue, forcing the savage in him to calm. "Never what?"

"Gone roller skating." She wriggled against him. "What do you think?"

Sean focused directly on her, gaze intense. "Then I am the first . . ."

"Naked man between my legs, yes." Andrea brushed fingers through his warm hair. "In my pack, if a female let a man in her bed, he pretty much stayed there for life. We only had about one female for every ten males. Everyone was desperate for mates."

"The first." Sean drew a shuddering breath. His eyes changed again, the Shifter in him wanting to roar his triumph. He'd touched her *first*. Before any other male could claim her.

Sean fought his way back to sanity. "Then why don't you stop me?"

Andrea's foot glided up to his thigh, her light touch erotic. "Because I don't want to."

"Sean?" Kim's voice cut through the darkness, followed by Connor's.

"Sean! Is Andrea all right? Where are you? . . . Oh."

Connor and Kim stopped, out of breath, to stare at the couple on the ground. Sean moved protectively to cover Andrea; she was small enough to be hidden under him. Kim clapped her hand to her mouth and spun around, her laughter snorting out of her, but Connor gave a happy whoop. "Did she accept the claim then, Sean? When's the ceremony?"

Sean growled. "Be off with you before you embarrass her."

"It's all right." Andrea said to Connor around the wall of Sean's body. "We're just playing, Connor. Be a love and fetch some clothes from my house?"

"I'll do it." Kim started back across the yard. She was shaking as she walked, and when she was out of earshot—for a human—she shouted with laughter.

"Stop gawping, lad," Sean said.

"Get a move on, Sean," Connor said. "Our house needs more females. And cubs. Our family's in danger of dying out."

"Don't be daft, lad. I can't very well persuade her to do the ceremony with you standing over us in the mud."

Connor heaved a sigh of aggrieved youth. "Fine, fine. Just hurry it up, will you?" He spun around and loped back toward the Morrissey house.

"And get those burgers off the grill before they burn the house down."

"Already did it," Connor sent back over his shoulder, and then the back door banged behind him. He'd probably already eaten one too.

"Why don't you shift back?" Sean asked Andrea. He was looking down at her, eyes glittering with the anger of a male interrupted from doing a favorite male thing. "You can shift back and run off home. You didn't need Kim to fetch your clothes."

Andrea smiled at him. "Maybe I just wanted to have a few more minutes alone with you."

"Don't tempt me, love." Sean's voice shook. He leaned to her, nuzzled her cheek, breath hot. "I want much more than a few minutes."

Andrea licked his chin. "Then don't waste them," she said, and kissed him.

Sean let himself get buried in her kiss, his mouth roving her throat and neck, down to her soft, tight breasts. But Kim was far too swift in fetching Andrea's clothes, and they had to part, Sean shifting to save himself embarrassment from just how damned desperately hard he was.

"Excuse me, what the hell are you doing?" Andrea demanded half an hour later.

Andrea had been hot and horny while Sean walked her the few steps home and accompanied her upstairs. Once in her bedroom, instead of pursuing their interrupted mating, Sean shifted back to his human form and dressed himself. He'd laid the Sword of the Guardian across the top of Andrea's dresser, and now he'd opened a drawer and started removing her underwear.

"*Sean.*" Andrea planted her hands on her hips. "I asked, what the hell are you doing? Trying to figure out what size *I* wear?"

"I'm cleaning out a space for my own clothes."

"Why?"

"Because I'm moving in here, love. While you're dreaming up Fae warriors, I need to be with you to stop the dreams."

Andrea huffed out a breath. "Glory can do that. I'll have her sleep in here with me."

"Glory's not here, is she? Trust me, she's off looking for Dad, and when she finds him, she'll hole up with him awhile."

"What? Leaving poor, helpless me all unprotected?"

"She knows you're protected. By me."

Andrea snapped her brows together. "You can sleep in the spare room."

"That's not on, love. I can't wake you up if I'm not sleeping with you. If you're summoning things or they're using your dreams to make a hole from Faerie, I'm going to be right next to you to stop it."

Goddess help me. Sean cuddling up to her the last couple of nights had warmed and soothed her, but what they'd done in the clearing had left her burning. The memory of his firm arousal pressing to her so-slick opening hadn't faded, and in fact excited her even through her anger. If he got into bed with her tonight, she'd never be able to hold herself back. She'd give in to him completely, and then the mating ceremony would be a mere formality. Shifters did have casual sex without mating—all the time—but this wouldn't be casual, and both of them knew it.

"Why are you doing this to me?"

Sean turned from the dresser. "To keep you safe. What else? And to figure out that's going on. That Fae appeared in the trees while I was home grilling burgers. No warnings—he was just there."

"Don't look at me; I don't know why."

"That's why I'm going to hang around you, to find out why."

Andrea sat down on the bed and put her head in her hands.

One second later, she sagged against him on the mattress, his thigh against hers, his arm around her shoulder. "We'll figure this out, love," he said. "I won't let you be hurt."

"That's not it. I mean, that's partly it. I thought that when I came here, my troubles would be over. Instead, I'm more confused than ever. I have a Feline who likes to climb through my window and go through my underwear, I have nightmares that scare the shit out of me, and now a Faerie creature pops into existence because I dream his voice. Instead of peace and quiet and shopping with my aunt, I'm shot at by humans and pursued by a Feline who's on the edge of mating frenzy."

"Welcome to Shiftertown," Sean said. "And I don't want to force you, love, no matter how frenzied I am."

"You're a Shifter male. It's what Shifter males do."

Sean raised his brows instead of growling in rage, showing her once again that the unreadable Sean wasn't behaving like he was supposed to. He took away his comforting embrace and rose from the bed. "Those bloody Lupines that raised you must have been right a piece of work."

"My stepfather is a kind man." A dart of pain pierced her heart. Her stepfather, Terry, wasn't strong; Andrea knew that, and yet he'd been simple and loving. She missed his warm smile, his embrace, even the way he liked to put onions on absolutely everything he ate. She'd cried and clung to him when he'd put her on the bus in Colorado, leaving behind the only Shifter who loved her. But Terry hadn't been allowed to come with her, by both human and Shifter law.

"The fact that you didn't run to this Jared, tail between your legs, makes you remarkable, love," Sean was saying.

"Huh. According to my pack, it made me ungrateful, untrustworthy, defiant, and bitchy. They thought my mating with Jared would be good for me, because I'd be moving up. The fact that Jared is a sexist, sadistic pig didn't matter very much. Except to me."

"Andrea."

Andrea looked up in surprise. Usually Sean called her *love* or *lass*, and never spoke to her in that quiet voice. "What?"

Sean watched her with a guarded expression. "You shouldn't have been able to resist Jared at all. Not with you so low in the pack. Not with him so high in the hierarchy and that determined. And you're not afraid of me, are you?"

Not in the way he meant. Andrea was afraid of the way

she reacted to Sean—the *wanting* that beat through her blood whenever he was near. Sean brought out the playful side of her as no other male ever had. She wanted to tease him, flirt with him, buy him underwear, tumble with him in the woods. She wanted him to chase her; she wanted to turn the tables on him when he caught her and take him down. Then she wanted to make love to him—deep, passionate, longing love, which she would have done in the clearing if they hadn't been interrupted.

Sean was trying to pin her with his dominant stare, his blue eyes hard and hot. She met that stare, which—he was right—she shouldn't have been able to. Not according to all Shifter instincts and laws of the pack.

"No," she said. "I'm not afraid of you."

"And that's what makes you unusual. And dangerous."

"I'm not dangerous." Andrea drew her legs up under her.

"It made you dangerous to *them*. To all packs in your old Shiftertown."

"All I know is that I don't want anything to do with them. Ever again."

"So you invoked a Shifter law that says a woman can refuse an insistent mate-claim by leaving the pack and heading off on her own. Clever, love."

"Jared still thinks it's the old days, when a female didn't have much chance of making it outside her pack. But these days it just means moving to a different Shiftertown. Jared didn't think of that."

"Smart of you."

"More like desperate."

Sean sat down beside her again. The bed felt so right with him on it with her, as though it had been missing something until he arrived. "You have no more need to be desperate," he said. "I wish you'd believe you're safe here."

Andrea slanted him a smile. "Except for the second-in-command who is obsessed with my underwear."

An answering spark lit his eyes. "I'd say you were obsessed with mine, sweetheart." He cocked a brow. "Smiley faces?"

"Hey, I thought they'd look good on you."

"And you think my ass is fine, do you?"

"Oh, yeah. There's a reason all those women rub themselves on something when you walk by."

Sean blinked in surprise. "You're dreaming that."

"No, I'm not. I'm jealous and possessive." She mimed scratching with her claws.

Sean smiled. "I'm liking the sound of that."

"Of course you do, feral cat."

Sean pulled her up to him and gave her a deep, heart-rending kiss before he got to his feet. "Don't go anywhere, love. I'm off home to grab my stuff; then I'm coming back here and locking us in."

"Promise?"

Sean's next kiss curled her toes. "That's a definite promise, love."

Later in the night, with Sean curled behind her in the bed—wearing the cupid's arrow briefs and a black T-shirt—a twig scraped across Andrea's window.

Andrea. Come to me.

Andrea lifted her head and looked across the room. The window was tightly closed, the curtains shut, but moonlight streamed through a gap in the fabric.

The voice whispered in her head. *Andrea.*

Andrea looked down at Sean. He was frowning in his sleep, but he didn't move. Slowly and carefully, Andrea slipped out of the bed, grabbed her clothes, and left the room.

CHAPTER NINE

Sean woke, knowing Andrea was gone. It wasn't only the empty bed that gave him the clue; it was the absence of warmth, of the feel of her, the scent of her.

Not only that, she'd left the house. The glow of the clock next to the bed told him it was a little before three in the morning, and the tingle that had announced the presence of the Fae was back in a big way.

Sean stripped out of his underwear on the way down the stairs and shifted as soon as he unlocked and opened the back door. Andrea's scent was clear as soon as he was a wildcat, her scent trail glowing like moonlight.

He tracked her to the precise spot where he'd found the Fae earlier today. The Fae warrior was back, and Andrea stood in front of him. She'd dressed in jeans and a sweater—looking very human—and she was reaching out to touch the Fae man's hand.

A snarl left Sean's throat as he leapt at Andrea and knocked her away. She yelled as she went down, and she started fighting. Sean shifted back to human form so he could lock his hands around her wrists.

"Get *off* me, Sean."

"What the hell is the matter with you? If you touch him, he can cross. He's a fucking Fae."

"He's my *father*."

Sean stopped, staring openmouthed. Andrea glowered up at him, gray eyes beautiful and enraged.

"That's right," she said. "The man who sired me."

Sean snapped his head up to look at the Fae, but he was gone, the clearing empty. Sean softened his hold on Andrea. "Why the hell didn't you tell me that before?"

"I didn't know before. He'd just revealed it before you came blundering in. Now, will you please let me up?"

Sean got lithely to his feet and pulled her up beside him. "Why the bloody hell did you run out here to see him alone?"

"I wanted to know why a Fae wanted to talk to me so bad. I knew you'd never let me out if I woke you."

"Damn right I wouldn't have. What else did he tell you?"

"Nothing. You interrupted."

Her anger was strong, but so was Sean's. "Just because a Fae says he's your dad doesn't make it true. You can't trust the bastards."

Andrea jerked from his grasp. "Watch it. I'm one of those bastards."

"Not what I meant, and you know it. I don't think of you as Fae anyway."

Now her gray eyes became chips of ice. "Well, I *am* Fae. You want to mate with me and sleep with me, but you've only seen the Shifter side of me. There's another side, and it's as much a part of me as the Shifter is. You don't get one part or the other; you get the whole package."

Sean gentled his voice. "I know that, love."

"Are you going to run to Liam now, tell him everything?"

"He'll need to know."

"Go on then." She spun around and marched back to the house without waiting for him.

"Damn it, Andrea."

Andrea heard the frustration in Sean's voice but didn't

look back. She couldn't. If she stayed near Sean, he'd see the worry in her, which had sprung there the moment her father—if he was her father—had spoken to her. The Fae had not only claimed to be her father, but he'd asked Andrea to bring him the Sword of the Guardian.

Under roiling clouds and cold the next day, Andrea studied her ley line maps with renewed intensity.

She was alone to do it. Sean had left as soon as it was light, kissing her good-bye but not bothering to tell her what he was off to do. Glory had appeared after breakfast, but she'd been moody and unhappy, Dylan nowhere in sight. After lunch, Glory had reemerged from her bedroom in tight black leather pants, a lacy blouse, mile-high shoes, and perfectly coiffed hair, her body doused with perfume. She told Andrea with a sweet smile not to wait up and drove off in her small car.

The day was full of clouds and wind and rain, which matched Andrea's mood. Andrea's ley line maps weren't helping—she had traced the line through the river valley that wound through Austin but not the offshoots of that line. Since she didn't have the transportation to do it herself, the next best thing would be to see whether someone else had mapped them, but she'd need a computer to find that out. Though Glory had an old PC, not all Shifters were approved for Internet access, and then they were only allowed dial-up. But if Andrea used Sean's computer, she'd have to tell him why she wanted to and get into explanations that made her uncomfortable.

Then again, Sean wasn't home. Liam had ridden off to do whatever Shiftertown leaders did, and Connor was at school. Andrea put everything back into her folder and went next door.

Kim was home by herself, working in the kitchen. She'd started a law firm to represent Shifters and also to study human-Shifter law and try to change some of the inequities Shifters had gotten stuck with. It was a slow process, but

Kim and her friends were trying. Kim had an office, but some days Kim found it easier to work from home.

Kim was happy to lead Andrea upstairs to Sean's bedroom and his computer. Sean's room was small, compact, and neat, except for a pile of clothes crumpled near the bed. Andrea felt a tingle of Fae magic from the polished wooden sword case on his dresser, but she knew without looking that the sword wasn't in it. Sean had taken it with him wherever he'd gone.

The computer was old, and Andrea expected it to be of limited use, but the connection went through quickly and the Internet was open for business. Andrea blinked in surprise at the speed. Shifters were only allowed dial-up connections, no cable, no DSL.

Kim smiled at her confusion. "Last year I helped out a Shifter who is very good at computers. He and Sean 'enhanced' this one."

"That's Shifters for you," Andrea said, typing in her search strings. "They won't break laws, but they'll bend them into all kinds of weird shapes."

Kim laughed. "A good way of putting it." She patted Andrea's shoulders and left her to it.

Some local Wiccans had mapped ley lines in the Austin area. The lines veined out from the riverbed, one running straight down Lamar, one snaking under the university's main campus. Long ago, another had followed what was now Mopac, but that one had withered and died when the railroad with its iron rails that had been laid there.

Andrea enlarged and printed out maps, tucking them into her file folder.

"Don't forget to delete your search history," Kim said from the door, as Andrea finished up.

"Sorry?" Andrea stared at the computer. She'd used the Internet before, but her access to computers had been limited to the two at the community center in her Shiftertown, a place she hadn't visited often.

"If you don't, Sean will know what you were looking up. I take it you don't want him to?"

"I can erase that?"

"Yes, but if you simply erase the whole thing, he'll know you were looking for stuff you don't want him to know about. And then he'll bug you to tell him."

"No kidding." Andrea glared at the plastic box. "Where is Sean, anyway?"

Kim looked surprised as she slid into the chair and started clicking things. "He left early this morning, I supposed on Shifter business. He didn't tell you?"

"He sleeps with me, but he's not exactly verbose. He expects full disclosure from me but doesn't return the favor."

"That's a Shifter for you. Liam talks and talks and talks, and tells you nothing at all. The gift of Blarney, he calls it." Kim smiled at the computer, her eyes filled with love for her talkative mate. "This will be fun. I'll delete your trail and load it with legal questions. Sean's eyes glaze over when I talk about legal issues. Or I can fill in with searches for shoes. Or baby furniture."

"You're a treasure, Kim."

"So they tell me. I won't ask you what you're trying to keep from Sean, but take some advice." Kim looked up at Andrea with dark blue eyes that had seen and accepted much. "Trust Sean. He's an amazing man, and there's much more to him than he lets anyone see. He feels things, deeply."

Andrea had seen that already. "I know his brother's death hit him hard and that Sean blames himself for it."

"It didn't so much hit him hard as change his life. Sean was close to Kenny, and having to watch him die makes Sean doubly protective of everyone he cares about. Sean's never said all this to me; but you live in the same house with someone a while, and you notice things."

And now Sean was trying to move in with Andrea. "I'll keep it in mind."

Kim and Andrea shared a hug, and Andrea departed with her maps.

The most interesting thing she'd found, she thought as she descended, was that a ley line streaked right through the heart of Shiftertown.

Not surprising, really. This entire area had fallen into disuse and urban decay long before it had become a Shiftertown. The Shifters had been put here precisely because no one wanted the real estate. In the twenty years since then, real estate a mile away had shot sky high, then dived again when the market crashed. But Shiftertown remained unchanged.

A half-Fae human had worked with human governments to devise the Collars that kept Shifters tamed. Had he also advised humans where to put the Shiftertowns? Maybe he thought a bit of Fae magic running through it would keep Shifters quiet?

It also could open a gate to Faerie.

Andrea stashed her file in her room and then went back out to the place where she'd seen the Fae.

The ley line, according to the maps, ran in a more or less straight line behind the houses on this street. Walnut trees, which caught the mists on still, wet days, towered overhead.

Gates to Faerie were rare. There were places in the world, Andrea had learned, where the gates could always be found—in stone circles in northern Europe, near temples and other sacred places in South America, in deep canyons of the American Southwest, in the soaring mountains of Asia. Fae who knew the spells could cross between standing stones and other thin places in the fabric of the universe, but this ley line wasn't that strong.

But gates could be created with a burst of very strong magic along a ley line, or possibly through the dreams of someone loaded with Fae magic. The link to this Fae was Andrea and her nightmares.

Andrea stood on the very spot the Fae man had appeared, closed her eyes and concentrated. Nothing. If there had been a gate here last night, it wasn't here now.

What had the Fae wanted? Was he really her father, and had he, after so many years, had a sudden jones to see his daughter?

Not likely. He'd wanted the sword, and now Andrea was in a position to steal it for him.

As a child, Andrea had envisioned her Fae father as a great prince, a beautiful man who would one day reach out from Faerie and take Andrea into his kingdom. There, she'd become a princess at his side. She'd wear gossamer robes and ride a beautiful white horse and be loved by one and all.

As Andrea had grown older and learned more about the Fae, her childish dreams had died. As poorly as the other Shifters treated her, the Fae likely would be even more vicious to a half breed. Fae apparently didn't like diluted blood, being very snobbish about breeding with "lesser" beings. Besides, Andrea had grown to love her stepfather deeply and couldn't imagine him not being part of her life.

So here she was, standing in a grove of trees in a Shiftertown far away from her beloved stepfather, trying to figure out whether the man she'd seen last night was her true father.

Not likely. And damned if she would simply hand the Sword of the Guardian to a complete stranger because he claimed to be her long-lost papa.

"Hey, Fae-girl."

Andrea snapped her eyes open to see four male Shifters drifting her way. One of them was a guy called Nate, who had a military haircut and build. He worked for Liam as a bodyguard and tracker or in situations when Liam needed extra muscle. Nate didn't have much in the way of brains, but he was fiercely loyal to his clan leader, whoever it might be.

He was also a shit who shared Jared's idea that females should be kept shut away to be screwed as often as the male Shifter wanted, plus he thought half breeds should be neutered. He let his opinions be known to Andrea, though never in Sean's hearing. Nate was at least that smart.

Andrea hadn't mentioned his shit-ness to Sean, because she refused to go running to him every time someone said something mean to her. Nate couldn't do anything to her, because the mate-claim made Andrea off limits, and Nate knew it.

Andrea folded her arms and stood her ground. She had a perfect right to wander back here, no need to scramble home because Nate and his bully-boys showed up.

Nate didn't like her blatant eye contact, but she refused to look away. "I heard you brought Ely Barry back from the dead," he said.

"He wasn't dead," Andrea said coolly. "He was almost dead. Big difference."

"I heard you stuck your hand above his crotch, and *wham*, he was all better." Nate held up his finger. "I cut myself this morning. Want to touch my crotch and see if you can heal me?"

Yuck. "Sorry. Not interested."

"Why not, sweetheart? Because the healing magic thing is all bullshit?"

"No," Andrea said. "Because you're a dickhead."

Nate's friends guffawed, and Nate's look turned ugly. "You need to learn your place, Fae-bitch."

His eyes went white blue, but Andrea held her ground. If she broke gaze first, he'd establish his dominance over her, and then she'd never have any peace from him.

"This *is* my place," she said.

Nate's Collar emitted tiny sparks in his fury. "Morrissey only made the mate-claim to make himself look generous. The minute he dumps your ass, you are so screwed. Once he cuts you loose, I'll fuck you until you remember you're nothing but a submissive Lupine Fae-get."

Don't look away. Glory wouldn't look away. "A Lupine Fae-get whose healing ability might be your only hope for fixing your very small penis."

More snickers from his friends. They were enjoying the show, but Andrea had no illusion that they wouldn't help him beat her if they thought they needed to.

Nate's Feline fangs extended. "I don't care if you are the Guardian's. You need to be taught who's in charge, bitch."

Andrea still didn't step back. In her old Shiftertown, if a dominant smacked a submissive, it was considered the submissive's fault for provoking one higher in the food chain.

So Andrea's pack leader would say while Andrea's ears rang with his hit. Andrea had never had learned to respect the hierarchy. But this was the Morrisseys' Shiftertown, and she already knew the rules were a little different here. If Nate tried to discipline her, he'd be toast.

That didn't mean him starting for her, his eyes white, didn't scare the crap out of her. She got ready to run.

But Nate's snarls abruptly broke off, and his friends moved a few paces back, sudden fear shining in their eyes. Released from Nate's glare, Andrea whirled to see what had scared them.

Dylan watched from a few yards behind her, the man doing nothing but standing there with his hands in his jacket pockets. The breeze ruffled his hair, but Dylan didn't say a word. He didn't have to.

Nate swallowed. Without defiance, without offering words of explanation, he and his friends quietly turned around and walked back the way they came, the smell of their fear sharp.

Of course, this left Andrea alone with the most frightening Shifter in Shiftertown, the man who could rip Andrea to pieces and walk away without breaking a sweat. She knew deep in her bones that if Dylan ever wanted to kill her, he would, never mind the Collar, never mind the rules, never mind his own son having claimed her. No piece of Fae technology or Shifter custom could stop Dylan Morrissey from doing whatever he damn-well pleased.

Before she could speak, Dylan said to her, "I was looking for Glory. Have you seen her?"

CHAPTER TEN

Andrea blew out her breath. "Glory? No, I thought she was meeting you."

Dylan's eyes sharpened, and Andrea regretted her hasty answer. "Why did you think that?" he asked, voice edged.

Because she went out all dressed up, like she was meeting a lover.

"I don't know. I just assumed . . ."

Dylan flicked his gaze down the row of trees but not before Andrea saw the flash of pain in his eyes. That surprised her. The way Glory told it, Dylan was the one with the casual interest in their relationship. He could take it or leave it, according to Glory.

"Has she gone to see someone else?" he asked, not looking at Andrea.

"Dylan, this is so not my business."

The predatory gaze fixed on her again. "Just answer the question."

"I haven't the faintest idea. I swear to you."

"Then why did you think she was meeting me?"

Goddess, he wasn't going to let go of this. "Why not call her? I'm sure she's just shopping or something."

"I did call. She didn't pick up."

Andrea's worry overrode any concern about herself. Humans were randomly shooting at Shifters; Glory had gone out alone; Glory wasn't answering her phone.

Andrea pulled her cell from her belt and tapped in Glory's number. Glory answered after the first ring. "Hey, there!" she sang.

Andrea turned around, walking a little away from Dylan. "Glory? Where are you? Dylan's looking for you."

"Is he? Too bad. I'm busy."

Through the phone, Andrea heard music and laughter—deep, male, throaty laughter.

"Where the hell are you?"

"Having a good time."

"What am I supposed to tell Dylan?"

Glory's voice was muffled as though she'd turned to talk to someone else, then she said, "You tell Dylan that I'm not going to wait for him to get around to seeing me. Until he makes a mate-claim, I'll go out as much as I want with whoever I want."

"I'm not telling him that! Do it yourself."

"Sorry, honey, gotta go." Glory laughed at a male voice in the background, and the phone went quiet.

"*Glory.* Shit." Andrea clicked off, her heart sinking. She pivoted to face Dylan, wondering how much he'd overheard, and found Dylan gone. The clearing was empty, quiet, as though Dylan had never been there.

Andrea scented him, though, male musk and anger. So much anger.

Damn it. Andrea tried to tamp down her worry and went back to the Morrisseys to find Kim.

"I'm pregnant, not an invalid," Kim snapped. "I'm in better shape than I've been in years."

Andrea eyed the car keys in Kim's hand, wondering if she could snatch them without hurting the woman. "I know that. But you have to understand. We've watched so many Shifter women die trying to have babies that we're a little paranoid about it."

"I'm perfectly healthy. My gynecologist is amazed at how healthy I am."

"Yes, but, Kim, if you get sick or hurt on this little expedition—if you so much as skin your knee—Liam will disembowel me and play jump rope with my guts." Andrea assessed the distance to the keys again. "Don't make me wrestle you for them."

Kim heaved a sigh. "Liam has become so protective, it's incredible. I mean, I like being cherished, but, sheesh."

"Liam's terrified of losing you. My mother died trying to have another child. Trust me, I know how awful that is."

Kim deflated. She blew out another sigh and handed over the keys to her Mustang. "Fine. Go get her. But not a scratch on that car, do you hear me? I've seen the way Shifters drive."

"Sweet." Andrea closed her hand over the keys. "I won't hurt it a bit."

"What do I tell Sean when he comes home?"

"That I stole your car and went joy riding. Or you can tell him the truth. I don't care." Andrea caught Kim in a hard hug. "Thanks. I'll be in touch."

She danced down the porch steps to the driveway and slid into the little sports car she'd been dying to try out since she'd arrived.

Now to find Glory. Andrea didn't have much to go on except Kim remembering Glory talking about a bar called Bronco's in north Austin that she liked to go to. Kim had looked it up on Sean's computer and printed a map to it.

Andrea studied the map before she pulled out. Since coming to Austin, she had realized that directions to places here could consist of a bewildering array of turns and little jogs down tiny streets that connected to giant thoroughfares.

In her old Shiftertown, "down the highway to the first left" had been the extent of the complication. Here, she needed a list of directions to get to the nearest gas station.

She sped through downtown Austin and turned off on Lamar to head north. She tried to follow the map's directions, but somewhere she took a wrong turn and found herself going back south on the wrong road. She cursed and looked for a street sign, but the next intersection was small, the street sign for some reason missing.

A car full of human males pulled up next to her. She gave them a nervous glance, but though they were youngish, in their twenties, they looked more inclined to wear colorful shirts and party than shoot Shifters. They were probably from the university, taking a day off, legit or not. When they saw Andrea look at them, they began the male ritual of showing off.

Peacocks. They were good-looking in a human way, and they obviously didn't realize that Andrea was a Shifter. With her jacket zipped high against the cold, her sunglasses hiding her eyes from the glare, she could pass for human. She wondered what these guys would think if they knew she'd been alive for forty years already. Forty for a Shifter was still very young, the equivalent of a human in her early twenties. Plenty ripe for mating. Sean at nearly a hundred was in his prime, his thirties as humans would measure things.

To her, these guys were still cubs. Older than Connor, yes, but not by much.

"Nice car," one in the backseat called to her.

"Hey," another said. "Want to go to Red's with us?"

Andrea smiled sweetly. "Sorry, I'm meeting a friend."

"Where? We'll go there instead."

Glory would eat these guys alive. "Do you know how to get to Bronco's?"

The two in the back looked blank, but the guy in the front passenger seat became suddenly grim-faced. "You don't want to go there. That's a Shifter place."

Andrea shrugged. "I'm curious."

"You meeting your friend *there*?" Front-seat guy gave her a onceover. "What are you, a Shifter groupie?"

"Not hardly," Andrea said.

"Those places are bad, girl. Y'all shouldn't go."

Andrea shrugged again. "Just tell me how to get back to Lamar?"

"Not from around here?" The young man patted the car as the light changed. "Follow us."

Andrea let them pull ahead. If they led her back to the right street, fine. If they tried to get her lost, she'd drive away and call Kim for help. The day she couldn't handle herself against four puny human males—unarmed—would be a bad day, indeed.

They were at least honest and took her back to Lamar. They signaled her to follow them north on it, and she pulled in behind them. A couple of turns later, and she found a small square building with a sign above its door that read "Bronco's."

Bronco's was low-key, no beer signs in the windows, no advertising that this was a good place to get fine drinks. According to Andrea's map, the bar was about a mile from the small Shiftertown that lay on the north edge of Austin. Like the bar where Liam worked, this one was probably human-owned but didn't turn away Shifter clientele.

Andrea pulled into the tiny parking lot and the guys stopped their car behind her. Two got out with her.

"You really don't want to go in there," the one from the front seat said. He was tall and lanky with brown eyes that looked as though they could be intelligent and kind. "Shifters can be weird."

No kidding. Two Shifters were talking to each other just outside the front door, Ursine from the look of them. They'd be able to scent that she was Shifter and that the young men weren't. They'd also be aware of Andrea's Fae scent. The Ursines' Shifter hearing had picked up on the word *weird*, and they stopped talking.

"I need to look for someone in there," Andrea told the

young human man, aware of the Ursines' gazes hard on her. "That's all."

"But this bar is really bad," he said. "So I hear. Really. We'll take you somewhere else. Somewhere nice."

He seemed very distressed she wanted to go inside, which made Andrea all the more curious and determined. She smiled at him and approached the Ursines.

The two bear-men closed together, staring down at her from their nearly seven-foot height. Andrea had gotten used to Ronan, who was one of the nicest guys imaginable, but these two made her feel like a lost hiker approaching a pair of grizzlies.

Show no fear. They'd smell it on her, but she bravely removed her sunglasses and met their gazes. "I'm looking for Glory," she said.

The two bears relaxed. One rolled his eyes, and the other grinned. "Yeah, she's in there."

Andrea gave them a warm smile. "Thank you." She shoved her sunglasses back on and approached the door. The brown-eyed student caught the door handle.

"Really. Let's go someplace else." He looked anxious, terrified even.

"My friend is in there," Andrea said. "I need to get her. Then we'll go." She'd drag Glory out by the hair and back home if she had to.

"I'm coming with you," the young man said.

He was human; he could go wherever he wanted to. Andrea shrugged and let him open the door. Humanlike, he gestured for her to go first. Such a weird custom. Who knew what danger waited on the other side?

The noise and smell of the place hit her hard. Smoke, beer, and body odor, mostly Shifter body odor. Music and lots of voices. It was dark inside, incongruous with the white glare of the afternoon. Andrea tucked her sunglasses into her pocket and scanned the interior.

The bar where Liam worked was more like a family place. Cubs couldn't enter until they reached the human age of twenty-one, but grown families congregated there to meet friends and other families. But no one would encourage mates and cubs to come here. These Shifters weren't from one enclave—she could scent that. There were two Shiftertowns in Austin, Liam's and the north Austin one. Another, smaller Shiftertown existed in back Hill Country, up toward Llano. Andrea didn't know enough Shifters down here to place everyone, but living in communities, Shifters picked up the collective scent of that community. She smelled four or five distinct ones in here.

Glory was easy to spot, sitting on a barstool in her black leather and lacy top, chatting to the human bartender and the Shifter males around her. She saw Andrea and lifted her bottle of beer in greeting.

"Hey, Andrea. Did Dylan send you running after me?"

"No." Andrea edged against the bar and gave Glory a hard stare. "I came running after you on my own. What are you doing here?"

"Enjoying myself. Who's your friend?" Glory gave the human who'd followed Andrea her widest, most tooth-filled smile. "He looks edible."

"He and his friends gave me directions."

"Oh, he has *friends*, does he?"

"Glory."

The young man looked from Glory to Andrea, and his face changed. "Aw, fuck, you're a *Shifter*."

Andrea stifled a sigh. "I never said I wasn't."

"Damn it, I was trying to *help* you."

"Why were you?" Andrea fixed him with a stare. "Why didn't you want me to come in here?"

The guy clammed up. He wasn't good at hiding things; humans often weren't. Something about this bar scared him, though Andrea couldn't tell whether it was simply because it was a Shifter place or something more sinister was going on.

He gave her an ugly glare worthy of Nate the tracker. "Forget it, bitch. It's your funeral." He spun and strode away.

"We need to go," Andrea began, but Glory clamped her hand on Andrea's arm.

"No," she said in a hard voice, though she kept smiling. "You need to stay."

Andrea stopped. "Why?"

Glory leaned close, bathing Andrea in heavy perfume. "Because there are some very interesting conversations in here."

"Meaning?"

"Just listen."

Andrea slid onto a barstool and signaled for the bartender to bring her a beer. Good Shifter hearing let Andrea eavesdrop while accepting the cold bottle the bartender put in front of her. If she'd been in her Lupine form, her ears would have been twisted hard behind her.

A table full of Felines had the most interesting conversation, and Glory nodded ever so slightly when Andrea focused on snatches of their talk. They were confident, Andrea thought. They must recognize Glory—she stood out, even for a Shifter—but they didn't seem to worry about her overhearing. The Felines talked for a while, and Andrea went cold. Something was going on, and it didn't take her long to figure out what.

When Andrea pulled Kim's car into the driveway an hour or so later, it was to face three Morrissey males: Sean, Dylan, and Liam. They stood with arms folded, right in front of the car, frowning like a tribunal ready to pronounce sentence.

Glory parked her own little car next to her house and leisurely exited her vehicle. Andrea got out of the Mustang and closed the keys in her hand, ready to return them to Kim. Without acknowledging the three watching men, she started for the porch, but Sean stepped in her way. His blue eyes glittered under the black slash of his brows, and his face was hard with anger.

"I take the blame, Sean," Dylan said behind Andrea. "I made her worry about Glory."

Andrea saw movement inside the house. Kim and Connor watched from the other side of the living-room window, making no move to greet Andrea.

Andrea looked from Sean to his brother and father. "What is this?"

"What did you think you were doing, lass?" Sean said, his voice deceptively soft. "You didn't tell Liam, or Dad, or even Ellison where you were going. Instead, you coerced Kim into helping you and told her to keep quiet."

Andrea stared at him. "I didn't realize I wasn't allowed to leave Shiftertown. Even the humans are all right with me doing that."

"Alone." Sean's voice was a growl. "When humans have been shooting Shifters." He was furious, his eyes blue white, but he only stirred her own anger.

"First of all, Sean, I can pass for human. Second, Glory was out there, and I wanted to bring her home before *she* got hurt. Third, I couldn't tell you about it, because I didn't notice you anywhere around today. Where the hell have you been?"

"Colorado."

Andrea stopped. "What? Why?"

"Taking care of business."

"What business? And anyway, how did you get there and back so fast?"

"There's this fine invention called an airplane."

"Which Shifters aren't allowed on. That's why I had to take that stupidly long bus ride to get here."

Kim opened the front door, despite Connor's obvious attempts to pull her back. "Leave her alone, Sean. You're getting to be as bad as Liam."

Glory strode unapologetically up the porch steps, passing Dylan without a word. "Instead of snarling at Andrea, you all need to hear what we have to say." She walked past Kim and into the house. Kim opened the door all the way, inviting the rest of them in.

* * *

Sean's anger tasted fiery as he led Andrea inside. He was rarely angry like this, but when he'd returned to Austin and found Andrea gone off alone, all reason had left his brain. When Kim, worried, had volunteered the information that Andrea had left to look for Glory, Sean's feral rage had taken over. Liam had tried to hold Sean against a wall to keep him from charging off to tear apart the city, but Sean had twisted free of Liam and slammed out of the house just as Andrea had driven up in Kim's car.

She'd emerged from the Mustang with that cool look that disdained Sean's protectiveness. But she was his *mate*, damn it, or as near as. One glance into Andrea's gray eyes told him she didn't care. The woman was driving him over-the-edge insane.

Sean stood right behind her in the living room. Andrea didn't like that, but too damn bad. Her scent aroused the fires inside him, rage and wanting all mixed together. He recognized the primal urge of a male in mate frenzy, and he clenched his teeth against it. He'd left town thinking she was protected, and returning and finding that his father had let her leave Shiftertown, unescorted, had made his dominant anger explode like a geyser. Liam had had to hold him back from that fight too.

With effort, Sean wrenched his attention from Andrea and focused on Glory's words.

"These Shifters were going on about how they don't want Shifters and humans mingling anymore," Glory was saying. "They say it's diluting us, making us weak. Interesting, don't you think?"

"I heard them too." Andrea stood so close to Sean that he could easily wrap his arms around her, though he knew that if he did, she'd only elbow him in the gut. "I thought they were reacting to the shootings, but then they went on about how the they thought the shootings were a good thing. The incidents would widen the distance between humans and Shifters, as it should be, they said."

"The Shifters were from north Austin?" Liam asked.

"From everywhere, Liam," Glory said. "North Austin, out by Llano, plus from this Shiftertown right here."

"The bastards," Connor spat. "Shifters in this Shiftertown should be loyal to Liam."

Liam rubbed his forehead. "Shite, this is all we're needing."

"A faction." Dylan's voice was grim. "Shifters from different clans and Shiftertowns forming their own power group. Were they different species?"

Glory shook her head. "All Feline."

"Hairballs, every single one of them," Andrea put in.

Sean wanted to touch her. He wanted to run his hands along her shoulders, lick her from neck to the base of her spine.

"We need to be having a chat with these Felines, I'm thinking." Liam looked at Sean, eyes flat and angry. "Up for some confrontation, Sean?"

"Yeah," Connor said eagerly. "Send Sean in to kick some ass. Can I watch?"

Sean's attention was pulled from Liam and problems in Shiftertown to the curve of Andrea's cheek, the way her black ringlets brushed it when she turned her head. He could lean down and nuzzle her, smell her hair, taste the salt of her skin. A low growl left his throat.

Liam's waiting stare didn't pull him out of it. The whole family knew damn well how distracted Sean was with this unfinished mate-claim. Liam and Connor were taking side bets on how long it would be before Sean combusted.

Liam looked away. "Dad?"

Dylan shrugged. "It's your call now, son. I'll back you up if it comes to a fight, but the first approach must come from you."

Liam acknowledged that, and even in his distracted state, Sean could tell Liam wasn't happy about it. Liam hadn't worn the mantle of power long, and it still bothered him to have his father defer to him. Sean understood; his own anger at his father today disturbed him underneath it all. Changes in the hierarchy were hell.

Sean knew that someday he'd slide in dominance beneath

his own son, and the thought of having a son brought him back around to thoughts of mating. With Andrea. Sean let his fingers drift under Andrea's hair to the smooth skin of her neck. She flushed but didn't shake him off.

Glory laughed. "Well, we know Sean's priorities today."

"He can't help it." Liam slanted a smile at Kim, the mate for whom his frenzy hadn't yet cooled. "Trust me, I know how it goes. Take Andrea home, Sean. We'll kick some Feline ass later."

CHAPTER ELEVEN

"I don't need to be taken home," Andrea said as Sean opened the door of Glory's house. He went inside first to check that the way was safe and gestured her to follow him.

The house was dark and empty. Glory and Dylan had remained at the Morrisseys', Dylan helping to reassure Connor that Andrea wouldn't be punished. Andrea had been a bad wolf, and so had Glory, but the mean alphas were going to cut them some slack for the good intelligence they'd brought home.

Andrea went straight to the kitchen and grabbed the coffeepot. The cold day was getting darker and colder, and she needed coffee.

Sean divested himself of his sword and then leaned his fists on the breakfast bar, muscles tightening. "I'm damn sorry if you walking into danger bothers me, Andy-love. I'm funny that way."

"I only went to find Glory to talk her into coming back home. I have to live in this house; I don't want the walls falling down around me because Glory and Dylan have a knock-down, drag-out fight."

"Dylan wouldn't do that."

Andrea noisily ran water to fill the pot. "No, he gets all cold and disappears, and then I have to live with Glory's bad temper. Why can't the two of them just mate and get it over with? Then the rest of us can sleep."

"Because it eats him up inside, my mother's death." Sean's fists were even tighter, his knuckles whitening. "It was a long time ago, but he hasn't gotten over it. The grief, it destroyed him."

Andrea let out her breath as she scooped coffee grounds into the top of the pot. "I understand. I saw what my mother's death did to my stepfather." Grief could be a terrible thing. Her stepfather hadn't truly recovered from it, and it had been more than thirty-five years.

"My mother was a little bit like Glory," Sean said. "Very in your face. Kind of like you." The corners of his mouth quirked in a tight smile. "I think if Glory weren't so like my mum, it wouldn't be so hard for Dad. But he's not sure he can give himself to Glory, not sure he has a right to. He's a complicated man."

"Whereas you are so simple." Andrea plugged in the pot and waited impatiently for the heavenly sound of percolation. Shifters could have automatic-drip coffeemakers, but Andrea thought it tasted better in an old-fashioned pot anyway. It was satisfying to watch the coffee burble into the little glass knob on the top of the pot as the water boiled. And the scent was glorious.

"I am simple," Sean said. "I wait for people to die so I can send them to the Summerland. I fill in the time between that messing with my computer and hoping to mate before I die myself."

"Don't overwhelm me with sentiment." Andrea faced him across the counter. He really had no idea that he was one of the most complicated and changeable males she'd ever met. One minute he was growling and controlling, the next so protective she thought she'd never feel in danger again, the next grieving for his dead brother and feeling compassion for his father. Which one was the real Sean Morrissey? Answer, all of them. Sure, Sean, real simple.

"What were you doing in Colorado anyway?" she asked him. "How did you pull off flying there? Shifters aren't allowed on planes."

"Not being allowed and not doing it are two different things, love. I have human friends who own airplanes."

"Oh, now you tell me after my bus journey across three states."

Sean had the gall to smile. "I was in a hurry."

"Are you going to share why you went there?"

"To ask your stepdad about your Fae father. I wanted to know everything your mother said about him, things you were too young to remember, and I wanted to be face-to-face with him when I asked it."

And now she had Sean the intelligence gatherer, who probed all the way to the root of the problem instead of just baring his teeth at it.

"You saw my dad?" Andrea's eyes prickled with tears. "How is he?"

His tone gentled. "He's fine, lass, though he's missing you. And he was happy to talk about your mum. Seemed like he was glad to have someone to talk about her with."

The tears threatened to spill out, and Andrea blinked them back. "I'm so glad you two got along."

"We did. You were right about your stepdad. He's a fine man, and brave for his rank in the pack. He's relieved that you're here, and safe, and happy. He sent his love."

Oh, damn you, Sean Morrissey. Andrea was trying to stay angry at him for being rabidly overprotective, and suddenly he moved back to being the Sean who knew exactly what Andrea needed. He'd gone not only to ask about her Fae father, but to bring back reassurance that Andrea's stepfather was well and that Terry didn't blame Andrea for what she'd done.

"I also saw Jared," Sean said.

"You did?" She smiled. "I'm kind of sorry I missed that."

"He's still pretty pissed off, especially since there are no other unmated females of age in your old Shiftertown. But don't worry, love. He'll not do a bloody thing to you ever again, not unless he wants to challenge me. I almost hope he does, so I can wipe the floor with his sorry ass."

Sean's protectiveness was rising again, but Andrea couldn't help but feel grateful for all he'd done. Being harassed and stalked wasn't something a woman just got over. Being stalked meant waking up every morning wondering what terrible thing would happen next, looking over your shoulder with every step, falling asleep wondering whether you were safe to do so. Because of Sean, Andrea could now wake up without fear.

"Why are you doing this to me?" she asked.

"Looking after you?" Sean sounded surprised. "I mate-claimed you. I take care of you now. I told you that when I first met you."

"I didn't mean that, exactly." She'd meant the easy way Sean disarmed her, the way he turned what made her angry into something wonderful he'd done for her. The way he was making Andrea care more and more about him. "And anyway, it's only a claim, not an official mating. You're not obligated to take care of me, yet."

Sean's eyes narrowed. "All of that is shite, and you know it. We follow the rituals of mate-claim and mate blessing because we'd just give ourselves to the frenzy if we didn't, no holding back. We'd be ferals, bloody barbarians." Sean leaned toward her, the scent of musk and leather reaching her, the look in his eyes heating her blood. "I'm very close to the frenzy now, love, and I'm not going to be able to wait for coffee."

"It *is* kind of warm in here, isn't it? Maybe you're just flushed."

Sean's smile went sinful. "It's bloody freezing in here. You're feeling the frenzy too, aren't you, love? Maybe a touch?"

More than a touch. Damn him.

Sean came around the counter. Andrea held her ground as he took a stance behind her, like he'd done in Liam's house, his tall body warming her all the way down. He leaned to her, his body heat like a blanket, and she felt his teeth on her neck. "You're the one who was buying me all the underwear," he murmured into her skin. "Want to guess which pair I'm wearing?"

"Sean . . ." The happy bubbles died across the kitchen, a rich aroma permeating the air. "The coffee's done."

"Unplug it."

"I'm dying for coffee."

"I'm dying for you." Sean licked Andrea's neck, his breath hot. "I can't hold back, love. I'm trying, I'm trying damn hard, but I can't."

Andrea looked straight up at him with those smoke gray eyes. If this had been a hundred years ago, when Shifters were wild, Sean wouldn't have waited for her decision. He'd have scooped her up and taken her. After all, she was his mate, she belonged to him, and the frenzy was killing him.

It makes you want to fuck or die, Liam had once said.

Or die if I don't fuck, Sean thought. A better way of putting it.

Even so, he knew that his frenzy wasn't just for sex, wasn't just the biological drive that ensured that more cubs were born. Sean's frenzy was for Andrea.

For her clear gray eyes, for her sweet curves, for the way she said his name. For the way her clothes clung to her body, for her sense of humor, for her buying him underwear with smiley faces on them. It was the way she smelled, the way she liked coffee, and the way she winked at the Shifter groupies in the bar and left them speechless.

It was her Fae scent and her fine skin, her breath, her warmth, and the fact that she walked upon the earth.

Andrea's eyes darkened as she slid cool hands up his arms. "You're burning up."

"With fever. I want you, damn your beautiful eyes."

Andrea burrowed her hands under his T-shirt. "Maybe taking this off will help."

Sean liked how her appreciative smile touched her lips as he nearly ripped the shirt from his body. She returned to running her hands over her skin, tracing the muscles of his chest, her lashes flickering as she examined his torso.

Sean smiled a hot smile. "I showed you mine. You show me yours."

His control slipped as Andrea stepped back and pulled her shirt off over her head. Her bra was silver lace today, a sweet and petite slash of fabric that cupped her full breasts. Sean itched to take his teeth to the little bow in the center.

Sean folded his arms, pretending not to shake. "All of if, love."

Andrea's smile widened. She reached behind her back and unhooked the bra and let it fall softly to the kitchen floor.

No more holding it in. Sean went to her and slid his arms around her waist. He gently pushed her backward until she arched against the counter, and then he licked her throat and down between her breasts. He turned his head and caught her nipple between his teeth, filling his mouth with her round breast, suckling, tasting. Andrea let out a sigh of satisfaction and drew her hand up his back.

Lovely, lovely breasts. Sean could feast on them all day. He was hard, straining against his pants, his mouth happy to lick and nip and suckle. She was so soft, yet so firm, flesh like satin.

Andy-love, you taste so damn good.

Sean felt fingers at his belt, his jeans loosening. "I showed you mine," Andrea said as she worked the button open, the zipper down.

Sean let go of her long enough to toe off his boots and shove his pants down. He waited for her laughter that he'd worn the "Fine" briefs, but Andrea's eyes darkened as she looked him over, then she slid her arms around him, fingers under the waistband.

He kissed her lips, taking her in slow, long strokes. Her mouth was hot, willing, tasting of whatever beer she'd drunk while out with Glory. Damn lucky beer to slide down her throat. Sean bit her lip and then traced the path the liquid would have taken until he swirled his tongue across her navel.

He tugged at the waistband of her jeans. "Your turn."

Andrea, bless her, gave him a show. She slowly undulated her hips as she stepped back from him, sliding her shoes from her feet. She unbuttoned and unzipped her jeans, the hips rocking, teasing him, enticing him.

Andrea turned around while she eased the jeans down, so that Sean saw her lovely dark hair falling down her bare back, her sweet ass coming into view covered with a bikini panty of gray satin. She stepped out of the jeans and glanced back over her shoulder.

Sean closed the distance between them in two strides, wrapped his arms around her from behind, slid his hands into her panties, and easily found the warm, wet core of her. She gasped as he touched her heat.

He'd seen her naked before—they'd both shed clothes when they'd shifted. But this was different; this was slow, and this was hot. Shifting was about the animal, and the animal didn't care anything about clothes or nakedness. It only wanted the feel of fur and fangs, wanted to give in to the instinct of the hunt. Screwing in animal form was basic, hard, and swift, and had nothing to do with nudity and sensuality.

What Sean did now was about loving, about savoring the goodness of her.

Sean licked Andrea's shoulder as he slid his fingers into her, Andrea warm and wet and open. Andrea, a woman who'd never felt a man inside her, stifled a groan.

He knew he needed to go slowly with her. The beast in him wanted to rip the panties from her, spread her legs, and lift her so that he'd fit against her from behind. His cock was pounding at him, telling him to do it and be done.

But Sean never could. He wanted to feel Andrea

surrounding him, wanted to watch her eyelids grow heavy as he loved her. He wanted her to give him that seductive smile as he licked the curve of her lips, see the shine of her eyes as she felt him inside her.

Andrea leaned back against him, eyes closed, as she enjoyed what Sean did. He could open her like this, with his fingers, get her used to being touched, entered. It would take time, and his body wanted him to hurry.

Too bad. I'm savoring this.

Andrea wriggled her hips, much as she had the night she and Sean had patched up Ronan in the bar's office. Then as now, she gave him a sly look and repeated, "Is that where you keep your sword, or are you just happy to see me?"

Sean nipped her ear. "Andy-love, don't play with fire."

"Why not? It's *fun*." The word ended on a gasp and a groan as Sean slid a second finger inside her.

The panties were cute but too much in the way. Sean eased his fingers out, trying not to groan when he heard her disappointed whimper, and snagged his hands through the elastic. He slid the panties down and off, then decided to stay there, on his knees, on eye level with Andrea's sweet little ass.

Not for long, because Andrea turned to face him. She was beautiful. Her waist nipped in above curved hips, and her tummy rose and fell as she took a nervous breath. Sean blew softly on the black ringlets awaiting him between her thighs, the curls already damp with her wanting.

"Spread your legs a little for me," Sean whispered. "That's my girl."

Andrea gripped the counter while Sean nuzzled her, her feet sliding apart. Sean leaned into her and let himself feast.

She tasted so damn good. *Andrea, my mate.* Salty and smooth, sweet and tart, a mixture of tastes that was all her own. And she belonged to Sean. No male had touched her or tasted her, only Sean. The knowledge spoke to primal forces deep inside him, the feral Shifter that wanted no other to touch the one he claimed. Long ago, the Fae had

bred so much animal into Shifters, and the beast in Sean
wanted Andrea.

He licked her, slowly at first, then speeding his attack
as she swayed her hips, little cries leaving her mouth. She
furrowed her hands into his hair, hands strong, her body
wanting to thrust against him.

Sean was dying for her, but it would be easier on her if
he first brought her to climax, opened her, relaxed her. He
could do that for her. And it wasn't like he didn't enjoy licking her, tasting her, nipping at the sweet berry that waited
for his tongue.

He felt her body start to open and respond, a basic, hard
reaction that erased all thoughts. It began with her drawing
a surprised breath, her legs stiffening, her hands clenching
at her sides. Then another gasp, followed by a wordless cry.
And then Andrea was writhing against Sean, calling his
name, hands in his hair, thrusting against his mouth and
begging him to do all he wanted.

Sean obliged, drinking her sweet cream. He teased her,
tasting her, his mouth pressed hard to her to suckle her. He
caressed her thighs, cradled her tight buttocks, loving the
smooth feel of her skin.

Finally Sean tilted his head back, satisfied, and looked
up at her. She gazed down at him, face soft with release,
red lips parted.

"Sean," she whispered brokenly.

Sean got slowly to his feet, letting his hands run up her
body as he rose. He finished by cupping her face in his
hands, then leaning down and kissing her mouth.

The kiss was deep, and she opened for him, even though
his lips were still wet with her. Sean ran his hands down
her back, lifted her to him, kept on kissing her. He was
rock hard for her, but he still wore the briefs, and rubbing
against her was not relieving the pressure.

Sean broke the kiss, traced her cheek with his thumb. "I
want to finish this."

Andrea nodded, as though it weren't even a question.

She felt her feet leave the ground as Sean lifted her into

his arms. He was strong, never faltering as he went up the stairs.

Damn, this was dangerous. Knowing Sean could make her feel like *that* took away Andrea's power. She'd wanted him before, to explore his body, to discover him, to touch and tease. Now Sean had turned the tables, letting her know he could mold her like clay any time he wanted to. All he had to do was touch Andrea, and she'd do anything he asked.

She couldn't lose herself like this. But she found no words to deny him as he carried her into her bedroom and laid her on the bed.

Sean didn't wait to close the curtains or shut the door or make small talk. He stripped off his briefs and let them fall, red letters flashing on black fabric.

He didn't hide his wanting either. As Sean climbed onto the bed, Andrea couldn't stop herself from closing her hand around his thick, hard cock.

Sean stopped, his eyes flicking to white blue. "I don't think you want to do that, lass."

In answer, Andrea squeezed. Sean always brought out the playfulness in her, the teasing that Lupines loved.

She licked her lips as Sean groaned. "Why shouldn't I, *Seanie*? You had so much fun with me."

"That was different. I was readying you to take me."

"I see." Andrea formed a teasing pout. "It had nothing to do with making me feel . . ." She squeezed again. "Like that?"

Sean took a sharp breath. "Well, maybe it had something to do with that."

"Besides, aren't I readying you?"

"No, you're torturing the hell out of me."

"Poor little alpha," Andrea said softly. "Can't handle one of your pride?"

Sean scraped her hair back with a strong hand. "You're not in my pride. Yet. And I don't want to *handle* you. I want to mate with you."

She pretended to look startled. "Golly, there's a difference?"

"Dad tries to handle Glory. See how well that works?"

Andrea ran her foot up the back of Sean's leg. "Maybe wolf-girls don't like to be leashed."

Sean's answering growl shuddered excitement through her. His eyes were white, pupils flicking to slits, the Feline in him aroused.

She smiled up at him, ran her finger down his nose. "Tomcat. What are you going to do with your little bad wolf?"

His growl strengthened. Sean was losing control, and instead of that terrifying her, Andrea wanted to laugh. Who said Sean could steal all her power?

She let her fingers drift across his cheek, which was flushed and hot. "I'm ready."

Sean's hand was hard as he stroked it around her breast. "Be sure, love. I'm big."

"Bragger."

"'Tis true. And you're not fully Shifter."

Shifters were larger—in all ways—than human males. Kim had told Andrea that salient fact, along with measurements. Eleven inches was common. Female Shifters, according to Glory, were built to accommodate, but Andrea was part Fae, her build more slender than that of most Shifter women. But Kim had learned to accommodate Liam—even without the obvious evidence of her pregnancy, the noise those two made next door proved it.

"I'm willing to give it a shot." Andrea lifted her foot, toes teasing the back of Sean's thigh up to his buttocks.

The movement opened her to Sean, and his tip slid straight in. Andrea stopped laughing, her breath speeding at the feel of him inside her. Only a few inches inside her, but she already wanted more.

She rubbed her foot on his thigh, encouraging him. His size was surprising but also exciting. What would it feel like when he was all the way in?

"Sean. *Please*."

His eyes were his wildcat's, no trace of the human left. But he softened his touch, gently kissing her lips as he slid his way into her wet and open passage.

Andrea's head went back on the pillow, her thoughts scattering. Sean was hard and hot, heavy on her, and yet, he touched her with such tenderness that her eyes filled with tears.

"Andrea, love." Sean closed his eyes on a groan as he slid in. He opened them again, the dark blue returning as he looked at her. "I've never seen anything as beautiful as you."

Andrea tried to answer, but only a groan came out of her mouth. She lifted herself against him, using her legs to pull him in and *in*.

It didn't hurt. Not exactly. Kim had told her that the first time for human females could be painful and about the hymen, a barrier that had to be broken. As far as Andrea knew, Shifter women had no such barrier. Shifters had been bred to mate, and anything that kept them from that had been left out of their physiology.

But Sean stretched her, entering a place that had never been touched. Andrea's heart soared. Sean had rescued her, making sure that her first time was with a male like him—a hard-bodied, protective, beautiful male who cared about her. Who cared about *her*.

"Sean." She loved saying his name, and this was a heartfelt cry of joy.

He was all the way in. Andrea opened her eyes, stared right back into his.

"Andy-love," Sean rasped. "I don't know if I can do this slowly. I don't want to be hurting you."

"I'm pretty strong, Sean Morrissey," she whispered.

"You are, but so am I. Stronger."

More excitement. "Let's see what happens." To emphasize her point, Andrea leaned forward and bit his neck.

Sean growled. His eyes flicked from blue to Shifter, back to dark blue again. "You asked for it, love."

She had. And she loved it. Sean slid almost all the way out of her and then firmly back in, Andrea's body opening for the stroke. He stayed all the way in for a few seconds, stretching her wonderfully, then he drew back and did it again. And again.

Andrea lost coherence. She held on to him with both hands, one leg wrapped firmly around his thigh, and gave in to ecstasy as she met his thrusts with her own.

They didn't hold back. Sean stroked into her again and again, and Andrea cried his name and begged with her body for him to give her more.

The bed scraped against the floor, but it didn't matter. There was no one downstairs to hear, no one in the world but herself and Sean. He was big, he was hard, and she loved every inch of him.

Sean gave up trying to go slowly. After a while, they were riding each other, bodies arching and moving together in a rhythm so perfect that Andrea knew her entire life had been hurtling her toward this wonderful moment.

When she started to climax, she looked straight at Sean. What she saw looking back at her were Sean's dark blue eyes, intense under black brows, pupils widening as he rode her.

Andrea couldn't look away. His dominant gaze held her, pinned her, and yet, it was the most beautiful thing she'd ever seen. He was looking straight into her heart. Something inside Andrea started to sing, like a violin string that had been out of tune suddenly tightened and made right.

The vibration warmed her heart, warmed her entire body. She tingled with it, and it poured out of her mouth in her cries of excitement, threatened to flow from her eyes as tears.

Sean shouted her name. He held her gaze as he started to climax, and Andrea couldn't look away. Sean was buried deep inside her, his thrusts generating little shocks as they locked together.

Shifters mated for life. He was part of Andrea now, as he scalded her inside, his body loving hers. At last Sean squeezed his eyes shut, breaking the gaze, and threw back his head with a fierce, lionlike snarl.

Mine, the Shifter in him was saying, and the Shifter in Andrea answered.

Mine. My mate. My love.

The mate bond. It twined around her heart, tightening as Sean opened his eyes and looked down at her again, his face softening in his pleasure.

The mate bond would fetter her far tighter than Sean's mate-claim or the claim Jared had tried to put on her. It was a bond of Andrea's own making, and she knew she'd never escape it.

Instead of anger or fear, Andrea's heart spread warmth through her. She wrapped her arms around Sean and pulled him down to her, burying herself in his heat, feeling joy.

CHAPTER TWELVE

The sword was calling to her.

Andrea lay still in the moonlight, listening, wondering whether she were dreaming. Sean's arm was heavy around her, pinning her in his sleep.

The words weren't English. They were liquid sounds, flowing like music. Andrea had never learned the language of Faerie, or the Celtic or Gaelic that Shifters from Ireland and Scotland knew. She wasn't even certain that what she heard was a language at all.

The sword was downstairs still, yet she had no doubt that the whispers that snaked into her mind came from it. The sound was tinged with silver, though practical Andrea knew sound had no color. This one seemed to.

Andrea carefully slid out from under Sean's arm, shivering as her skin met the cold air. Sean frowned in his sleep as she left the bed, but he didn't wake.

Andrea moved softly down the stairs, knowing the house was empty. The rooms were dark, no lights to betray her to anyone walking by outside.

The sword was in the living room, lying across a table

like a sentinel, an oblong cross in its plain sheath. The runes on the sheath and hilt glowed faintly in the moonlight.

The whispers increased as Andrea approached, the sounds more rapid. Andrea folded her arms across her chest, certain she didn't want to touch it.

Bring it to me, the Fae man had said. He'd stood out there under the trees, tall and beautiful in his shimmering armor, his eyes dark gray, almost black. *Bring me the Sword of the Guardian. It is the most important thing you will ever do.*

The arrogant Fae had been surprised when Andrea had put her hands on her hips, cocked her head, and said, *And why should I believe you?*

For an instant, he'd shown his rage, fury that a mere half-Fae woman would disobey him. Then his look had softened, and he'd said, *Because I gave life to you. Your mother was my only love, and you, Andrea Gray, are my daughter.*

The shock of his words had dried her mouth, but Andrea shook her head. *Weak card, Fae-man. Even if I did believe you, it wouldn't make me give you the sword. My father was a complete bastard who deserted my mother because he didn't care about anyone but himself.*

He'd gazed at her with Fae-dark eyes, black in his pale face. *I had to leave. The time between has been long. And now, you . . .*

You've been coming to me in my dreams, and now you claim to be my father. If you think I'll fall on my knees and beg to obey you, you're a complete fool.

To her surprise, the Fae had smiled. *Ah, Andrea. You are so like your mother.* He reached for her. *Her death took the heart out of me, child. Perhaps you could put it back.*

Don't even think about touching me.

The Fae dropped his hand to his side. *No. You must touch me. Touch my skin, and I will prove it to you. I will show you . . .*

Curious in spite of herself, Andrea had been reaching for him when Sean had barreled into her, and the Fae had blinked out.

Andrea had been angry at Sean for stopping her, but she understood, when she'd calmed, why Sean had done it. Fae were treacherous. They weren't as strong in the human world as they once were, but that didn't mean they couldn't do plenty of damage if they managed to cross over. Just because this Fae knew Andrea's name and said heart-wrenching things about her mother didn't mean he told the truth. He could be anybody, could have forced knowledge out of her real father, and for whatever purpose the man wanted the sword, it couldn't be good for Shifters.

The sword continued its rapid, musical whispers as she approached. The runes glowed and quivered, and Andrea's sleep-blurred eyes saw a glow rise from the hilt in fine threads, the same as she'd envisioned when she'd healed Ely.

Andrea reached for the hilt. A strange reluctance to touch the sword stole over her, but she let her hand hover just above the metal. The threads of light reached for her, touched her palm, tingled.

She jumped, but this touch was different from the touch of the threads in her nightmares. Those threads tried to bind and suffocate her; these caressed her skin and continued their tingling dance. The feeling was warm, comforting.

Andrea moved her hand down the sword, and the threads followed. The sparks were tiny, barely discernable, and moon-light gleamed hard down the length of the sword.

Sean's sword. Part of him and now trying to be part of her.

Andrea had to smile. His *other* sword had been part of her tonight too. Sean had truly claimed her, and she'd loved every second of it.

Bring it to me.

The Fae's remembered command echoed in her head. Andrea pictured herself taking up the sword and carrying it outside into the moonlit clearing to hand it to the tall Fae who would be waiting.

Except there shouldn't be a moonlit clearing, because it was raining outside. Droplets of rain pattered outside the window and had been this entire time, but Andrea hadn't noticed them. As soon as she glanced at the window, whatever had passed for moonlight died, though the threads continued to seek her hand.

When she'd healed Ely, she'd cut herself on the blade. She studied the streak across her palm and noted that it had narrowed and dried to a very thin streak.

The sword had touched her blood, and her blood was on the sword.

Did that mean something? Or nothing at all?

"What are you doing, love?"

The floorboards creaked as Sean crossed to her, and then he was behind her, six and a half feet of naked male leaning over Andrea's equally naked body. His skimmed kisses to her neck, his breath heating her.

"I think your sword likes me," Andrea said.

Sean's chuckle sent ripples of warmth into her ear. "Oh, my sword certainly does, love."

"I meant the one on the table."

"I didn't."

The firm length of him rubbed her buttocks, making her smile. Her thoughts of the Fae, threads, healing, and the Sword of the Guardian dissolved and fled as she turned around and buried herself in Sean's kiss.

"I'm thinking this one needs your touch, Sean," Liam said the next morning.

Sean's surprise that Liam wanted him to go solo got buried beneath his memories of waking up next to Andrea. They hadn't opened their eyes long before he was making love to her again, feeling himself surrounded with all of her. The scent of her filled his thoughts and every breath he took.

Glory had come home while they'd kissed and whispered afterward, and she'd called up the stairs that if they were finished humping each other, she'd make them breakfast. Then Liam had phoned, asking for Sean's assistance.

"Go talk to them as the Guardian," Liam said. "Flash your sword. They'll get the message."

In other words Sean's message would be: *If you think I'm scary, wait until you meet my brother.*

Sean thought he understood a second reason why Liam was sending him. "Kim doesn't want you going after them, does she?"

Liam grimaced. "Kim's not being reasonable about this."

Sean wanted to laugh. He could imagine *that* argument. "She's right, though. You need to stay nearby." A man needed to protect his mate and his unborn cub. "I'll take Andrea along."

"You think that's a good idea?"

Sean thought it was a good idea never to stray far from Andrea's side again. "She'll be able to point out who was saying what, help me figure out who is the ringleader so I can take him out first. Besides, I'm not leaving her alone here." Not with Fae men popping into Shiftertown, and Andrea deciding to run off places by herself.

"She's not alone anymore, Sean." Liam's eyes changed to dark blue, as they did when he was deeply contented. "She's family now."

"I'm still trying to convince her of that."

Liam's knowing look said it all. He'd known damn well when Sean had walked in here this morning that Sean and Andrea had made love most of the night and on into morning. Deep, satisfying love.

Liam pulled Sean into a tight embrace and nuzzled his cheek, one brother congratulating another. "Go explain to some Felines what we're trying to do here, Sean. We split into factions among ourselves, we'll never get these Collars off and ourselves out of Shiftertowns. Don't kill anyone, though. The last thing we'll be needing is having to explain to the humans why a few Shifters have become dust."

Sean released Liam and gave him a caressing pat. "No deaths today. Got it."

"Doesn't mean you shouldn't hold back on the threats, though."

"I wasn't planning to. I'll be my intimidating best, don't you be worrying."

Liam's look turned serious. "And if any of those bastards know who put Ely in the hospital, beat it out of them. The shooter's going to pay for that."

"Consider it done," Sean said, and he departed.

Glory watched Sean and Andrea ride off in her car she'd agreed they could borrow at the same time Dylan's pickup pulled to a stop in front of her house. She hadn't seen him since yesterday afternoon at Liam's, which had only made this decision easier.

Still, her stomach churned acid as Dylan left the truck and mounted the porch stairs, his stride measured, his head down, thinking about something. Glory was willing to bet that the something wasn't her.

Glory's first floor was one large square, the kitchen and dinette open to the living room. She came around the counter as Dylan closed the door, slid off his jacket, and laid it on the sofa. His eyes flickered when he saw her, as though he had to force himself back from wherever he'd been to the here and now. Or *her* and now.

He didn't reach for her; Dylan rarely did so right away. Glory sensed that he was troubled about something and didn't necessarily want to talk, but she made herself look him straight in the eye. If Andrea could do it, so could she.

"Dylan," she said calmly. "Get out."

Dylan blinked in surprise for one second, then he pinned her with eyes of hot blue, the dominant focusing on the immediate problem.

Glory swallowed but stood her ground. "Did you hear me? I said, get out of my house."

"Why?" The word was quiet, unworried.

Her temper splintered. "Why the hell do you think? You always assume I'll be here, waiting for you, whenever you're finished with whatever Shiftertown business you have. Glory will be here, available to soothe your troubles. Did it ever occur to you that I get tired of waiting for you to decide to come around?"

"No, it didn't."

The honest answer hit her like a stinging slap. "That's why I want you out," Glory said, throat tight. "You remember me when it's convenient. Other than that, I don't matter to you. I don't need you, Dylan. There are plenty of other fish in the sea. Or Felines, Lupines, Ursines, and humans."

Dylan kept staring at her. The alpha stare, the dominant in him telling her to look away, back down, admit she had no right to tell him what to do.

"This is my house, Dylan," she made herself say. "Please leave it."

He continued looking at her with his hard assessment. "You really want that?"

"No." Glory's throat worked, almost choking her words. "What I want is for you to tell me that you love me, that you want us to be mated, that you want to stay forever. That's what I want. But I've finally made myself realize it's not what I'm going to get. So I'd rather you go, instead of having my heart torn out every time I look at you."

"Glory."

Damn him, he couldn't stop being the alpha. He wouldn't look upset or uneasy, couldn't show any sign of conceding.

"What?" she snapped.

"Things are difficult for me at the moment. My whole world has changed, and I don't know where I fit into it anymore."

His words tugged at Glory's heart, but he wasn't getting off that easy. "What has that to do with choosing a mate?"

"I chose a mate once upon a time. She died."

"I know that. I'm sorry. Really, I am. I lost my mate too, you know I did."

That had been a hundred years ago. Glory's pack and her mate's had lived rough in the heart of the Rockies, but they'd been happy. Glory was robust even for a Shifter female, but fecundity had been low in both packs, and she'd never conceived. Within a year of her mate blessing, her mate's pack had been attacked by ferals, and they'd been wiped out, down to the last wolf. Her mate had hidden her beforehand so that she'd be safe, a decision Glory had fought like fury, but she realized now that if she hadn't obeyed him, she'd be dead too. The ferals would have taken her, used her, and let her die.

Her parents' pack had found her days later, lying in shock among the dead. The Guardian had sent the souls of the entire pack to the afterlife, and Glory had been taken back to her family. She'd never wanted to mate again.

That is, until her pack had been relocated to this Shiftertown twenty years ago, and she'd moved in next door to Dylan. Life went on, she'd learned, even after horror.

"I know," Dylan said. Glory had told him the entire story, which he would have heard anyway from Wade, her pack leader, even if she hadn't. No one kept secrets from Dylan.

Glory drew a breath. "I'm not trying to tell you to get over Niamh. I'm saying I want more than an on-again, off-again affair with you. There is happiness in the world, Dylan, in spite of everything, and I want it. If you can't give it to me, then I don't want you here." She wet her lips. "I don't want you tearing me apart."

Dylan moved to Glory slowly, as he might toward a hurt cub. His hands on her shoulders nearly undid her. "You are so strong." He caressed her skin below her Collar. "So strong that I never knew you were hurting."

"I guess I hide it well."

"You do, that." Dylan leaned closer and nuzzled her. "I'm sorry, my girl," he whispered. "I'm so sorry I can't be what you want."

The tears slid out before Glory could blink them back. "Then you understand why I need you to leave?"

Dylan nodded. He nuzzled her again, and his lips grazed her cheek. When he backed away, she thought she would die of grief.

Not the same, her common sense told her. He's not dying; he's just leaving. But right now, her heart couldn't tell the difference. Gone was gone.

"You'll want your things," she said in a strangled voice.

Not that he'd brought much into her house; the entirety would fit into an overnight bag.

"Throw them away. Or leave them outside the door and I'll have Liam fetch them later. Your choice."

Possessions meant so little to a Shifter, especially this Shifter. "What will you do?" she asked.

Dylan shrugged, gave her a little smile. "Who knows? But I'm good at taking care of myself. Didn't I have to raise three sons on my own?"

Glory nodded, unable to speak anymore. Dylan wiped a tear from her cheek and pressed a gentle kiss to her lips. "Be well, love."

And then he left her, walking out the door and back down the porch steps in the same even stride he'd used to mount them. Without stopping, looking back, or even glancing at his own house, he got into his pickup, started it, and pulled smoothly away.

Glory waited until the sound of the truck had faded into the distance, then she walked upstairs, entered her bedroom that still smelled of him, and pulled down the shades. Only then did she let herself fall across the bed and weep until she had no tears left.

"So what did you think of my dad?" Andrea asked as Sean drove rapidly down Thirty-Fifth. "My stepdad, I mean."

Sean glanced at her, his eyes still holding the fires they had last night and this morning, and again when he came to tell her that Liam wanted them to go back to the bar in north Austin. The throbbing of the bond hadn't gone away. She felt it wrapping around her heart, squeezing tight.

"I liked him," Sean was saying. "You said he was a good man, and he is, I could see that."

"I miss him." Andrea sighed.

"I can try to have him transferred here, if you want. And if he'd be wanting that. It would mean leaving his pack."

"You can do that? The humans told him he couldn't come with me, and then a pack here would have to let him in . . ."

"You let me and Liam worry about that."

He had such power and spoke about it so casually, hands resting lightly on the wheel. His generosity touched her.

She grinned at him. "If you're this nice to all the girls you get into your bed, I'm surprised you don't have a line at your door. Maybe stretching all the way down the street."

Sean glanced at her, fire dancing between them. "Only ones I want for my mate, love."

"So the rest of them must just be after your fine ass."

"No woman's ever bought me underwear for my ass, that's for certain. But what can I do? Lupines like to play. You throw a stick, they race after it. Cats wouldn't dream of doing that."

Andrea drew her finger across her lip, wetting it. "But you give cats a little . . . nip and they go insane."

Sean stared at her a moment longer before traffic on the curving road dragged his attention back to it. He moved in the seat, as though something in his pants had tightened. "And now, it's the tease."

"I don't have much else to do. Teasing you fills the time."

Another sideways glance, the sparkle in his eyes stoking the fire high. "Would you be willing to fill it with something else?"

"Not right now," Andrea said. "You're driving, and we're on a mission."

"Mmm, I'm thinking some Shifters are going to be damn sorry they're pulling me away from the mating frenzy."

"Maybe it's why Liam wanted you to do this instead of him."

"Could be. If they take too much time messing with me, I might tear them up for interrupting us."

"Don't get too carried away. Your Collar will go off, and they'll just laugh at you."

"Don't worry about that, love. I'll time it just right."

Andrea wasn't certain what he meant by that, and by the way he stopped talking, he didn't want her to ask. Andrea shrugged to herself and looked out the window as they turned and wound northward through town.

Bronco's, the bar where she'd found Glory yesterday, sat back from the road in a littered parking lot. Behind it, an old wooden fence separated the property from a creek, and beyond that lay suburban houses. To either side of the bar were one-story shops. A vacuum repair store occupied one of the buildings; the other held an antique store and a tobacconist. All closed for the day, Sunday.

The bar was also closed, but a few vehicles were parked around it. From the age of the cars and trucks plus the fact that they'd been kept well, Andrea could tell that they belonged to Shifters.

Sean smiled in anticipation. "Let's see what they're up to in there, shall we, love?" The sun gleamed off the sword on his back, and Sean's smile added to the deadly picture he made. No wonder Liam had sent him as liaison.

The door to the bar was locked. No grate had been pulled across the door, and it was fastened with a simple dead bolt. Sean wrapped his fingers around the door handle, let his hand become his powerful lion's paw, and yanked. The lock splintered, and the door opened.

"Nice trick," Andrea said. "Wish I was a big, bad Feline."

"I'll teach you someday, if you're good."

"Mmm, I'll never learn it, then."

Sean's answering grin stoked the heat already burning in her, and then she fell in behind him as he strode inside.

"Hey, we're closed," someone yelled.

Sean didn't stop. The bar was thick with cigarette smoke, which meant humans. Shifters didn't smoke. A knot of people sat around a table in the back, and a human worked behind the bar, likely prepping to open the place later that afternoon. The bartender had been the one who'd yelled.

From the scent beneath the gagging smoke, three of the men at the table were human. They wore jeans and biker vests, their guns in shoulder or belt holsters evident. But it wasn't just their scent that betrayed them as the ones who'd been responsible for all the shootings. One human rose as Sean came in and pointed a black pistol at him.

Sean drew his sword, the silver glittering, the blade

ringing as it swept out of its sheath. The human laughed, but one of the Shifters knocked the gun from his hand with the swipe of a claw.

"He's a Guardian," the Shifter snarled.

The human opened his mouth to jeer, looked at the Shifter faces gone hard and cold, and sat back down. He retrieved his pistol from where it had landed on the other side of the table and shoved it into a shoulder holster.

Sean brought the sword around and rested the point of it on the table, the hilt rising like a cross. He scanned the faces that turned to him, Sean quiet and unafraid, the Shifters tense and worried. Sean's gaze stopped as he picked out a Shifter to address, and that Shifter shrank back in his chair, looking like he wanted to wet himself.

"So tell me, Ben O'Callaghan, of me own clan," Sean said to him. "What exactly have you been up to?"

CHAPTER THIRTEEN

Sean smelled Ben's fear even before the man spoke. "You should leave, Sean."

Sean rested his hands on his sword hilt, driving the point a little way into the table. "Now, why would I be wanting to do that? We had some humans shooting at Shifters, and then I walk in here and find humans with pistols sitting at this very table. A suspicious man might make a connection."

Ben's blue eyes clouded with worry. "You really need to go. Pretend you never walked in."

"I'm not good at playing pretend, me." Sean caressed the hilt while he scanned the faces of the other Shifters. "Why don't I join you, and we'll have a nice little chat?"

"No one's talking about anything," another Shifter said. He was a Feline Sean recognized, but he wasn't from Sean's clan, and he wasn't from Austin. "Especially not with you," the Feline finished.

"*She* can stay," another of the human men said. He grinned at Andrea, showing unnaturally straight teeth.

The Feline growled. "She's Fae."

"Half Fae," Andrea shot back.

The Shifter's brows lowered. "Abomination."

"I've heard that before." Andrea looked right at the fur-ball, not dropping her gaze like a good submissive should. It pissed off the Feline and made Sean want to laugh.

"Callum Fitzgerald, isn't it?" Sean asked him. Callum was an alpha, a pride leader. Sean knew this from the data-base he maintained of information on all Shifters but nothing much about him.

"The great Sean Morrissey knows my name," Callum said. "I'm honored."

He couldn't meet Sean's eyes, though. "The honor's all mine," Sean said. "Or it will be if you tell me what the hell is going on."

"So you can run back to your brother and tell on me?"

Sean reached into his pocket. The humans tensed, but Sean only pulled out his cell phone. "If you'd like me to have Liam and my father join us, I'm happy to call them."

A ripple of discomfort circled through the Shifters. Dealing with Sean was bad enough; dealing with Dylan was nothing any Shifter wanted to do on a good day. Callum didn't look worried at all, which was a bad sign.

"You'd summon the might of your clan to interrupt Shifters having a private drink on a Sunday morning?" Callum asked. "I'd heard you Morrisseys liked to abuse your power."

"Having a beer, is it?" Sean picked up a half-empty bottle on the table, looked at the label, shook his head, and put the bottle back down. "I don't call this much of a beer. And just yesterday my friends heard you saying you thought Shifters should have nothing to do with humans, but here they are. So, which is it, Callum?"

"Your friends are mistaken."

Sean glanced at Andrea, who gave him the barest nod. These were the assholes she and Glory had overheard, all right.

"I trust them." Sean looked up and down the table again. "Tell me, Callum, which one of these is the man who shot Ely Barry?"

The wave of fear that came off the humans made Sean's

nose curl. "Hey, we didn't aim to hit anyone," the one sitting right next to Sean said. He had long hair pulled into a ponytail and a scar across his jaw. "He jumped in the way."

"So you think it's not your fault that my cousin lay dying?" Sean asked him. "Thinking he'd not live to see his grandchildren born? But that's all right, because *you weren't aiming for him?*"

Sean watched fear dive deep inside the man and erupt as wild fury. His face went red, his scar white. "Fucking Shifters." The man jumped to his feet, drew his pistol, and jammed it, cold and hard, against Sean's jaw. "What are you afraid of?" he snarled at the other humans. "They can't hurt us. Those Collars will hurt them worse."

Sean heard Andrea's growl, a sound that built into a wall of vibrating rage.

"Shit," Ben whispered.

Shit was right.

Sean let go of the sword. It stayed upright, in the table. When the human with the pistol glanced at it in surprise, Sean whipped around and crushed the pistol from the man's grasp. The breaking metal bit into Sean's skin, bloodying it, but he didn't feel a thing.

Sean also didn't feel the sparks that burst from his Collar as he wrapped his hand around the human's throat and lifted him high. The human made choking noise and clawed at Sean's fingers. Sean casually threw him across the room.

The other two humans sprang to their feet. Shifters weren't supposed to be able to hurt humans; the Collars were in place to prevent that. Sean's Collar was sparking, but he ignored it as another human yanked out his gun and opened fire.

The bullets went wide as Ben plowed into the man. Callum shifted, his clothes ripping, and he launched himself at Sean. Sean met him, his hands changing to claws as Callum's wildcat landed on him. Callum's Collar went off, but he went for Sean's face with his fangs

The shouts of the other Shifters were drowned by the fearsome snarl of the huge wolf that hurtled at Callum. The wildcat was knocked aside by a hundred and fifty pounds of wolf, her fangs bared, aiming right for Callum's throat. Andrea's Collar went off, blue arcs of electricity whipping around her neck, but it didn't slow her a nanosecond.

Andrea went down with Callum, Callum fighting and clawing. Still Andrea didn't stop. She was within a heartbeat of ripping out Callum's throat when Sean wrapped both arms around her and dragged her back.

"*No.* Don't kill him. Don't, love. You've got to stop."

Andrea snarled and fought. Her Collar snapped and sparked and sizzled, but it might have been an inert piece of metal for all her reaction.

"Andrea!" Sean put every ounce of force he had into the word. "Stop! Now!"

Andrea finally went slack in Sean's arms but breathed hard, wolf eyes hot with rage. Sean let her go, and she sank to her haunches next to him, pressing her shoulder hard into his hip.

Callum morphed slowly back to human. Blood dripped from his face, his throat blackened from his Collar's sparks. "Bloody Lupine," he grated.

"I want no Shifters dying," Sean said. "Not today."

"To hell with what you want," Callum said.

Andrea growled and jerked forward, but Sean stopped her with his hand on her back. He drew out his cell phone again. "I'm not letting Shifters die," Sean repeated. "But the cops get the humans. They're paying for Ely. I suggest all Shifters clear out, unless you're wanting to explain your presence to the human police."

He punched numbers, then paused with his thumb over the button that would send the call.

"Bloody hell, Sean," Ben rumbled.

Callum spat blood. "Just like a Morrissey to only believe one side of a story."

Sean snarled at him, feeling his eyes change. "Humans are shooting at Shifters, and you're getting cozy with the same humans. Doesn't take a genius to figure out that you're in on it with them."

"Because mixing ourselves with them and their world makes us weak," Callum said with heat. "Going to their bars and shops, our cubs wanting their toys like stupid cell phones and satellite dishes. They've forgotten that Shifters are supposed to be fighters, warriors, a hell of a lot better than humans."

"So you're putting Shifters in danger because your son's been bothering you for a nicer computer, are you now?" Sean asked. "Good logic, that. Now, Callum, are you going to run or stay and pay the price?"

"Don't be an idiot. You won't call the police."

Sean rotated his thumb over the button. "But I will. This human toy, you see, lets me talk to people from far away."

"He's right, Sean," Ben broke in. "If the cops take the humans, they'll just tell them we hired them. The police will come after us then. You'll make it even worse for us."

Sean knew that, had known it, hated that. In retrospect, it was a good thing that Kim and Silas, and Sean, hadn't been able to convince the human police to take the problem more seriously. The detectives would have found Shifters at the end of the trail. Shifters would be rounded up, guilty and innocent alike, interrogated, not likely to be let go in a hurry, probably punished, which mean being put to death. Shifters did not need a lockdown and arbitrary arrests, especially not just now with Liam and Dylan performing their experiments on the Collars. Callum's little plot to keep Shifters pure could be the death of them all.

Sean smiled, thumb still poised. "What do you suggest then, Callum. We kill your humans?"

Callum liked that solution, Sean could see, and the humans saw that he liked it too. But as much as Sean wanted to tear off their heads, he knew that dead humans were another risk they couldn't take.

"You want it too much, Callum," Sean said in a quiet voice. "So what I'll do is call my dad. He and my brother's trackers will escort these humans out of town, somewhere far, far away, where we won't ever see them again. Ben, why don't you and some of the Shifters you trust here help with that? Take them somewhere that I or my brother won't happen on them. Either that or I take them to San Antonio and let them face Ely's mate."

Andrea growled in agreement. Female Shifters defending their mates were the most dangerous Shifters of all. They didn't care who died, as long as those who'd attacked their mates bled. A lot.

"We'll help your dad take care of it," Ben said quickly.

Two of the other Shifters disarmed the humans so fast they didn't have time to react. Sean's adrenaline eased the slightest bit. Ben would be smart enough to see the wisdom of hiding the mess and throwing the police off the scent. Whatever evil deed they'd been planning here today wouldn't happen.

Callum, on the other hand, wasn't about to obey. "I think it's time the Morrissey clan had a new Guardian."

He leapt at Sean, shifting to his wildcat in midair. Sean blocked Andrea from attacking, at the same time half shifting so that he caught Callum in a claw-filled embrace. Callum's Collar was sparking, the electricity from it singeing Sean's skin, but it didn't slow Callum much.

Sean's own Collar bit shocks deep into him, but he clenched his jaw and kept the pain at bay, as he'd trained himself to. Andrea was snarling in fury, barely holding herself back. Sean fought himself away from Callum's vicious teeth, and in a lightning-swift move, he hurled Callum across the room. Callum crunched into the wall and slid down it.

Breathing hard, Sean dialed his cell phone again and got Spike, one of Liam's trackers, loyal and the smartest of the bunch. Spike had been waiting for the call, in fact, Liam telling him to stand by in case Sean needed backup. He was there in a few minutes, followed by the other trackers and Dylan. Dylan looked white and almost ill, but he ignored Sean's look of concern as he pulled Callum off the floor.

Andrea remained a wolf, still growling at Callum. Sean retrieved his sword and swept the remaining Shifters a stony look.

"Go home. It's over."

Sean deliberately turned his back, showing he didn't need to keep them in his sights to make sure they obeyed. He also knew none of them would try to take on Dylan. They were at least that smart.

Andrea had left her clothes in an almost tidy pile on the bar. Sean scooped them up and stared down the human bartender, who cowered in a corner.

"My advice?" Sean said. "Find another job."

He yanked open the door and walked out at a deliberate pace, Andrea, still in her wolf form, trotting beside him.

"My underwear, Sean?"

Andrea unfolded herself from her cramped position on the floor of the car. Normally she wouldn't worry about her nakedness after shifting, but like hell she'd let those gun-toting humans see her in all her glory. She'd waited until Sean had driven out of the parking lot to shift to human form, and now she didn't feel like flashing greater Austin while Sean sped them home.

Sean pulled a tiny pair of panties out of his jacket pocket. He looked good for a Shifter whose Collar had just shocked the hell out of him, very good, even better dangling her underwear just out of reach.

"The black lace again," he said. "I like these."

Andrea snatched them. "Great. I'll buy you a pair."

"Have you taken over all my underwear shopping now?"

Andrea had pulled on her shirt and now wormed her way up to the seat, which was cold to her bare behind. She lifted her hips to get the panties up over her butt. "I never said that."

"But you rushed to defend your mate from attack in there. That was sweet."

Andrea's face heated. "Of course I did. Callum is an asshole. He's responsible for Ely almost dying, and I wanted to kill him."

"Agreed. But no one's ever leapt to my rescue like that, not since I was a cub. It felt good."

Andrea looked at him in surprise. "Never?"

"Never." His words were emphatic.

"I probably didn't need to," Andrea said. "You could have torn Callum apart. Your Collar wasn't stopping you."

"Could have, yes. Did I think it wise? No. Shifter deaths, they'll only cause problems. That's a certainty."

"You're evading the question, Sean. Why didn't your Collar bother you?"

"Why didn't yours?"

Andrea shrugged. "The Collar doesn't work on me."

He gave her a swift, startled look, sunglasses hiding his eyes. "Why? Is it defective?"

"No. I mean it's never worked on me. I don't know why."

Sean looked back at the road, his face still. "And how many people know this fact?"

"No one but me. And now you. I decided it would be wise not to mention it."

"Very wise, I agree. Is it to do with your Fae blood?"

"I haven't the faintest idea." Andrea looked out the window as she zipped up her jeans, but she barely saw the picturesque sight of downtown Austin floating toward them. "All I know is, the day the Collars were put on us twenty years ago, I didn't understand why the Shifters around me were screaming in pain. It took me ten seconds to realize I'd better start moaning and writhing with everyone else." She remembered the terrible agony of the Shifters around her, how she'd grabbed her stepfather's hand and tried to ease his hurting while pretending to be in pain herself.

"Aye, I remember the blissful day we took the Collar. They made Connor's mum put one on, even though she was so close to term with Con. I think it's why he came early, that pain, and why she died giving birth to him."

Andrea heard the sad anger in Sean's voice, and she covered his hand on the wheel with hers. It was a terrible thing for young mothers to die, and until recent years, it had happened to Shifters all too often, including Andrea's own mother, who'd died trying to deliver a son.

"I'm sorry," she whispered.

"Aye." He caught her fingers between his. "Let me tell Liam about your Collar."

"Why?" Sean was the first person she'd ever told apart from her stepfather.

"He'll keep it a secret, I promise you," Sean said. "But he'll want to know. And I can't tell you why until I talk to him."

Andrea gave him a shrewd look. "Does it have anything to do with why *your* Collar didn't work?"

"Oh, it did work, Andy-love. In time, I'll pay, and pay like hell."

"What does that mean?"

Sean flinched, body jerking. Andrea didn't need to see his eyes to know they'd gone Shifter white behind the sunglasses.

"Damn, I thought I'd have time to get home," he said softly. "But I was worried about you, and Callum and his humans enraged me."

"Sean, what the hell are you talking about? What's wrong?"

Sean swerved the car, and Andrea grabbed the seat as they careened off the main road and down a street that headed toward the river. They flashed past the entrance to a park, to which hundreds of people had flocked this fine Sunday afternoon.

"We're not allowed down here," Andrea said. Glory had showed her a map when Andrea had arrived, with "no-Shifter" zones marked in red. This park was one of the reddest.

Sean kept driving, leaving the park behind. A few miles ahead, he turned down a quiet road that snaked along the river. Trees closed overhead, blotting out the glare of the day. Sean halted the car on the very banks of the river and turned off the engine.

He nearly threw himself out of the car, and Andrea scrambled out as well. She had taken two steps when she found herself pinned against the car by a large, virile Shifter with white blue eyes, sunglasses gone. He was half shifting, snarling in pain.

"Sean, is it the Collar?"

"You should go," he rasped. "You should run from me."

Not that she had a choice smashed against the car by his body weight. She lifted her chin. "No. I'm not afraid, and you're obviously hurting."

"I know you're not afraid. And you should be." Sean's hands closed on her shoulders with fingers that could crush her bones. "You should be terrified of me, love. Low in your pack, here at the mercy of the most powerful Shifters in Hill Country. You're bound to us, obligated. You should be groveling, grateful that you have your Fae healing gift to give us in return."

Andrea gave him a little smile. "Forget that."

"Aye, and here I stand, worried that I'll hurt you, a Lupine, a half Fae, a woman I'd never met until she turned up at a bus station and looked me with the most beautiful eyes I'd ever seen." He leaned closer, his body hard against hers. "What are you, Andrea Gray, that you make me feel like this?"

Trapped between the metal car and Sean's strength, she knew he was right—she should be afraid—but fear was the last thing on her mind. "Maybe it's the mating frenzy talking."

"It's more than that." Behind his anger, Andrea sensed Sean's confusion, his struggle to understand the one thing that didn't fit his world—her. "In that bar just now, you should have been hiding behind me in terror, letting me protect you, and yet you attacked Callum, a pride leader, without hesitation. He should be way out of your league."

"He messed with you." When Callum had gone for Sean, Andrea's emotions had snapped. Her wolf had answered a primal need, and she'd pulled off her clothes with only one thought ringing in her head. *Protect the mate.*

She ran restless hands up Sean's arms. "He wanted to kill you. I couldn't let him do that."

Instinct was a hell of a thing. Her rage at Callum for attacking Sean had overridden all fear, all reason. She'd only wanted to taste Callum's blood and make him pay.

If her fighting instincts had overwhelmed her, her mating ones were now filling her with fire. Sean bent her back against the car, his growl animal-like as he brought his mouth down to hers. His hands slid, warm, under her shirt, touching, molding, sliding around her waist and under her breasts, bare because Andrea hadn't bothered to put her bra back on. His mouth opened hers, the kiss claiming her, possessing.

They were so alone down here, with only the chatter of birds filling the air and the swish of water rushing past trees. No one might come back here for hours.

Sean broke the fierce kiss to nip Andrea's cheek. He thrust her shirt down to nibble his way to her shoulder, his thighs hard against hers, his arousal even harder.

"Sean."

"Don't stop me." His words were whispered, savage. "I need this. Don't stop me."

She wouldn't dream of it. "I just like saying your name," she said.

Sean raised his head. His eyes were almost white, the beautiful blue swallowed. Every line of his face was tight, his mouth pulling in pain.

"Fucking hell," he whispered. "No. Let me have this."

"Sean?"

Sean collapsed to his knees, his hands so tight on her wrists that Andrea went down with him. They ended up in the mud near the wheel of the car, Andrea crouching, Sean folding in on himself.

"Where do you hurt? Let me see."

Sean curled one arm across his belly. "Everywhere. You're right, it's the Collar."

Andrea stared at Sean's Collar, but it was a silent silver-black streak on his neck. She'd seen it shock him deeply in the bar, but he'd fought first the human and then Callum, as though he felt nothing. And then he'd said, *I'll pay, and pay like hell.*

"Delayed reaction?" she asked. "But Collars don't work like that. Do they?"

"We've learned." The words jerked out of him.
use . . . adrenaline . . . to keep the pain away. But onl
so long. Then . . . payback." His words faded, the Shifter i.
him fighting the hurt.

Andrea wrapped her arms around him. His skin was
slick with sweat, his breath coming fast, his heart going in
rapid-fire beats.

"You should go home, love," he whispered. "This won't
be pretty."

Andrea didn't bother to answer. She kissed his damp
hair, rested her head against his, and closed her eyes.

The pain wove through Sean in bright, hot lines that
streaked from his Collar and around his body like fishing
line—strong, tight, strangling. It was somewhat like what
caught her in the nightmares, though not as arbitrary and
terrifying. This was almost organized, technology making
the magic threads ruler-straight.

Andrea eased her concentration under the threads and
slowly, slowly started to loosen them. The pain clamped
Sean hard, the Fae magic almost gleeful. He'd cheated the
magic, and now the magic wanted its revenge.

No, Andrea told it. *You will obey* me.

Magic wasn't an entity. It was a force, without intelligence. But Andrea fought it now, and it fought back like
an enemy.

In her mind's eye, Sean's Collar gleamed on his throat
like a white-hot band, the Celtic knot a tangle of bright
energy. When fighting adrenaline flowed through a Shifter,
the Fae magic sensed it and triggered the shocks. The man-
made electricity was enhanced by the magic to make the
pain excruciating, plus the magic also made certain the
Collar never ran out of power and could never be removed.
Andrea knew all this intellectually, but seeing the pain
with her mind, feeling it with her fingers, made her very,
very angry.

The Collar's spells were strong, locked hard in place.
Andrea knew she couldn't negate the power, but she could
at least ease its intensity.

It took longer than she'd have liked, but Andrea managed to snake her healing magic beneath the Collar and loosen the wires of pain. Sean's body began to relax, as, one by one, the bright wires unwound themselves from him and retreated.

Sean drew a long breath. When Andrea opened her eyes, he was looking at her, his irises calmed back to lake blue.

Andrea exhaled in relief. "Better?"

Sean's answer was a growl. He dragged Andrea into his arms and brought his hard mouth down on hers.

CHAPTER FOURTEEN

His *mate*. Andrea had leapt to his defense, ready to fight for him, and then, when Sean had collapsed in mortal pain, she'd pushed her Fae magic into him and healed him. He'd felt the Collar's agony cease and slink away, as though she'd commanded it to go. He'd opened his eyes to find Andrea's head bowed, eyes closed, her brow puckered in a little frown as she concentrated on easing his pain.

She was the most beautiful thing on this earth.

The ground was wet, cold, uncomfortable. Sean dragged Andrea up with him, kissing her as he rose to his feet with newfound strength. He pushed her down against the still-warm hood of the car, and she smiled and wrapped her arms around him.

Andrea's mouth was a point of heat. Sean licked it. He liked the taste so much he continued licking across her lips, and then down her chin and her slender throat. Her shirt was tight against her body, and Sean reached to tear the fabric away.

"Don't." Andrea's hands came up.

Sean drew back a little, his heart pounding, dying for her. He couldn't stop his snarl of frustration, and she laughed.

"Let me. I don't want you to rip it; it's one of my favorites." Andrea grasped the hem of the shirt and slipped it off over her head.

There she sat, on the hood of Glory's car, bare from the waist up. She was so beautiful, smiling up at him with her breasts naked in the winter sunshine. It was cold, which tightened her nipples into dark points, but when he touched her, she was warm, so warm. Sean leaned down and drew a nipple into his mouth, suckling her as he pushed her down on top of the hood.

"Not fair." She hooked her finger into his waistband. "Take these off. If you get to look at something, so do I."

Sean barely registered her words. He yanked off his boots and then his pants. She raised on her elbows to watch him and laughed, her eyes sparkling.

"You're wearing them. The smiley faces."

"I wanted to make you laugh. But not just now." He tugged off the underwear and tossed it on top of his jeans.

Andrea's laughter died as she roved her gaze to his very obvious wanting. She lingered there, her smile returning, sly and a little bit smug.

"What is so damn funny?" he asked.

"I was blessing my luck that the alpha who volunteered to claim me wasn't ancient. And limp."

"I haven't been limp since I laid eyes on you, Andy-love."

"That must have made for some painful moments."

"It is pain." Sean climbed onto the car over her. "It's pain to watch you when I'm not inside you, not having you all the time."

"We'd never get anything else done."

"And why should I be caring? There's plenty of others to get things done for me."

"Must be nice to be at the top of the food chain."

"It is. I have the privilege of claiming the best female Shifter in the world and bringing her out here where no one can find us."

He tugged her jeans open and down her hips. Andrea helped, pushing away the fabric that kept him from her. The lace panties came off and followed the rest of the clothes to the ground.

Sean exhaled as he slid inside her. He belonged here, safe inside Andrea Gray, his beautiful love.

They fit together so snuggly, but when he began to move, it was hot, slippery, fiery, and fine. The awkward position, the fact that they were on a car in the woods, made the excitement burn. Andrea held his hips, her head going back as she felt it. *In, in, in, all the way in. Goddess, you are beautiful.*

How crazy to be naked out here, the river sliding by not five feet away, while he pumped and pumped and pumped inside her. This lovemaking wasn't slow and lovely, like their first time. It was all animal, hard and fast and needy. This was like being feral, back in the wild days when humans had never heard of Shifters, back before anyone had tried to tame them.

Andrea moved beneath him, her little cries winding him hard into the frenzy. Sean was making noises too, panting like a crazy man, grunting and groaning. He couldn't get enough of her.

Their mouths came together, tasting, devouring. Sean felt the wildcat in him wanting to come out, his claws sprout on his fingers. Damn what he wouldn't give to have her in his wildcat form, when mating was basic and mindless.

But this was even better. He could kiss her lips, watch her eyes, touch her face, have *her*. When they were fully mated, they'd shift and go for a run, and then he'd take her down and not stop.

Sean's breath grated in his throat, Andrea's breathing was as rapid, her hands skating over him as she pulled him down on her.

"Andrea," he said between kisses. "Mate. I don't care about sun and moon. You're my fucking *mate*."

"I am right now," she said in a throaty voice. She drew her fingertips down his chest, nails barely scratching him.

Damn it, why did she always have to laugh and tease and play? And then gaze up at him with those beautiful gray eyes, as though she wanted to peel back all his layers and look at the real Sean?

As it had last night, the mate bond reached out and wrapped around Sean's heart. The iron bands of it were more painful than the Collar's torture, because while the Collar lay quietly until provoked, the mate bond would tighten forever. Once begun, it would never die. His father was fighting the pain of having that mate bond ripped from him, and it gave Andrea the power to destroy Sean.

You belong to me. Mate, lover. Mine!

Sean shouted her name as his climax grabbed him and squeezed him hard. His seed sped out of him to be swallowed by the heat of her sheath, but still he went on, thrusting again and again inside her. Andrea arched to him, her own climax taking her, but Sean never wanted to stop.

And with his mate smiling that sultry smile, sliding arms around Sean and groaning his name with her beautiful red lips, he never would.

Both Sean and Andrea were panting as they wound down, the residual warmth of the engine keeping the cold from their bodies. Not that Sean would ever feel cold again. The mate bond, and Andrea, would see to that.

He looked into Andrea's stormy gray eyes and saw the mate bond reflected there. She was going to break his heart.

"Andrea," he whispered, just to say her name. "Andy-love."

"Feeling better?" Andrea drew her nails lightly down his chest.

"I don't think I'll ever feel better than this."

"Is that right?" She smiled up at him, so hot and good, and then her fingers squeezed one of his nipples, and she bit his neck.

Sean growled long and low as the mating frenzy reared up, hard, and he drove into her once again, until they were both crying out in joy.

* * *

The best place for talking about serious shit was on the front porch with beer. Sean and Liam sat alone that night as the moon rose, bottles in hand. Liam had his booted feet up, but Sean rocked back on the porch swing, trying to focus on the problem at hand and not the fact that Andrea was in the house next door, warm and waiting in her bed.

Sean had reported all to Liam on their return home, but Liam had listened, nodded, and said nothing. Not until after dinner was over and the world was dark had Liam indicated that he and Sean should talk. Sean understood how Liam worked—he listened, digested, thought, and then made decisions. Andrea had gone home, perceiving that Liam wanted to talk to Sean alone, but the promising look she'd given Sean made him very impatient to be done.

"This is not good," Liam said.

"No," Sean agreed.

They drank in silence.

"The humans are taken care of?" Sean asked after a time.

"Dad reported. They're gone."

"Dead?"

"Alive," Liam said. "Shitting themselves to do whatever Dad wanted, so he said."

Sean nodded, and they went back to the beer.

"That's not the end of it," Liam said.

"Aye."

"Callum, who claims to want nothing to do with humans, hired humans to shoot up bars and restaurants," Liam said, spinning it out. "I told the other clan leaders in his Shiftertown what he's been up to, and they're not happy. His clan is protecting him from me and them. As long as they sit on him and keep him quiet, fine, though I'd love to kill him over Ely."

"So would I. Not to mention his family."

Liam shook his head, his eyes flicking to cat slits and

back again. "If we start a clan war, there will be too much bloodshed, and the humans will come down on us, and all Shifters will suffer. Damn it." He drank his beer, a leader unhappy that the simple solution wasn't going to work. "If this was the wild, he'd be dead."

"If this was the wild, it wouldn't have happened at all," Sean said. "Shifters hiring humans to terrorize Shifters? Never. This is a problem that could have only happened after the Collar."

"Which brings me back to why he bothered. He had his humans shoot up bars and restaurants where Shifters like to go. Causing the human owners to get jittery and forbid Shifters entry, and causing other Shifter-friendly businesses to start banning Shifters. Widening the divide between Shifters and humans." Liam took a thoughtful sip of beer. "Why?"

Sean shrugged. His heart thrummed with the mate bond, distracting him, his body pounded with the mating frenzy. His mind was reliving Andrea lying against the hood of the white car, smiling at him, sunshine on her bare breasts while her black curls spread across the hood.

"Humans to Callum are nothing," Sean said. "Tools to be used and discarded."

"It's more than disdain of humans though, isn't it?"

Sean knew without expressing it, and Liam knew too, that they'd stirred the surface of a current that ran deep. "I can see Callum's way of thinking. We're stronger now, healthier, better organized. He's wondering why Shifters try to integrate with humans when we can kill them instead."

"They were all Felines at that bar, you said," Liam mused. "I'm guessing they don't want Lupines or bears joining their little party."

"Didn't seem that way. They looked at my bringing in Andrea as an insult, and not just because she's half Fae." Sean grinned. "You should have seen their faces when she attacked Callum and took him down. It was priceless."

Liam shared his smile. "Next time, take a picture and show me. She's a treasure, that one."

"I know." Sean's entire body sang, thinking about her. She'd soothed his hurts and made all the pain go away. "I treasure her."

Sean's gaze wandered to the house next door, and he caught Liam watching him with a knowing smile. "She's good for you, Sean. I've not seen you this interested in—well, anything—in a long time."

Not since Kenny died, he meant. Sean shrugged. "I'm not fooling myself that Andrea hasn't rejected the mate-claim because she adores me. She doesn't have much of a bloody choice."

"So let her go. Tell her you release her. We can keep it to ourselves so Jared will stay away from her, and Wade won't give her hell."

Sean's deep-seated rage flared. For some reason he wanted to launch himself at Liam, to slam his brother to the ground for even suggesting Sean release the mate already bound to his heart. Andrea's scent was so mixed with his that he couldn't separate them anymore.

When Sean's vision cleared, he saw Liam laughing. Laughing hard.

"Damn it, Liam."

Liam kept chuckling. "I'd react the same if you told me to let Kim go back and live among her people."

Sean sat back and took another drink of beer. "I'm thinking I'm so screwed."

"That's the mate bond, that is. You know you'd die if she went away. You'll fight the world to keep her at your side and keep her safe."

"Exactly."

Sean thought about what he'd explained to Andrea, that his father still struggled with the pain of his broken mate bond. Dylan hadn't been able to keep his first mate safe, and recently he'd slipped in the hierarchy, so what made him think he could protect a second one? That must eat him up.

"Kim told me Glory kicked Dad out," Sean said.

Liam nodded. "And he hasn't come back here."

Sean started peeling the label from his beer bottle. "Dad can take care of himself. He's damn good at it."

"That's what I keep telling myself."

"Someday we'll believe it?"

Liam laughed. "He'll expect us to take care of this Shifter problem without asking him for advice."

"That bites." Sean savored the dark taste of another sip of beer. "Why do we get stuck doing the hard work?"

"Because Dad raised us well, and now it's up to us not to shame him."

"Sure, no pressure." Sean took another drink, sank back into the swing. "Callum and his friends, they at least haven't figured out how to override the Collars. How's that going, then?"

Liam glanced off into the dark, nostrils widening as he searched the wind for scent. "Slowly," he said in a low voice. "I'm not letting anyone else be hurt because of it."

Sean leaned forward, and very quietly told Liam about Andrea's Collar. A spark danced in Liam's eyes, and he traced the lip of his beer bottle. "Does she know why?" Liam asked.

"She says not. I believe her. But she pulled magic from my Fae sword to heal Ely, and she eased the pain of my Collar. Something about her healing touch, maybe, that makes her Collar not hurt her."

"I wonder if any other half-Fae Shifters have the same immunity."

Sean shrugged. "If they do, I'm not thinking they plan to tell anyone."

"I wouldn't." Liam gazed off into the night again, winter cold returning with bite. "Would she help us, do you think?"

"She might. If we asked her nice."

Liam's eyes crinkled in the corners. "Is that your other sword talking? Does she draw magic from that one too?"

"You're a funny man, Liam Morrissey. I think she will help us, in time. As long as you don't piss her off. She's kept the secret of her own Collar forever; I think she'd be amenable to keeping ours."

"Let me think on it, talk to Dad."

"In the meantime, what about Callum?" Sean asked. "His clan might be sitting on him, but who knows how many of them agree with him?"

"Aye, I've got my eye on him and his friends." He scowled. "The idiots. Their impatience will only bring human wrath down on Shifters, set us back another twenty years."

Sean couldn't help looking at Glory's house again, at Andrea's bedroom window. "Dad could help. All he has to do is look at them, and they'll be properly terrified."

"Don't I know it."

The brothers shared a grin. They both would have been dead long ago without Dylan, that was certain. Sean thought back to long winters on the lonely coast of Ireland, when food and fuel ran short, and they'd curl together in their cat forms to warm each other—three brothers with their father. Dylan would disappear and return with food; not kills or stolen potatoes, but fresh vegetables and pheasant and fish prepared for rich men's tables. He wouldn't say how he'd obtained them, and Liam, Sean, and Kenny had decided it was wiser not to ask.

"I guess Dad's decided it's time to stop saving our asses," Sean said.

"It's high time we started saving his."

"You have the right of it." Sean rose and set his beer bottle on the table. "I'll be off home, then."

Liam grinned. "You might want to try actually sleeping, tonight."

"It's overrated, sleep. Far more fun things to do in bed."

The twinkle in Liam's eyes told Sean that he agreed. Liam rose and the brothers shared a tight hug. Then Sean walked next door, his frenzy mounting with every step.

Sleeping with Sean was supposed to keep away the nightmares. Andrea snuggled down against Sean's warm body as they both drifted off that night, limbs heavy with afterglow, and found herself instantly tangled in the white threads of her dreams.

This time, Andrea couldn't move, couldn't make a sound. She was bound in a cocoon, breathless, dying.

Fight it, Andrea.

The voice of the Fae cut through her panic. She punched her fists into the white threads and started to break them. When she'd ripped enough away to see through the cocoon, she found herself not safe in bed with Sean, but in a gray misty place that was neither one world or the other.

Wake yourself, but quietly, and come to me. I need to speak with you, daughter.

The white threads started to tangle her again. Oh, right, how was she supposed to fight them *quietly*?

She heard whispering music, familiar now, like dozens of voices calling to her. The Sword of the Guardian, which she knew gleamed like flame where Sean had left it on the dresser. Andrea envisioned using it to slice through the white threads, and instantly, the cocoon cringed away and vanished.

Ah, wise choice.

Andrea opened her eyes to silence. Sean was sound asleep beside her, his head pillowed on one muscular arm. Her heart caught as she looked down at him, a damn sexy man curled up in bed with her. Even with his blue eyes closed, his face relaxed in sleep, he was strong, and the memory of his weight on top of her body made Andrea warm. He was awakening deep emotions inside her, emotions that threatened to tear her apart.

Andrea slid silently out of bed, her movements so fluid that Sean never stirred. She retrieved her clothing and carried it downstairs to dress in the living room. The house was pitch-black, but Andrea had never had trouble seeing in the dark.

The Fae waited for her in the clearing, in the precise spot he'd stood two nights ago. He was tall, his face thinner and longer than a human's or Shifter's, and his white braid fell down his back, thick like silk rope. The silver mail he wore shimmered in light that didn't come from this world. The moon over Austin was hidden by a thick layer of clouds. In Faerie, the moon shone brilliant and white.

"Daughter." The Fae looked at her empty hands and frowned. "You did not bring it."

"No, I didn't bring it," Andrea said. "If you're going to insist on invading my dreams, let's start with a few questions, all right?" She counted off on her fingers. "Who are you? What's your name? Why do you insist on calling yourself my father? And why do you want the sword? I want your answers, in that order. You can start right now."

CHAPTER FIFTEEN

The man could do a good sneer; Andrea gave him that. The curl to his lip told Andrea he wasn't used to being questioned, especially not by what he considered lesser beings. Well, too damn bad.

"If you do not bring me the sword," the Fae said, "the Shifter you've claimed as your lover could die."

"So you say." Interesting choice of words, *the Shifter you've claimed as your lover*. Andrea claiming Sean, not the other way around. "Why should I believe you? You're Fae. Fae created Shifters, Shifters freed themselves from Fae, and now Fae hate Shifters. Tell me, why on earth should I believe that giving you the Sword of the Guardian would be a smart thing to do?"

His gray eyes went fierce. "Because I am Fionn Cillian, and what kind of honor would I have to lie to my own daughter? My own men would flay me alive, and I would deserve it."

The words came with such force that Andrea almost believed him. She folded her arms. "Sorry, never heard of you."

"This place has made you ignorant, including ignorant of what you are."

"You're not answering the questions. All right, we have your name; now, let's continue. Why do you keep saying you are my father, and why do you really want the sword?"

"I say I am your father because I am. Your mother was Dina Stewart, a wolf Shifter I met one night, in the wild, when the moon was full. The way between Faerie and this world had weakened, and I saw her in a clearing in dark woods. She had just shifted from her wolf, rising tall and naked in the moonlight. She was the most beautiful creature I'd ever beheld." His voice softened as he spoke, his gaze going remote.

Andrea swallowed. "I barely remember my mother."

"You look like her, Andrea. She had the same dark hair, the same gray eyes, the same stubborn tilt of the chin." Fionn's arrogance left him as he looked directly at Andrea. "When you stand there defying me, you sound just like her too."

She wanted to believe him. Andrea wanted to be with someone who'd known her mother, who could share memories of her, as she did with her stepfather. She needed that so much that she wondered whether this Fae had sensed her need and was playing on her emotions.

"Why are you here?" Andrea asked in a hard voice.

"I am Fionn Cillian, head of the Cillian clan, warriors of Faerie."

"You said that already."

His look turned sharp. "You demand explanations, and now I am explaining. My clan is the chosen of the emperor. We are his guards, his fighters, his military advisors. It is said that whoever protects the emperor controls the realm of Faerie."

"And your clan protects him?" Andrea's brows rose. "And you're the head of the clan? Are you saying that *you* control the realm of Faerie?"

"I do." It was a quiet statement, flat and without boasting.

"No wonder you're so full of yourself," Andrea said. "But

if you're this bad-ass warrior-protector for the emperor, when did you have time to meet and have an affair with my mother?"

"It happened when we were at war. Battles raged all across Faerie, clans fighting clans for control of the empire. I found myself cut off and alone in a wild place but discovered a way to the human world. The gate opened, and I startled a she-wolf who'd come to the woods for solitude. She wasn't exactly glad to see me, but I stood before her, transfixed. I fell in love with her on the spot."

"Except that Fae despise Shifters. We were bred to be your fighters, and you consider us no better than animals."

Fionn gave her a derisive look. "Shifters were bred well before my time, and the Shifter-Fae war happened before I was born. I'm not *that* old. I'd never seen a Shifter before. She was my first."

"So you saw each other, and it was instant love?" Andrea couldn't keep the skepticism from her voice.

"Not on her part. I had to beg her to pull me through the gate to save my life. She did that—pitying the wreck that was me, I suppose—then I had to follow her about for a long time before she'd even let me near her. And then . . ." Fionn swept his hand in front of him, palm up. "What we had was beautiful. And now, at last, I can see what came of our love."

Andrea cocked her head to study him, but her heart was hammering. "I believe that you were probably good at persistence, plus you're not bad looking, for a past-it Fae. But I'm not a complete idiot. Any Fae could pop out here on this ley line and pull a Darth Vader on me."

"Pull a what?"

"*Andrea, I am your father.* It's not as though your name is on my birth certificate or we can do a paternity test." Andrea paused. "Although, to be fair, he really was Luke's father."

Fionn looked puzzled—as puzzled as an impossibly tall warrior in chain mail could look. "I do not understand these words. Your world is confusing to me."

"As yours is to me. How do you even speak English?"

"I knew a little from academic studies on Earth languages, which are required curriculum. Your mother taught me much more. I studied on my own after that, so that when I saw you again, I could communicate well with you."

"*When* you saw me? Not *if*?"

"I always planned to find you when I could. I have been watching you, waiting until it was safe."

Andrea's anger boiled out of her. "Watching me? What the hell? If you really were my father, and really were watching me, why didn't you burst in and stop all the bad things that happened to me? Where were you when the pack leaders wanted my stepfather to strangle me at birth? How about when my mother died? Or when I was shunned for most of my life? How about when Jared tried to force a mate-claim, with the entire Shiftertown to back him up? And when Jared went on to stalk me and terrorize me? Tell me, Daddy Dearest, where the hell were you then?"

"Hiding you. Keeping you from my enemies."

Andrea's words faltered. "What?"

"Daughter, when the Fae wage war, it's brutal and ruthless. I am the head of my clan. If the leader of my rivals knew I'd fallen in love with a Shifter, that I'd sired a child on her, your life and hers wouldn't have been worth a breath. The other leader wanted to win at any price, and you would have been part of that price. He slaughtered half my men, almost all of my Fae family. Dina died here in this harsh world from illness when she tried to have a Shifter child, and I didn't dare go to her for fear my rival would find you. You were all I had left. When I say I watched you in secret, I mean I kept it secret from everyone. Which means it had to be a secret even from you."

Andrea listened in growing shock. "And this guy, this rival. Where is he now?"

"Dead." The word held triumph, simple and raw. "I myself ran my sword through his black heart. And so now I am free to reveal myself to you, my beautiful daughter, and to bring you home to me at last."

Andrea stepped back, putting herself well out of the man's reach. "When you say *home*, you mean in Faerie, with you?"

"It is where you belong, Andrea Gray. You are the only child of a warrior lord, the warrior who essentially rules the land of Faerie. You belong at my side, a highborn lady in your own right."

A bubble of hysteria worked its way upward and burst out as a laugh. "You mean I really *am* a Faerie princess?"

"Essentially, yes. The equivalent rank of one, though you wouldn't be of the royal house."

Fionn's deadpan explanation made Andrea laugh harder. He scowled as she wiped her eyes. "Sorry," she said. "This is a lot to take in. And to believe."

"You must believe me, child. Take my hand, come to me, and I will show you. I will give you visions of how I met your mother if you want. If that will convince you."

"Oh, right." Andrea took another step back. "Why don't you just come out here and get me yourself?"

"You know that I cannot. I need your touch to come to you. But why should I? Yours is a dirty world, full of cold iron. You come into Faerie and be with me."

"And then what happens? You laugh maniacally, say 'I've got you now, my pretty'? Maybe you are my father's enemy trying to fool me in order to get to him."

Now, he grew annoyed. "God and Goddess, what will it take to convince you?"

"Let me think about it for a while. What you say could be true, but I'm not gullible enough to drop to my knees, throw my arms around your waist, and scream *Daddy*."

He gave her an impatient look. "I was right when I said you were just like your mother. She drove me insane before she'd even let me touch her."

"Good for her. If you really are my father, you'll be kind enough to give me time to accept what you say."

Fionn frowned again, obviously not used to people who didn't simply obey his every command. He was a bit like Dylan in that respect.

"Time is a mutable thing," he said. "Don't take too

much of it. And while you are thinking, daughter, let me have the Sword of the Guardian."

Andrea laughed again. "You are amazing. If I steal the sword—and worse, hand it to a Fae—the Shifters will kill me. Why would you want that to happen?"

"If you don't bring it to me, Shifters will die for it. The stirrings among the Shifters are dangerous, and disaster could come of it. You need to give me the sword."

His words, especially after what had happened with Callum at the bar, made her nervous, but she kept her voice steady. "I'll need to think about that one too. Good night, Father." Andrea turned around and walked away, pretending nonchalance.

Fionn called after her. "You will regret so much if you do not listen to me."

Andrea gave him a cheery wave and kept walking. Something flashed behind her, and she knew that if she turned around, Fionn would have vanished, the way to Faerie closed again.

She didn't turn, though. She also wasn't surprised to find Sean on the back porch of Glory's house, scanning the darkness for her, ready to start after her. He growled as she came out of the trees, his eyes Feline slits.

"Don't even ask me where I've been," Andrea said, walking past him and into the house. "Right now, I'm very tired of males expecting me to do everything they say."

Andrea went into the house and slammed the door behind her, not waiting to see whether Sean would follow her in or not. He did, but he didn't ask questions. He simply made love to her in fierce silence until they fell asleep, curled together in blissful exhaustion.

Bloody females made him bloody furious. Sean's legs were cramped from sitting in the booth at the bar, but damned if he was going to leave until Andrea was done working her shift. She was closing tonight, so that meant he had to stay here at least until two.

She hadn't spoken to him much today, not to tell him why she'd been running around outside near dawn or whether she'd seen the Fae again, although Sean knew damn well she had. He'd smelled the stink of Faerie wafting in from the clearing when she'd come in, like acrid smoke laced with mint.

Sean had spent the day following up on the Callum problem, visiting his clansman Ben to let him know he was taking a personal interest in the situation. The humans were long gone, Spike had told Sean, and Ben had confirmed, headed back east somewhere. Callum's clan leader wouldn't let Sean see him but assured Sean that they were taking care of the problem internally. By Shifter law, Sean had to leave it at that, but he and Liam would watch.

Sean had returned home in time to see Andrea getting ready to go to work. He'd objected, and she'd pointed out that the human shooters were gone. Arguments that who knew whether the humans' friends or one of Callum's zealous followers would try to take revenge on Sean and Andrea were ignored. Andrea clearly wasn't going to stay safely at home unless Sean chained her to her bed. He almost did that, except that Kim and Connor intervened when they came over to see what the noise was about.

The compromise Kim forced on them, that neither of them liked, was that Andrea went to work but Sean went with her. Andrea refused to wait on Sean's table all night but smiled sweetly at the other customers.

Look at her. Sean watched Andrea over the beer Annie had brought him. *Swaying her hips in those tight pants, and her top looking like it's painted on.* The shirt bared her shoulders, making even the Collar around her throat sexy. The humans she waited on liked what they saw, if the drool dripping down the sides of their mouths was any indication. If any of them touched her, they'd lose fingers.

Sean's view of Andrea was cut off as someone stopped in front of his booth. He looked up to find Dylan gazing steadily back at him.

"Dad," Sean said as Dylan dropped into the seat opposite.

Sean reached for Dylan's hand, squeezed it. "You all right? Where are you staying?"

"At a friend's." Dylan didn't respond to Sean's touch, and Sean withdrew, troubled.

"I'm hoping you don't mean a female friend. I don't need Glory exploding while I'm living in her house. I'm not getting much sleep as it is."

Dylan looked surprised. "Glory told me to go. Why would she care?"

"She didn't mean for you to be running to the next woman on your list. You know that."

Dylan gave him a tight smile. "You flatter me if you think I have a list." He signaled to Andrea, who nodded and turned to the bartender. "Kim is kindly letting me stay in her house, if you must know."

Kim's family had left her a big house north of Lake Austin near Mount Bonnell, and though Kim now spent all her time in Shiftertown, she still owned the house, which was large and posh.

"Cushy crash space," Sean said. "With cable. Now I envy you. Kim's a sweetheart."

"I had to promise not to get cat hair on the sofa," Dylan said.

"That's our Kim. What do her neighbors think?"

"Her neighbors don't know I'm there."

They wouldn't, not if he didn't want them to. Dylan could be the master of stealth.

Andrea floated over with a bottle of Guinness. She smiled at Dylan as she set down the bottle, her dark hair dancing across her cheeks. Sean wanted to pull her down, kiss her red lips, wrap his arms around her, and get down to serious business.

Andrea didn't even look at Sean. "That beer's on me," she said to Dylan. "Nice to see you again." She deliberately ignored Sean as she sashayed away.

"Trouble in paradise?" Dylan asked with a glint of humor.

Sean growled. "Goddess, Dad, she is the most bloody

stubborn, smart-assed, frustrating female I've ever met. Did I mention stubborn?"

Dylan's smile took on a touch of sadness. "She's like your mother. Niamh had that same trick of looking at me as though she didn't give a damn about anything I said until I apologized—for whatever it was I'd done to piss her off that time. If I didn't know what I'd done, that just made things worse."

"Aye, I remember. And, aye, I'm thinking Andrea's the same way."

Across the room, Ellison started up the jukebox with a rocking country tune. Ellison liked all music, as long as it was country and the singer was from Texas.

Dylan leaned across the table to Sean. "Where did you put the sword?"

"Liam's office, like always. Why?"

"Liam's in there?"

Sean glanced around. The office door was closed, and Liam hadn't emerged. "He is."

"If he's not back there to watch it, I don't want it out of your sight."

"Why, Dad? What's up?"

"They had plans to steal it," Dylan said around blare of the music. "Callum and his Feline faction. That's interesting, don't you think?"

CHAPTER SIXTEEN

Sean stared. "Why the hell should they want the Sword of the Guardian? It's not like anyone can just pick it up and use it."

Dylan shrugged as he lifted his beer. "Who knows? To intimidate you, our clan . . . this entire Shiftertown, maybe. If Shifters think their souls are in peril because you lost the sword, will they be trusting you?"

"Are they crazy?"

Sean recalled the night he'd been chosen as Guardian, when he'd been barely past cub age. He remembered shivering on a windswept Irish promontory under January moonlight, while the dead body of the previous Guardian lay on the ground, the naked sword across his chest. Sean remembered his dismay as white-hot Goddess magic turned his own blood to fire, his absolute knowledge that *he* would be the one to lift the sword and drive it into the former Guardian's heart. He'd been terrified that night, Dylan and Niamh so proud.

"Most Shifters know that the Guardian has to be chosen," Dylan was saying. "But if the Guardian isn't strong enough to protect the sword, how quickly will they choose a new Guardian, or kill the old one?"

"Bloody hell, Dad. I'm flattered that Callum and his friends thought I had so much power. But the sword is a sacred relic. They'd have messed with that?"

"I'm thinking they would have."

Sean knew full well that some Shifters now believed they could get to the Summerland without the Guardian to turn the body to dust and release the soul. The sword had been forged for the purpose of keeping Fae from trapping or torturing Shifter souls, but the Fae were no longer around, and having the soul trapped was not a likely danger.

Then again, Sean also knew that superstition died hard. Shifters might *say* they didn't believe they still needed a magic sword, but Guardians had been around for centuries. Beliefs got lodged deep inside and were not easily pried out.

"Would it scare you, Dad?" he asked out of curiosity. "If the Guardian wasn't around when your time came?"

Dylan thought as he took another drink. "It's something we grow up with, the cycle of life: birth, mating, cubs, then the Guardian's sword at the end. It's a relief, knowing that you won't be ending alone, because the Guardian will be there to help you to the Summerland. There's no evidence we need a Guardian anymore, but why take the chance?"

Sean nodded. "I think that too. I'm betting every Shifter in this bar does."

"So you see how powerful a Sword of the Guardian would be in the wrong hands? Keep yours safe."

Sean needed to see the sword now, to know that it still leaned against the wall in Liam's office with his big brother keeping an eye on it. He glanced toward the office door, but his gaze was arrested halfway there.

Andrea had moved in front of the jukebox, and now she started to dance. A hip swinging, undulating, sexy, gyrating dance. The gaze of every unmated male—Shifter and human alike—swiveled and fixed on her. Ellison whooped and started swaying behind her, beer held high, his body nearly touching hers.

A growl tore from Sean's throat. Dylan rescued Sean's beer as Sean sprang from the booth and hurtled across the room to Ellison. Sean's fingers turned to claws as he latched onto Ellison's shoulder and jerked him away from Andrea.

Ellison's Lupine eyes flashed gray white. "Hold on there now, my old friend. We were just dancing."

"Stay away from her." Sean's voice was grating, throat clogged with rage.

The song wailed to an end, and the jukebox clicked off. Silence descended on the room as the two males faced each other. Andrea breathed hard from the dance, her breasts rising most distractingly under her low-cut shirt.

Ellison saw his sideways glance at her and laughed. "Woo, Sean." He clapped Sean on the shoulder. "You're walking on a knife edge, my man. Better get this thing blessed, or you'll be challenging every male who even looks at her."

Sean knew he should calm himself, laugh it off, but instincts were a bitch. He stepped to Ellison, everything in him wanting to gut the Lupine for coming near Andrea.

Ellison lifted his hands, beer still in one. "Steady, big guy. I'm leaving." He backed slowly out of range, making sure not to turn his back on Sean.

When Sean didn't pursue him, the bar relaxed and conversation and laughter started up again. A blood-drenched conflict had been avoided, and Shifters could go back to drinking and enjoying the night.

Andrea was glaring at Sean, hands on hips. "I was dancing, Sean. Get over yourself." Before Sean could reach for her or say a word, she slammed away from him and marched back to the bar.

After the bar closed, Andrea stashed her apron in the office and left through the back door, only to find Sean waiting for her. The sword's hilt rose above his shoulder, glittering in the moonlight.

The night was brisk though not as cold as previous nights, spring at last touching the air. The sky had cleared, and the moon was a round disk of white.

Andrea said a silent prayer to the moon goddess and pretended to ignore Sean as he fell into step beside her. He was still angry at her for dancing with Ellison, she felt that, and she was still angry at him for trying to keep her home tonight. The Ellison thing had been partly her fault—she'd been dancing to show Sean what he was missing by being so high-handed.

They reached Shiftertown without either of them saying a word. Though it was late, Shifters lingered on porches, enjoying the brisk night and the bright moonlight. "Now then, Sean," they called out, in a friendly fashion. "Andrea."

Sean raised his hand in greeting, and Andrea waved too, secretly pleased that they greeted her by name. The Shifters here were gradually accepting her, and the thought warmed her. She wasn't fool enough to think they'd welcome her half Faeness with open arms without Sean, but even so, she liked the feeling of belonging.

Glory wasn't home, the house dark and silent. Dylan hadn't asked Andrea about Glory tonight, and he'd departed right after Sean had interrupted Andrea's dance. Andrea had sensed Dylan's sorrow when she'd brought him the beer, but she doubted he'd make the first overture to Glory. It was too bad. They were two lonely people who needed each other. No, correction, two lonely, *stubborn* people.

Speaking of stubborn, Sean followed Andrea upstairs and into her bedroom. Andrea sat down on the bed, pulled off her shoes, and stretched her aching feet as Sean unbuckled the sword and laid it across the dresser.

Andrea studied the moonlight on the sword as she rotated her ankles. "Can anyone wield the sword but a Guardian?"

Sean gave her a quick, questioning look. "Legend says no." He skimmed his fingers over the sword, then came to sit on the bed next to her. Right next to her. The mattress dipped with his weight, and as annoyed as Andrea was at him, she realized she'd come to like the sensation.

"Does that mean you're not sure?"

He shrugged, his shoulder brushing hers. "It means legend says no. The Guardian must be descended from the original Guardian of the clan, and he is chosen in a spiritual ritual."

"So I hear. What I mean is, if *I* took the sword and stuck it through a dead Shifter's heart, would he turn to dust?"

"Actually, I have no idea, love."

Love. It was difficult to stay angry at him—not that he was right—when he called her *love* in that warm voice. "As I understand, the original sword was made by a Fae, right?"

Sean nodded, looking curious at her questions. "Created by a Shifter smith and a Fae woman who wove her magic through it. A Fae bastard had wanted a sword made so he could trap and torture Shifter souls with it, but the Fae woman, his sister, turned the tables on him and made it so the sword released the souls instead. That's the story, anyway."

"And she made it so the sword can't hurt Shifters, right?"

"I didn't say that. If I stick its sharp point into a live Shifter's body, he'd be a bit pissed off at me. But I'd only stick it in someone if he was dying already or into a crazed feral who needed to go down."

"*You* would," Andrea said. "But what if someone else got hold of it?"

Sean's gaze went sharp. "Has my dad been talking to you?"

"Dylan? No. Why?"

"Because he told me tonight that Callum had planned to grab the sword. He'd wanted to use the fact that he had it to intimidate other Shifters into following him. It could work, I think."

Damn Callum anyway. Was this what the Fae warrior had been talking about? The danger if she didn't bring him the sword? Why would a Fae care if Shifters were angry at their Guardian? It made no sense to her.

"Doesn't Callum's Shiftertown have its own Guardian?" Andrea said. "Why not take *his* sword?"

"Mine is the original sword made by Niall O'Connell and his Fae mate. The others are later copies. Much more symbolic if Callum stole this one. Besides, his Shifter-town's Guardian is a bear, and I'm not thinking even Callum would risk pissing off the Ursines. But Liam is new at being leader, and Shifters like to test new leaders. Callum's clan's protecting him now, but they know as well as Callum does that if he tries anything else, we'll take him down, and that will be the end of him."

Andrea drew her feet to the bed and wrapped her arms around her knees. Sean spoke with firm finality, no regrets about the violent justice he'd mete out. But Shifters walked a tightrope now that they lived in Shiftertowns—if they turned against each other, it would be a disaster.

"I think Callum just got bored," she said. "In Colorado, we were still pretty close to basic survival, no thoughts of conspiracies and that kind of thing. Survival, mating, and raising cubs—that was it."

Sean looked at her sitting next to him, all folded in on herself, her eyes gray like a misty evening. What male *wouldn't* want Andrea under him in the night, those beautiful eyes darkening with desire?

"I think Callum's not wrong that we've gotten a little comfortable," Sean said. "We have food and shelter, time to pray and love and play. Families are staying together and growing larger. So of course we have to start fighting each other for power."

Andrea gave him a wry look. "When you force different species to coexist on the same patch, there's bound to be friction. Look at your Dad and Glory."

"I'm not wanting to at the moment, thank you very much. A better example is you and me."

"Cross-species mating?" Andrea said with a little smile. "Can it possibly work? We could go on an afternoon talk show."

"I want it to work." Sean turned the full force of his gaze on her. "Because when I first saw you, love, I started to believe in forever."

* * *

Andrea gazed back at him with gray eyes so filled with loneliness that Sean's heart squeezed hard. He wanted to make all her hurts go away, and damn it, he would.

"You thought that across a crowded bus station?" she asked in a light voice.

Sean leaned closer, breathing her heat. "You said you didn't want a mating without the bond. Well, that bond is here, in me. I'm feeling it—I'm not feeling anything else these days but that. It's yours for the taking, love."

Andrea drew her legs even closer to her chest, curling into a ball like a frightened cub. "Sean, I don't know who I am. How can I decide whether to accept a mate-claim when I don't even understand what I'm supposed to be?"

"You're supposed to be my mate."

She shook her head. "No, I mean, *what* am I? I've got a Shifter mother, Fae father. I know what I am as a Shifter. Nothing—too far down in my pack to be anything but a cub producer."

His eyes flashed. "Goddess, what asshole told you that?"

"Who do you think? The brilliant leader of my Shifter-town and his son. Not to mention everyone in my stepfa-ther's pack. I grew up being told that that was all I'd ever be good for, over and over again—that is if anyone wanted my tainted Fae blood in their cubs."

"I'm hoping you didn't believe all that, Andy-love."

"When I grew older, it started to piss me off. But there, in that Shiftertown, they weren't going to let me be any-thing else."

She looked so sad that she broke his heart. "Oh, love." Sean scooped Andrea onto his lap and closed his arms around her. Earlier tonight when Andrea had given him her scathing glare, so angry at his protectiveness, Sean had told himself that he understood. It wasn't that Andrea minded being protected—she didn't want to *need* to be protected. Sean snarling at every male within range only reminded her of her situation, over which she had little control. Didn't mean Sean would stop snarling at them; it just meant he understood.

"But you're here with me now, and you can do whatever you want—well, whatever humans will let us do, but we'll not be under their thumbs forever. What *I* want is you, the woman for me. My whole life has become wrapped around you. And I'm liking it that way."

Andrea liked it too, but the revelations she'd had were complicating things. "*My* whole life has become . . . I don't know. Insane. Everything I knew and thought I understood is gone."

"From what you just told me, that's a good thing, love."

Sean's gaze held anger, difficult to meet even if the anger wasn't directed at her. *You are the child of a warrior,* Fionn had told her. *A highborn lady in your own right.* Perhaps that part was true.

"That's not the point," she said. Sean's sandpaper chin was at kissing level, and Andrea barely resisted licking it. "When you're a child and a certain way of life is all you know, it's truth to you. It's your world; there is nothing else. Even when I wasn't happy, I knew what to expect every day. Now, I have no clue what to expect. Humans shoot at us, the Feline next door makes me care about him, a Fae pops out of my dreams and claims to be my father, and my aunt likes to wear black-leather bodysuits."

"Aye, Glory has some interesting tastes."

Andrea looked past Sean's strong face into his beautiful blue eyes—the eyes of a wildcat who'd taken in a stray and made her feel safe. "You never have told me why you stepped up to mate-claim me. To keep the peace, you said, but you and Liam could have strong-armed someone else into doing it. Ellison, for instance. Why would you risk mating with a Lupine half Fae you'd never even met?"

The look he gave her was dark, intense, and vastly lonely. "Because I was selfish enough to grab the opportunity. Females have their pick of males, and I knew damn well no female would willingly choose a Guardian. But if she didn't have a choice . . ."

"Sean Morrissey, don't tell me females in this Shifter-town don't drool over you. I see them—like Caitlin your neighbor, and Rebecca. I see how the unmated honeys eye you in the bar, and it makes me crazy jealous. If you tell me you've been celibate all your life, I'll know you're lying."

Sean's answering blush confirmed it. "A tumble for fun is one thing," he said. "But females have made clear that they have no intention of being mated to a Guardian. Guardians rarely mate or have cubs—their lives are about the sword and about death. What female wants that?"

"It's not about death; it's about caring."

Something flickered in his eyes. "Goddess, aren't you a sweetheart? But I've become more a symbol than a man. I can't save lives, only take them. You tell me, Andy-love, what the hell is that good for?"

Andrea heard his bitterness, and her heart wrenched. She imagined the night he was chosen, a young Sean blinking blue eyes in shock when he was handed the heavy sword. His entire life changed, any plans and ambitions taken away. A Guardian was a Guardian for life.

"Guardians like you remind us we won't always be enslaved," she said in a low voice. "In death, your sword frees us."

"You believe that, lass?"

"A Guardian released my mother's soul when I was three. I remember being grateful to him for what he did. Even if my mother couldn't be with me and my stepdad, we knew she was safe in the Summerland."

"You were three years old, love. Barely able to shift yet."

"I was still grateful." She touched his cheek, a man so strong and yet so vulnerable. "You relieve grief, Sean; you don't cause it."

"But the Shifters have made the sword more important than their lives. That's why Callum wanted to steal it. They've made it more important than fighting to stay alive."

"I'm not sure that's true . . ."

"Love, it's why my brother died." His voice grew choked, eyes wet. "Kenny was fighting to keep some feral Shifters from stealing the sword that night. He chose to die rather than risk the Sword of the Guardian, and me. How does a man live with that?"

"Goddess," Andrea whispered. "Sean." She wrapped her arms around him and pulled him down to her.

Sean closed his eyes and sank into her warmth. He'd never voiced these thoughts to anyone, not even Liam, the man he was closest to. And now this Lupine woman with her beautiful gray eyes comforted him in a way no one else had been able to. He'd seen the compassion in her eyes and the understanding.

"He loved you," she said in her whispery voice. "If Kenny was anything like Liam or your dad or Connor, he loved you. He was fighting to save *you*, not just your sword."

"And now he's gone. He's gone, and we'll never have him back."

His heart gave up to grief. Sean thought he'd been done with this, emptied of tears, but the pain welled up as fresh as it had been that night. He buried his face in his mate's neck and wept.

Andrea held him close, tears in her own eyes. She stroked the hot silk of his hair, kissed it. Her own heart twisted with his grief, which made this strong, strong man break down. Andrea hated those ferals, whoever they'd been, for hurting this family and driving such pain into them.

"Sean, I'm so sorry."

Sean lifted his head, kissing her cheek. He wiped tears from his face and pressed his forehead against hers. "Thank you, love."

He held on to her still, for a little longer. Andrea kissed his lips, light kisses of compassion and caring, with only a taste of wildness. Andrea's anger at him for trying to keep her home dissolved into understanding. Sean had watched his brother be slaughtered. He lived in terror that he'd have to see that happen to anyone else.

"Sean, I need to tell you something."

Sean looked up at her in mild surprise, but only mild, as though his emotions had been all used up. "What's that, love? You bought me more underwear?"

"You're funny. No." Andrea slid from his lap to her feet and walked to the dresser, where Sean had laid the sword. She drew a breath. "The Fae warrior asked me to steal the Sword of the Guardian."

There was dead silence behind her.

Andrea resisted touching the sword on the dresser, feeling Sean's gaze burning her back. She'd known she couldn't *not* tell him, but she worried about what Sean would do with the information. She wanted to question Fionn some more about his claim to be her father and about her mother, but telling Sean he wanted the sword would probably kill that chance.

It shouldn't matter. Fionn was probably lying about who he was to get what he wanted. Or, even if he truly was her father, his goal must be to get the sword and nothing more.

Let it go, Andrea whispered to herself. *The Fae told you what you wanted to hear so that you would do what he wished.*

But part of her cried out, yearning to know the truth.

"Bloody hell," Sean said. "What did you tell him?"

"That I wasn't stupid enough to snatch the Sword of the Guardian and take it to him because he gave me a line about being my father." Andrea turned around. Sean remained on the bed, face quiet. "But if *I* don't take Fionn the sword, what if he convinces someone else to? That's why I wondered what would happen if a Fae wielded the sword. What would it do?"

"In theory, nothing."

"Then why would he want it?"

"The same reason Callum wanted it, most like. To wake Shifters' fear of soul death. To make them wonder what a Fae would do with the sword. Just knowing that a Fae had it and we might never get it back would make Shifters crazy."

Andrea made a noise of frustration. "I don't know what to do."

"That's easy, love. Don't give it to him."

"But . . . Oh, hell, Sean, what if he really is my father?"

"Would that make you give him the sword?"

"No, of course not. Even if Fionn is telling the truth about being my father, why would I trust him? I mean, he left my mother and never went back for her. Or me. He told me it was too dangerous, that he was hiding us from his enemies, who wouldn't hesitate to kill us. But damn it, that could all be total bullshit. How would I know?"

"Do you want to cross into Faerie and find out?"

Andrea shuddered instinctively. She'd been raised to hate the Fae, the cruel people who'd bred Shifters to be their hunters and fighters. Faerie was a terrible place, so Shifters said. Cold and harsh, full of glittering Fae who would kill you in an instant, or worse—trap you and display you as a prize, maybe letting other Fae torture you for their pleasure.

"Not really."

"I'd go with you."

Andrea blinked. "What? You've got to be kidding me. Why?"

"You want to find out who you are, don't you?"

Sean regarded her quietly while he made what was probably the most generous offer in Shifter history. A Feline volunteering to enter Faerie so his half-Lupine, half-Fae girlfriend could resolve her identity issues?

"Are you crazy?" she asked. "That's way too dangerous. Then the Fae would have the sword *and* the Guardian."

"I'd leave the sword with Liam for safekeeping."

"And if they killed you? No, Sean, I couldn't risk that."

"I see you hurting, love," he said calmly. "I don't like that."

"Now you're acting like you can make everything all

better." She gave him the tiniest smile. "I'm not wrong about you being full of yourself, hairball."

He came off the bed and to her, warming her with his strength and power. "I *can* make it better, little Lupine. I want to make everything better for you. I want to hold on to you and keep you from harm. I want to for the rest of my life."

She shivered in excitement at the fierceness in his voice. "You can't by taking me to Faerie. That's crazy, Sean."

"I'd rather take you than have you run off there by yourself." He growled low in his throat, that mate protectiveness rearing again.

Andrea put her hands on her hips. "You're going to start arguing with me again about me wanting to work at the bar, aren't you?"

"'Tis dangerous. I'm not wrong about that."

"We've been through this. I know it's dangerous, but you can't lock me away. You told me that I had the freedom to do what I wanted here, that I had freedom I didn't have in my old Shiftertown. You can't have it both ways."

More growling, but his eyes stayed human blue, which meant he wasn't as enraged as he'd been. Something had warmed between them, something that wouldn't be undone. "Fine," he said. "Work. Enjoy yourself." His powerful hands went to her shoulders. "But no more dirty dancing with anyone but me."

She smiled. "Jealous, were you?"

"You make my blood hot, sweetheart. I wanted to rip you away from him and break his neck." He cupped her head in his hands, strong fingers on the back of her neck. "I want you so bad it's fucking me up inside." He smiled, a tall and virile Shifter male.

His kiss bit deep, stirring the fires that would never die inside her. Dancing tonight had been for Sean, not just for the joy of moving to the music. Yes, to tease him, but also because she wanted him to want her. She'd wanted *him*, not Ellison, to get up and come to her, to slide behind her and gyrate against her backside. This is what the mating frenzy did—threw caution to the wind.

Andrea's hands went to his T-shirt, skimming under it to find his heart beating as fast as hers under his hot skin. "So don't go."

He shook his head, face pressed against hers. "I won't leave you alone, unprotected. It's my job to keep you safe. I can at least do my job."

"While we're going mad with mating frenzy?"

"I asked Ronan to guard the house. He's happy to. He should be down on the porch now."

"Good." Andrea tugged Sean's shirt off over his head while his hands went under her shirt, undoing her bra, pushing everything from her skin.

The sword began to sing as they went down on the bed, Sean's mouth all over her. He kept amazing her, this man who'd claimed her. Wanting to keep her safe yet offering to help her find out who she truly was; fearing to lose her, yet wanting her to understand that she was free. His guilt and sorrow for Kenny tugged at her, making her want to hold him until his hurting went away.

She kissed him as Sean divested her of her pants and clawed out of his own, and then they were body to body, skin to skin, the frenzy winding them hotter and higher. Andrea cried out as he entered her; she was already open for him. Sensation after sensation swamped her, his thrusts spreading her until she twined her legs around his hips.

Sean, my mate. Mate of my heart.

Shifter bodies were made to respond like this, needing to mate until they couldn't walk. The Fae in her couldn't eradicate the wanting. Or maybe it was Sean himself who brought out that need in her.

The thought opened her eyes, opened her body, and made her cry his name in climax. Sean came seconds later, his body slick with sweat, his eyes wide and dark blue. The sword sang its joy at their joining, the threads twining within her and with the mate bond. Andrea had no idea whether Sean heard it too, because before she could ask him, he kissed her deeply, pinned her hands above her head, and started loving her all over again.

"These pancakes are great, Sean." Ronan put his big elbows on the table and shoveled in another mouthful. "Mmm, blueberry. My favorite."

Sean, at the griddle, ladled batter in a careful circle, filling in the middle as the pancake sizzled. His eyes felt sandy, his temper just as gritty. His mating frenzy hadn't let him sleep much nor had his worry for Andrea, though he was pleased that her nightmares hadn't returned last night.

The shower running upstairs told him Andrea was awake . . . and wet and soapy and naked. Why Sean was downstairs cooking breakfast for Ronan, he wasn't sure.

"I know things are tough right now," Ronan said around bites. "But it'll work out."

"Whist, aren't you the confident one?" Sean said.

"And I know that when you start saying things like *whist* that you're pissed off. I'm trying to help. Don't take it out on me."

"Sorry. Didn't sleep well."

"I know you didn't. I heard all that crazy, banging makeup sex. You don't exactly keep it down. Here's my advice: Just let the mating frenzy take over completely, and you two won't have time to argue. Or the energy."

Sean had almost forgotten about what he and Andrea had been mad about last night. Oh, yeah, her at the bar. Ellison. Didn't seem to matter as much today. "I'll keep it in mind."

The bathroom door slammed open upstairs, and Sean and Ronan fell silent, Ronan to eat, Sean to cook and fantasize about a wet and naked Andrea.

Andrea came down the stairs in a T-shirt and jeans, her damp hair tousled. "I smell pancakes."

Ronan held up his last forkful. "Sean's wicked good with them."

Sean flipped the batch from the griddle onto a plate and put it on the counter. Andrea smelled good, far better than the pancakes, and the sight of her mussed hair shot his temperature high. Her black ringlets were thin corkscrews against her face and neck, and Sean wanted to burrow among them, licking her still wet skin.

"That's yours," he growled, pushing the plate at her.

Andrea took it with a nod and carried the plate to the table. Sean had already laid out butter and syrup, knives and forks, juice and coffee. He was at least good at feeding his bloody stubborn potential mate.

Andrea poured syrup over her pancakes and licked her finger. Sean froze as he watched her catch the sticky drop of syrup on her tongue. His throbbing erection, which had risen when he'd pictured her in the shower, tightened still further.

"That's the solution, is it?" Andrea asked Ronan as she licked her lips. "Sean and I should have sex until we can't remember why we're mad at each other? Or anything else?"

Ronan grinned and swallowed his last mouthful. "Hey, it would work for me. You have good hearing, Lupine-girl."

"I'm part Fae." Andrea lifted a forkful of pancakes. "I have quite a few traits that are . . . enhanced."

Ronan burst out laughing as Andrea popped the bite into her mouth. "I get why you like her, Sean."

Sean got why too. Her shirt was clinging to her, her gray eyes were on him, and sticky syrup lingered on her lips. What they'd done all through the night hadn't sated him at all. Andrea swiped away a drop with her moist, red tongue, and Sean stifled a groan.

"Hey, who's that?"

At Ronan's tone, Sean came alert, forcing his attention from Andrea. A Shifter was cutting across the yard toward the house next door, one Sean had never seen before. He knew no one was home over there—Liam had taken Kim and Connor out for breakfast.

"Stay put," Sean said to Andrea, and signaled Ronan to follow him out.

CHAPTER SEVENTEEN

Sean watched from the shadows while the unknown Shifter walked up onto the Morrissey porch and peered through the living room window. Ronan waited next to Sean, folding his arms and looking formidable.

When the Shifter left the front door and moved to circle the house to the back, Sean vaulted over Andrea's porch railing and landed in front of him.

"Can I help you, friend?" he asked.

The Shifter stopped with a growl, and Sean gave him an answering one.

The man was tall, hard-muscled, and dark-haired, Feline by the scent of him. He met Sean's gaze with eyes of deep jade green. "Who are you?" the Shifter demanded.

"This is my territory," Sean said, "so it's me who gets to ask you."

The Shifter turned, but Ronan had closed in behind him. Ronan showed all his teeth in a grin. "It's not *my* territory," he said. "But it's a good question."

The Shifter gave Ronan a steady stare, not intimidated in

the slightest. He was obviously an alpha, and Ronan, ~~~~
his size and strength, was a bit lower in his bear clan.

Sean stepped between them before Ronan could weaken. Sean met the green gaze without flinching, two alphas facing off. Sean had the advantage of territory, and finally the unknown Shifter flicked his eyes away and gave him a nod.

"The name's Eric Warden. I've come to see Dylan Morrissey."

"I'm Sean Morrissey." Sean didn't offer information on Dylan's whereabouts or what his relationship was to Dylan.

Eric's gaze moved briefly to Sean's Collar. "I've been in touch with Dylan for a few weeks now. He invited me here."

If so, Dylan hadn't informed Sean or Liam. "From?"

"Las Vegas. I'm Shiftertown leader there."

Sean kept him pinned, but annoyance bit him. He wished Dylan had bothered to mention an impending visit from another Shiftertown leader. Humans forbade such visits without formal permission, fearing to give Shiftertown leaders any chance to conspire. Not that Shiftertown leaders paid much attention. They'd long ago decided that what humans didn't know wouldn't hurt Shifters.

"Where's your backup?" Sean asked.

Eric shrugged and spread his hands. "I came without."

"Insane, are you?"

"Probably."

"Ask him what he wants to see Dylan about." The voice was Andrea's, and it came from the porch. She looked down at Eric, unafraid, the naked sword of the Guardian in her hands.

Eric's brows shot up in surprise. "Easy, girl."

Sean's outrage battled with laughter, and Sean settled for humor. Here he was, facing an alpha as powerful as himself or Liam, and his sweet little mate-to-be had charged out to protect him.

"She's a little headstrong," Sean said with a smile. "Don't provoke her."

"Your father told me that *you* were the Guardian," Eric said.

"I am. She just likes handling my sword."

That got him. Eric tried to keep his expression stern, but his lips twitched. Behind him, Ronan gave up and burst out laughing.

"Very funny, Sean," Andrea said. "You still haven't asked what he's doing here."

"My business is with Dylan." Eric's quick recovery told Sean he wasn't about to discuss it with anyone but Dylan.

Sean gestured to the Morrissey house. "Come in, and I'll see if I can round up Dad and my brother."

He led Eric to the front door, but as soon as they stepped inside, Andrea was there, following them in, the sword resting on her shoulder.

"Andy-love . . ."

"If you think I'm letting you walk in here, alone, with an unknown Feline, you're crazy."

Sean gave up. "Andrea stays. Ronan, do you mind standing guard outside?"

"Hey, you make me another mountain of pancakes, and I'll do anything for you, Sean." He grinned at Eric. "Sometimes he puts mini chocolate chips in them. Culinary genius." He gave them a casual salute and left, closing the front door behind him.

Sean led Eric and Andrea to the kitchen, where the table was littered with notebooks and textbooks Connor had left behind. Andrea pushed them neatly to one side, laid the naked sword on the tabletop, and sat down. "Why don't you make us some coffee, Sean?"

That won her another irritated look, and Eric said quickly, "I don't need coffee."

"I'd love a cup," Andrea said, smiling at Sean.

Sean sat down. "You know where it is."

Andrea remained seated. "So, are you going to tell us why you traveled all the way from Nevada to visit, Eric Warden? Especially one as high-up as you?"

Eric looked uncomfortable, also a little confused ab____ Andrea's role here. He'd have scented by now that she was half Fae and understand that she wasn't an alpha female, but not why she didn't defer to Sean or to him. Not that Andrea was going to bother to explain. This Eric might be telling the truth about his appointment with Dylan, but then again, he might be on Callum's side. He might have other Shifters lying in wait for a chance to snatch the sword. Someone in this needed to be smart.

"I think I should wait for Dylan," Eric said.

"How's Callum?" Andrea asked.

Eric looked blank. "Who's Callum?"

Sean said nothing, only sat back and watched.

"Handy that you've come to talk to a Shifter who hasn't been around much lately," Andrea said.

"I can't help that. Dylan arranged to meet me here. We left the time vague—I didn't know when I could get here to the minute."

"How *did* you get here?" Andrea asked. "Hitchhike?"

"I have my ways." Eric made a point of inhaling her scent. "I had no idea I was coming to be interrogated by a Fae."

"Half Fae. To be exact, a half-Fae warrior princess."

Andrea couldn't help smiling when Sean tried to suppress his start. "Ah, is *that* why you're such a smart-ass, love?" Sean asked.

"Could be." Andrea fixed her gaze on Eric, meeting his green eyes without showing fear. It would be easy to fear Eric Warden, because he had power, as much power, Andrea sensed, as did the Morrisseys.

"Let me put it this way, Eric," Andrea said. "If you're involved in any way with gangs of human gunmen or Shifters who follow Callum, I'd advise you to stop now. This isn't your territory, and when Sean and Liam put Callum in his place, you don't want to be caught up in that."

Eric's eyes widened slightly. "Son of a bitch, what the hell is going on down here?"

"Internal problems," Sean said. "Nothing to worry about."

"I can see my timing is less than stellar." Eric lifted his hands. "All right, I give you my word, Sean Morrissey, on the sun and moon, that I have nothing to do with whatever troubles you're dealing with on your patch. I connected with Dylan on another business entirely and fixed this day to meet him."

"He did."

Dylan's voice rumbled from the back door, and he walked in a moment later, hands stuffed into the pockets of his leather jacket. Eric rose to meet him, as did Sean. Andrea kept her seat.

Dylan clasped Eric's hand and pulled the man into the brief embrace reserved for dominant males who didn't know each other well. *I welcome you,* the embrace said, *but don't try anything involving my territory, mate, or cubs, or you'll swiftly die.*

Eric and Sean performed the same ritual, before Dylan moved to the kitchen and started making coffee.

"Warrior princess?" Dylan threw over his shoulder.

Andrea shrugged and didn't answer. This was new to her, and delicate, and she didn't relish spilling it all to Dylan.

"Andrea has a fine sense of humor," Sean said. He sat down again, taking the seat next to Andrea's. He rested his hand on her thigh, and Andrea suddenly felt a little less brittle.

Eric focused sudden attention on them. "Now I understand. You two are mated."

"Not yet," Andrea said. "Sean's made the mate-claim, but I haven't given him my final answer."

Eric shook his head, grinning. "No. You're mated."

Even Dylan looked amused as he finished setting up the coffeepot and sat down.

"Are *you* mated?" Sean asked Eric.

Eric took on an empty look, the same one that Andrea's

stepfather always wore, the same one Dylan had when he talked about Sean's mother. "Was," Eric said. "She is gone. I have a son, Jace. He's of age now and my third-in-command."

Andrea heard the pride in his voice when he said the last. Not all children of alphas stayed high in the hierarchy. "Who's your second?" Andrea asked.

"My sister." More pride. Females didn't always achieve such high status, not because they couldn't be dominant, but because of archaic Shifter laws. Alpha females were rare, because alpha males were allowed to kill them.

"Cassidy lost her mate too," Eric said. "A couple of years ago."

Andrea felt a stab of sadness. She whispered a quick prayer, echoed by Sean and Dylan, then reached across the table and touched Eric's strong hand. "Please send her blessings from me."

"Thank you." Eric's face softened in his gratitude. "She'd appreciate that. It hit her hard."

"Which is part of the reason you're here," Dylan said. "Sean knows, and Andrea . . . well, she'll know sooner or later."

Eric nodded silently. He remained just as silent as Dylan rose to fetch the coffee that had finished brewing. Without complaint, Dylan poured four cups and brought them to the table. He didn't offer cream or sugar since most Shifters drank it black, and Eric didn't ask for anything.

"The Collars," Dylan said. "That's why Eric's here. He heard about our ability to override the Collars, and he wants to learn it."

"Andrea knows about it already." Sean sent Andrea a quick glance.

"I saw a vivid demonstration by Sean," Andrea said.

Dylan shot Sean a concerned look. "You all right?"

"Fine. I didn't mind beating on Callum a little."

Eric listened, brows raised. "You got a war going on?"

"Trying to prevent one," Sean said.

"Using your half-Fae warrior princess?"

Sean gave him a little grin. "If necessary."

Andrea took a gulp of coffee and got to her feet. "Obviously you all don't need me here. I'll just be going." She took up the sword, which hummed in a muted way when she touched it, like a child singing under its breath. "Back to pancakes."

Sean, of course, followed her out. Ronan remained in place on the porch, giving them another salute from the porch swing. He'd stay, Andrea knew. Ronan was still distrustful of this stranger.

Sean didn't reach for the sword as they walked back to Glory's house, but let her carry it, as though she had every right to. "Should you leave your dad alone in there with him?" Andrea asked as they mounted the porch.

"Dad seems to have it under control." Sean opened the door and went in first, checking for danger.

"You're trusting."

"I know Dad. He wouldn't invite another Shiftertown leader out here if he wasn't certain about him. Plus Eric has to know that if he makes a wrong move, Ronan will be on him, and if he gets past Ronan, he'll have to deal with me."

Sean's quiet confidence always amazed her. Unlike Liam, who joked and charmed, Sean simply looked at a person with calm blue eyes, and that person fell all over himself to do whatever Sean wanted. He had power in his silences.

"Now, Andy-love, what's this about you being Xena, Warrior Princess?"

Andrea laid the sword in the case Sean had left on the table. "Fionn told me a lot of things. Some of them might even be true."

"At least he gave you his name."

"Fionn Cillian. So he said. But what good does that do?" Andrea sighed, spreading her hands. "What do I know about warrior lords of Faerie?"

"You don't have to know anything. You just need a name. Now we can look him up."

* * *

Glory's computer wasn't very sophisticated, but Sean didn't seem bothered by that as he sat at the desk in the living room and fired it up.

Andrea pulled a chair next to his. "If you plan to Google Fionn Cillian, you can't do it from here. Glory hasn't been given Internet clearance."

"I don't need the Internet." Sean frowned at the screen as he typed in letters. "I have my own database."

"A database bigger than the Internet?"

"No, but one much deeper and more precise." On a black screen with a blinking cursor, Sean typed in five letters. They came out as runes, the same kind of curlicues that were on the Sword of the Guardian.

"Those are Fae runes."

Sean leaned to study the screen in surprise. "Are they now? How about that." As Andrea rolled her eyes, the screen blanked out. Sean typed in another set of runes. "There we go."

The screen went blank for a few seconds before words shone out at the top: Welcome, Guardian.

"What on earth is this?" Andrea asked.

"The Guardian Network. That's the half-assed name we gave it. It's information that Guardians have collected over the centuries—about the Fae, the sword, Guardians, about Shifters in general. It used to be written down in a book, but when computers got practical, a Guardian in New Orleans built a database for it and input all the information. Made it searchable. Now we can add information to it when we need to or contact other Guardians through it."

"But how do you access it without Internet?"

He smiled. "Andy-love, just because not all Shifters are allowed on the great human Internet, doesn't mean we haven't created our own network. You just need a server and the ability to tap into the lines. Wireless has made it even simpler. All those remote connections out there just waiting to be used."

Andrea raised her brows. "You're a hacker."

"A good hacker. I can get into all kinds of places."

"I see. That's handy."

"And geeky, according to Connor."

Andrea knew she'd never explain how attractive she found geeky Sean, so she didn't mention it. "Aren't you worried someone will hack into *your* network and steal all the Guardian's secrets?"

"Most of it isn't secret. But only Guardians know how to use this thing, and the codes are pretty intense."

Andrea looked at the runes that appeared in response to his tapping, the program obviously translating the standard Roman letters on the keyboard. "Okay. I believe you."

Sean hit the Enter key, and the screen blossomed into colorful pictures, links, and columns of text. "This is everything Guardians know about Fionn Cillian."

Andrea leaned against him to peer at the information, which was at least in English. Sean slid his arm around her waist as she read it.

Fionn Cillian was several hundred years old, the text told her. Born somewhere in Faerie in a place whose name was unpronounceable, he'd became leader of his clan when he hit his ninetieth year, fairly young for a Fae. Next came a list of what Sean said were battles won by Fionn as a general. The list was quite lengthy. By age one hundred and fifty, he'd been instrumental in winning a war that put him and his clan in control of the emperor of Faerie.

The database showed lists of various heroic deeds Fionn had performed since then, battles fought and won in the name of the emperor, honors awarded him. It listed a wife, a highborn woman from a rival clan, Sean said, but no children. Doubtless it had been a political marriage, he speculated, undertaken to end a dispute. The wife had died about a hundred years ago, leaving Fionn alone and childless.

Andrea took in the information in amazement. She'd always pictured Faerie as a misty place of white trees and mountains, with Fae hanging out in gauzy robes, riding unicorns, hunting with hawks, and doing other Fae-like activities. The database was showing her a real place full of intrigue and power shifts, alliances and relationships, reminding her of what she'd read about shoguns in historic Japan. The land of the Fae stretched back thousands of years, and she was seeing history as complex and intricate as that of Shifters or humans.

Sean clicked on a link that revealed pictures of Fionn Cillian—line drawings and paintings, because Fae didn't have photography.

"That's our guy," Sean said, looking at the haughty face and dark eyes that were like windows to eternity.

"See any resemblance to me?" Andrea asked.

"Hard to say. He's very much a Fae, and you, love, are a hell of a lot sexier than he is."

"Hmm, maybe you should check his underwear."

"I'm thinking I shouldn't be getting within a hundred miles of his underwear. If he wears any."

Andrea's smile faded. "All right, so we know he's who he says he is. But how do I know that he's my father? I don't see any record of me in here."

"There wouldn't be, would there, if he wanted to keep you secret?"

Andrea pointed at the computer. "Where does that info come from?"

"Various sources, but it's all official records or personal observation by Guardians over the centuries. If this Fae didn't want anyone to know about you and your mother, there won't be any record of you."

"How does he expect me to believe him, then?"

Sean gave her a quiet look, no teasing or anger. "You want to believe him, don't you?"

"I want to *know*."

"Don't worry, love. We'll find out."

"I don't see how."

"We'll wrap his ponytail around his neck and threaten

to strangle him with it unless he tells us what we want to know."

Andrea started laughing. "I'd like to see you doing that to a Fae warrior. He looks pretty tough."

"Then I'll pull him into this world. He'd be weaker here, what with all the iron around. I could stuff him into Dad's pickup and drive him around until he talks."

"I think I'd pay to see that." Andrea leaned against him, wishing her anger and confusion would drain away. "Why are you helping me, Sean?"

With one touch of a key, Sean shut off the database. "I'm curious too, love. I want to know what this Fionn is up to."

"I mean with everything. You admitted last night that you first claimed me because you thought it would be your only chance to have a mate, and there I was all helpless."

Sean chuckled, eyes warming. "The day you are help-less, love, is the day the moon falls out of the sky."

"Very funny."

Sean nuzzled Andrea's hair, his breath hot on her scalp. "Maybe it was the reason why I jumped at the chance for the mate-claim before I met you, but not after. Love, I want you for my mate because you have eyes the color of smoke. Because you are wicked sexy, because you're fearless and have a smart-ass mouth, and because you kiss like fire. Why wouldn't I want a woman like you around me the rest of my life?"

He could melt stone, this one. He smelled good too, musk and heat and the soap from his shower.

"You could charm a girl," she said. "You and your Irish accent and beguiling flattery."

"It's not flattery, Andrea. I want *you*. I want to touch and hold you. I want to keep you safe. I'm wanting you in my life."

"In that case . . .." Andrea stopped, her heart beating so hard she could barely get the words out. "In that case, Sean, let's have the mate blessing and get it over with."

Sean's blue eyes blazed with his sudden smile. "Andrea, love, you like to ask for trouble." He stood up so suddenly she nearly fell, but he caught her hands, lifting her to her feet. "But all right. The sun is high, and Dad is here." His smile went positively sinful. "I say we go have us a mate blessing."

CHAPTER EIGHTEEN

"You sure about this, Sean?" Liam asked.

"Just get on with it."

Liam had arrived home in record time after Dylan had called him with the news. The rest of the family had materialized as well, as though they'd all been hanging on their cell phones, waiting for the call.

"It's always best to make certain." Liam was grinning at Sean, an excited light in his eyes. A few feet away, Kim fixed a garland of flowers to Andrea's hair, the two young women chattering animatedly about whatever women liked to chatter about at these times.

"He's sure," Connor said. He wrapped lanky arms around Sean from behind and squeezed hard. "We'll have more and more cubs, and it will be a grand thing. Is she already pregnant, Sean?"

"None of your bloody business," Sean said, but he gentled his voice and returned his nephew's hug.

"Well, if she's not, get a move on, man." Connor let Sean go, spun around to Andrea and gave her an equally hard hug that lifted her off her feet. "Welcome to the family, Andrea. You and Sean can have my room—it's the biggest one in the house. I'll take Sean's. It's like a closet. No room for cubs there."

"I thought I'd move myself in with Andrea and Glory," Sean said as Connor set a flushed Andrea down. "Kim and Liam will be needing all the space they can get."

"Aye, that's true," Connor said. "And Glory needs a man about the place." He glanced meaningfully at Dylan, who waited a little way away for the ceremony to start. "Now that Grandda' has moved out."

"Exactly." Glory walked toward them, dressed from head to toe in silver lamé, her silver platform shoes shining in the sunlight. Her finger- and toenails and been painted to match her outfit and decorated with thin-lined Celtic designs. "We ladies need protection."

"Huh," Connor said. "One look at you, Glory, and your enemies fall over in fear."

"Well, that's true." Glory smiled, showing every tooth. "I welcome Sean and look forward to a lovely stack of pancakes each morning. It will be nice to have someone to take out the trash, clean the gutters, rake the leaves, fix the sink . . ."

Sean broke in with a growl. "Stop before I change my mind."

Glory covered her mouth in mock fear. "Ooh, wouldn't want that."

They were laughing, eager, and the air was tinged with joy. Another mating in Shiftertown, another strengthening for the Morrissey family and its pride and clan, another strengthening of Shifters in general. Kim was nearly dancing with happiness, and Sean wouldn't have been surprised if Connor broke into cartwheels. The young man bounced around, making whooping noises as neighbors came out of houses to join them.

Liam stepped to Sean and pulled his brother into his arms. Liam's embrace felt good; the brothers were of equal strength. The two men had comforted each other through so many years and hardships, so much grief and pain. Sean had rejoiced when Liam had found Kim, his perfect mate, and now Liam thumped Sean on the shoulders, nuzzled his neck, and finally smiled into his face.

"Ready?"

Sean nodded, impatient. "I've been ready for weeks. Can we do this?"

Andrea came to him, and Sean warmed when she ducked under his arm and stood against his side. Liam raised his hands, and the little crowd went quiet.

The sun blessing was not as formal as a full-moon blessing, the more sacred of the two. The immediate family arranged themselves in a circle around the couple, and the neighbors formed a ring outside them. Eric was in the family circle, invited as a family friend. Kim stood next to Liam. As the clan-leader's mate, she had the right to participate in the ceremony and add a blessing of her own. Not all clan mates exercised this right, but Kim liked the idea.

Likewise, clan leaders didn't need to say more than a few words to complete the ceremony, but Liam cleared his throat and launched into a speech.

"Friends, my brother, Sean, has at last chosen himself a mate." The crowd fell silent as Liam's voice broke the afternoon. "'Tis a romantic tale, one of a man reaching out to help another Shifter and then falling for the lass when he at last met her in the flesh. Sean has taken a mate outside our clan, as is custom, but she's also outside his species. Andrea has Fae blood, which can provoke some hardness of feelings against her from some Shifters. But let this be known." Liam's gaze took in all present. "Andrea Gray is now accepted into our pride and our clan. She is protected not only by Sean, her mate, but by me, the pride leader, clan leader, and leader of the Austin Shiftertown. If anyone wishes to dispute this decision—well, too late, because here I am making it. 'Tis done."

Connor let out a cheer. Liam opened his mouth to continue, but Kim nudged him. "Just finish it."

Liam grinned. "My mate, she's anxious for the celebration. In that case . . ." He rested one hand on Sean's shoulder and the other on Andrea's. "By the light of the sun, the Father God, I recognize this mating."

Connor launched himself into the air, screaming at the top of his lungs. He came down and grabbed the nearest person—Glory—and spun her into a hug.

"The Father God go with you, Sean," Liam said, embracing his brother again then Andrea. "And you, sister."

Andrea's eyes were moist when Liam let her go, and then Kim clasped both Sean's and Andrea's hands. "My turn. I've never done this before, but here goes. May your mating be blessed and you be forever bonded. And may you be blessed with many cubs." She smiled. "How was that?"

"Perfect." Andrea pulled Kim into a hug, then it was Sean's turn to show his sister-in-law some affection. After that, the rest of the crowd surged forward, wanting theirs.

It was a Shifter thing. The tactile acknowledgment of a mating, the reassurance that the pride, the clan, and the species would continue.

Liam's acceptance of Andrea, even more than Sean's, seemed to work magic. The Shifters who might not have come near Andrea before suddenly wanted to hold on to her for a moment or two. Feline, Lupine, Ursine—didn't matter. She was one of them now, part of the chain of existence stretching far into the past and on into the future.

Ronan squeezed the breath out of Andrea and then let her go, laughing out loud. Eric too gave her a hard hug, congratulating her, the man who'd lost his mate happy to see another find one. Andrea's pack leader, Wade—now her former pack leader—also stepped up to embrace her. Wade was middle-aged, for a Shifter, which meant that he was about the same age as Dylan. He'd let softer living get to him and was forming a paunch, which did not look good on his wolf.

"Be well, Andrea," Wade said. The look in his yellow eyes was one of relief that he wouldn't have to deal with the problem of half-Fae Andrea anymore.

"Thanks." Andrea supposed that Wade had felt pressure from his clan and his pack about letting her come to Austin. A good pack leader didn't simply obey his own whims but tried to do what was best for the pack. She could feel sorry for him. Almost. A good pack leader also needed balls.

Ellison was a Lupine who obviously hadn't resented her coming to Austin. His hug lifted her off her feet.

"Congratulations, Andy-girl. I got your back anytime. Even if you've mated with a fucking Feline."

Andrea dragged in a breath once Ellison let her go. "Thanks, Ellison. You're a treasure."

"For a Lupine," Sean said from beside her. "Shifters who chase their own tales. What a travesty."

Ellison put his Stetson back on with one hand. "At least I don't cough up hairballs." He grinned and sniffed the air. "Hey, time for some good old-fashioned Texas bar-bee-cue."

Sean drew Andrea a little from the crowd as Ellison ran off. "I love my family and my friends, but damn." He circled his arms around her neck. "You're mine, not theirs."

"Give them a break. A mate blessing is a happy time. We need those."

"True." Sean pressed a kiss to her mouth, then another. "But right now I'm thinking the mating frenzy will overshadow the Texas barbeque."

"I think so too."

"Well, then," Sean said into her ear, teeth on her lobe.

Andrea wished she didn't like kissing him so much. Sean tasted like sunshine and salt, his mouth splendid against hers. She rubbed fingers under his warm hair and inhaled his scent, a Shifter aroused.

Another scent came to her, this one sharp like mint. A cold breeze slapped her, and Sean jerked her away to growl at the white gap that was opening in the trees, a little way from the celebrating Shifters.

Fionn stood in the opening, the mists of his world swirling around the gleaming silver of his mail. It was raining in the land of Faerie, though the sun shone in the human world as hard as it could.

Andrea walked to him, Sean right on her heels. The other Shifters hadn't seen, but they would, and who knew what they'd do once they knew a gate to Faerie could open behind Glory's house? How Fionn had opened the gate without Andrea being asleep and dreaming, she didn't know either. But she would be sure to ask him.

As she neared him, Fionn reached out a hand gloved in finest leather. "Andrea. Child. Take my hand. Let me cross."

"Don't touch him," Sean rumbled.

Fionn's eyes flashed anger. "Can you not let me come to my own daughter's wedding?"

"It's a mate blessing under the sun," Andrea said. "Not the same thing."

His voice softened. "Please."

Andrea saw something other than arrogance and rage today in Fionn's dark eyes. Sorrow. Loneliness. Need. The Shifters partied by the Morrissey house, the scent of barbecued ribs floating on the breeze. Here in the grove behind Glory's house it was quiet, mists drifting from Faerie to dissolve in the Texas sunshine.

"All right," Andrea said. "If you promise to behave yourself."

Sean stopped her. "Andrea, no."

"Come on, Sean. I need to know."

She hadn't told Sean what she'd planned if she saw Fionn again, and she didn't have time to tell him now. Without giving herself time to think about it, Andrea shook off Sean's hold and held her hand out to Fionn's.

The moment Andrea touched him, Fionn's expression turned from sorrow to triumphant glee. He grabbed

Andrea's wrists and yanked her toward him, and she heard Sean yell as she went hurtling toward the gap.

Fionn started to laugh, a laugh that cut off in a scream as Andrea slapped the first steel handcuff she'd pulled from her belt around his wrist. Fionn stared in disbelief. Andrea smiled hugely as she clicked the second cuff around his other wrist, hooked her finger around the cuffs and dragged Fionn into the human world.

CHAPTER NINETEEN

The Fae warrior wrenched away from Andrea and fell to his knees, his chain mail rattling as he clawed at his wrists. "They're burning! Get them off me!"

Sean whipped his sword from its sheath and rested the point against Fionn's neck. "Sun and moon, Andrea, where the *hell* did you get handcuffs?"

"Glory." At Sean's amazed look, she added. "Don't ask."

"Don't worry. I'm not wanting to know."

Andrea gazed sternly down at Fionn. "So, the great Fionn Cillian, now that you're here, do you still maintain that I'm your daughter?"

"Of course I do. No other would dare bind *me*."

Sean let out a laugh. "I see where you get your self-confidence, Andy-love. What do you want to do with him, now that you have him trussed?"

Andrea crouched down to face Fionn. He glared back at her with eyes as black as night.

"Prove it," Andrea said. "Prove that you sired me, and I'll let you go back to Faerie land."

"My word should be good enough."

"Oh, sure, because no Fae would ever lie to a Shifter."

"Damn you, child, these manacles are killing me. Take them off and I'll tell you what you want to know."

"Tell me what I want to know, and *then* I'll take them off."

Anger and fierce pride surged on Fionn's face. "There's no doubt to me that you're my get. Here." He thrust shaking hands under his mail coat and pulled a chain from a hidden pocket. Delicate silver links shaped like leaves formed a bracelet, and a unicorn charm dangled from every other link. "This was hers, your mother's. She gave it to me that last night, when I left her, knowing I could never return."

Andrea had seen bracelets like this in the shops she and Glory had gone to in SoCo, though this one was of real, heavy silver. It was definitely human-made, however; a trinket that a Shifter woman might have seen and liked.

"That's Dina's."

Glory stopped next to Andrea, her face stricken. Andrea became aware that most of the Shifters had moved this way, the conversations stalling and drifting to silence.

Glory yanked the bracelet out of Fionn's hands. "Damn you. That was my sister's."

"Are you sure?" Andrea asked her.

Glory's eyes blazed. "Of course I'm sure. I gave it to her. Why does *he* have it? Don't tell me this is the fucking Fae who seduced her."

"Yes," Fionn said without flinching. "I am that fucking Fae."

Glory screamed and let fly a kick, her five-inch heel driving toward his face.

Fionn had reflexes a Feline would envy. Even with his hands bound, even in pain, he caught Glory's foot as it went by, flipped her onto her back, and got to his feet, all the while evading Sean's sword.

"Cowards," he spat. "Shifters, fighting a man caught and chained. Is that the best you can do?"

Dylan's savage growl filled the clearing as Glory struggled up, mud all over her silver lamé. Andrea turned and stepped in front of Dylan.

"Get out of my way," Dylan snarled at her.

Dylan had never looked more terrifying, but Andrea couldn't afford to back down. If she let him tear through Fionn, she'd never know the truth.

"Don't touch her, Dad," Sean warned.

"Dad! Sean!" Liam's voice cut like a whip. Dylan and Sean remained locked in place, eyes on each other. After a long moment, while Andrea's heart froze, Dylan dropped his gaze from Sean's and turned away.

Liam's whole body was tight with fury. "To avoid any Shifter blood spilling on this fine day, I suggest we let the Faerie man speak." He switched his glare to Fionn. "Tell Andrea what she wants to know, and if you're sweet about it, I might decide not to rip you to shreds. I might let Sean and my father do it instead."

Fionn's lip curled. "Goddess, Andrea, how do you live with these . . . *creatures*?"

"I never had much choice, did I?" Andrea took the bracelet from Glory, her breath catching as sunlight danced on the unicorn charms. Her mother had always loved unicorns. They were gentle beasts, she'd said, in spite of their horn and some stories that painted them as fierce. "How did she know so much about unicorns?"

"I showed them to her," Fionn said. "I risked taking her to Faerie to show her the unicorns, because she was so fascinated by them. I wanted to give her that much."

His dark eyes swam with sorrow for a deep-felt love that had been torn from him too soon. For all his Fae arrogance, Fionn Cillian had loved and lost. Andrea touched his hand.

"My daughter." His stern voice broke and his eyes grew wet. "I've waited so long to find you."

Andrea swallowed. "I think I believe you."

Fionn raised his manacled wrists. "Then will you have pity on your poor old dad?"

"Oh." Andrea turned to Glory. "The key?"

Glory had her arms folded, her expression forbidding. "There is no key."

"Then what are these for?" Andrea held up her hands. "No, please don't tell me. Sean, can you help?"

The handcuffs were ordinary steel, the same as the police used on human captives, but they would be no match for the strength of a Shifter. Sean sheathed his sword, worked his fingers between the cuff and Fionn's gloved wrist, and twisted one handcuff open. He did the same with the other, and Fionn quickly stripped off his gloves.

"Let me see," Andrea said.

Fionn held out his hands. Below the tunic he wore under his mail shirt, his bare wrists held red marks in the exact shape of the cuffs. The metal had burned him right through the gloves.

Andrea brushed her thumbs over the wounds and closed her eyes, reaching for her healing magic. She saw the tangle of threads around Fionn's hurt skin, blackened and burned, but the aura of the rest of his body was amazing. He was like silver and light, shimmering strength.

She'd seen some of that glittering silver in her own body. As she touched the threads of Fionn's being, they wrapped around her, familiar, loving, welcoming.

She also sensed Sean beside her, as she had when she'd healed Ely. Tall and strong, like a bright fire, Goddess blessed. The magic of his sword ran through him, and she reached for it and for Sean, who was bound to her now through the mate blessing.

It was real, this mate blessing, she realized. Not just words spoken by the clan leader in a social agreement. The Father God had been in the words and in the sun kissing their skin. She saw the bond between herself and Sean, gold and strong. Real.

Under her hands, Fionn's wounds closed. When she opened her eyes, Fionn's wrists were whole and unblemished, and he was watching her with an amazed expression.

The silver threads of his being still wrapped Andrea,

seeking her own. "I see it, the substance of your aura in mine," she said. "Yours and my mother's."

Fionn's eyes were fathomless. "Well, yes, child. 'Tis only natural."

He was part of her, and she of him. Andrea had been conceived by this battle-hardened, proud warrior, and a gentle and loving Shifter woman.

Tears trickled from her eyes. At last, after years of shame and fear and withdrawing into herself, Andrea knew who she was. She belonged, both to the Fae holding her hands and to the Shifter at her back who'd just made her his mate, bound to her body and soul.

*M*y mate. Mine.

Sean shuddered with release in the darkness, surrounded by the feel, the scent, the warmth of Andrea. Her lips, her hands, her breath, touching his skin. She gasped along with him, her sexy little noises making him wild.

He kissed her face, her hair, her mouth. He'd lost his power of speech, and he kept silent, simply kissing and touching, arching his body to drive himself deeper inside her.

Her lips were soft with desire, as were her eyes, which were silver-gray in the moonlight. Fionn had looked at Sean with the same kind of determined arrogance Sean had so often seen on Andrea's face. They were related, all right.

Andrea was so elegant, and Sean felt nothing but brutal frenzy. He'd spilled his seed but was hard again, ready, still inside where she could squeeze him.

Andrea touched his cheek, her fingers featherlight. "Sean," she murmured. "You all right?"

Sean let the growl come, and with it, his words returned. "I'm buried inside my sweet, hot little mate. How are you thinking I am?"

"Horny. A mate-frenzied male."

"You bet."

"Now you sound like Ellison."

Sean thrust again. "Don't mention that Lupine idiot while I'm making love to you."

Andrea laughed, the little beauty who teased him raw. "You're so easy, Sean."

"You're *mine*. Mate blessed. Which means we get to screw until we both can't walk."

"Half mate blessed." Andrea's smile was languid as she ran fingers down his back. "I saw it, you know. While I was healing my father. The bond between you and me."

Sean stopped, heart thumping. "The mate bond?"

"I don't know. But I saw it. The blessing isn't simply words and traditions. It's real, the Father God binding us together."

"Is it, now?"

Andrea smoothed his hair. "It is, now."

"Are you going to become a true believer, like those Shifters who wear white and meditate in stone circles all the livelong day?"

Andrea's foot caressed his bare calf. "I wasn't thinking I would. I have plenty to do right here."

"We do. Connor's not going to be happy unless we tell him tomorrow that a cub is on its way."

"Do you want children, Sean?" Andrea's voice was hesitant. "I'm not Feline. The child will be born human, and we won't know which animal it will become until later. Plus it will have Fae blood."

"I know. It will be—entertaining—to see what our child will be." He nuzzled her, finding her beautiful scent. "But, yes, I want cubs. With you."

But pregnancy meant risk for Shifter women. Fear caught in Sean's heart, so hard he couldn't breathe for a few seconds. His logical mind told him that a female's odds for survival were so much better now that they had access to medicine and doctors, and besides that, Andrea had healing magic. But Sean had seen too many females die bearing cubs or just after, sometimes the cubs dying as well, to be completely worry-free.

"I'll be all right." Andrea traced his cheek, sensing his fears. "We're safe here, and I have so many people to look after me now."

Sean knew the mating frenzy was pouring dire scenarios into his head, making him fear, so that he'd stay with Andrea and rut her all night and on into the next day. And the next night.

A biological drive, Liam had speculated once. Making the Shifter *need* to make cubs, giving him any excuse to have his woman under him. In the wild, Shifters had simply given in to it. Civilized Shifters felt the same mating frenzy, *But we ponder about it a bit more,* Liam had said. From what Sean had observed, Liam and Kim didn't ponder about it much.

Sean touched her Collar. Liam wanted to try removing it, but Sean didn't want him to now. Liam's curiosity could put Andrea at far too much risk.

The smile Andrea gave him heated his blood. "So what do you want to do next, Sean? You're my first, but I'm not innocent. I've heard about all kinds of interesting things we can do."

Sean's already fast pulse sped. A sudden vision flashed through his mind: Andrea on her hands and knees in the woods, he coming behind her, folding down over her while he drove inside her. The feel of her soft backside against his groin, smelling the fine silk of her hair, tasting her neck.

"Goddess, you make me want to do things to you," he whispered. "But I don't want to hurt you."

"I'm Shifter. I'm resilient."

"You're also Fae." He touched her wrist, slim and dwarfed by his hand. "Smaller than most Shifter women."

"Fae are pretty kick-ass too." To demonstrate, she hooked her legs around his and rolled, landing on top of him. "See?"

Sean had let her do that. Not that he minded having his beautiful mate on top of him, her breasts pressing his chest, her smile wide in the evening light. "Aren't you the wicked one?"

Sean traced Andrea's Collar again, letting his fingers drift down her chest. Would risking Andrea be worth getting all Shifters free? *No.* She was his mate, in all ways, and his instinct was to protect her with everything he had. Even if every other Shifter in the world had to die, it didn't matter, so long as Andrea was safe. To a mate-frenzied, dominant Shifter male, that was *right*.

Sean growled. His fingers became claws, which he retracted before he could scratch her. Andrea's growl answered. She leaned down and licked his throat.

The snarl that came out was pure feral. Reason, concern for all Shifters, even romance, went right out of Sean's brain. He dragged her down to him, rolled over her, and entered her again with one swift thrust.

Andrea's answering growls made him crazy. He thrust into her again and again, her arms and legs encircling him, pulling him into her warmth. She started to shift and came back, her smile wide, her gray eyes beautiful. She didn't shift *all* the way back. Sean felt wolf claws on his back, which pushed him into madness. The world went a little black, but it was all right because his mate was under him to guide him and keep him safe. The mate bond locked around him, the mate frenzy drove him on, and Andrea's sweet smile broke his heart.

"I know you don't much want to see to me," Glory said on the porch next door. "But the air in my house is crackling. Your son is noisy, Dylan."

Dylan, lounging on a chair in the shadows, didn't answer. Liam sat with his arm around Kim on the porch swing, and the Feline called Eric Warden sat with a beer on another chair, his long legs stretched out. He was a handsome devil, that Feline. His hair was a rich dark brown with little highlights that told Glory that he spent much time in the sun. Maybe with the sun kissing him all over? And his eyes—the color of jade with the intensity of fire.

Liam chuckled in response to Glory's comment. "You're

always welcome, Glory. The noise, it runs in the family, I think."

"Tell me all about that," Connor said from his perch on the porch railing. "I have to wear earplugs every night."

"Your time will come, lad," Dylan said.

"And then we'll be making fun of you," Liam put in.

Glory wished Dylan's voice didn't make her long for him so much. She missed him with every breath. Dylan was the best of lovers, alternately fierce and gentle, whatever his mood and the situation. And not only did she miss him in bed, she missed *him*. Dylan was the only one who truly listened to her. She wasn't top of her pack, didn't have the power someone like Dylan deserved, and Dylan didn't seem to care.

She crossed her legs, noting that she'd chipped paint off one toenail. Damn the Fae who'd made her charge across the yard in open-toed shoes to Andrea's rescue. Fionn, the bastard, had gone back to Faerie. Glory was sorry Andrea had let him out of the handcuffs.

"I was talking to Wade today," Glory said. "He thinks Callum's plan was idiotic but says he wouldn't mind if all Felines take each other out. Then Lupines would have the edge."

Liam listened with a calm expression. "Aye, he would say that."

"Don't underestimate Callum," Dylan said, his voice quiet. "His clan's protecting him, meaning we can't touch him, but who knows when they'll try to turn it into a clan war."

"Aye, Dad, and if that happens, we'll fight them."

Dylan's eyes glittered in the darkness, but he went silent. Glory thought she understood. Dylan wouldn't lecture Liam in front of the others, even if he thought Liam wrong. The first few years a Shifter took over his pride or clan were the toughest; others would test his power again and again until the new leader either fell or proved he couldn't be moved. Callum's rebellion was one such probe. If Dylan protected Liam too much, guided him too closely, the other Shifters would never respect and obey Liam.

Of course, Glory wasn't high enough in the hierarchy to tell Liam this. She could only listen, bring him intelligence, and let Liam make his decisions.

And I wanted Dylan to be impressed with me for finding out that Callum had put the humans up to the shootings, she thought in disgust. *How pathetic am I?*

"So tell me, Feline from Las Vegas," she said, to stop herself from looking too much at Dylan. "What's your interest in our problems?"

She made her voice go a little throaty, casting a suggestive look at him. Yes, she did it just to annoy Dylan, and she resisted glancing at Dylan to see how he took it.

"I don't mind helping out," Eric said.

Eric was here to learn about Collars, Glory knew. They'd trusted Glory with the information, and she'd kept her silence. Did Dylan remember that? Admire her for her discretion?

Goddess, I might gag.

Glory fidgeted and crossed her legs the other direction. "How do we know Eric won't tell our fractious Felines all about what you're doing?"

"I gave my word." Eric sounded surprised. "Swore on the sun and moon."

"He won't tell," Liam said.

"No," Dylan added with finality.

Damn, but Glory missed his voice. She missed that deep baritone whispering sexy things to her deep in the night, missed his tender nips on her skin as they made love. If she sat in Dylan's presence any longer, she'd burst into tears or something, making a complete idiot of herself.

Glory jumped up. "I'm off. For a walk. It will be a while before those two back off enough to let me sleep."

No one rose with her except Kim. Shifters didn't stand when a woman did; they stayed put and watched for danger. Kim, human, said she found this rude, but it seemed natural to Glory that males waited so they could spring on an enemy if necessary. How humans had survived this long with their strange customs, Glory had no idea.

Kim came to Glory and gave her a quick hug. "Thanks, Glory. Good night."

Glory hugged her back. She'd grown to like Kim, especially now that Kim had erased the sorrow in Liam's eyes. Andrea was busy erasing the same kind of sorrow in Sean. Now if only Dylan would let Glory try with him.

Time to leave.

"Good night." Glory gave Kim a kiss on the cheek, squeezed the hand Eric held out to her, patted Connor on the shoulder, and descended the porch stairs. She put a little wiggle in her hips, hoping that Dylan noticed.

I so need a run.

West of town lay hills that folded along the river, wild spaces where Shifters could pretend they were free. Glory drove there, parked her car well off the road, stripped off her clothes, shifted to her wolf, and started to run.

It felt good to pound along the hills, under the wide sky and the bright moon. She smelled water and woods, damp earth and open spaces. The wind was cold but just right for a wolf with a thick coat of fur.

Glory wanted to throw her head back and howl for the joy of it, but she kept a grip on herself. The land wasn't truly wild; it was owned by farmers and developers now, humans who didn't want to hear wolves on it. The other wild animals out here—coyotes, rabbits, snakes—kept silent, sensing her.

Glory slowed, then sat on her haunches and sniffed the air, trying to calm herself. Dylan was finished with her. She needed to come to terms with that, even if it broke her heart.

The run helped a little, but Glory was still restless by the time she made it back to her car. Shifting back to human, she stretched, dressed, started her car, and drove back to town.

It was only eleven, and Glory wasn't ready to go home yet. She turned along streets until she found a bar she occasionally visited on the outskirts of town. The bar wasn't a Shifter hangout, but when a woman was six feet tall with a well-packed body and blond hair, the clientele seemed happy to accept her. Now that the shooters had been driven off it was a relatively safe place where she could sit and brood.

She believed in its safety until she walked out to her car again two hours later, which she'd parked at the edge of the lot. A human male stepped out of the dark, shot her twice in the torso, and disappeared again.

Glory's Collar sparked as she instinctively tried to attack, but all feeling left her limbs, and she slid down the side of her car in a mass of pain. She quietly collapsed on the pavement, the gravel cutting into her face.

As she lay there bleeding, dying, she felt great regret that she'd never see Dylan again. She'd never be able to apologize for her stupid pride, which had made her throw away what little he was able to give her. That giving had cost him dearly, and Glory had thrown it back in his face.

A wolf scent came to her, sharp and pungent. She recognized the scent, which surprised her. Before she could form either hope or fear, the Lupine, in wolf form, walked up to her and sniffed her face.

CHAPTER TWENTY

"You've never been inside a grocery store, love?" Sean asked Andrea. "What, never ever? You're missing a grand experience."

Andrea gazed at the vinyl-tiled aisles stretching away from them with some trepidation. Not only did the aisles go on forever, they were filled with shelves upon shelves of boxes, cans, bags, and jars that all looked alike. "How is anyone supposed to *find* anything?"

Sean leaned on the handles of a wire cart, a luscious man out to do his morning shopping. "You soon figure out where they put the things you like."

"I thought you handed a list to someone, and they found the food for you."

"That was the old days. The village grocer would get in what he knew you liked and make up an order for you, in his friendly little shop on the high street."

"Even for Shifters?"

Sean shrugged. "Back in Ireland, no one, supposedly, believed in Shifters, but we were the best customers. We always paid our bills, and we were grateful for the sacks of flour and salt and the coffee our village man would get in. We hunted a bit more then, but the day we discovered we could get rabbit in a tin, well, it changed our lives."

Andrea studied his straight face. "You are so full of shit."

Sean let himself smile, but his eyes held worry. He was trying to distract Andrea from her thoughts about Glory, who'd not come home last night. Glory often went out and stayed out until the next morning, but Andrea didn't like that Glory hadn't even called. With Callum out there still plotting, Andrea worried.

Another problem with Glory not returning was that they'd run out of groceries, and Andrea had been stumped about what to do. Back in Colorado, the stores in town hadn't wanted Shifters in them but had grudgingly let a few Shifters shop for the entire Shiftertown. One person in Andrea's pack had been assigned to collect food orders from the families each week, then he made the run into town and brought back said food and supplies.

Andrea hadn't realized things how differently things were done in this Shiftertown. Glory always asked Andrea what she wanted from the store, never suggesting Andrea do the shopping, so she'd assumed that Glory was a designated shopper.

Andrea had written up what she needed this week, but the list was still on the refrigerator, and food was running low. When she'd told Sean, puzzled, he'd laughed at her, put her on the back of his motorcycle, and driven her to the grocery store closest to Shiftertown.

Andrea gazed at boxes stacked inside a long row of refrigerators with clear glass doors. "I don't even know what most of this stuff is."

"Ready-to-eat frozen meals. I've tried them. They pretty much taste like the package they come in."

"Why would anyone want to eat it then?"

"They're for the perpetually busy. Humans work non-stop, and then throw away all the money they make on cardboard food because they're so busy working they don't have time to cook real food. Ironic, that is."

"Do they have coffee here?"

"Love, they have everything here."

Sean led the way down the bewildering array of colorful offerings to a row of coffee in cans plus bins of coffee beans at the end of the aisle.

Andrea watched Sean fill a small bag with fragrant coffee beans, his intense gaze fixed on the task. "I never thought I'd need a mate to help me navigate the mysteries of a grocery store," she said.

"Mates are good for something, then."

Mates were good for far more than that, but Andrea wasn't about to flatter Sean's vanity with that remark. He'd been extremely proud of himself ever since they'd done the mating ceremony yesterday, and the fact that she was sore all over today was testimony to his joy. Sean had a few scratches and bite marks on his flesh as well, silent signals of Andrea's mating frenzy. She wondered what would happen when they really let themselves go. Wonderful thought.

"You don't think Glory went off with someone?" Andrea asked. "Eric, maybe?"

Sean shook his head as the stream of coffee topped up the bag. "Not right under Dad's nose. Glory's mad at him, but I don't think she'd go that far. Not yet."

Andrea agreed, but she'd prefer her aunt holed up consoling herself with a younger man than out-and-out missing.

"Or maybe she went to face my father again," Andrea said, "and he took her into Faerie." Far-fetched, but Andrea was trying not to think of the alternative—Glory hurt somewhere. Maybe Callum had found her and was using her to gain a hold over Dylan.

"I'm thinking Glory doesn't want to be within smelling distance of Faerie or Fionn."

"Damn it, I keep trying her cell, but she doesn't answer." Shifters weren't allowed voice mail, so Andrea couldn't leave a message. The phones could call one another, but that was about it.

"Once we're done foraging for food here, we'll go see Liam again," Sean said. "We'll make a search if we have to. If Glory gets pissed at us for interrupting whatever she's got going on, that's her problem."

"I'm glad you're so calm."

"I'm not, but going into hunter mode in the middle of a human grocery store would be a bad idea." Sean folded up the coffee bag and put one hand on her shoulder. "We'll find her, love. I promise you."

At last they were finished, carrying the bags of food Sean had paid for and heading for Sean's motorcycle. Sean had calculated buying just enough to fit the saddle bags and no more. He settled everything, and Andrea climbed on behind him. She liked holding on to his waist as they moved through the streets to Shiftertown. Sean was strong, warm to lean into. She rested against him and closed her eyes, breathing his scent.

Liam was home when they walked next door, but Dylan had gone again.

"I wish he'd stay put," Andrea growled.

"He has a lot to think about." Liam looked from Andrea to Sean, his blue eyes grim. "I'll put out a lookout for Glory, but I haven't heard anything."

A step sounded on the stairs, and Eric descended, his face a bit white, his gait shaky. "Are you all right?" Andrea asked him.

"We tested the Collars last night," Liam answered for him. "Eric's getting good at it, but it's still hell."

"Hell is one word for it," Eric said. He wore jeans and a T-shirt but was barefoot, his hair damp from a shower. "Damn painful is another."

"You don't know where Glory is, do you?" Andrea asked him. "You didn't arrange to meet up with her?"

Eric looked surprised. "Are you kidding? With Dylan watching me? I'd be bloody stupid to step between the two of them."

"I bet Dylan went out looking for her," Kim said.

"I just hope he finds her." Liam looked both worried and annoyed. "I'll call Spike and have him start a search for her—discreetly. Sean, can you help me today?"

The way he said it told Andrea that he expected Sean to understand what he meant. Sean's eyes flicked to Feline white blue and back again.

Liam also shot a pointed gaze at Eric, who took the hint. "The less I know about this, the better, right?" Eric asked. "I'll go for a walk."

His green gaze was speculative, but he brushed by Liam on the way out, showing that the two Shifter males had become friends.

"All right," Andrea said once Eric was gone. "Mind telling me what's going on?"

"Liam wants to try to remove your Collar," Sean said.

Her eyes widened. "*Remove* it?"

Sean put a protective hand on her back. "He's trying to find out how to remove all Collars, but doing it can make the Shifter crazy, even more feral than before. But you." Sean traced the design of the Celtic knot. "Your Collar doesn't affect you. Liam wants to study it, to see whether he can safely remove it from you."

Interesting. "Ooh, I've always wanted to be a lab rat."

"I won't let him if you don't want to." Sean's voice took on a hint of growl. "I'll protect you from him with my last breath."

Andrea found Liam's gaze on her, his alpha stare matching Sean's. Wasn't that wonderful? Two powerful Felines pinning down a little Lupine. She smacked that gaze right back at them.

"Yes," she said to Liam. "The answer is yes. I'm curious, and it might be worth it to find out."

Sean did not want this, and he let Liam know with every bit of body language that he didn't. Liam, damn his eyes, pretended to ignore him.

Connor was at school, so they didn't have to explain why they'd left him behind to go to the innocent-looking garden shed behind another Shifter's house; Kim was at her office. Eric didn't like being left out, but Eric understood. The less he knew, the less culpability he'd have if humans found out what they were doing. Eric and his Shiftertown didn't need to pay for the Morrisseys' experiments.

The inside of the garden shed looked innocent as well. Tools hung on the walls, an old lawn mower sat in the corner, and the whole place smelled of grass, earth, and oil.

Liam removed a small tarp hanging on the wall and took down his tray of instruments. No one who didn't know would understand what the little files and probes were for—to fix the lawn mower, maybe? Liam kept them deliberately grimy, sterilizing them only if he needed to nick Sean's or Dylan's or his own skin.

The Shifter to whom this garden shed belonged wasn't home, but Liam came and went here as he pleased. Kim had saved that Shifter's life, and the grateful Feline and his mother who lived with him obeyed Liam's every wish.

Liam had Andrea sit on a stool. Andrea did, betraying no fear, but Sean knew her enough to read her by now. He saw the minute flicker of her lashes, the small nervous movement of her hands as she brushed a speck of dirt from her jeans.

"I'd love to tell you this won't hurt," Liam said. "But I have no bloody idea."

The Collars were fused to the wearer's skin, so they never moved, never slipped. Liam touched a probe that looked like a small flashlight to the Celtic knot at the base of Andrea's Collar. A spark leapt from the knot to run around the Collar, and Andrea jumped. Sean snarled.

"No, I'm all right," Andrea said quickly. "It just—I wasn't expecting that."

"Don't hurt her, Liam." Sean knew he'd die if Andrea was hurt. He'd be scrambling around like a madman trying to save her, the mate bond closing like iron around his heart. If Liam hurt her, clan leader or no, brother or no, Sean would attack him.

Andrea's hand on his calmed his craziness, her gentle touch a link to sanity. "I'm really fine, Sean. Is that it?" she asked Liam.

"No." Liam took out another instrument that looked like a scalpel, scrubbed it clean with some antibacterial wipes, and dipped it in alcohol. "I'll try not to cut you."

"Oh, that's reassuring."

Liam held up the knife. "I also have to ask you not to talk."

Sean squeezed her hand. "Andrea likes to talk."

"Especially when I'm nervous."

"Well, for now, resist the urge," Liam said. "Shifters have fine metabolisms, but not if I accidentally slit your throat."

Andrea opened her mouth to answer that, her lips shook a little, and she closed them again. Her fingers closed harder on Sean's as Liam very carefully slid the knife under a link in Andrea's Collar and again touched the probe to the knot.

The Collar loosened. Sean and Liam already knew that the technology to unfuse the Collars worked, as far as it went. They'd learned that last summer when they'd discovered the experiments that the Shifter who owned this shed had been performing in secret. But the technique had been rudimentary and either killed the Shifter outright or made him so crazy he went feral. Liam, Sean, and Dylan had been working on refining the process, but so far they hadn't been able to figure out a better way. They couldn't experiment much on themselves without risk, and it wasn't as though they could ask for volunteers.

Andrea sat still as stone as a link came free. Her gray eyes were large, the fear in them real. But it was only fear. No pain.

Very slowly, Liam loosened another link and another. A tiny drop of blood squeezed from Andrea's neck, and Liam dabbed it away with another antibacterial wipe.

Andrea closed her eyes and held Sean's hand, but as more links came away, she breathed easier. "It doesn't hurt," she told Sean. "Well, no more than would someone pulling staples out of your flesh."

Surface pain, she meant, not deep, profound, bone-jarring pain that made a Shifter insane. Sean had let Liam remove a couple of links of his Collar one night a few months ago, and he thought he'd die of the pain. Andrea simply sat there and watched Liam work.

Link by link, the Collar came away, until finally, Liam disconnected the Celtic knot. Andrew sat holding Sean's hand, Collar-free, her gray eyes clear. Sean's heart gave a throb of joy. His mate was free.

"Nothing?" Liam asked as he held the Collar delicately in one hand. "You don't, for instance, want to disembowel me or turn on Sean and rip out his throat?"

Andrea grinned. "Not about this."

"Amazing." Liam peered at the thin red line around her neck and then at the Collar. He pulled a microscope from a tool drawer, set it up, and studied the Collar through it, looking like a cross between an Irish biker and a biology professor. "This is a regular Collar all right. No different from mine or Sean's or the ones I have in case I run across crazy ferals."

"Is that good?" Andrea asked.

"It's a wee bit puzzling." Liam lifted his head. "Same technology, same magic, same everything. Different reaction."

"Fae blood or the healing," Andrea said.

"Or it didn't fuse to you correctly the first time." Liam leaned close to her neck again, causing Sean's mate-instinct to flare. He put a strong hand on Liam's shoulder and steadily pushed him back.

Liam's look was amused. "Don't worry, my brother in a mate frenzy. I won't touch her."

"Didn't fuse correctly?" Andrea repeated in a worried tone. "Does that mean if you put it back on, it might?"

"By the look of your neck, which no, Sean, I wouldn't dream of touching, it did fuse properly. You're right that it might be a Fae thing. You wouldn't mind if I put a drop of your blood on a slide?"

Andrea shrugged. "Sure."

Liam reached to her already cut neck with his scalpel,

and Sean couldn't stop his growls. "Down, lad," Liam said, his lips twitching that annoying, amused way. He flicked one drop of Andrea's blood onto a slide, closed another over it, and eagerly went back to his microscope.

"It is different," he announced. "Just a little. But who knows if that's the Fae in you or just you. I've not looked at a Fae's blood before. Maybe your father would be willing to give me a drop someday?"

"I could ask," Andrea said. "Don't hold your breath or anything."

"Maybe it's to do with the fact that she can touch the Fae magic in the sword," Sean suggested.

Liam looked up in surprise, then broke into a grin. "You can feel the magic in Sean's sword? I'm thinking that makes for interesting evenings."

"You're funny, Liam Morrissey," Andrea said.

It was a good question though—perhaps her ability to use the Fae magic in the sword was connected with negating the effects of the Collar. She seemed to do both instinctively. Something to investigate when they had the time.

As Liam bent over the microscope again, Sean leaned down and nuzzled her. His eyes, so close to hers, were warm, inviting. Andrea had just touched her lips to his when her cell phone went off.

She snatched it up anxiously. "Glory?"

The answering voice was not one she wanted to hear. "No, it's Wade. You need to come over here. You and your Feline."

"Why?"

"It's important. Get here." He broke the connection, and Andrea was left staring at the silent phone.

"What?" Liam's head was up, sensing Andrea's and Sean's tension. "What did he want?" He would have heard Wade's voice too. Liam had Shifter hearing, and the man didn't exactly speak softly.

"No idea," Andrea said.

"Your old pack leader no longer has authority over you,"

Liam said. "I'm the one you have to grovel to now." He grinned as he said it, but the look in his eyes told her he didn't want Andrea answering the summons.

"It might be something about Glory."

"Don't worry, love," Sean said. "We'll go."

"Sean." Liam's look was stern, but Sean met it fearlessly, and Liam stopped. Liam might still have precedence over Sean, but Liam no longer had ultimate authority over Andrea. The mate's hierarchy overrode the pride leader's and the clan leader's, even the Shiftertown leader's. If Liam ever decided he needed to attack Andrea for some reason, he'd have to go through Sean first. The protection of the mate was a male Shifter's ultimate concern, and by the way Sean looked at Liam, he was going to protect her to the death. Instead of annoying her, Andrea felt a burning joy inside her at his need to protect, to cherish. The mate bond was a crazy thing.

"My Collar?" Andrea said. She lifted her hair out of the way, as though expecting Sean or Liam to snap it back on as they would a necklace.

Liam closed his hand around the Collar. "I'm keeping this one. You can wear this." He pulled a chain out of a drawer that looked exactly like a Shifter Collar. Andrea could tell the difference when she took it from Liam's hand—the slight touch of Fae magic that ran through all Collars was absent.

Andrea raised her brows at it. "Nice."

"I'm not risking putting the real one back on you," Liam said. "The fusing process will be bad, and as I said, we can't take a chance that your first one simply didn't activate right. This one will pass for a Collar except under close examination. And I know your wild mate here will never let anyone close enough to examine you."

Sean clicked the fake Collar around Andrea's throat. The Collar looked real, and Andrea winced only because it rubbed her abraded neck. But Shifters healed quickly, especially Andrea with her healing gift, and soon no one would be able to tell that the first Collar had been removed.

Looking at Sean, Andrea knew Liam was right that Sean wouldn't let anyone else come close enough to check.

"Go on then," Liam said as Sean helped Andrea down from the stool. "Call if you need backup."

They went, Sean with his sword strapped to his back, his hand in Andrea's.

When they reached Wade Sawyer's house two blocks east and four south, Andrea recognized the scent of the second male Lupine inside even before Sean knocked on the door.

Sean did as well. He growled, but he rubbed between her shoulder blades, his voice reassuring. "Don't worry, love. We'll see what they're up to. You're safe with me."

Wade's mate answered the door. She gave Andrea a worried look but said nothing, only ushered them inside. Sean entered the living room first and remained in front of Andrea as the second Lupine rose to join Wade on his feet.

"You remember Jared Barnett," Wade said.

Jared looked the same: dark hair, blue eyes, slouch to his overly muscular shoulders. Andrea realized something new, though, as his scent curled inside her nostrils—Jared was a weak Lupine who'd been given precedence in the hierarchy by the power of his father. Jared hadn't been strong, just protected by his sire.

Back in Colorado, the sight of Jared had triggered Andrea's fight-or-flight reaction—dismay, fear, the need to be anywhere but near him. And now, nothing. Andrea felt no desire to run. Jared no longer had importance in her world. Sean had given her this gift. He'd set her free.

"What do you want?" she asked Jared.

"Be nice to me, Andrea," Jared said. "And I might be nice to you later."

Andrea rolled her eyes. Sean's low, wild-sounding snarl made the color drain from Jared's face, but Jared tried to pretend he didn't hear. Idiot.

Andrea switched her gaze to Wade. Wade didn't have

anywhere near the presence of Sean, but he was the dominant Lupine in the room, and it was clear that he didn't think much of Jared.

"Why did you let him come here?" Andrea asked Wade.

Wade shrugged, pretending indifference. "You are of my pack so it was natural for him to come to me about you."

"She's no longer of your pack," Sean said. "She's in our pride now. Or were you forgetting?"

Sean didn't even have to raise his voice. The simple syllables in his Irish lilt spoke of danger lurking below the surface. The fear scent in the room rose sharply, and sweat formed on Wade's upper lip.

Wade brought his fingertips together in a nervous gesture. "That's a little tricky. Andrea is still not quite in your pride. You've only been blessed under the sun, and one more mate blessing is needed. Technically she's got one foot in both camps, and on that technicality, Jared can make his request."

"What request?" Andrea demanded.

"A challenge," Jared said. He couldn't meet Sean's gaze or Andrea's, so he looked at Wade. "Witness that I challenge Sean Morrissey of the South Texas clan for the mate Andrea Gray. Or, I should say, I accept *his* challenge, since I made the mate-claim first."

"Done," Sean said before Andrea could speak. He took Andrea's hand, and Andrea felt his rage matching her own. "Wade, set up the time and place. Andrea and I have things to do."

"It's ten feet under the trees, Ronan," Andrea argued. "You can walk next to me the whole time. Or behind me, whatever you want."

"That's where the Fae appeared," Ronan said, his dark eyes narrowing. Seven feet tall and full of muscle, Ronan still had to flick his gaze aside when Andrea pried him with hers.

"I know that," Andrea said. "I want to talk to him. I have some questions to ask him."

"Oh, come on, Andrea. Sean will kill me."

Sean had escorted Andrea back to the Morrisseys' house to leave her under the protection of Ronan while he, Eric, Dylan, and Liam joined the hunt for Glory. Andrea wasn't thrilled by Sean's easy acceptance of Jared's challenge, but more because she worried about Jared trying something treacherous than Sean's ability to defeat him. That Jared thought he had the right to challenge, and that Wade agreed with him, made her taste rage.

"Kick his ass, Sean," Andrea had told him before Sean left. Sean had smiled, said, "That's my girl," and kissed her.

Now Andrea faced Ronan. "Sean wants you to protect me from Jared. And so do I. Fionn is my father, he's not going to harm me, and I need to ask him some serious questions. Now hurry, before everyone gets back."

The problem with leaving Ronan as a protector was that, while few could best him physically, Ronan was not as dominant as Sean and Liam. Andrea might find it a challenge to get her own way with the Morrisseys, but Ronan only groaned at her demands.

"Ten feet," Ronan growled.

"I promise."

Ronan held up his hands. "All right. All right. We'll walk out there. You'll talk to your dad. Then right back inside."

Andrea patted his shoulder. "You're a sweetie, Ronan."

Ronan marched so close to Andrea as they crossed the yard that their bodies touched. Andrea felt him quivering hard with fighting instinct.

Andrea stopped at the weak spot on the ley line, her skin tingling as she neared it. "Father," she called.

The air split, and a pale, cold light touched her. Fionn Cillian stood tall and strong in the shimmering entrance to Faerie.

Andrea held out her hands. "I need you. Can I talk to you?"

Fionn smiled, his warrior face filled with triumph. He caught Andrea's hands in his, ignored Ronan's cry of surprise and outrage, and tugged Andrea, alone, into Faerie.

CHAPTER TWENTY-ONE

Sean checked Glory's usual haunts and turned up little. Glory was more adventurous than most Shifters, liking to hang out in human bars and dare the patrons to make something of it. No one could mistake six-foot-tall Glory for anything but a Shifter, but she enjoyed letting humans be fascinated by her.

In a bar way out on the west side of town, Sean finally found a trace of her. Glory had told him about this place a few years ago, though Sean had never taken her up on her offer to visit it. It was closed this early in the day, but Sean didn't need to go inside to catch Glory's scent.

The scent was strongest at the field beyond the parking lot, where asphalt crumbled into waist-high weeds. No cars lingered in the lot, including Glory's, but here, he smelled blood. Not much—someone had cleaned it up, and he couldn't smell who under the stench of blood. But he knew the blood was Glory's.

Sean stood up, heart thumping, pulled out his cell phone, and called his father.

* * *

Faerie wasn't what Andrea had expected. Instead of shimmering mountains of ice or trees of silver, she saw ordinary-looking trees stretching up to gray sky, the muddy ground laced with ferns and other undergrowth.

On second glance, the trees weren't ordinary. They were a species she'd never seen, with dark green needles, somewhat like pine, but the trees were studded with blood-red berries. Fallen berries littered the forest floor, scarlet juices staining the mud where the berries had burst. Behind Andrea, the rent in the fabric between the worlds snicked shut. She searched the air but found no sign of the bright light that marked the doorway.

Fionn let go of Andrea's hands and pulled her into a bone-crushing embrace. "My daughter. I knew you'd come to me at last." He released her and looked her up and down. "Now, where is the Sword of the Guardian?"

Andrea put her hands on her hips. "As a matter of fact, I came here to ask you about that. Why do you want the sword so much?"

Fionn's dark eyes filled with fire. "Daughter, that sword has unbelievable magic. It is the original Sword of the Guardian, did you know? The first one forged by a Fae woman and her Shifter mate."

"Yes, Sean told me."

"That Fae woman, Alanna, was the daughter of kings, and her magic was great. It runs in the family. Our family."

Andrea stared. "Our family? What are you talking about?"

"We are descended from Alanna's brother. He was an evil bastard, I'm sorry to say, but we can trace our line to him through his pure-Fae offspring. Thus, the magic in her family has passed to me, and so to you."

"And that means what?" And who actually used the word *thus*? "That I can wield the sword? I doubt that. Sean is the Guardian, chosen by the Goddess. And please don't tell me I'm related to him, even distantly, because that would just be too weird." Shifters had an even greater horror of inbreeding than did humans.

Fionn shook his head. "Sean is descended from the Shifter sword-maker's sons by his Shifter wife, not from Alanna. He is pure Shifter as our family is pure Fae. But it means that both you and Sean are connected through the sword. By magic." Fionn put a hand on her shoulder. "Think, Andrea. The sword speaks to you, does it not? It connects with you."

Andrea thought of the way the sword's threads wove through her fingers, how it seemed to whisper whenever she drew near, how she'd drawn in its power to heal Ely. "Yes."

"That means it will connect to me too. We will defeat our enemies if we have it."

Andrea growled. "It's not for *you*. It's Sean's, and it's not a weapon of war."

"I never said it would be. Andrea, our Fae enemies want it. They know its power, and they know its power over Shifters. They want Shifters under their control, and having the sword is one way to get it."

"*Fae* want it? But . . ."

"Daughter, the enemy Fae clan believes that if they have you and they have the sword, they will gain power over Shifters again. They'd be able to bring Shifters back where they belong, as slaves of the Fae."

Andrea grew cold. Mist was forming under the trees, and Andrea already missed the dry blue sky of Austin and the wind from the river valley. "Slaves of the Fae? How? Shifters will never let that happen again."

"Think it through. If they capture the Guardian's mate and the Guardian's sword, won't your Sean come charging in here to find them? And his brother and father will rush in after him, leading an army to best the hated Fae. So there we have it—some of the strongest Shifters on your earth, already weakened by the Collars, now in Faerie surrounded by thousands of Fae. It's a trap, child, an elaborate trap. The Fae will defeat your Shifters, strengthen the magic of the Collars, and settle down to breed even more captive Shifters. And after that, what wouldn't they be able to do with hundreds of Shifters forced to fight for them?"

Andrea listened, her heart constricting with each word. She knew damn well it could happen the way Fionn outlined it. If Andrea were trapped here, Sean wouldn't hesitate to search Faerie to find her, and Liam and Dylan would come right behind him. They'd organize a rescue, and if it came to a fight, they'd fight.

She imagined them, all the friends she'd made in the last weeks—Ellison and Ronan, Connor and Liam, Dylan and Eric, Ely and his sons, the regulars at the bar—surrounded by armed Fae warriors. The Fae wouldn't have to fight very hard, just wait until the Collars weakened the Shifters enough before taking them captive. Even Liam and Sean and Dylan being able to override the Collars wouldn't help them for long. The pain would catch up to them all too soon, and then the Fae would have them.

"Holy shit," she whispered. She wondered whether the Collars had been part of a grand Fae plot all along. A half-Fae human had come up with the concept and the magic for the Collars—what if he'd been employed by the Fae to help weaken the Shifters? The Fae resented Shifters for winning their freedom long ago, and Fae were just stubborn enough to wait centuries for their revenge.

"What makes you think the sword would be safe with you?" Andrea asked when she could speak again.

"Because if I have the sword, the other Fae would have to fight *me* and my armies. And they're hesitant to do that. My armies are the best in the world." Fionn said it without conceit—he was stating a fact. "I've been trying to keep you safe, child, from these ambitious Fae. What do you think your nightmares have been about?"

Andrea thought about the bright, white threads that tried to smother her in her sleep, how the voice had said, *Fight them!*

"The white threads are from those Fae, trying to trap

me in my dreams," she said slowly. "You've been there too, trying to stop them."

"Yes, daughter. When you moved here, so near a ley line, they tried to use your dreams to connect to your Fae magic. And it is my fault." He looked suddenly ashamed, this tall, proud warrior.

"Your fault? How can it be?"

"Because in my arrogance, I thought it safe to contact you. I thought my enemies were down forever. I knew where you dwelled in the place you call Colorado, and I thought it safe to tap your dreams. And it was safe, until you came here. That's when my enemies found you."

When the nightmares had started. "But I was looking for you," Andrea said. "I'd decided to start looking for you not long before I left." Fear about Jared had begun her quest—her need to find out who she really was, her way of gaining some control.

"I put the suggestion in your dreams," Fionn said. "And you went at it with determination. That's what allowed me to find you again along this ley line, but my enemy Fae found you too. They seized the opportunity to enslave you or at least influence your mind. But you were so strong. They tried again and again to make you go to them, to become their tool against me, and you never let them. You are a Cillian, without doubt." He radiated pride. "But you have no need to fear any longer. I will defeat my Fae rivals, kill their clan leader, and take command of their opening on the ley line. And I will teach you to resist all other attacks on your dreams. You have the strength; you simply need the training." He spoke so casually, certain of his success.

"You'll do all this if I bring you the sword?"

"I will teach you regardless. Sean has been able to help you resist them too, with the Goddess magic in him."

Sean's presence had kept the nightmares at bay until the calling had become too strong. "I'm right then," Andrea said. "Sean is Goddess touched."

"Of course he is. There has to be a way to choose a Guardian besides someone simply grabbing the sword."

"Does Callum know that?" Andrea asked, half to herself. She'd bet that most Shifters didn't know that Guardians had actual Goddess magic in them, that it wasn't the *sword* that was important, but the man who wielded it. Or maybe Callum did know, and his ploy to get the sword was more like a ploy to get Sean. Hell.

Fionn went on. "Those Feline Shifters who have decided to fight against Liam Morrissey and his family play right into the hands of the Fae. The weak Shifters will easily lose the sword to the Fae who encourage them."

Andrea's heart squeezed again. Liam had been so certain that Callum would be kept down by his own clan but not if Callum's clan aided and abetted him. Now Glory was missing.

"Damn it, Father, why the hell didn't you tell me all this before?"

"I didn't know. About my Fae enemies thinking about getting their hands on the sword, yes; about them seducing disgruntled and ambitious Shifters to help them do it, no. I was lucky enough to capture and interrogate a Fae spy yesterday. Before I killed him, I learned that this Callum person is ready to strike. Which is why you should have brought me the sword." Fionn stopped, blinked. "Child, did you realize? You called me *Father*."

Andrea had, but she was too distracted to think about that right now. "So Callum thinks he's using the Fae, but the Fae are using *him*."

"You have grasped it," Fionn said. "My enemies can be beguiling. They probably put the idea in his head that he could unite Feline Shifters without this Callum even realizing it."

"Goddess, Sean is out there looking for Glory. Alone."

"You must find him and bring him to me. You will both be safe in my keeping while I defeat the Fae who seek the sword."

Finding Sean made sense to Andrea. Fionn's request

that he have the sword for safe-keeping still didn't—or it did, but Andrea wasn't sure how much to believe him. If Fionn were beguiling *her*, and she handed the sword over to him, then *he'd* have the hold over the Shifters. But she'd work all that out once she connected with Sean.

Andrea whirled, but the woods looked the same to her in all directions. "Where is the damn door?"

Fionn's hands on her shoulders guided her to the right place. "I can't come with you," he said. "I'm strong, but in your city, there is too much iron. Far too much for me."

Andrea hadn't expected him to help. The wolf in her wanted one thing and one thing only.

Protect the mate.

Andrea dove through the slit that appeared to find herself back in Shiftertown—a Shiftertown too quiet and too still for a fine spring day. No cubs ran in backyards, no parents moved between houses, no one worked in yards or sat on porches. Everyone was inside or gone, the houses shut and dark. *This Callum person is ready to strike.*

In this unnatural silence, Andrea punched Sean's number on her cell phone, but he didn't answer.

A Lupine presence loomed up so strongly while Sean bent over the blood-stained grass that he had his sword out and at the other male's throat before either of them could blink.

Jared Barnett stared at Sean down the length of the sword.

"What the bloody hell are you doing here?" Sean demanded.

Jared shrugged his massive shoulders. "I followed you. What are *you* doing here?"

"Looking for Glory. I found her blood. If you had anything to do with that, this blade goes into your throat."

"I haven't seen anyone but Wade and his mate since I got here."

Sean inhaled, but Jared's scent spoke the truth. Sean smelled only the strong odor of Jared himself and the fainter ones of Wade and his mate, the scent from their house. Nothing of Glory. He lowered the sword.

Jared smiled. "In fact, I had a good night's sleep and I'm feeling energetic. So let's do this."

Sean gave him a look of disgust. "I don't have time to fight you right now. Besides, a mate challenge has its proper rituals, as you should know. Wade should have kept you away from me until time."

"Wade Sawyer is weak. We didn't have to wait in the old days. If a Shifter wanted to challenge for a woman, he went after the other male, no rituals, no declarations. They just fought to the death."

"That's what you want, is it? A fight to the death?"

"Yes."

No wavering. Jared's scent of fear was smothered by that of anger and determination.

"Are you stupid, lad? If I fight to kill, I'll kill you."

"Maybe you will. Or maybe I'll kill you. But it doesn't matter. Because of you, Guardian, I lost Andrea—a submissive, half-Fae bitch who was my only chance at having a mate. There is no other unmated female of mating age in our Shiftertown, and I am the Shiftertown leader's son. I'm expected to carry on the line." Jared shed his jacket and tossed it on the grass. "So I have nothing to lose. If I kill you, I get Andrea. If you kill me, I avenge my honor."

"I said I'd fight you," Sean said, holding on to his patience. "I accepted the mate challenge. But not right now. I don't have time."

Jared pointed at the ground. "Right now. No referees, no rules, no one stopping us from killing each other. Just two Shifters fighting to kill or be killed. Like in the old days."

"You're bloody obsessed with the old days. What about your Collar?"

"I'll fight through the pain."

"You've got a death wish, lad."

"I have no honor left. What do I care?"

Sean knew that the idiot would attack whether Sean was ready or not. Sean slid his leather jacket from his shoulders, laid the sheathed sword on the grass, and dropped his coat on top of it. "Can't wait an hour, can you? Glory's in trouble somewhere, and I need to meet up with my dad and find her."

Jared shrugged again, then moved his shoulders in circles to stretch out his muscles. "No," he said. "Now." And he attacked.

"Ronan?" Andrea called into the Morrissey house. "Liam?" She walked through the empty rooms and peered up the staircase. "Eric?"

She mounted the stairs and knocked on bedroom doors, finding the rooms behind them empty. The big attic where Connor slept was also empty. "Where the hell is everyone?"

Back at Glory's house was the same. No notes, no messages, nothing. The entire Morrissey family had vanished.

Andrea crossed the street to Ellison's, but no one answered the door. Ellison lived with his sister and her two cubs, who were nearly grown young men, but none of them were home. In rising panic, Andrea knocked on doors down the block, but no one seemed to be around.

What the hell?

Panic made her heart speed. She forced herself to stay calm, to reason out what could have happened while she was in Faerie talking with her father. If Callum or the Fae had come for all the Shifters in Shiftertown, there would have been a big fight. The Shifters wouldn't simply disappear—Felines and Lupines and Ursines alike. Therefore, the Shifters must have gone to ground or were hiding the mates and cubs in preparation for a fight, which would happen who-knew-where.

Andrea heard a car turn down the street. Without hesitation, she sprinted back down the street and ducked around Ellison's house. The car didn't slow but carried on past Shiftertown and toward downtown Austin without stopping.

Andrea ran across to Glory's house and around to the back. She stopped, panting, in the grove of trees. "Father!" she shouted.

Fionn didn't answer. Instead, a strong hand closed on her shoulder and another clamped over her mouth when she opened it to scream.

Jared fought like a crazy thing. He didn't bother sliding out of his clothes before Shifting; he simply morphed into his wolf form, his clothes splitting to rags. Sean didn't have time to undress like a civilized being before Jared was on him.

Damn it, I liked this shirt. Sean's claws tore fabric from his body as his wildcat took over. Jared ran smack into him, and the two went down in a tangle of limbs and claws.

Jared, with nothing to lose, had no reason not to kill Sean. He was fighting for his honor, not Andrea, while Sean fought to stay alive to save her from Jared.

Sean sensed his sword in the tall grass where he'd left it, the blade waiting to see which Shifter it would send to the afterlife. It offered no help while he and Jared tumbled through the field, wildcat on wolf, kicking up dust into the clear blue sky.

Jared's Collar sparked around his neck, driving blue veins of electricity into his body, and Jared snarled in pain. Sean's Collar did the same, but adrenaline ran so high that they both went on fighting.

Jared hooked a claw around Sean's Collar and twisted. One link that Liam had dislodged before easily came loose, giving Sean a surge of feral-spiked rage.

Sean roared and shook his head. Sean's sides were already bloody from Jared's claws, Jared's dark fur dripping scarlet from Sean's. For seconds they stood back to catch their breaths, and then they were fighting again. Grappling, clawing, ears back, each trying to close jaws over the others' throat.

Savage snarling filled the air, but it didn't come from Sean or Jared. Before Sean's enraged brain could reason out what was going on, a half-dozen Felines sprinted across the parking lot and leapt on them both.

Sean rolled from Jared and fought this new attack. His nose told him who they were—Callum's followers he'd seen in the bar. Of Callum or Sean's clansmate Ben, there was no sign.

The Felines had one thing on their minds: to rip Sean and Jared to pieces. Their Collars sparked too, but they fought right through the pain.

Sean turned on them. He roared a mane-shaking roar, proclaiming to all who heard that he was in command here. One Feline started to back away, but the other four didn't give a damn who was in charge and renewed their attack.

Jared, the idiot, didn't run off, go for help, or even join the others to kill Sean. This wasn't his fight, and yet he turned and started battling the Felines alongside Sean.

Sean roared and plunged, snapped teeth and raked claws, fighting furiously. He saw and sensed the Feline who'd dropped back make for the sword.

The sword. Damn it.

But if Sean broke away and made a dash for the sword, the Felines would tear Jared to pieces. If Sean didn't, the shite slinking toward the Sword of the Guardian would snatch it and run off. Sean couldn't let that happen.

Dimly he heard cars squealing to a halt in the parking lot, and far away, the sound of sirens. Help coming?

From the scent, the people who piled out of the cars were human. Ben had assured them that the human shooters they'd hired had gone, so were these friend or foe? Sean couldn't afford to wait around and find out.

He sprinted for the sword, knocking aside the Feline that had almost reached it. Sean's Collar was sparking like fireworks and the later payback would be hell, but he didn't have time to worry about that right now.

Sean morphed to human as he rolled over the Feline, landing on his human feet and sweeping up the sword. The Feline backed off, looked up at Sean with red-rimmed eyes, and turned to dash back to the fight around Jared.

"Jared, you gobshite. Run! Get out of it!"

Jared continued to fight, and the Felines continued to

savage him. They were in a killing frenzy, instinctively taking out the Lupine, the competitive predator. Jared, enraged at the interrupted challenge, was fighting for all he was worth.

So this was Sean's choice—again. Help Jared and risk the sword, or watch Jared die, just as Sean had with Kenny. Jared was nothing to Sean but the asshole who had persecuted Andrea, but the situation was the same. Sean guarded the sword, and others died for it.

Sean dropped the sword and shifted. He bounded into the tangle of wildcats shredding Jared and fought them hard. The humans from the cars moved toward them. They had weapons, but they stood at the edge of the fight, watching.

Sean shoved one of the Felines in front of him, snarling as he rolled over and over with him toward the five humans. Sean came out of the roll and barreled into the human men, scattering them like bowling pins. They cursed and shouted and then they started shooting.

The sirens grew louder, nearer. Two of the gunmen ran, jumping into a car and peeling away. The other three remained. A bullet sliced across Sean's chest, and he gave up trying to be nice.

He took down two humans, raking claws across the arms that held the guns, digging deep. The men screamed, trying to get away, weapons dropped and forgotten. A few smacks from Sean's huge paws put them out, and he turned to jump on the next one.

The man rose and aimed at Jared, Jared's Lupine form standing out among the Felines. He fired. Jared howled and fell, and Sean's claws tore across the shooter's back. The man landed on the ground with his fellows, and Sean smacked his gun out of his reach.

The Felines converged on Jared, but Sean dove between them, flailing and fighting. The Felines were tiring finally, reacting to their Collars. Sean fought on but he knew his own pain would creep up on him soon.

Two of the Felines morphed back to human, breaths grating, and started dragging the bleeding, mewling humans to the cars. Another Feline went for the sword, but Sean intercepted him, jaws snapping on the Feline's spine.

The Feline squealed and limped away, his fight done, but it was the end of Jared. One of the remaining Felines dragged a paw down Jared's face as he lay unmoving, opening it to the bone. The Felines turned to look at Sean, faces bloody, sides heaving.

Sean stood over the sword and snarled at them, the blade between his front and back paws. Two came back to Sean, circling him.

Sean lunged at one Feline, and the wildcat backed off, tail swishing. The other tried to get behind Sean, but Sean was too fast, his paw catching that one and sending him to the ground.

The sirens drew near. By tacit agreement, the Felines turned and made their painful way back toward the cars. Sean felt no triumph as he watched them morph into bloody, battered humans and crawl into their vehicles. They were giving up for now, but there was nothing to say they wouldn't simply call others to come and take him while he was here with the sword and wounded. He needed to get the hell home, but it would be a long way for him to ride, broken and bloody, on his motorcycle. As if in response, one of the cars slowed where Sean had left his bike near the door of the bar, and fired five rounds into the motorcycle's engine.

Bloody bastards. Sean lay down, panting, the sword hard under his body, as the cars moved off and disappeared down the empty street. The sirens neared the scene and went past on the next block, never coming close. Whatever emergency the vehicles were responding to, it wasn't this one.

Sean couldn't get his breath. He'd fought too long and too furiously, and the wounds in his side, plus the chunk taken out by the bullet, segued into the Collar's payback pain. But if he passed out or even died here, he couldn't risk anyone else picking up the sword.

He scratched in the earth, using the last of his strength to dig deep. He moved as much of the wet earth as he could before shoving the sword into the hole and piling mud on top of it. The field was so gouged with the fighting, this last gouge didn't look any different from the others.

Sean morphed back to human, and then his world went black as the Collar's agony took over. Vaguely he sensed another presence and smelled Lupine, not Jared, but nor was it Andrea.

Andrea. Love.

I love you.

As Sean lost consciousness, he felt himself being lifted by the armpits and dragged away. Behind him, dying sunlight picked out Jared lying alone and bloody in the litter-strewn parking lot.

CHAPTER TWENTY-TWO

Dylan's white pickup barreled through traffic on MLK Boulevard, and Andrea hung on to the swaying seat. Dylan's face was set, his dark blue eyes almost black with fury.

"So where did they all go?" Andrea asked. Once she'd calmed down from the shock Dylan had given her, he'd ordered her to come with him, striding away before she could ask questions.

"Callum and his clan declared war on Liam," Dylan said in clipped tones. "Liam gave the order—all cubs and vulnerable Shifters to be taken to safety. But each family has to look after its own, because the collective hiding places aren't safe, not when Callum and his faction know where they all are."

Which meant each family or pride or pack had gone to ground in their own secret hideaways. They'd have these places, because even though Shifters now lived in communities, the instinct to protect the mates and cubs from other Shifters still existed. Shifters worked together now, yes; but they all had private places into which they could disappear if they needed to.

"What the hell were *you* doing?" Dylan demanded. "Liam wanted to take you to stay with Kim and Connor, and Ronan tells us you forced him to let you go to that Fae. Liam decided you'd be all right with him, but he's bloody pissed off at you. And Ronan."

"Don't blame Ronan. I needed to talk to my father—to Fionn. He said that Fae were helping Callum. They want the sword—the Fae, I mean."

Dylan grunted, not sounding very surprised. "Betraying Shifters to the Fae. Callum dies for that." A simple statement, but the chill with which he said it emphasized the walking danger that was Dylan Morrissey.

"Sean was looking for Glory," Andrea said worriedly. "I know some of the places she likes to go, but not all."

"Doesn't matter; I know where Sean is. Or at least, where he was."

"You do? How?"

"He called me. I was on my way to meet him when Liam summoned me and told me to stay behind in case you popped back out of Faerie."

He snapped his mouth shut, and Andrea didn't have to be a mind reader to know how he felt about that. Dylan turned abruptly onto a little-used street that wound behind empty warehouses.

"Sean told you he was out here?"

"He said he was in the parking lot of a bar Glory likes to go to. He found her scent and some blood."

Andrea felt sick. "Blood?"

Dylan was pale and drawn, his fear for Glory coming off him in waves. "Not enough to show Sean what happened."

"Where exactly are we going?"

"Here." Dylan jerked the truck into a parking lot.

Andrea saw the familiar bulk of Sean's motorcycle by the front door of the closed bar. Dylan glanced at it, and then tires screeched as he rode the breaks to avoid hitting the body of a man lying motionlessly on the pavement. The stench of burning rubber filled the air.

Andrea was out of the truck and racing to the man's side before Dylan switched off the engine. She dropped to her knees and pushed blood-matted hair out of the face of Jared Barnett.

"Jared. What the hell?"

Jared's flesh bore the deep marks of the fully extended, razor-sharp talons of a Feline Shifter. The cuts went to the bone, Jared's naked skin blue white where it wasn't covered with blood. He was still alive, barely, his heart fluttering in faint, rapid beats.

Jared opened his eyes, but they were filmed over, gaze unfocussed. "Andrea?"

"What happened? Did you see Sean? Did he do this?"

Jared swallowed, fighting for air. "Felines. Sean tried to save me."

"Sean tried to *save* you? Where is he? What happened?"

"Gone. He was taken. The sword."

Dylan crouched on Jared's other side. "What about the sword?" he demanded.

"The sword," Jared whispered. His eyes drifted shut, but breath still rasped in his throat.

Andrea cast her gaze around the parking lot. Much blood had been spilled, red soaking into the crumbling gray asphalt. She smelled more Shifters than just Sean and Jared. Felines, several of them, some of whom had been in the bar with Callum.

The parking lot ended in a field covered with weeds and tall grasses. A creek cut through the bottom of this field, ensuring the place stayed nice and wet. The field had been torn up by the fighting, leaving gouges of mud through the tall weeds, but no bodies lay here.

Neither did the sword. Nowhere did she see a glint of sliver, the hump of its hilt, but as she stood at the edge of the field, she started to hear it. The familiar shimmering sound that the sword made when she neared it rang inside her head, growing louder and louder until Andrea clapped her hands over her ears. An instinctive move—one glance back at Dylan and Jared told her they couldn't hear it.

The sword was here, calling to her. Gritting her teeth, she followed its song, which grew louder and more joyful as she neared it.

Andrea dropped down and dug in the grass and soggy earth. She had to go down a long way, covering herself in muck before her hand encountered something hard. She pulled it out of the gripping mud, the sword singing with all its might.

So the sword was here, safe and sound. But where the hell was Sean?

The ground around where the sword had lain was saturated with blood. Sean's blood. The blood was drying, no longer fresh, but the dampness of the grass ensured that her fingers came away red.

Andrea hoisted the sword, ran back to Dylan and Jared, and crouched next to Jared.

"What happed to Sean?" she demanded. "Tell me."

"They tried to get the sword," Jared whispered. "Sean fought them so hard. Drove them off."

"But what about Sean? Who took him away?"

"Don't know. Didn't see."

Andrea put her hand on Jared's chest, again felt the flutter of his heartbeat, so swift and faint. It was useless to ask him any more questions. "Lie still. We'll get an ambulance."

"No. Human hospitals will kill me."

He was probably right, and Andrea didn't have the heart to argue with him. But she could try to help him at least. Jared was cruel and nasty and selfish, but he didn't deserve to die in such pain and alone, so far from home.

Andrea pressed her hand to his chest and closed her eyes, searching inside herself for the healing magic.

Except that she already knew that her magic would not be strong enough. The threads that were Jared's life force were snarled, too tangled to unravel. He'd been battered, bones broken, muscles and organs tattered by claws and by bullets.

When she'd healed Ely, Andrea had boosted her power with the Fae magic of the sword. Shaking, she wiped as much of the mud and grass from it as she could, laid it across her knees, and wrapped one hand around the blade.

The sword kept singing to her, not as loudly now, and she understood with abrupt clarity that the runes etched on the blade and hilt were forming words in her mind. They must be part of the spells made by the Fae woman long ago, and the words spoke of peace.

The sword's threads flowed into Andrea's body then out through her fingers, joining with her own healing magic that she poured into Jared.

But it wasn't enough. The sword helped a little, but Andrea felt nowhere near the surge of magic she'd experienced when she'd healed Ely.

Come on. Give me more.

Even as she thought it, she knew that there would be no more. The missing factor from this healing was Sean.

When she'd helped Ely, Sean had held the sword's hilt while Andrea had held the blade. The sword had drawn from Sean's amazing Goddess-touched aura and combined it with Andrea's healing gift to make Ely whole again. Sean the Guardian was the second part of the equation. The magic of the sword's original makers—the Shifter man and the Fae woman—had manifested again in Andrea and Sean. Both of them were needed to make the healing work.

Beneath Andrea's hand, Jared's body weakened. She saw in her mind the faint threads of his aura suddenly fade and wink out.

Andrea gasped. She plunged her healing magic again into Jared, but she found the threads brittle and black, snapping under her touch. *Andrea,* Jared's voice came to her, sounding happy, and then he was gone.

Andrea opened her eyes and jerked her hands from Jared's body. Dylan leaned down and gently closed Jared's blind eyes.

"You tried, lass," he said softly.

"But it didn't work. I wasn't strong enough."

"He was already gone. You eased him into his death, let his end be painless."

Andrea stroked the silver blade on her lap, the runes still whispering to her, trying to comfort her. She and Dylan sat silent a moment, as was traditional when a Shifter died, each sending a prayer to the Goddess.

"If Callum or his Felines took Sean, they wouldn't have left the sword," Andrea said as Dylan helped her to her feet. "So that leaves who? If it was someone trying to help him, then why did they leave Jared?"

"I don't know, lass. Maybe whoever it was thought Jared was already dead. Or maybe they just didn't give a damn. But we'll find him." Dylan's voice held determination.

Andrea's breath hurt, but with her fear came rage, a killing anger. They'd taken her *mate*. A female defending her mate was the most fearsome of Shifters, and whoever had done this to Sean didn't yet know the meaning of terror.

A ndrea and Dylan couldn't leave Jared's body behind for the humans to find. Though Jared had been an asshole who'd made Andrea's life hell, every Shifter deserved to be sent to the afterlife by the Guardian. Andrea helped Dylan wrap Jared's body in a tarp and ease it gently into the bed of Dylan's pickup. Dylan laid another tarp on top and secured the tailgate.

They followed Sean's blood trail through the grass onto the pavement behind the closed bar, and there the trail vanished. By the scent, someone had backed a vehicle there and must have then driven away with Sean's body. There were no tire tracks on the solid asphalt, nothing to indicate what kind of vehicle it had been or in which direction it had gone.

Andrea didn't want to give up and drive away, but there was nothing they could do. Dylan started the truck, and Andrea held the sword in her lap, her hands around both hilt and blade, as though the sword would give her some clue. It didn't; the damn thing only kept whispering musical words that she couldn't understand.

When they pulled into traffic, Dylan's cell phone rang. Andrea jumped, and Dylan's hand shook as he pulled the phone from his pocket. He handed the phone to Andrea and went back to dodging traffic at its densest.

"Andrea?" Liam yelled into the phone when she answered. "Where's Dad?"

"Driving. Did you find Sean?"

"What?" Liam stopped. "What do you mean, find Sean? I thought Dad would be meeting up with him after he found you."

Andrea's chest tightened. "Where are you?"

"Fighting. We need Dad. And Sean and the sword. Damn it."

"I have the sword. I don't have Sean."

Liam's voice trailed off into a snarl. "Tell dad to get here. We're at home. Callum's Felines are all over the place."

"What about Sean?"

In the silence she sensed Liam's terrible fear for his brother fighting with his duty as a leader. "Dad needs to take you to safety and get here. We'll have to look for Sean later."

The phone went silent. Andrea looked over at Dylan as she clicked it off. "He wants you to help him fight Callum."

Dylan's hands tightened on the wheel. "Then that's what I'll do."

"We can't stop searching for Sean."

"I know that, lass, but I have to go to Liam. Or I'll lose another son, and who knows how many others."

"Then let *me* look for Sean."

Dylan's lips were white. "Like hell I'll let you run around the city by yourself. Besides, there are Shifters following us, and I can't risk taking you to Kim's in case they aren't on our side."

Andrea looked back past the billowing tarp to see another pickup, this one dusty black, with two male Shifters she didn't recognize in the cab. They didn't do anything but follow, but they stayed on Dylan no matter how much he dodged through traffic.

"The Morrisseys' safe house is Kim's place?" Andrea asked, turning back. She'd been there once, a large, richly appointed human house with a terrific view.

"She has a state-of-the-art security system, a basement we can lock down like a vault, and if any strange Shifters go poking around her house, her human neighbors will call the cops." His look turned wry. "Besides, she has cable, which we figured could bribe Connor to stay put."

But with fighting like this, the cub must be chafing. Even the sword seemed to be anticipating battle, its singing excited.

"When we get to Shiftertown," Dylan said, "you go to ground in the safest place you can find. I'll keep them away from you and the sword. Callum's obsessed with Felines only, Shifters only, and you're both Lupine and Fae. He'll kill you and bathe in your blood."

Andrea was past caring about Callum. "I'd like to see him try."

"Well, I wouldn't. I'm aging, child. If you carry Sean's cub, I want you alive to bring it into the world. I want to see Sean's and Liam's cubs grow up. If that means hiding you in the basement while we fight, I'll do it."

What he didn't say was, *If we've lost Sean, I don't want to lose his offspring too.*

Andrea fell silent as streets whipped by. Traffic was thick but Dylan navigated with the ease of long practice. As he drove, he directed Andrea to dial the cell phone and hand it back to him. Mostly Dylan got no answers, which meant the Shifters he tried to call were already fighting, on whichever side. Others simply hung up on him.

Dylan finally threw down the phone. "I don't know who I can trust. Gobshites."

He drove straight into Shiftertown, screeching the pickup to a halt in front of Ellison's. As they got out, Andrea heard shouting, snarling, and enraged growls, the sounds of battle.

The Shifters who'd been following them nearly slammed into them before they stopped, leapt out of their truck, and sure enough, tried to go for the sword.

Dylan tore out of his clothes and shifted as he attacked the other two. He might claim to be feeling his age, but his wildcat was still fast and ferocious as the three rolled and tumbled in fierce Shifter combat.

Andrea hurried across the street to look for Liam. The heart of the battle converged around the Morrissey house, about fifty or so Shifters battling it out in knots of fights that spread down the green behind the houses. The beasts were so entangled Andrea couldn't distinguish one from the other, though she saw Eric shift to wildcat to fight near Liam. There were only a few Lupines—Ellison was one, Annie from the bar another.

Andrea still held the sword. Dylan had told her to go to ground, but there was nothing to say one of these Shifters wouldn't peel off and follow her into Glory's or the Morrisseys' or Ellison's place and kill her there. But if she stayed to fight, she'd have to shift and drop the sword. If she simply stood here, clinging to the sword in her human form, she'd be a sitting duck to the Felines who wanted it. She couldn't hold on to the sword in her Lupine form, but she couldn't fight as well in her human form. Sean had to make this kind of decision in every fight. No wonder being Guardian drove him crazy.

One thing was for certain, she couldn't stand here and wait for one of Callum's Felines to attack her. An idea came into her head, one that made her smile. She headed for Glory's house, not bothering to keep out of sight.

Three Felines broke ranks and charged Andrea, and she started to run. Not into the house but down the green and under the trees behind it.

The Felines attacked her. Andrea swung the sword, feeling Shifter glee when bright blood coated one wildcat's striped shoulder. The sword at this moment was not so much sacred relic as handy weapon.

"Come on!" Andrea shouted at them. "What are you afraid of?"

They snarled and circled her. *Good, Andrea.* She might be the daughter of the greatest warrior in Faerie, but that didn't mean she was practiced at sword fighting.

First thing I do after I find Sean—hook up with my new dad and have him give me a few sword lessons.

"Father!" Andrea shouted as she swiped the sword at the Felines. She thought she was in the right place, on top of the ley line, but she didn't have time to be certain. "Fionn Cillian! I need you!"

The Felines attacked her, all three at once, intent on slaughter. Their Collars were sparking like crazy but that didn't seem to slow them down.

Andrea swung the sword again, slicing through fur, but the Felines were dexterous enough to avoid her more deadly thrusts. They jumped and circled like domestic cats around a snake, avoiding the sword's strike.

"Any day now, Father!"

White light broke the shadows under the trees. The fabric of reality rent about six feet away from her, and Fionn appeared in the opening to Faerie, his chain mail glittering. He had a bow in his hands, arrow knocked, the fury in his black eyes matching that in Dylan's.

Fionn let an arrow fly straight into the haunch of one of the Felines. The big cat roared and fell, but he was up almost instantly, his paw turning human long enough to wrench the arrow out of his leg.

The three Felines launched themselves at Andrea, ready for the kill. Andrea turned to face her father.

"Dad!" she shouted. "Catch!"

She threw the sword at Fionn. Fionn let go of his bow, reached out his hand, and caught the sword by the hilt. He laughed, flourished the blade, and vanished.

The Felines stopped as one in front of Andrea. The air behind her was smooth and unbroken, the way into Faerie gone.

The cats turned their gazes from where Fionn had been to where Andrea stood now. They bled from shallow cuts she'd given them, and the one who'd been stuck with the arrow limped. But they weren't dead, not by a long way. Yellow eyes narrowed; breaths burned hot.

Andrea turned and ran, shedding clothes as she went. As soon as she flowed into her wolf, she whirled around, teeth bared, and attacked the Felines who'd dared hurt her mate.

CHAPTER TWENTY-THREE

Sean opened his eyes to a Lupine nose right in his face. "Oh, beautiful," he croaked. "Dog breath."

He tried to open his eyes wider but found that he couldn't see much past the black and wet nose. "Where the hell am I?"

The Lupine growled, and while Sean had lived a long time among Lupines, that didn't mean he understood every nuance of every sound they made. He raised a hand to his face, noting that no part of him did not hurt. He'd been clawed and shot, beaten, and half electrocuted by his Collar.

He lay in a dry cave, but that didn't much help him figure out where he was. The hills around Austin were sprinkled with caves, some of which were tourist attractions, some known only to weekend spelunkers. Sean assumed that this cave was in the last category; that is, if he was still anywhere near Austin at all. There were plenty of caves out in the middle of nowhere.

As Sean's senses returned, so did his intense pain. He closed his eyes, as though that would force it away.

The sword wasn't here. Its presence was unmistakable, Sean's link to it formed the day he'd been chosen as Guardian.

He hoped to the Goddess that he'd buried it well enough, that he could get his hands on a cell phone so he could call Liam or his father to go find it before anyone else did.

The Lupine was sniffing him again. *If he drools on me, I'm killing him.*

Sean opened his eyes to see the Lupine shift back to the man Sean had already placed by scent—Wade, Andrea's pack leader. Sean hoisted himself into a sitting position and then spent a few minutes huddled against a wave of pain. "I feel like shit."

Wade backed away. "You were pretty far gone. You might want to lie down again."

Not if you're going to keep poking your nose in my face. "How did you find me, anyway?"

"I was following Jared. I feared he'd gone to harm Andrea, and that's against the rules."

"Bugger the rules. Jared was after me. What happened to him? We were fighting, and he went down."

"He's dead. I didn't have room to bring you both."

"Dead?" *Poor, stupid sod.* "So you left him for the humans to find?"

"I told you, I didn't have room for him. You're lucky I got you away. Jared was a fool and above himself."

"Yes, he was a thrice-damned idiot, but he was also under your protection. What are you going to tell his dad, who is a Shiftertown leader?"

Wade shrugged. "That Jared broke the rules and suffered the consequences. Shifter law is Shifter law."

What a piece of work. Wade was the worst kind of pack leader—enforcing rules to the letter without any thought of mercy.

"I have to go back," Sean said. He started to push himself to his feet but fell back with a gasp. "Shite."

"You're hurt. Rest a while."

"Did you call for help? Call Liam—why haven't you already?"

"Your cell phone is broken, I don't have one, and Glory's wasn't on her. I wanted to get you to safety."

Sean's eyes narrowed. "Yeah? Why didn't you take me back to Shiftertown? To my house or even yours?"

Wade avoided his gaze. "There's fighting there."

"What kind of fighting? Callum, is it?"

"I think so, yes. They attacked Liam when Liam returned from sequestering his female."

Sequestering his female. Sean wondered what Kim would think of that phrase.

"Then we should be back there," Sean said. Again he tried to get his feet under him, and again, his legs refused to obey. "I appreciate your tender loving care, but damn it, we need to help Liam."

Wade didn't move. "You're not going back yet. Wait until it finishes."

"No matter how it finishes, they'll need me."

"No." Wade's voice went hard. "Callum's Felines will win. Accept it, Sean. The Morrisseys' power in this Shiftertown is over."

"Oh, you're sure about that, are you?"

Wade's voice was flat. "You and your family will lose. Callum will lose too, because he's an idiot. But the Lupines, we will win."

Mother Goddess help us all. "Don't be daft, man. Whichever faction wins will be damn strong, strong enough to take out a bunch of overconfident Lupines." And Sean would make sure the faction that won was Liam's.

"No, it won't. Callum has the advantage, and he'll kill you all, but he bought his power at too high a price."

"Price? What the hell are you talking about?"

Wade tried to shut up and look wise, but Sean reached out and easily caught Wade around the throat. Sean squeezed, ignoring the agony in his own arm. "What price?"

Wade gasped for breath, eyes bulging. "Goddess, Sean."

Sean didn't relent. "Talk or I snap your neck."

"Fae," Wade rasped. "Callum made a bargain with some Fae."

Sean loosened his hold, but only slightly. "What bargain? Tell me, damn it."

Wade dragged in air, coughed. "The Fae promised magic to dampen the effect of the Collars while Callum's Felines fought this battle, to give Callum the advantage. In return, Callum pledged his men to aid the Fae whenever they call."

Holy crap. "Aid the Fae? What Shifter would make a bargain like that?"

Wade smirked, a neat trick while Sean was holding him by the throat. "My intelligence gathering is better than yours. You and Liam are so arrogant, thinking no one can displace you. Callum went behind your back, hooked up with the Fae, and now the Fae are going to kick your asses."

Sean released Wade with a jerk of his hand. "I'll kill him," he said as he tried to make his legs work again.

"You only have to wait for Callum to pay the price," Wade said. "The Fae will summon him and his friends to Faerie, and they won't be able to resist. They'll be Fae slaves, and then Lupines will rule Shiftertown."

"With you as its leader? Don't flatter yourself. Ellison will never follow you, nor will Glory."

"Won't they? How do you know? *You* treat them like shit. You call Ellison your friend, yet you nearly killed him the other night for dancing with Andrea. I was there—I saw. Glory's in love with your father, but he can barely bring himself to notice her. No I think both Glory and Ellison will be happy to take their vengeance against the Morrisseys."

Sean didn't like that Wade might not be far from wrong.

"As for your half-Fae mate," Wade said. "The Fae can have her after I kill you."

"Fuck you." Damn it, if Sean could just make his body obey, he'd break Wade's neck and run off to find Andrea. His body had other ideas, like collapsing, hurting, dying maybe.

"Sean." The whisper came out of the darkness, a woman's whisper. A weak one but not Andrea's.

"Glory?" Sean turned his head sharply and scanned the depths of the cave. "You've got Glory in here?"

"She was wounded by Callum's humans. One of my trackers found her and brought her here to die in peace."

"Damn it, why didn't you tell us?"

"Why? You're Felines. Glory is a Lupine and of my pack. I do with her what I please."

Gobshite. "Glory, where are you?"

"Sean," she whispered again, her voice far too weak. "Don't listen to this asshole."

Sean's heart pounded as he glared at Wade. "Why didn't you at least take her to a hospital? What the hell are you thinking?"

"I don't like humans touching my pack. She's dying. Let her go."

Sean snarled. With all his strength, he pushed himself to his feet, noting Wade's sudden alarmed expression. Satisfying. Sean was half dead, and yet Wade Sawyer was still afraid of him.

Sean stumbled in the direction of Glory's voice. He found her after a few moments of painful searching, a body stretched out in the dirt, Sean barely able to see her in the darkness.

"Sean," she whispered in relief.

Sean's legs folded up, and he fell beside Glory, unable to do anything more than stroke her tangled hair.

Fear tore at him. Sean had to get to Andrea, had to warn her about Callum and his deadly bargain. He had to keep Andrea safe. The mate bond beat at him in panic and rage, and still, Sean couldn't make his body move.

Andrea knew she fought a losing battle as the three Felines circled her. She'd give the fight all she had, would possibly even wound the Felines along the way, but in the end, she'd lose.

The Felines' sparking Collars didn't slow them down at all. How they'd managed that, Andrea had no idea. Her fake Collar had expanded and stretched when she'd shifted, almost like the real thing. Liam had prepared well. But being unhampered by a Collar was no advantage at the moment, because these Felines were busy being happy they got to kill her.

They attacked. Andrea fought—snapping, clawing, feinting, striking. Claws ripped through her skin, teeth tore her fur. The pain made Andrea fight back with savagery she never knew she had, but in the long run, it wouldn't be enough.

A roar of rage cut through the grove, and the ground shook as though a tank battered its way through the trees. A huge bear barreled through the knots of fighting Felines, scattering them left and right, the ruff on his neck expanding with his anger. He flung a wildcat foolish enough to attack him through the air, rose to his full Kodiak bear height, and roared his power. The air vibrated with fury, and the Felines attacking Andrea fled.

Thank the Goddess he's on my side.

Andrea ran to Ronan, thinking that she'd give him as many of Sean's pancakes as he wanted. The nearby Felines hesitated, fear radiating from them, but beneath their fear was hard determination. They wanted to win.

They were smart enough to realize that attacking Ronan directly would be pointless. So the Felines used their cat swiftness to dive at Andrea, forcing Ronan into a defensive position. Of course, Ronan outweighed the three Felines collectively by about fifty pounds, and his razor-claws were at least eight inches long. He lifted one Feline that had closed teeth into Andrea's fur and threw him aside with ease.

Andrea realized a slight disadvantage as they fought on, however. Ronan wouldn't go for the kill. In spite of his massive size and strength, Ronan was a kindhearted male who didn't like to hurt anyone. Frighten them, yes, give them a good thumping, any day. Kill, no. That was why he'd jumped in front of bullets but hadn't dragged the human shooters out of the car to break their necks.

The Felines caught on and attacked with renewed viciousness. *They* had no problem with going for the kill.

Ronan was happy to rough them up plenty, though. His arms moved like sledgehammers, paws throwing bodies left and right. His ears were flat against his skull, his teeth bared for all to see, and his roars filled the clearing. Andrea leapt and snarled and snapped beside him.

The Felines were bleeding, breathing hard, Collars sparking, though the look in their white blue eyes told Andrea they weren't finished by a long shot. But they were slowing a little. Ronan's growls sounded more like laughter now as he fell to all fours and charged, scattering the cats like fallen leaves.

But just when Andrea thought the Felines would abandon their attack and run back to the main fight, light rent the air, and she smelled the sharp scent of Faerie.

Fionn? She wasn't ready for him to bring her back the sword, not until the risk that Callum's Felines could snatch it was gone.

She noticed that the Felines didn't look too worried, and then she saw that the tear happened not in the grove where she usually spoke to Fionn, but farther along the ley line, closer to the end of the block.

She remembered what Fionn had said about his enemies and Callum, and her blood froze. "Dylan!" she screamed.

One of Callum's Felines stood by the opening, and he pulled through five Fae warriors. They were tall and nasty-looking, armed with bows, and silver swords glittered on their backs.

A Fae spotted Andrea where she stood gaping, raised his bow, and fired. Andrea threw herself flat on the ground, but it was Ronan leaping in front of her who took the arrow. It drove deep, but Ronan was up again in an instant, his bear hide thick, and he ran for the Fae.

When Ronan faltered after he'd taken only a few strides, Andrea realized that the arrow must have been poisoned. Elf-shot, Shifters called it—spelled poison that paralyzed a Fae's enemies until the Fae could make the kill. They didn't always make the kill right away, she'd heard. Fae liked to play with their victims.

The faces of the tall Fae were ghost white, eyes burning black, mouths set with hatred and determination. But as fearsome as they were, the Fae couldn't come far into this world without weakening, which gave Andrea a spark of hope. Iron sapped their strength and would send them fleeing back to Faerie. That didn't help this instant, while the

Shifters fought in animal form, without weapons, no iron in sight. But Andrea could change that.

Andrea forced herself into her human form. Her wolf wanted to stay wolf and fight, and she had to battle her own instincts to complete the shift.

"Back to the house!" she shouted at Ronan soon as she could form words. "There's iron and steel there. We'll hold them off."

Ronan roared at her and didn't obey. Andrea couldn't speak Ursine, but she understood the gist—good-natured Ronan had finally found beings he wanted to kill.

"You've been elf-shot," Andrea called. "We've got to get rid of them so I can help you."

Ronan's dark eyes lit with fire. He knew he'd been poisoned, but he was determined to take the Fae out with him as he went. He completely ignored Andrea and charged the Fae warriors.

Andrea said foul words while she forced herself back to wolf. It took too long—by the time Andrea made it to fur and fangs, Ronan had engaged the Fae.

The Fae warriors ran out of arrows and attacked with swords. Andrea darted around Ronan and sank her teeth into the sword arm of the tallest Fae. The Fae shook her off but dropped his sword, bleeding from her bite.

Ronan staggered and fell. The Fae moved in, horrible joy in their eyes.

Andrea shoved one aside, grabbed the back of another's mail coat, and started dragging him toward the grove of trees behind Glory's house. The warrior fought but couldn't reach around to jab her with his sword. When he drew a silver knife, Andrea let him go and bounded into the grove. She didn't have time to shift and scream for her father, but she could throw her head back and howl.

It was a full wolf howl, one made to echo from hilltop to hilltop across wide plains. It filled the clearing and bounced up and down the human-made houses, proclaiming that for all their domestication, Lupines were still wild, still powerful, still deadly.

Andrea heard a tearing sound and then felt the chill wind of Faerie. Fionn was there, reaching out.

"Touch me, Andrea. Quickly!"

Andrea ran at him. Fionn put one hand on the fur on her neck and stepped from Faerie into Shiftertown.

At almost the next instant, Fionn had a bow knocked, raised, aimed. Arrows flew—one, two, three. Three of the Fae warriors who had been sprinting for them dropped in rapid succession. The remaining two had the sense to flee back into the trees.

Fionn grabbed Andrea and nearly threw her through the gate to Faerie. Ronan, staggering badly, but not down yet, ran in after her, followed by another Feline who hit the ground, rolled, and came to his feet in the form of Dylan Morrissey.

Dylan had his hands on Andrea's arms, dragging her up even as she shifted. He shook her, hard, eyes blazing with alpha rage. "What the holy hell did you do?" he shouted. "You've given the Sword of the Guardian to a gobshite Fae!"

CHAPTER TWENTY-FOUR

A long-fingered grip wrenched Dylan from Andrea. "Take your hands off my daughter."

Dylan's voice was hot with fury. "I don't care what tales you told her, I still don't believe you're her father. She's my son's mate, and I'm not letting any Fae have power over her."

"But having her in *your* power is better?" Fionn asked. "A Feline Shifter who hates her Fae blood?"

"She is my son's choice. That means I protect her."

"But who protects her from you, Shifter? How do I know your son is worthy of my girl?"

Andrea growled, her wolf fury unchecked as she stepped between them. "Could you two stop playing 'Who's the Better Dad' for two seconds? Ronan needs help."

Ronan lay on the ground like a big bear rug, his eyes closed, his sides rising and falling with labored breathing. Andrea knelt beside him and stroked his broad head and his muscle-filled ruff. Ronan acknowledged her with a little sigh but didn't open his eyes.

Andrea focused on the fur under her hands, soft as down

yet wiry and tough, just like Ronan himself. Beneath the fur she sensed the threads of Ronan's aura growing black and brittle, much as Jared's had.

Smooth fabric dropped over Andrea's shoulders. Andrea looked up in surprise as Fionn draped a cloak of light green silk around her body, its cool folds pooling in her lap.

"You needed to cover yourself, daughter."

Andrea didn't miss Dylan's look of disgust. Shifters didn't find nakedness shameful or embarrassing, but Fae did.

Fionn knelt next to Andrea and touched Ronan's side. "He's quite big. What is he?"

"Brown bear," Dylan rumbled above them. "One of the biggest kind, from the Kodiak islands. Ursines breed closer to wild species than other Shifters."

"What Fae was mad enough to make Shifters from *these* creatures?" Fionn said in wonder. "The Felines are bad enough."

Dylan growled, and Andrea ground her teeth. "Please? Can we focus?" she said. "Those other Fae might be back any minute."

Fionn removed a pouch from his cloak. "What other Fae?"

"The ones you shot at. Remember? You hit three in about two seconds."

"I fired too slowly, I know, but I didn't have time to adjust for the air currents on your world. Otherwise, I'd have taken the other two as well."

"Your modesty amazes me. But the others will just come charging back through here, won't they?"

Fionn looked puzzled a moment before his brow cleared. "Ah, I see your mistake. Have no fear, child. Whatever way they found to your world, it is leagues from here. They would never dare to try to cross into my territory."

"What do you mean, leagues? It was twenty yards, if that."

"Yes, along the ley line in your world," Fionn said. "That gate will not necessarily lead to the same place as the one I use. Their gate will open to the lands of their clans, which is a three days' journey from here."

"Oh." Andrea needed to adjust her thinking, that was certain. "What says they can't dive in here through *your* gate?"

Fionn opened the pouch and sprinkled what looked like plain sand into his palm. "Because only I can activate it, just as only their leader can activate theirs." He traced the sand with one finger. "This will heal your bear, but it will hurt him. Can you ensure that he will not turn and kill me?"

Andrea lifted Ronan's head into her lap, and Ronan huffed an unhappy sigh. Andrea stroked his fur. "Did you hear that, Ronan? The big Fae warrior is afraid of a little teddy bear like you."

"You do have your mother's sense of humor," Fionn said. "Yes, I am afraid of him. He is large and could decapitate me with one swipe of his paw. Please tell him to stay calm."

Andrea scratched between Ronan's eyes. "I'm sorry, Ronan," she said. "He'll help you, but I need you to promise to let him live. He's my dad, and I haven't had time to get to know him yet."

Dylan knelt on Ronan's other side, put his hand on the bear's shoulder. "Easy, lad. Let the Fae bastard try. I want you back with us, my friend."

Ronan heaved another sigh, opened his eyes, and gave Andrea a long-suffering look.

"He'll be all right," she said to Fionn.

Fionn finished smoothing out the sand until a thin layer coated his hand. Then he slammed the hand, palm down, onto Ronan's side, right where the arrow had gone in.

Ronan's eyes popped open and a stifled roar came out of his mouth. Fionn kept his hand solidly against Ronan's fur, flattening his lips in concentration as Ronan's body began to heave.

"Hold him steady," Fionn said.

"What is it doing?" Dylan asked.

Andrea knew before Fionn answered. In her mind's

eye, she could see the magic of the dust leach into Ronan's blood, muscles, and bones, searching for the taint of poison and then eating through it like acid burning away rust.

It had to hurt like hell. Ronan writhed under Andrea's touch even as she laced her healing power down to help him, his moans of pain almost howls. As the counterspell traveled through him, Ronan's movements grew stronger, until finally he shook off Fionn and Dylan and sprang to his feet. He roared as he rose on his hind legs, all twelve feet of him, and he morphed into his human form in midroar.

"Ow, that fucking hurts! Enough!"

Andrea pulled the silk wrap about her as she stood. The cloth was soft as air but opaque, hiding her completely in its smooth folds. "You all right?" she asked Ronan.

Ronan shuddered, hands coming up to scrub his face. "What the hell was that? It was like being eaten by ants from the inside out."

"A very powerful magic charm," Fionn said, dusting off his palms. "Without it, you'd have been dead."

"Oh." Ronan rearranged his expression. "Thanks. I mean that."

"I'd not have bothered, but my daughter spoke well of you. I did it for her."

"No, really, don't keep explaining. I'm fine. Thanks, Andrea."

Andrea squeezed his big body in a hug. "Anytime. You saved my life out there."

"Plus, the Guardian's not here, so it's just as well I didn't die." Ronan glanced around, as though Sean would come crawling out from under the nearest fern. "Where is Sean? I thought he never strayed two feet from you."

"He's not here," Dylan said grimly.

"We need to find him." Andrea chewed on her thumbnail, her anxiousness returning full force.

Ronan looked from Andrea to Dylan. "What the hell happened to Sean?"

"We don't know," Dylan said. "We found blood . . ."

Fionn was the only one who didn't look concerned. "You can find him, daughter."

"How? Someone took him away, who knows where, and we don't even know whether he's alive."

"You have the answer," Fionn said. He gestured to the sword, which he'd left leaning against a tree.

Andrea glanced at it, waiting so patiently for the Guardian's return. "What, I point it and say, *find Sean*?"

"It's a magic blade, forged by a Shifter and a Fae, and the two of you are connected to those who made it. More importantly, you share the mate bond."

She heard Ronan's gasp of delight, but Andrea couldn't look away from Fionn. Dylan rumbled behind her. "Is that true, Andrea? You and Sean have formed the bond?"

Of course Andrea felt the mate bond; it had been probing at her since the night she'd seen Sean at the bus station. Andrea had taken one look at Sean's dark blue eyes and lost herself. She understood that now.

She smiled a little. "Yes. We share the bond."

"Hot damn!" Ronan said. "Congratulations, Andrea." The mate bond didn't always happen between a couple, and when it did, Shifters rejoiced for them.

"How did you know?" she asked Fionn. "I don't remember telling anyone."

"I felt it when you healed me," Fionn said. "I saw it in you, fierce and strong. I saw that in your mother too. For me."

Andrea lost her smile in sadness. She'd known that her mother had loved her Fae, and Fionn had just confirmed it.

Dylan took Andrea's hands, the tall, blue-eyed man who looked so much like his son. "Because you share the bond, you'd know if Sean wasn't alive. You would know, Andrea."

Andrea thought she understood. She didn't exactly feel a tether to Sean, but she knew she'd feel its absence if the bond between them severed. Her entire body would know the difference. She realized now what Dylan must have gone through when he'd lost Sean's mother—when the mate bond had been wrenched from him. The loss had scarred him so deeply he'd taken more than fifty years to heal.

"I think he's alive," Andrea said slowly. "But I still don't know where."

She went to the sword and lifted it, passing her hand over the runes that the long-ago Fae woman had etched with her magic. The sword was as bound to Sean as he was to Andrea, as they were to each other.

Ronan grinned. "So maybe you do just point it and say, *find Sean.*"

Andrea drew a breath. "What the hell? The worst that can happen is I look like a fool."

She wrapped both hands around the hilt and lifted the sword. She pointed the blade into the air and said, "Find Sean."

The sword jerked to the right, nearly impaling Ronan, who jumped out of the way just in time. The blade dragged Andrea's arms around before the sword sliced through the air with a white-hot light.

"**G**lory."

Sean's whisper sounded loud, even to himself. Glory's answer was a soft groan. She was dying.

"I need to apologize," Sean murmured to her. "For what I have to do."

Glory's eye cracked open. "Kick his ass, Sean."

For a Feline to kill a Lupine pack leader was against all protocol and Shifter law. Shifter species traditionally despised each other, but they'd made it a policy to avoid fighting each other rather than wipe each other out. They'd have all died out long ago if they hadn't.

Then again, if a Lupine was a clear danger to a Feline pride, then he was fair game. Glory's words meant she would be witness to this, her offer tantamount to the pack's acceptance of the kill.

The question might be academic, however. Sean wasn't

in position to kick anyone's ass, Lupine or otherwise. His entire body was a mass of pain right now, and strength was a vague memory.

But he had to get them out of here and back to Shiftertown. Glory needed medical attention, and the Goddess only knew what Callum's Felines were doing to Andrea—not to mention Liam, Dylan, Connor, and Kim. If Callum were daft enough to make a pact with the Fae, Shifters were screwed. The Fae were strong, treacherous, and deadly. They'd happily wipe out or enslave all Shifters and not worry too much about it.

Heartless, cold bastards. And stupid, stupid Callum.

Sean closed his eyes and directed all his remaining energy into shifting to his wildcat.

He spent the next ten minutes gasping in blinding pain. Shifting itself shot agony into his body, coupled with the pain of his wounds and the torture from his Collar. *This is what I get for being compassionate. I should have let Andrea rip out Callum's heart when she had the chance.*

Andrea. Hell. Sean was supposed to be her great protector, and now here he was, weaponless, weak, and in too much pain to get himself free to help her.

Wade claimed he didn't have a phone, so Sean needed to find out where Wade had stashed whatever vehicle had gotten them out here and go for help. That is, if Sean could get himself up off the floor.

Wade walked toward him but stayed out of reach. "Don't try it, Sean. Or you'll watch Glory die."

Sean hauled himself to his feet and shook out his mane. It hurt to do it, but mane-shaking always looked intimidating. Sure enough, Wade took a step back.

Roaring was out of the question. Sean could barely draw a breath, could barely even see. He settled for a harsh rumble in his throat that seemed more threatening than it was.

"Seriously, Sean." Wade put his booted foot on Glory's bare side. "I'll kill her."

Glory, with the last of her strength, grabbed Wade's foot and shoved upward. She was too weak to do much, but

Wade lost his balance, and that gave Sean his opening. He sprang.

Gravity worked to Sean's advantage. He was able to shove Wade to the ground and land on him, using his weight to hold him down. But Sean grew dizzier as Wade struggled, and he knew he'd pass out if he made much more effort. Glory tried to crawl toward the cave mouth, but she'd moved only a foot or so before she collapsed.

Wade started to shift, wolf claws digging into Sean's side. Wade's Collar went off, but even with that, Wade was stronger and more rested than Sean. The wolf would kill Sean and Glory both and claim that they'd died of their wounds.

Andrea. Sean's consciousness started to drift. *Love you.*

"Sean?"

He heard her voice, the sweetest music. Sean pictured Andrea's gray eyes that had looked at him so saucily that first night at the bus station, the black ringlets of hair he liked to catch between his lips. He loved every curve of her body, her red lips, her tender and skilled hands that liked to explore him. Sean liked her wolf too, the noble Lupine with Andrea's cool gaze.

There was no finer woman than Andrea Gray, and she belonged to Sean.

"Sean!"

A white light blinded him. Damn, wasn't it enough that Wade had them cowed without the man beaming light in his eyes?

A stench went with it, a cross between smoke and mint. Cold wind blasted through the cave, and suddenly it was filled with people. Sean could scent them: the acrid mint odor he'd come to associate with the Fae, the rather ripe smell of a pissed-off bear, the scent of his own father, and the cool honey tones of his mate.

Andrea.

Sean opened his eyes. At the same moment, Dylan reached down and hauled Wade, half shifted, to his feet.

Dylan's eyes were white-hot with rage. His Collar sparked,

but Dylan, the best trained of them all against the Collars, wouldn't feel it. Behind Dylan, the tall Fae drew a sword.

Wade gibbered in terror. "I was keeping them safe. I was keeping them safe!"

"Lying shithead," Glory whispered.

Sean let out his breath and turned his head to inhale the goodness of Andrea. She dropped the Sword of the Guardian and wrapped her arms around him, burying her face in Sean's mane.

"I found you," she sobbed. "Sean, my *mate*. I found you."

CHAPTER TWENTY-FIVE

Healing Sean was a joy. Andrea felt her magic connecting with the shimmer of Goddess magic inside Sean to soothe his hurts and heal him. He slowly shifted back to human as she worked, the threads of his pain unsnarling and smoothing at her touch.

Andrea knew when Sean felt better, because she felt his gaze fix on her, strong and blue. He snaked a hand around her wrist, fingers hard, and pulled her down to him. Andrea came willingly, sensing their threads twine together, the mate bond tightening.

"Thank the Goddess you're all right," she said.

The look in his eyes told her he had more than prayers of thankfulness on his mind. Sean rolled her over into the dirt, and his mouth landed on hers, hungry and desperate, seeking with primal need. His body was hard and heavy on hers, hot through the silk.

Ronan chuckled. "Looks like he'll be okay."

"Glory." Dylan's moan of anguish made Andrea break the kiss at the same time Sean did.

Dylan had Glory's head in his lap and was stroking her

hair. Sean picked up the sword and moved to them, Andrea right behind him.

Together they healed her. Andrea grasped the blade, letting the edge nick her hand as she had when she'd healed Ely. Sean held the sword steady as the magic poured from him, the blade as a conduit. Andrea directed the heady magic into Glory and watched her wounds close, her strength return. Glory had been hurt far worse than Sean, shot and left to bleed out, but Glory's healing, boosted by the combined strength of the Guardian and the sword, was swift.

Glory at last drew a long breath, smiling up at Dylan with her usual verve. She was a long way from completely well, though. She'd lost a lot of blood, and she'd need a doctor.

Andrea let go of the sword and leaned back against Sean. "You'll need to get her to an ER," she said, her body warm and tired. "That's all I can do."

Dylan's eyes were wet when he looked up, Glory still cradled in his lap. "You've done enough, child. Thank you."

"Now, we need to save Liam's butt," Ronan said. "Especially if Fae are popping out of nowhere and shooting poisoned arrows."

"Indeed," Fionn said. "Leave the Fae to me. My own fighters are standing at the ready, and they've not had a good battle in a long time."

Sean's scowl was fierce. "Fae are shooting poisoned arrows at Shifters?"

"Yep," Ronan said. "They got me, but Fionn here has this magic powder . . ."

Fionn interrupted. "My warriors know they are to be of assistance to my daughter on her command. They always will be." Fionn gave Sean a pointed look. "You'd do well to remember that."

Sean's brows climbed, and Andrea wanted to laugh. "Hey, I'm a warrior princess, remember?" she said.

Sean growled as he leaned into her. "A warrior princess with lacy underwear." He pressed a promising kiss to her mouth. "Now, let's go kick us some Feline ass."

"Love to," Andrea said.

Dylan stayed behind with Glory. He told them he'd get her to a hospital, and then he'd deal with Wade. He sent the unconscious Lupine a vicious look that didn't bode well for him.

"You sure, Dad?" Sean asked. His sword gleamed, his naked body tall and strong, the Guardian ready for battle. "We could use you."

Dylan shook his head. "This is your fight, Sean. Yours and Liam's. It's time for me to focus on different things."

He was conceding his place to his sons. Firmly and finally. The tender way Dylan looked at Glory and the gentleness of his touch told Andrea what decision he'd reached. Sean squeezed his father's shoulder, understanding.

"Don't worry," Ronan said, his energy restored. "I'll make sure Liam and Sean win. And then we'll party."

"Bears," Sean said. "Always wanting their honey."

"And beer. Don't forget the beer."

"Are you sure you want to stay with these animals, daughter?" Fionn asked.

Andrea took Sean's hand. "Very sure."

She used the sword to open the way. Light flashed, along with the sharp, clean stench of Faerie, and then the four of them were gone.

W ade remained unmoving on the ground, but he wasn't dead. Dylan suppressed his instinct to stroll to the man and snap his neck, much as he wanted to.

Glory's lovely body was covered with dirt and blood, but her skin was warm, her breathing even. "I feel like shit," she said.

Dylan touched her face. "But you're alive, love. That's the important thing."

"Yeah, you're right, that's pretty important." Glory tried to sit up, and Dylan had to support her against him. "I heard what you said to Sean," she said, "but they really will need you back there. Callum's crazy, and if they've got Fae on the loose . . ."

"I made my decision." Dylan's words were sharp, final. "I'm taking care of you, and that's all." Dylan pressed a gentle kiss to her forehead. "For always, Glory."

Glory's eyes widened. "That sounds perilously like a commitment."

"'Tis not a joke. I need you in my life, my girl. It's empty without you."

"You're very flattering. Is that because I was almost dead?"

Dylan ran his hand through her sleek hair. "Knowing you'd gone missing, thinking I might lose you forever . . . Everything in my life suddenly lined up, from most important to least. At the top was finding you."

"Oh, yes?" Glory's smile was a pale shadow of her usual one, but her eyes glinted. "What was number two?"

"Bringing you back into my life. Permanently."

"I think I like this priority list."

"It's not easy for someone like me to ask for forgiveness, love. Alphas don't have to talk—we just stare at people until they fill in the words for us."

Glory's smile grew stronger. "A good way of putting it. Are you saying you want to move back in with me?"

"I'm saying that—using a word Andrea likes—I've been a dickhead. It was easy for me to leave for weeks at a time when I knew you'd be there when I came back. I took that for granted. You were right to kick me out."

"I know." Glory touched his cheek. "But I also think I'm right to give you a new key to my house."

"I still have the old one. I kept it, just in case."

"What if I've changed the locks?"

"You didn't."

Glory smiled again. "You're such a know-it-all, Dylan. What are we going to do about you?"

Dylan leaned to her again, and this time he licked her ear. "I'll show you when we get home."

"Mmm, sounds good to me." She looked across the cave at Wade, still unmoving. "But we'll have to do something about *him*."

Dylan followed her glance. "I'm thinking there needs to be a challenge for pack leader. If you want to make it, I'll back you."

Now Glory sat up, her delectable naked body brushing his. "A female pack leader? You're kidding me. How very modern, how cutting edge."

"I can't think of a better one than you, love. You're far stronger than you think you are—than *they* think you are. You'd make a hell of a leader."

"And if I lose?" she asked. "I admit that if I could fight the challenge using sarcasm, there'd be no contest, but I might have to battle Wade's nephews tooth and claw."

"If you lose, then we retreat and lick our wounds, ask Liam for protection. Maybe go to a beach somewhere, lick our wounds there."

"I like the way you think, furball."

Dylan cupped her face in his hands. "I like you, Lupine. No, Glory, I love you. You're crazy and you piss me off, and you make me do insane things, and I love you to pieces. I'd be more than honored to have you as mate."

Glory's usual smirk dissolved. "You damned irritating, high-handed, full-of-yourself, shithead alpha male."

"Does that mean yes?"

Glory's answering kiss was smoldering. "*Yes*. I love you," she said between breaths. "Damn it, Dylan, I love you so much."

She smiled her triumph, but Dylan didn't mind. As long as this tall, beautiful, sanity-stealing woman was in his life and in his arms, he didn't mind much of anything at all.

Shiftertown was in chaos. There was too much fighting, too many Shifters on the ground bleeding, and Sean started growling even as they stepped through from Faerie.

Andrea was right behind him, like a living goddess in that body-hugging silk. He wanted her with a fierceness that threatened to overwhelm him, but first, they had to fix this mess. From the determined look on Andrea's face, she agreed.

Sean ran toward the Morrissey house, sword in hand, in time to see Connor go down under two Shifters, a Fae pointing an arrow into the mass.

Sean froze, rage and fear pouring through him. *Take care of Con for me,* Kenny had whispered as he'd died. *Promise me, Sean.*

That day flashed back to Sean, the feral Felines attacking Sean and Kenny as they tracked them through the brush alongside the river, the snarls in the darkness as the Collarless Shifters turned and fought. Sean weeping after the fight as he covered Kenny's fallen body with their discarded clothes, then calling first for an ambulance and then his father and Liam. Kenny had died before they could reach him.

Dylan crouching down and covering his face when he beheld Kenny's lifeless body, Liam standing stiff and still, face wan with grief and shock. Sean had unsheathed the sword while Liam had watched with tears pouring down his face. Dylan hadn't been able to look up.

Sean had said the prayer to the Goddess in a broken voice and plunged the sword into Kenny's chest. Sean had followed the sword down as Kenny had gone to dust, landing flat beside the ash that had been his brother. And then Sean and Liam held each other hard while they cried, while Dylan still hadn't managed to unfold.

All this flashed through Sean as he saw the Felines go for Connor. Callum circled, ready to attack Sean to get the sword, and Sean heard Connor scream.

Fucking, bloody hell. Sean snarled as he started to shift. Screw the sword. No way was an ancient relic more important than Connor's life. *I won't let him die, Kenny. I promise you.*

"Sean!"

Andrea shouted at him. Sean turned, saw her outstretched hand, the strength in her eyes, Fionn right behind her.

"I'll take care of it," Andrea cried. "Me and my dad."

The empty places in Sean's heart filled as Andrea met his gaze. He already loved her with intensity that made him insane, but right now he loved her more than ever. Andrea understood exactly what was going through Sean's head as he watched Connor struggle, knew exactly what Sean needed. She was offering Sean a solution with her brave generosity. She was his mate all right.

You should see my girl, Kenny. She's beautiful.

Sean threw back his head and laughed. "All right then, Xena. You look after that now."

He tossed the sword high in the air, the blade glittering in the sunlight. It flew end over end, perfectly balanced, singing as Andrea stepped forward and caught it by the hilt, her silk robes billowing around her. Fionn closed in behind her, his bow and arrow ready, and Ronan, a bear again, stood defensively in front of her.

Still laughing, Sean shifted. Strong with Andrea's magic, he lifted his head and roared.

The roar echoed up and down Shiftertown, proclaiming that the Guardian was there, the second-in-command of this Shiftertown, mad as hell and ready to fight. An answering roar came back to him, filled with family pride, Liam tearing it up.

Sean pounced on Callum, lifted the wildcat high with his paws, and threw him. Callum tumbled through the air, crashed into the Fae with the bow, and went down with him. While they fought to untangle themselves, Sean charged the Shifters fighting Connor and burst them apart.

Connor rolled from the ground, teeth bared, his eyes red with fury. His wildcat's mane wasn't well developed yet, Connor barely more than a cub, but his rage was plenty strong.

Sean took the brunt of the fight, but he let Connor battle it out alongside him, knowing the lad wouldn't be happy to be *too* protected. Connor's Collar was already slowing him down, but he bravely stayed on his feet and helped drive the other Shifters back toward Liam.

Sean heard Andrea shouting at the Felines around her

Ronan roaring as he fought them away from her. He knew Fionn had her back, and that fact warmed him. *The family that fights rogue Shifters and upstart Fae together . . .*

Liam charged through the clearing to complete the family togetherness. Liam leapt on Callum at the same time the slit to Faerie opened and about a dozen or more Fae warriors boiled through with the help of Callum's Shifters.

They were way too close to Liam. Sean crashed the last of the Shifters he fought to the ground and ran to help his brother.

The Fae looked smug as they pointed knocked arrows at Liam. But Fionn was bellowing in an alien language, and more Fae popped out of *his* hole to Faerie, these armed with wicked-looking swords. The first set, alarmed, turned and tried to fire at the second set.

The Fae fought dirty. While Sean knew Liam wanted the battle settled with as little Shifter bloodshed as possible, the Fae killed each other without remorse. It was chilling to watch one of Fionn's men drive his sword clean through another Fae and laugh as his enemy's blood showered over him.

Callum's Fae were defeated. Cut off from retreat by Fionn's warriors, they died to the last man. The remaining one who struggled up from under Callum saw what was happening and took his revenge by turning on Callum.

Before Liam or Sean could reach them, that Fae clenched an arrow in his hand and drove it straight into Callum's heart. Callum bellowed in agony, paws scrabbling in the dirt, and the Fae wrapped his arms around Callum's neck and broke it.

That Fae died an instant later when Fionn's sword swiped his head from his neck.

As soon as the last Fae fell, whatever Fae spell had been helping Callum's Shifters fight despite their Collars dissipated. Feline Shifters howled in pain and dropped all over the clearing. Liam loped to Sean and rose, shifting as he stood.

Eric, the Shiftertown leader from Las Vegas, shifted to

stand beside Liam and survey the battlefield. "Sun and moon, what a mess."

Sean remained wildcat, his nose wrinkling at the stench of dead Fae. Fionn's warriors began carrying them back to Faerie, the bodies of friend and foe alike. Callum, they simply left where he was.

Fionn stepped back to let the last of his warriors go through. As that door to Faerie winked out, Fionn wiped his sword clean on the grass.

"The rest will be taken care of on my side," Fionn said to Sean. "It is finished."

"Sure about that, are you?" Liam asked him.

Fionn shrugged. "I am a Cillian. We always prevail." He walked away, his stride long and still energetic.

"And *he's* going to be your father-in-law, Sean," Liam said. "Whew. Better you than me."

"Hey, he helped save our asses," Connor said. He'd shifted back to human and sat, panting, at Sean's feet, looking a little green from the effects of his Collar.

"So did Sean." Liam's hand landed on Sean's mane. "Thank you, brother, for coming to Connor's aid. I couldn't reach him in time."

"Yeah, good save, Sean," Connor echoed.

Good save. Sean wanted to laugh and settled for a Feline growl. *I'll always save you, Con. Kenny never has to worry about that.*

Liam turned a sudden furious eye on his nephew. "And what the bloody hell are you doing in Shiftertown anyway, Con? You're supposed to be guarding Kim at her house."

"Kim insisted we come back," Connor said. "And I wanted a piece of these gobshites."

"You should have talked her out of it. Stolen her keys. Anything. I see we need to have a little chat about clan leaders and orders and shite like that."

Kim came around the house at that point, her Mustang in the driveway. It was over and she knew it, and she added her voice to what she thought about Shifters expecting her to stay away while they went out to nearly be killed.

Sean left them to it and returned to where his heart was. Andrea.

Andrea greeted him with a big smile and a hug around his wildcat neck. Sean decided to shift while her arms were around him and found himself against her delectable body. The silk that covered her let him slide against her in a delicious way.

"Sweet lady," he rumbled. "I'm thinking I can't wait for that moon blessing."

Andrea's answering kiss heated his blood. The fighting frenzy coupled with mating frenzy made him almost forget he was in the middle of Shiftertown surrounded by family, friends, and enemies.

"Sean," Liam's voice cut through his joy. "You're needed."

Sean eased Andrea from his arms with reluctance, but he knew Liam was right.

Callum was one of three Shifters who'd been killed in the fighting. Liam, Ronan, Eric, and Ellison helped lay all three of them out under the trees, surrounding them with fresh branches, murmuring prayers as they did so. They brought Jared from the back of Dylan's truck, his body still wrapped in the tarp, and laid him next to the fallen.

Andrea's hand slid into Sean's as they both looked down at Jared. Sean hadn't forgiven Jared for what he'd done to Andrea, but now the man was a mere pathetic heap of bones, as much a victim to Callum's schemes as Callum had been himself. Sean looked at him and felt sad.

Andrea handed Sean the sword. She stayed next to him, warm at his side, as Sean prayed to the Goddess for the safe passage of the four Shifters at his feet. Then he lifted the silver sword and sent each of them to dust.

CHAPTER TWENTY-SIX

The moon was two nights past full that night, but Liam decreed that they were within the time range for the moon blessing. Besides that, he added with a grin, Sean and Andrea would combust if they didn't get it over with.

Andrea once again stood in the clearing with a garland of flowers on her head, Sean at her side. This blessing was the more sacred of the two, and all Shiftertown was there, circling and celebrating. They had two things to celebrate: Sean and Andrea's mating and the fact that Shiftertown was once again peaceful—well, as peaceful as a bunch of Shifters living together could ever be.

Callum's men had pretty much surrendered to Liam the day before, now that their Fae backers had been defeated. Ben O'Callaghan was put in charge of seeing that the Felines followed Liam's strictures, Ben's penance for having joined the Felines-only movement in the first place. *One day, Ben,* Liam had told him, *the world will belong to us again. One day. But not today.*

They'd spent the rest of the day and evening recovering from the fight, Sean and Dylan and Liam having to face the delayed reaction to the Collars. It had been bad. Eric, who'd been testing out how much he could resist his Collar, hadn't fared much better.

Liam had sent out Spike and the other trackers to clean up the parking lot of the bar where Felines had battled Sean and Jared and to recover Sean's bike. Sean moaned when he saw the shot-up engine and gave the motorcycle a caressing hug while Andrea watched in sympathy. "I'll take care of you now," he'd said to it. "Me and Andrea. She has a wicked grip on a wrench."

Glory's car had been found as well. Dylan had discovered that Wade's tracker had driven Glory's car out to a road past the caves to the west of town and abandoned it, on Wade's orders. Glory hadn't been best pleased about that and made sure everyone knew it.

The human police had come to the bar outside Shiftertown to ask Liam about the reported noise in Shiftertown that day, and Liam had glibly told them, "Shifter games." He'd smiled his warm smile and let his Irish lilt roll from his tongue. Kim had backed him up, as had Silas the reporter. "Running and jumping and other frolicking," Liam had said. "Like your human Olympics but not as organized."

The police, who really hadn't wanted to deal with Shifter problems, bought his explanation and went away.

That night, as the moon rose, the Shifters were rested and joyous and now slightly drunk.

"Under the light of the moon, the Mother Goddess," Liam said, his smile so broad that Andrea was surprised he could speak. "I recognize this mating."

Simple words, but they meant everything.

Liam didn't get a chance to make a speech this time. As soon as he pronounced the blessing, Shifters around them went crazy, whooping and shouting, howling and bellowing, and Sean swept up Andrea for a deep, possessive kiss.

"I love you, Sean," she whispered, her heart in the words.

She couldn't kiss Sean long, however, because the family was all over them. Andrea got squeezed into a round of hugs—Connor's enthusiastic, Liam and Kim's loving,

Eric's strong, Glory and Dylan's warm. Glory had dressed in her favorite leopard-print pants and spike heels, and she smiled with newfound happiness. Neither she nor Dylan had mentioned a mate blessing, but Andrea felt in her bones that it wouldn't be long coming.

The celebration lasted all night, Fionn there celebrating right along with the Shifters. Fionn had softened a bit, observing his daughter's happiness with Sean.

Dina had loved this man, Andrea thought as Fionn held her after the mate blessing, no matter how strange their relationship might have been. They'd shared the mate bond. Andrea now felt love from Fionn for her as he hugged her close.

Ronan came to thank Fionn for saving his life and started a discussion with him about beer. Apparently Fae liked ale as much as Shifters, and Andrea left Fionn to Ronan, Ellison, and Eric, who began introducing Fionn to a succession of beers from across America.

In the small hours of the morning, Sean took Andrea by the hand, winked at her, and crept away with her from the mad festivities to Glory's empty house.

Glory watched them go as she slid her fingers through Dylan's. "I'm thinking we should stay somewhere else tonight, or we'll never get any sleep."

"Kim offered us the use of her house," Dylan said, taking a sip from his bottle of Guinness.

Glory smiled. "Kim's generous." She couldn't stop herself from feasting her eyes on the man at her side—tall, blue-eyed, hard-bodied, with a quiet strength that belied the ferocity with which he'd fought earlier today. She watched him draw beer from the bottle, his mouth moving as he savored it, and her female places squeezed.

"Kim knows," Dylan said. "Sean and Andrea will be wanting their space, and Kim said she got in enough food to satisfy even Shifters."

"Plus she has cable. Luxury."

Dylan stopped, his eyes quiet. "I don't mind anywhere we stay, as long as I'm with you, my girl."

Glory felt the mate bond for him wrap around her heart, and she nearly dissolved with its warmth. Taking a mate for the second time would be different, but the love would be no less intense. She understood that now.

She leaned into Dylan. "I'm feeling a bit of that mating frenzy coming on myself. Think anyone would notice if we slipped away?"

"I'm thinking they wouldn't miss us."

The smile Dylan slanted her was primal, and Glory's excitement doubled. She slid her hand to his fine ass as they walked around the house to his truck, and then she leaned her head on his shoulder while he drove her across Austin and up into the hills.

Sean and Andrea didn't make it upstairs before their clothes came off, pieces scattered down the stairs like a breadcrumb trail. Then Andrea was under Sean on her bed, right where she wanted to be.

The lovemaking was intense, Sean sliding into her while she opened to take him deep. Andrea knew in her heart a cub had already begun forming inside her, knew it with the tingle of warmth that was an extension of the mate bond.

She'd tell Sean later. Right now, he was pressing into her, his eyes flickering from blue to white and back again, the Collar gleaming on his bare throat. She arched against him, loving the feel of his strong chest on her breasts, stirring more and more fires.

He was hard, he was big, and he was driving Andrea into the bed for all he was worth. Sean's hands turned to claws as the frenzy drove them on, and so did hers, both of them growling as they suppressed the change to *keep on doing this*.

As the night moved on, Sean and Andrea kept loving each other, the mating frenzy claiming them, the mate bond winding them tightly together. Their bodies were drenched in sweat, their lips raw with kissing, their bodies twined so close that Andrea didn't care whether they ever came loose.

Eventually, as cold night warmed to day, their raw, frantic sex wound down into tender, gentle sex. That in turn wound down, more slowly, into sleep. They drifted off, cuddled against each other.

When Andrea woke again, the sun was high, and Sean and she lay together in a tangle of warm limbs.

It was quiet outside now, all of Shiftertown sleeping off a collective hangover. Mate blessings were few and far between, and Shifters didn't have much to celebrate in this world of captivity. Last night they'd celebrated both the mate blessing and the conclusion of a damn good fight, so they'd gone at it double force.

The sun warmed the window as Andrea watched Sean sleep, her heart full of love. Sean was a hot, hard-bodied male, and he belonged to her.

Sean opened his eyes, which were deep blue and clear of sleep. He gave her a smile. "I didn't have time to give you your gift last night, love."

"Gift?" Andrea grinned back. "You mean all that sex wasn't a gift?"

"Oh, aren't you the amusing one?" Sean kissed the tip of her nose, rolled away, and took a tissue-wrapped package from the nightstand drawer. "For you."

Andrea took it, feeling something soft beneath the paper. "I didn't get you anything."

Sean's eyes warmed. "Yes, you did."

Andrea paused to give him a long, satisfying kiss, then she tore off the tissue and lifted a pair of lovely black silk panties between her fingers. On the back of the panties, bright red script spelled out *Smart Ass*.

"Goddess, Sean, these are great. Where did you find them?"

"Same place you found mine. The girl there was happy to help me out."

Andrea remembered the young clerk in the store, the one friendly to Shifters and interested in Connor. She'd probably had a blast helping Sean pick them out.

Andrea swung the panties around one finger. "I'll have to wear them. But not, I'm thinking, just now."

Sean's look was wicked. "No, we definitely aren't needing any panties right now." He took them from her and dropped them to the nightstand as he pushed her back down into the mattress. His kiss was warm and languid but held an edge that said more wild lovemaking was to come.

They were deep into the kiss when Andrea heard a car door slam, and Sean raised his head again.

"My second gift has arrived," he said.

Much as she liked gifts, Andrea wasn't sure she relished the interruption. Gifts could wait. "How many did you get me?"

"Only as many as I know you need." Sean's eyes held a mysterious glint. "Don't you want to see what it is?"

With Sean lying on top of her all naked and fine? Andrea wet her lips. "They can leave the package on the porch."

Sean lifted away from her, removing his delicious warmth. "No, love. This is something you have to get yourself."

"Right now?"

"Right now."

Andrea gave him an impatient look. Why would a mate-frenzied male insist his mate get up and answer the door? He had to be insane.

Andrea rolled out of bed, groaning a little as she realized how sore she was. "All right, if it makes you happy."

She pulled on a T-shirt and the new panties and slid jeans over those. Stretching, she went to the window, looked down, and uttered a strangled cry.

Her stepfather stood on the driveway below, he and Dylan having just stepped out of Dylan's pickup. Terry Gray saw Andrea in the window and stopped.

"Andrea," he said. "My daughter."

"Father," Andrea choked out the word. "What are you doing here? No, wait, don't move, I'm coming down."

She spun from the window to find Sean behind her, dressed in jeans and nothing else, his Collar gleaming at his throat. Her libido took in what a delectable picture he made while she pointed at him with a shaking finger. "You did this. You brought him here."

"That I did." Sean gave her a quiet nod, a Shifter who didn't need to shout for everyone to understand how powerful he was. "It's all very well that you found Fionn, but I knew you'd be still be missing your dad."

Andrea felt the tears coming, but she smiled at Sean with all her heart. "I love you, Sean Morrissey."

He drew her into his arms and gave her a kiss that was at once gentle and full of fire. "I love you too, Fae-girl. Go on now."

Andrea kissed him one more time, then she dashed out of the room, nearly flew down the stairs, and burst out the door to be swept into the arms of her stepfather.

Sean watched out of the window as Andrea hugged her stepfather, his heart at peace. He caught the gaze of his own father, who leaned against his truck. Sean and Dylan shared a look that was full of understanding. Damn, it was good to be a Shifter today.

Across the room, the Sword of the Guardian gleamed in the sunshine, softly singing its happiness.

Turn the page for a preview of the next
Shifters Unbound novel by Jennifer Ashley

WILD CAT

Coming soon from Berkley Sensation!

CHAPTER ONE

Heights. Damn it, why did it have to be heights?

Diego Escobar scanned the steel beams of the unfinished skyscraper against a gray morning sky, and acid seared his stomach.

Heights had never bothered him until two years ago, when five meth-head perps had hung him over the penthouse balcony of a thirty-story hotel and threatened to drop him. His partner, a damn good cop, had put his weapon on the balcony floor and raised his hands to save Diego's life. The perps had pulled Diego to safety and then casually shot both of them. Diego had survived, but his partner hadn't.

The incident had left Diego burning with rage and grief, which manifested itself from time to time into an obsessive fear of heights. Even rising three floors in a glass elevator could make him break into a cold sweat.

"Way the hell up there?" he asked Rogers, the uniform cop who'd made the call for backup.

"Yes, sir."

Oh, just effing perfect.

"Hooper's pretty sure it's not human," Rogers said. "He

says it moves too fast, jumps too far. But he hasn't got a visual yet."

Not human meant Shifter. This was getting better and better. "He up there alone?"

"Jemez is with him. They think they have it cornered on the fifty-first level."

The *fifty-first* level? "Tell me you're fucking kidding."

"No, sir." Rogers gestured. "There's an elevator. We got the electric company to turn on the power."

Diego looked at the rusty doors then up through the grid of beams into empty space, and his mouth went dry.

This cluster of buildings had been under construction for years. An apartment complex, hotel, office tower, and shopping center in one, a little way from the Strip. The idea was to lure locals and rich out of towners from the more touristy hotels and casinos and have them spend their money here. The project had started to great fanfare, but so many investors had pulled out that building had ground to a halt, and the unfinished skyscraper sat like a rusting blot on the empty desert around it.

Tracking Shifters wasn't his department. Diego was a detective in vice, and this call should have been a simple case of trespassing. He'd responded to the plea for backup because he'd been heading to work anyway, and his route took him right by the construction site. He figured he'd help Rogers chase down a miscreant and drive on in to the station.

Now Rogers wanted Diego to jaunt to the fifty-first level, where there weren't even any floors, for crying out loud, and chase a perp who might be a Shifter. Rogers, rotund and near retirement, made it clear he had no intention of going up there himself.

A high-pitched scream rang down from on high. It was a woman's scream—Maria Jemez—followed by a man's bellow of surprise and pain. Then, silence.

"Damn it." Diego sprinted for the elevator. Like hell he'd let two uniforms die up there because he was a little nervous about heights. "Stay down here and call for more backup. Tell them to bring tranqs."

Fifty-first level. Shit. The lift rose through a few completely finished floors, then onto floors that were nothing but open beams and catwalks.

Diego had been chasing criminals through towering hotels for years; no need to get squeamish about it now. Hell, he and the sheriff's department had followed one idiot high up onto a cable tower two hundred feet above Hoover Dam five years ago, and Diego hadn't even flinched. A bunch of cop-hating meth dealers hang him over a balcony, and he goes to pieces.

It stops now. This is where I get my own back.

Diego rolled back the gate on the fifty-first level. The sun was rising, the mountains due west bathed in pink and orange splendor. The Las Vegas valley was a beautiful place, its stark white desert contrasting with the mountains that rose in a knifelike wall on the horizon. The visitors down in the city kept their eyes on the gaming tables and slot machines, strippers, and celebrities, uncaring of what went on outside the windows, but the beauty of the valley always tugged at Diego's heart.

Diego drew his gun and stepped off the lift into eerie silence. Something flitted in his peripheral vision, something moving too quickly and lightly to be Hooper, who was a big, muscular guy who liked big, muscular guns. Diego aimed, but the movement vanished.

He didn't fire. No sense in wasting ammo. He didn't feel like having to balance on a catwalk five hundred feet above ground while he reached for an extra magazine.

Diego stepped softly, keeping to shadows. A soft sound came from behind him. He swung around, stepping into the deeper shadow of a beam, making himself a lesser target. The catwalk groaned under his feet.

Something pinged above his head. Diego hit the floor instinctively, trying not to panic as his feet slid over the catwalk's edge.

What the hell was he doing up here? His heart was pounding triple-time, his throat so dry it closed up tight. He should have confessed his secret fear of heights a while back, gone to psychiatric evaluation, stayed behind a desk for a time. But no, he'd been too determined to keep his job, too determined to beat it himself, too embarrassed to admit the weakness. Now he was endangering others because of his stupid fear.

Shut up and think.

Whatever had pinged hadn't been a bullet. Too soft. He got his feet back onto the catwalk and crawled to find what had fallen to the boards. A dart, he saw, the kind shot by a tranquilizer gun.

Perfect. Put the nice cop to sleep, and you can do anything you want with him, including push his body over the edge.

Diego moved in a crouch across the catwalk to the next set of shadows. The sun streaked across the valley to Mount Charleston in the west, light radiant on its snow-covered crown. More snow was predicted up there for the weekend. Diego had contemplated driving up on Saturday to sip hot toddies in a snowbound lodge, maybe with something warm and female at his side.

Once he finished here, he was requesting leave. It was long past time. He'd go to Mount Charleston and then stay at his mom's house out in Baker and fix all the things she kept complaining about. She'd be glad to see him.

On the other side of the next girder Diego found Bud Hooper and Maria Jemez. Maria was fairly new, just out of the academy, too baby-faced to be up here chasing a crazy perp. They were slumped together in a heap, still warm, breathing slowly, out cold.

Footsteps, running. Diego swung around. Something moved upward in the middle of the building, not bothering with the lift. The shadow detached itself from the catwalk and rose in a graceful leap to the next level.

Another *ping* sounded beside him.

Diego let his instincts take over. He rolled, returned fire.

He heard a grunt, but he couldn't tell if he hit his mark. Then someone barreled at him, a second perp, not the thing that had so easily leapt to the floor above. Diego dodged out of the way and went down, landing on his side, but he didn't lose hold of his gun. He brought it around, but there was nothing to aim at.

"Drop your weapon and get on the floor," he bellowed.

Silence. Nothing but the rising desert wind humming through the building.

Diego saw the rifle barrel a split second before he rolled out of the way. Another dart struck the catwalk where his head had been. He fired once before the catwalk seemed to slide out from under his body, and he found himself falling, falling, falling through empty space.

Son of a fucking—

Two strong arms caught him. He looked into a ferocious face that was somehow beautiful, a mouth full of gleaming fangs, and white green eyes.

Before Diego could draw breath to shout, the creature deposited him on another catwalk and leapt away, the morning light glinting on the silver links of a chain around its neck. Diego heard a wildcat's scream, like a panther's, meant to terrify.

Diego lay still to catch his breath. It was one thing to believe that Shifters were rounded up, contained, Collared, rendered harmless. Another thing to lie in the darkness listening to one snarl, knowing that a wild beast with human intelligence was fifty stories in the air alone with you. Collars or no, Shifters were still damned dangerous.

Diego got up on his elbows. He heard running, a strangled cry, and then a clattering as the tranquilizer rifle skittered toward him across the catwalk. He rolled over, aiming, when two feet landed in front of his face.

Two human, female, naked feet. Diego lifted his head to find two strong female legs right in front of him, skin tanned from the desert sun, a thatch of dark blond hair between her thighs. He forced his gaze to continue upward, over her flat stomach with a small gold stud in her navel, to firm breasts tipped with dusky nipples. He forced his gaze past *them—* though he'd dream about them for a long time coming—to be rewarded by the sight of her breathtaking face.

The Shifter woman had a strong face, but it contained

the softness of beauty. Her eyes were light green, a shimmer of jade in the darkness. A mane of pale hair fell past her shoulders, and a chain with a Celtic cross fused to it glinted around her slender throat.

Damn. Diego had never seen a female Shifter before. His cases had never taken him to Shiftertown, which lay north of North Las Vegas, and he'd only ever seen the male Shiftertown leader, Eric Warden, on the television news. He'd had no idea that their females were this tall or this sex-humping gorgeous.

Her breasts rose in even rhythm with her breathing, and she expressed no embarrassment at her nakedness. She didn't even seen to notice it. "You all right?" she asked.

"Alive," Diego croaked.

He saw her light-colored eyes flick to the tranquilizer gun a few feet from him, watched her calculate the distance to it.

Diego brought up his pistol. "Don't try it, sweetheart. Get facedown on the floor, hands behind your back."

She blinked. "What? Why? I just saved your ass."

"You're trespassing, *niña*, and two cops are down. On the floor."

He gestured with the gun. The Shifter woman drew an enraged breath, eyes flashing almost pure white. For a moment, Diego thought she'd leap at him, maybe change into the wildcat and try to shred him. He'd have to plug her, and he really didn't want to. It would be a shame to kill something so beautiful.

The Shifter let out her breath, gave him an angry glare, and then carefully lowered herself facedown on the catwalk. Diego unclipped his handcuffs.

"What's your name?" Diego asked.

Her jaw tightened. "Cassidy. Cassidy Warden."

Related to the Shiftertown leader called Warden? This could get interesting.

"Nice to meet you, Cassidy," Diego said. "You have the right to remain silent." He droned on through Miranda as he closed the handcuffs on her perfect wrists. Cassidy lay still and radiated rage.

Diego's hands were shaking by the time he finished. But that had less to do with his fear of heights than with the tall, beautiful naked woman on the floor in front of him, hands locked together on her sweet, tight ass. The best ass he'd ever seen in his life. He wanted to stay up here and lick that beautiful backside, and then apply his tongue to the rest of her body.

He broke into a sweat, despite the cool wind wafting from below, and made himself haul her to her feet. The Shifter woman's look was still defiant, but he wanted nothing more than to crush her against him and kiss that wide, enticing mouth.

Diego cleared his throat and made himself steer her to the lift.

Not until they were rapidly descending did Diego realize that since Cassidy Warden had come into his view, he'd not once thought about how far he might have fallen had she not caught him and the spectacular splat he'd have made when he hit the ground.

THE NEW VICTORIAN HISTORICAL
ROMANCE NOVEL FROM
USA TODAY BESTSELLING AUTHOR

JENNIFER ASHLEY

*Lady Isabella's
Scandalous Marriage*

Lady Isabella Scranton scandalized London by leaving
her husband, notorious artist Lord Mac Mackenzie, after only three turbulent years of marriage. But Mac has
a few tricks to get the lady back in his life, and more
importantly, back into his bed.

"I adore this novel."

—Eloisa James, *New York Times* bestselling author

penguin.com

As Tracker for the SnowDancer pack, it's up to
Drew Kincaid to rein in rogue changelings who
have lost control of their animal halves. But nothing in his life has prepared him for the battle he
must now wage to win the heart of a woman who
makes his body ignite...and who threatens to enslave his wolf.

Lieutenant Indigo Riviere doesn't easily allow
skin privileges, especially of the sensual kind—and
the last person she expects to find herself craving
is the most wickedly playful male in the den. Everything she knows tells her to pull back...but she
hasn't counted on Drew's will.

Now, two of SnowDancer's most stubborn
wolves find themselves playing a hotly sexy game
even as lethal danger stalks the very place they call
home...

NEW FROM NATIONAL BESTSELLING AUTHOR
ALLYSON JAMES

Stormwalker

"*Stormwalker* boasts a colorful cast of characters,
a cool setting, and a twisty mystery!
A fresh new take on paranormal romance!"

—Emma Holly

Janet Begay is a Stormwalker, capable of wielding the
raw elemental power of nature, a power that threatens to overwhelm her. Only her lover, Mick, is able
to calm the storm within her—even as their passion
reaches unimaginable heights of ecstasy.

But when an Arizona police chief's daughter is taken
by a paranormal evil, they find themselves venturing
where no human can survive alone—and only together can they overcome the greatest danger they've
ever faced.

penguin.com